CONTENTS

CONTENTS

DANIELLE M. ROEMER AND CRISTINA BACCHILEGA

Introduction

This project began in 1996 when we proposed "Angela Carter and the Literary *Märchen*" as a "Folklore and Literature" topic for the American Folklore Society Annual Meeting in Pittsburgh, Pennsylvania. The response was invigorating, resulting in two well-attended panels and lively discussion. We decided to put out a general call for papers in scholarly journals and on the internet in an effort to reach international scholars across disciplines who were actively thinking about Carter's magic. For us, much of the pleasure of working on this project has derived from seeing a seemingly straightforward topic, "Angela Carter and the Literary *Märchen*," transformed into a fire-breathing beast of varicolored fur and plumage. And yet the fire's source is one: Carter's pleasure economy of images and words as she works in "the lumber room of the Western European imagination" (Carter, "Angela Carter" 29). As she said in an interview, "I do think that the body comes first, not consciousness. . . . I often shatter pure and evocative imagery with the crude. But remember there's a materiality to symbols and a materiality to imaginative life which should be taken quite seriously" (33). And the fairy tale as collective art has taken this materiality of symbols to heart.

This volume has no one thesis. But in presenting these contributions, we still wish to intervene in the debate surrounding Carter's texts in a variety of ways: by providing more information—at times erudite, at time mundane—about her knowledge of and playful commitment to folk and fairy tales; by actively seeking ways to shake easy labels from her work; by placing international perspectives in conversation with one another; and by opening the way for further research into her exploration of *Märchen* worlds.

The contributions to *Angela Carter and the Fairy Tale* focus on Carter's creative appropriation and adaptation of fairy-tale patterns, motifs, and content. In organizing this volume, which appeared originally as a 1998 special issue of the journal *Marvels & Tales*, we wanted to call attention to the striking diversity of Carter's approaches to the fairy tale. This heterogeneity, though, is not without heritage. The fairy-tale genre is neither monolithic nor the product of a single branching of literary history. Many oral and literary fairy-tale traditions have developed in Europe and the United States over the centuries. Because the contributions included here do not take as their expressed subject Carter's alignment or dispute with varying fairy-tale traditions, we wish to address elements of those relationships in the following pages. We survey the literary traditions of Germany, France, and Italy and the cinematic tradition of the United States, touching on aspects of genre definition, character and plot development, and sociopolitical stance.[1] In no way do we want to suggest that Carter's tales are derivative of these traditions; rather, we believe that an understanding of her work can be deepened if perceptions of it are refracted through a variety of fairy-tale contexts.

We begin with the issue of genre definition.

From 1812 to 1857, Jacob and Wilhelm Grimm collected, rewrote, edited, and published seven large and ten small editions of tales under the title *Kinder- und Hausmärchen,* that is, "Children's and Household Tales." According to the Grimms' *Deutsches Wörterbuch* (*German Dictionary* [1852–1960]), *Märchen* (a diminutive of *Mär* [an account]) meant simply a "fictional tale" (Goldberg 407). Under this rubric, the Grimms included a variety of narrative types, producing the "most complete [and] representative collection of miscellaneous narratives"(Dégh 68) available at the time. There were tales of magic and marvels, humorous stories, animal tales, saints' legends, and pious tales from the Middle Ages. All were considered *Märchen* and, as the Grimms' title suggests, "family fare." Subsequent nineteenth-century German compilers of collections tended to follow the Grimms in placing diverse subgroups of folktales within the larger category of *Märchen*; some even adopted the Grimms' title (Bottigheimer; Köhler-Zülch). Definitional problems arose, though, when such collections were translated into English. *Märchen* was typically rendered as "popular story," "wonder tale," or "fairy tale." Interestingly, the latter term derived not from any Germanic perspective but from the earlier translation into English of the seventeenth-century French term *conte de fées,* which referred to narratives with fairies (or other supernatural beings) as characters.[2] The result of this translation was a rather awkward semiotic disjunction. Henceforth, English-language collections, whether translations or not, were often identified by the term "fairy tales"—a term that described only a relatively small number of those collections' constituent narratives. With time, this metonymy was accepted as convention. However, under the surface, the terminological quandary remains: In speaking of the fairy tale, to which broadly or narrowly defined corpus is one referring?[3]

In contrast to the French tradition, Carter's attitude toward defining the fairy tale is inclusive, recalling the Grimms' practice. Her position is stated explicitly in the introduction to her first edited volume of tales, *The Old Wives' Fairy Tale Book*. There she defuses terminology by labeling "fairy tale" as a "figure of speech," moreover one used loosely to "describe the great mass of infinitely various narrative that was, once upon a time and still is, sometimes, passed on . . . by word of mouth" (ix). Thus, the term "fairy tale" for Carter is primarily a convenience of familiarity. What she does then in her own space of referential potentiality—the edited collections, *The Bloody Chamber*, and other writings— is to provide her readers with a striking diversity of fairy-tale narratives.[4] Among her literary fairy tales, for example, are ones that combine the marvelous with the gothic—"The Bloody Chamber"—and others that dabble in the macabre while trafficking in classical myth—"The Snow Child."[5] Each of these tales told on the slant presents a powerful kinglike figure who parthenogenetically "births" his own wives/daughter/muse/lover. Conversely, one finds tales in which a woman, Rapunzel-like, seeks to escape the life that either her family or myth has authored for her ("The Lady of the House of Love," "The Courtship of Mr Lyon," and "The Erl-King"). There are animal tales blended with romance ("The Tiger's Bride"), with horror ("Wolf-Alice"), and with awe ("Peter and the Wolf") in which a human character finds greater fulfillment in the animal side of her nature. There are tales of inverted biblical allusion and dark wonder ("Penetrating to the Heart of the Forest") in which Hansel- and Gretel-like children journey into a marvel-filled forest with mystery/knowledge/danger at its center. There are also questlike tales of bawdy humor that borrow from the literary picaresque ("Puss-in-Boots") or from the culinary memoir ("The Kitchen Child"). Carter's penchant for boundary crossing is further demonstrated with *The Bloody Chamber,* which can be read as a "gleeful, subversive commentary" on her own previous translation from the French of Charles Perrault's fairy tales (Gamble 131).

Another point also needs to be addressed—that concerning the folk "purity" of the tales as they were published in the nineteenth century. Contrary to today's popular stereotype, the Grimms did not go out into the farms and byways to take down verbatim the words of peasant storytellers. Rather they found their sources as convenience led them: in literary and manuscript collections as well as in easily accessible individuals, spanning the working, bourgeois, and even the aristocratic classes (Scherf). Believing that the tales illustrated the essence or soul (*Volkgeist*) of the German people, the Grimms acted in accordance with the romantic perspectives of their day in focusing on the material rather than taking into account the socioeconomic conditions of the tales' informants. These romantic perspectives also led the Grimms to rework the obtained material, sometimes heavily, to suit the family and educational values of their bourgeois audience (Tatar, *Off With Their Heads;* Zipes, *Complete Fairy Tales*). Thus the Grimms would take notes on the basic plots of the tales and then flesh out these verbal skeletons as their own perspectives inclined them. They reinforced the Christian aspects, the homey sayings, and the violence, while deleting sexual references. The Grimms were also responsible for changing the wicked mother figure in many tales to a wicked stepmother character so as not to challenge prevailing beliefs about motherhood. The resulting tales were not primarily indicative of peasant values but of those of the German middle class. The rub of the matter comes today with continuing assumptions that the conservatism of the tales is innate to the "folk" mentality, not only in the Grimms' corpus but, by extension, to all "real" fairy tales. This is not the case, especially not for those tales that either bridge or are firmly nestled within the domain of written literature, as we discuss below with the French *conte de fées* and the tales of Basile.

Carter was well aware of the extent of the editing/rewriting performed by many previous collector/editors, particularly those of the nineteenth century who wished to turn fairy tales "into the refined pastime of the middle classes, and especially of the middle-class nursery" (*Old Wives'* xvii). As a result, she avoided rewriting, collating, or deleting material, including the sexual, from her edited collections. Her explicitly literary fairy tales, even those that share "roots in the pre-industrialized past" (xvii), are another matter. Carter as well as other professional authors are of course free to draw on whatever heritage they wish. The intermixing of folk (however folk may be defined), literary, and, in the twentieth century, mass media versions of fairy tales, sets in motion, in Carter's words, the transnational and "endless recycling process" (xi) of storytelling. It is the "user-friendly" (xxi) nature of the tales which allows them to participate in a powerful "public dream" (xx).

In considering some of Carter's relationships to French fairy-tale tradition, we move from the topic of functional genre definition to that of character development and the sociopolitical functions of the tales themselves. Beginning in the 1630s in Paris, educated and accomplished women of the aristocracy organized gatherings called salons in their homes for the purpose of intellectual discussions of literature, art, and concerns on love, marriage, and proper manners and morals. Highly valuing wit and invention, these women, and eventually some men, were, in Jack Zipes's words, "constantly seeking innovative ways to express their needs and to embellish the forms and styles of speech . . . that they shared" (*Beauties* 2). As one source for new material, the salon participants turned to those tales of magic and marvels they had learned as children, which they then elaborated upon and experimented with in sophisticated ways. By the last decade of the century, salon participants began writing down their narratives for publication, and thus was born the literary *conte de fées.*

In 1690 salon participant and author Marie-Catherine d'Aulnoy embedded her invented magical tale "L'Isle de la Félicité" (The island of happiness) in her novel *Histoire d'Hippolyte, Comte de Douglas.* Her example quickly prompted a spate of literary fairy tales by other authors. Often lengthy and characterized by intricate plots, these narratives' "glitter and artificiality" were intentional constructs, intended to "contest the emerging association of fairy tales with the primitive" (Harries 153). In addition, the *contes de fées,* like the oral tales still being told at salons, had specific sociopolitical functions. Informed by female perspectives and featuring female characters, the *contes* offered their creators opportunities to critique conditions of the day, particularly the social institution of forced marriage and the general lot of women in a predominantly male-controlled world.[6] Thus it was no accident that in the tales ultimate power was held by the female stock character known today as the fairy godmother, who was described as having control not only of her own life but of others' as well. There was also good reason, though, for these authors to mediate their social commentary through the veil of fantasy. The efforts of these highly literate women, among them some of the best writers of the day, were necessarily conducted within a wider, markedly patriarchal system, one which advocated the "taming of female desire according to virtues associated with male industriousness" (Zipes, *Fairy Tale* 28). As a result, that system regarded the *contes de fées* as "deeply disturbing and suspect" (Harries 169). The work published by these women was criticized and dismissed as early as the 1690s. For example, in 1699, the Abbé de Villiers published the booklet *Entretiens sur les contes des fées* (Dialogues on fairy tales) in which he praised Charles Perrault—"a well-known member of the Academy" and one of the "fraternity of learned male authors"— for imitating so cleverly the "style and simplicity of 'nurses.'"[7] On the other hand, Villiers criticized the women writers of *contes de fées* for their "lack of learning" as well as for their invasion of the literary marketplace where, Harries summarizes, "lazy and ignorant women readers read the productions of lazy and ignorant women writers" (154). For the most part, by the mid-1800s, the French women's work had been overlooked in the developing fairy-tale canon in favor of the more acceptable male author Charles Perrault.[8] This dismissal occurred despite the fact that the women had produced two-thirds of the *contes de fées* written between 1690 and 1715 (Seifert 84).[9]

Relative to the *contes de fées,* we can see Carter's literary fairy tales not as departures from some simpler fairy-tale tradition but as intensifications and modifications of previously instituted and sophisticated narrative modes. The adult wit and glittering style of Carter's writing are, of course, her own but precedents were established during the *ancien régime* with the inventive style of the French women. Even certain metanarrative qualities in Carter's work were anticipated by the *contes de fées.* The *contes* were typically self-referential, making "self-conscious commentaries on themselves and on the genre [they were] part of" (Harries 161). They functioned, as Harries puts it, as "fairy tales about fairy tales" (161). By her own admission, Carter too wrote "stories about fairy tales" (qtd. in Makinen 5), although her metanarrative art has been little studied. Nor has the relationship of her narratives to those of Perrault or the French women authors been examined closely.[10] It is appropriate that Carter chose to reframe some of Perrault's tales in *The Bloody Chamber,* given the long-standing, positive reception of his tales. However, also given three centuries of patriarchal disdain for the "proto-feminist" efforts of the salon and *contes* women, it is ironically apropos that Carter, a feminist, should now speak through Perrault's tales.

In addition, certain character types popular in seventeenth-century narratives parallel some of those that Carter appreciated. Like those in Carter's collections of oral tales as well as in her literary work, the female protagonists of the salon tales and the *contes* could be "wise, clever, perceptive, occasionally lyrical, [and] eccentric" (Carter, *Old Wives'* xxii). Such a character is Finette of Marie-Jeanne L'Héritier's "The Discreet Princess" (1695–98) who, in contrast to her sisters Babbler and Nonchalante, is said to evidence "great judgment," "a wonderful presence of mind," and "good sense"—qualities, admittedly, that could serve different functions in the seventeenth century as compared to the late twentieth or twenty-first century. Women's skill in speaking well—however the quality of that skill is defined—is apparent in Carter's female characters. For example, the Red Riding Hood protagonist of Carter's story "The Company of Wolves," who knows when she confronts the (were)wolf antagonist that she is "nobody's meat" (219). Other character-types undergo a transformation under Carter's influence. For instance, the traditionally benign figure of the French fairy godmother can be inverted, with Carter, into the malevolent crone of "The Snow Pavilion" or into the aging movie queen of "The Merchant of Shadows," a woman who is actually her own husband.[11] Additionally and most importantly, like the salon narrators and the authors of the *contes,* Carter was drawn to the fairy tale as a vehicle of sociopolitical commentary. And like the characters created by the seventeenth-century authors and indeed like those women themselves, Carter's fairy-tale protagonists often face conditions of enclosure. To be sure, *The Bloody Chamber* has been criticized by some for its interest in motifs of entrapment (Duncker). However, just as female protagonists in *Chamber* typically find themselves within actual or perceived perimeters, they just as typically discover alternatives to them. In her lack of patience with essentialism and master narratives, in her penchant for inter- and intratextuality, and in her insistence on blurring the "boundaries which purport to fix reality one way or another" (Kappas 128), Carter produced a counterdiscourse to enclosure, always mindful though that a recognition of boundaries must precede their modification and dissolution.

Other fairy-tale traditions bearing upon Carter's fiction are the American tradition, specifically the productions of the fairy-tale film industry as it has been influenced by Walt Disney, and the Italian tradition, particularly the writings of the early seventeenth-century Neapolitan Giambattista Basile. Over much of the twentieth century, Disney created his own niche within a fairy-tale tradition long dominated by male collector/editors, authors, and illustrators. In the opinion of some, however, Disney was not only a descendent of this male line but one who capitalized upon it in markedly ideological and financial ways.

In Zipes's view, what was important to Disney was not the enhancement of the fairy-tale tradition or the visual exploration of oral/aural relationships between traditional storytellers and their audiences. Rather, what guided Disney's perspective was the desired impact that he as a "creator could have on as large an audience as possible in order to sell a commodity and endorse ideological images that would enhance his corporate power" (*Happily Ever After* 87). By the 1930s Disney had established key elements of his perspective with his animated film *Snow White and the Seven Dwarfs*: first, the selection of a familiar story line that by virtue of its simplicity would highlight the technical artistry and innovation of the film itself; and second the reinforcement of a patriarchal code that associated model male characters with action and power and marginalized model female characters by linking them with domesticity and disempowerment (71). Admittedly, Disney's innovations in animated film were remarkable. However, in Zipes's opinion, what Disney actually promoted was the "domestication of the imagination" (92). His fairy-tale films offer an "eternal return of the same" with their one-dimensional, stereotypical characters, their thematic emphasis on "cleanliness, control, and organized industry," and their encouragement of "nonreflective viewing" (*Fairy Tale* 94–95). And Disney's wider corporate efforts provide an emotionally comfortable (but lucrative for their producers) blending of the material and the marvelous through the merchandising of fairy-tale film-related books, clothing, records, and toys as well as the attractions of theme amusement parks.

In contrast to Disney's penchant for the "eternal return of the same," Giambattista Basile's *Lo cunto de li cunti* (*The tale of tales* [1634–36]) incorporates an eclectic range of styles and themes drawn from various traditions. Nancy Canepa comments that, in *Lo cunto*, "high and low cultures intersect to create an 'open,' heteroglossic text in which linguistic and cultural hierarchies . . . are rearranged" ("Quanto" 40). Mixing high and low cultures, for example, Basile's noble characters speak in the Neopolitan dialect, which, prior to *Lo cunto*, had been associated in written literature with "peasants, vagabonds, fools, and other butts of laughter" (41). He further challenges literary and social hierarchy with his collection's frame narrative, which begins as a tale of a princess who cannot laugh (but eventually does) and progresses into a series of fairy tales told to satisfy the aural cravings of a prince's wife who is pregnant (but who is subsequently deposed and, with her child in utero, killed). In this way, Basile's interest in leveling hierarchy is coupled with the motif of emergence, not of a child but of a literary domain, a pairing that effects, via his collection, the "entrance of the fairy tale into the authored canon of Western literature" (42).

Another example of Basile's interrogation of hierarchy is his version of "Puss-in-Boots," a tale retold by both Walt Disney and Angela Carter. In Basile's version, "Cagliuso" the title character inherits only a cat from his beggar father. The wily feline proceeds, through deceiving others, to gain for Cagliuso fame, fortune, and a princess for a wife. Later, to test her master's assertions of gratitude, the cat plots another deception, this time directed at Cagliuso himself. Her master fails the test, and the indignant and poorly repaid cat cries, "This is all the 'thousand thanks' for the rags I lifted from your back that were only fit to hang spindles on? . . . Go, and a curse be on everything that I have done for you, for you're not worth spitting on!" (Penzer 157). In its imbalanced ending, Basile's tale contrasts with both Disney's and Carter's. Apparently borrowing the motif of dual romance from Disney's 1922 short animated film *Puss in Boots* (Zipes, *Happily Ever After* 35–36), Carter's human hero links up with his sought-after young woman, but Puss also establishes a romantic relationship with the cat of the young woman's household. The happy endings for human and animal mirror each other.[12]

Though opting for the emotionally satisfying conclusion like Disney's, Carter's "Puss-in-Boots" sets Basile and Disney in dialogue with one another as well as with her own narrative. Both Basile's and Carter's cats illustrate the wily servant character-type who believes he or she can accomplish almost anything— an expectation Carter exploits in ebullient fashion. Her tale begins with Puss, the narrator, singing his own praises with allusions to the comedic/operatic character of Figaro. Puss exclaims, "Figaro here; Figaro, there, I tell you! Figaro upstairs, Figaro downstairs . . . he's a cat of the world, cosmopolitan, sophisticated . . . A tom, sirs, a ginger tom and proud of it" (170). This is a cat who believes he has no equal and who astounds even himself at times, as when he finally accomplishes the "famous death-defying triple somersault en plein air, that is, in middle air, that is unsupported and without a safety net" (171). Despite his egocentricity, Carter's Puss betters Disney's female cat who, though resourceful, relies more on twentieth-century technology (a hypnotic machine) than on innate skill (either physical or verbal) in achieving impression management.

In contrast to Disney's staid commitment to depictions of "clean" living and other "family values," both of Carter's primary male characters—feline and human—enjoy a reputation for frequent and raucous sexual escapades. The bawdy humor of Carter's story borrows from Basile, in part from his frame tale. There, the princess who cannot laugh witnesses the reaction of an old woman whose water jar has been broken maliciously by a "devil of a Court page" (Canepa, "Quanto" 44). Angered, the old woman loses "her phlegmatic compass bearings and charg[es] from the stable of patience [by raising] the stage curtain and reveal[ing] a woodsy scene" (44). Seeing the old woman displaying her genitals in frustration at her loss, the princess bursts into laughter. An analogous undoing of constraints is apparent—indeed, celebrated—in Carter's tale as her male Puss does not simply wash but repeatedly reports on washing his "privates" (172), the coal dust removed from his "sparkling dicky," doing so to pass the time as his master makes the "beast with two backs with every harlot in the city" (173). In Bakhtinian fashion, the low subordinates the high in fun and in challenge.

Carter also interrogates Disney's habit of disempowering his female characters by allowing her own young woman character (whom Puss and his master help to liberate from a suffocating life with a doddering and possessive husband) to participate fully in the bed-thumping sex. Initially described in courtly love terms as a "princess," "[r]emote and shining as the [star] Aldebaran" (172), her face like an "alabaster lamp lit behind by dawn's first flush" (173), the "divinity [Puss's master has] come to worship" (174), the young wife shows the "glimmerings of sturdy backbone" (180) in several ways, one of them during her second tryst with her new lover by "heav[ing] him up and throw[ing] him on his back, her turn at the grind now, and you'd think she'll never stop" (184). Carter does not allow her young woman to remain on a pedestal, and the guiling not only of the husband but also of the crotchety woman housekeeper suggests Carter's criticism of those of either gender who would insist on keeping their princesses pure.

By tarting up "Puss-in-Boots," Carter celebrates with Basile the vital energies of life while interrogating the corporate-driven reductiveness of Disney. Admittedly, both Disney and Carter tell tales of the "little guy" who wins out over the more affluent and more powerful classes. In Disney, Puss and her master dupe a king; in Carter, Puss and his tabby paramour engineer the "accidental" death of the elderly but rich husband. However, it may be no coincidence that Carter's Puss and his master, who are both working "men" and lusty after life in the spirit of Basile's tales, better the husband Signor Panteleone, who, through his name, is linked to Venice during the late Middle Ages and Renaissance, the center of an economic empire—perhaps an allusion to Disney himself.[13]

In the scholarship on Carter, particularly that dealing with *The Bloody Chamber,* mention is made of the conservatism of the fairy-tale genre and/or of Carter restricting her rewritings to the fairy tales of Charles Perrault. As we have tried to indicate here, both situations are more complicated than that. Whatever conservatism is suggested by fairy tales is not necessarily present because peasant folk put it there. Rather, fairy tales that have been altered from their oral versions come to reflect, to whatever degree, the ideological perspectives of their editors and reframers. To hypothesize the direct linkage of fairy tales to a peasant mentality is a hopeless quest for origins, one especially hopeless given the multiple reworkings of the "classic" tales even in just the twentieth century. Nor is it appropriate to center on Charles Perrault as Carter's exclusive source. Even within the French tradition, of which Perrault is often (erroneously) assumed to be the sole master, alternate voices of fairy-tale authors are available to be heard, their possible influence on Carter available for investigation. Further, recognizing interrelationships among Carter's multiple sources, such as with Basile and Disney, can enrich an understanding of the heterogeneous frames in which and with which Carter worked.

The volume's first three essays consider different aspects of Carter's relationship to the fairy tale in general—by exploring her role as translator and editorial advisor, the critical responses to her fairy-tale work, and the impact of the fairy tale on her oeuvre. The volume then offers essays on specific tales—principally "The Bloody Chamber" and "The Courtship of Mr Lyon"—as particularly telling examples of Carter's stance toward the genre. Following these are contributions on fairy-tale related texts that, in comparison to tales from *The Bloody Chamber*, have been little studied. These texts are drawn from Carter's stories for children, her novels, and her wonder- and legendlike tales. Also included is an interview that considers artistically creative responses to Carter and the fairy tale, providing insight to the illustrations of her two volumes of collected fairy tales as well as the film adaptations of her work. The concluding pieces combine commentary and fiction and reflect on Carter's creative vision. Visual commentary is provided through illustrations drawn from Carter's second edited collection of fairy tales.

It is appropriate that the first contribution of this collection is that of Jacques Barchilon, who founded *Merveilles & Contes/Marvels & Tales* in 1987 and who worked with Angela Carter when she was a member of that journal's editorial board. Barchilon's memoir, however, does not focus on the business details of their relationship but rather on more personal aspects of their long-distance communication. Remembering the accuracy of her English translation of Charles Perrault's fairy tales and the "magic of her style" (26) in her own tales, Barchilon refers to excerpts from letters he received from Carter, thus opening the door to an additional aspect of her writing. His references prompt one to hope that, sooner rather than later, Carter's correspondence will be collected and made available in print.

Stephen Benson's contributions review various scholarly and journalistic responses to Carter's fairy-tale work, published over the past twenty years. Benson surveys an impressive range of reactions, grouping them around the topics of intertextuality and pornography's relation to conceptions of female sexuality. He considers the latter in terms of connections between Carter's extended essay *The Sadeian Woman* and her literary collection *The Bloody Chamber*. With respect to the power of intertextuality in Carter's fiction, Benson views her fairy tales as materialist, historicizing, and "denaturaliz[ing of] the mythic pretensions of [their] source texts" (43) He then considers those treatments of Carter's tales that acknowledge the tales' relativizing power: their ability to mix modes in the service of process and re-vision.

In Lorna Sage's piece, she describes the transformational impact that fairy tales had on Carter's work by considering relationships between Italo Calvino's retellings of fairy tales and Carter's. Sage also takes up the issue of *The Bloody Chamber*'s relationship to pornography noting that Carter wrote those tales while rereading Sade. Explaining that both pornography and the fairy tale (as well as "novels, psychoanalysis, and suburbia" [68]) have contributed to the myth of the "good"-because-passively-suffering woman, Sage cites the Marquis de Sade's character Justine, the fairy-tale heroine Sleeping Beauty, and even Shakespeare's Ophelia as representatives of the "unimaginative woman" (71) who wears her sense of blamelessness as if a natural skin adhered to her soul. Those "bankrupt enchantments" (67) in which such women characters operate, in Sage's words, stultify rather than encourage the reader to discover the means to "take flight" (68). Sage argues that fairy tales can be read as providing this access if one knows how, as Carter did, to see past patriarchal bias by means of historically grounded and liberating perspectives.

Kathleen E. B. Manley's "The Woman in Process in Angela Carter's 'The Bloody Chamber'" is the first in a set of three essays on that story. Reading past the stereotype that would make a victim of the female protagonist, Manley argues that the Marquis's newest wife is a "woman in process, someone who is [beginning to] explor[e] her subject position" (83). Combining the metaphors of the blank page and the (un)stained nuptial sheet, Manley considers the fibers of emotional strength and the opportunities for independence that the protagonist has received from her mother and weighs these against the young wife's lack of self-confidence, naiveté, and romantic assumptions about marriage. The protagonist understandably oscillates between action and passivity in searching for her identity as a woman. Manley examines Carter's references to mirrors and to Richard Wagner's opera *Tristan and Isolde* in indicating the processes of discovery by which the protagonist "escapes the tale patriarchy wished to tell of her and instead tells her own story" (92).

Cheryl Renfroe's "Initiation and Disobedience: Liminal Experience in Angela Carter's 'The Bloody Chamber'" takes a different approach toward the story by drawing on anthropological interpretations of rites of passage. Renfroe combines these interpretations with a view of intertextuality as a simultaneous vision of past and present/future, and she recognizes two subtexts in the story whose interrelationships reflect this dynamic. The first, that of the Marquis's initiatory testing of his new wife with the intent to subjugate her, is informed by the second, that of the wife's crossing a crucial threshold from subjugation to free will. The tension between these subtexts, in Renfroe's opinion, opens a liminal space in which the reader can reconsider patriarchy's mythic and entrenched role in the cultural initiation of women. Also useful in identifying this space is Renfroe's intertextual rethinking of the role of the biblical Eve with whom the wife is identified in the story. Rather than viewing the wife as someone who ends paradise and thereby condemns herself to a life of misery, Renfroe sees both Eve and the wife as emancipatory figures, as women who win the right of self-determination.

In "The Contextualization of the Marquis in Angela Carter's 'The Bloody Chamber,'" Danielle M. Roemer takes yet another route into the story, examining the role of allusion. She concentrates on patriarchy's control of the processes of signification, specifically those concerning the construction of the ideal woman. Associating the Marquis with three "Oriental" tyrants, either directly or indirectly alluded to in the story, Roemer examines Carter's treatment of the consuming passions of patriarchy in its obsession with display and its lack of respect for individuality—and even life. Linking the young wife's exploration of her husband's castle with the reader-activated investigation of allusion, and contrasting these modes with the Marquis's and his avatars' domination of meaning, Roemer points to Carter's investigation of curiosity—one in which curiosity develops into either life or death, depending on the energies of its construction.

In "The Logic of the Same and *Différance*: 'The Courtship of Mr Lyon,'" Anny Crunelle-Vanrigh considers Carter's treatment of the "canonical" fairy tale "Beauty and the Beast." In contrast to assumptions of singularity implied by the status of canonicity, however, Crunelle-Vanrigh finds that by rewriting fairy tales, a genre based on the act of retelling, Carter "places repetition and difference at the core of her enterprise" (128). While examining repetition and difference as imitation and variation from a narratological viewpoint, Crunelle-Vanrigh also considers the dynamic as *différance* from a deconstructionist perspective, and as the dialectic of Same and Other from a feminist stance. Comparing "Courtship" to other Carter stories—"The Tiger's Bride," "Wolf-Alice," and "Peter and the Wolf"—she argues that "[P]resence is replaced by . . . volatile and unstable identity—beast or beauty, tiger or bride, wolf or girl" (139), in which each new identity/signifier gives "meaning to the previous one and so on 'forever after'" (139).

Elise Bruhl and Michael Gamer take a different track in questioning singularity in their essay, "Teaching Improprieties: *The Bloody Chamber* and the

Reverent Classroom." Reporting on the reception of the collection in several undergraduate classrooms and in a law clerks' reading group, Bruhl and Gamer found reactions similar to those demonstrated in professional scholarship on Carter: that the collection tends to polarize readers, often producing either "unmitigated praise [or] unabashed anger" (147). Bruhl and Gamer suggest that the collection provokes unease because it provokes examination of readers' assumptions about readerly pleasure. However, the potentially rocky road of classroom reception for *Chamber*, Bruhl and Gamer suggest, can provide a valuable pedagogical resource. Acclimatizing students to the heterogeneity of Carter's approaches can serve as a way of getting students to think about the politics of convention and revision, not only in Carter's fiction but also in the students' own perspectives on reading and writing across various contexts.

Moving beyond tales from *The Bloody Chamber*, Zipes's essay "Crossing Boundaries with Wise Girls: Angela Carter's Fairy Tales for Children" concentrates on an overlooked area of Carter's fiction, her picture books for children. Zipes explains the ways in which *Miss Z, the Dark Young Lady* (1970) and *The Donkey Prince* (1970) anticipated Carter's future work with adult revisionist fairy tales. He finds that the female protagonists of both books prefigure those later characters who are wily, strong, and, most importantly, marked by some form of difference. These are not protagonists who strive above all to marry the prince; these are women who explore unknown and potentially dangerous territory, returning home wiser for their effort. Nor have these protagonists been created expressly for children, in Zipes's view. Instead, they inhabit what Zipes terms "crossover" tales, which, like their protagonists, "break down accepted definitions, norms, values, types, and forms" (165) to create a literary and imaginative space amenable to both children and adults.

Considering the amount of criticism generated in response to Carter's literary fairy tales, fairy-tale elements in Carter's longer fiction have garnered little attention. Kai Mikkonen addresses this neglected area in his essay "The Hoffman(n) Effect and the Sleeping Prince: Fairy Tales in Angela Carter's *The Infernal Desire Machines of Doctor Hoffman*." Focusing on the literary devices of polygenetic intertextuality and parody as well as the use of an unreliable narrator and the treatment of characters as figures of speech, Mikkonen considers Carter's rewriting of E. T. A. Hoffmann's romantic tales and her reframing of the Grimms' "Sleeping Beauty." Conducting this discussion through frames provided by romantic, surrealist, and modernist aesthetics, Mikkonen explains that alternative readings of Carter's work—with its "texts embedded within each other in a potentially endless and all-pervasive combination" (170)—encourage a model of reading as "circularity and metamorphosis" (175). The resulting opposition between stability and change adumbrates structural transformations of the traditional "Sleeping Beauty" story (e.g., is it really the prince figure who is sleeping?). Mikkonen further argues that Carter's treatment of characters as figures of speech problematizes issues of the semiotic construction of the subject, both within and without the novel. For example, with *Infernal Desires*, Carter's treatment of desire raises questions about the role of the reader of the romantic fairy tale and reinterprets that position as oscillating between voyeurism and its critique.

Betty Moss provides an alternative slant on the project of reinterpreting prevailing stances. In her essay, "Desire and the Female Grotesque in Angela Carter's 'Peter and the Wolf,'" Moss brings Cixousean and Bakhtinian perspectives to bear on this little-studied tale of wonder. Arguing that for Carter "continual exploration and regeneration are an imperative responsibility" (199), Moss locates the story's most potent sign of potentiality in the female wolf-child's grotesque body, specifically in its genitalia. By means of this image of otherness and difference, Moss suggests, Carter's tale contrasts male arguments of a void of finality with female assertions of a domain of abundance. The result, in Moss's opinion, is a narrative of defamiliarization, materiality, and process, one which prompts the reader's unease with masculine priorities of domination and transcendence.

Investigating the act of literary storytelling across genres, Janet L. Langlois's essay "Andrew Borden's Little Girl: Fairy-Tale Fragments in Angela Carter's 'The Fall River Axe Murders' and 'Lizzie's Tiger'" examines fairy-tale fragments in Carter's retellings of the legend of Lizzie Borden, the woman accused of killing her father and her stepmother in Fall River, Massachusetts in 1892. Langlois argues that, always sensitive to the impact of shifting narrative forms, Carter explores Borden's representations as woman/princess-daughter/murderer/icon/enigma by intertextually playing her treatment of Borden against her own previous rewrites of "Little Red Riding Hood." Langlois's examination of the companion tale "Lizzie's Tiger" extends her tracking of *Märchen* elements through another legendlike story. Here Langlois posits relationships between Carter's fictional history of an event in Borden's childhood and the fairy-tale quest of "Hansel and Gretel," on the one hand, and one of Carter's "Beauty and the Beast" tales, "The Tiger's Bride," on the other. Throughout, Langlois suggests, Carter intermingles a reaction of horror at Borden's violence with a not unsympathetic portrait of Borden's containment within patriarchal and Victorian codes.

Although the film adaptation of Carter's tale "The Company of Wolves" has attracted scholarly attention, other image-centered renderings of her work have generally been overlooked. Cristina Bacchilega addresses this oversight through interviews in her contribution "In the Eye of the Fairy Tale: Corinna Sargood and David Wheatley Talk about Working with Angela Carter." Sargood, a London-born artist and longtime friend of Carter's, illustrated the two Virago books of fairy tales edited by Carter; Wheatley, an award-winning director, directed the film *The Magic Toyshop*, adapted from Carter's 1967 novel. Interviews with both focus on the process of collaboration between writer and illustrator or director; on Sargood's and Wheatley's understanding of and involvement with fairy tales, independent of Carter; and on these visual artists' fascination with Carter's work as well as their knowledge of Carter's "luggage" (226) of images. Kate Webb's observations bridge the two interviews and contribute to place Carter's fascination with film in a larger context of image and word re-production.

Three of Corinna Sargood's illustrations from *Strange Things Sometimes Still Happen* are included in this volume. They illustrate Carter's tongue-in-cheek and yet symbolically layered approach to the fairy tales she had selected for her second anthology: the squatting frog is more than a symbol of fertility in the Hungarian "The Midwife and the Frog"; the trompe-l'oeil basin where the young bride in "The Sleeping Prince" will wash is made with the head of the old witch; and in "The Werefox," the treacherous and foxy Chinese spirit who takes on the form of a lovely woman to tempt a horseman, turns into dry bones in the end, but only after her "flesh and bones flowed away like a stream" (75). Sargood's images visualize Carter's attention to transformation—its eeriness as well as its quotidian instances. "The Bloody Chamber" linocut, which Sargood created specifically for the special journal issue and which is used for the cover of this volume, is more complex in its combination of metaphorical and narrative axes. Sargood's image, like Carter's story, foregrounds the four elements—air, water, earth, and the fire of passion along with the mother's revolver *firing* its "single, irreproachable bullet" (142)—those life forces which the deadly husband thinks he can submit to his own will. In Sargood's visualization, the bloody chamber of violence against women is blown apart, opened up for the world to see, but also reframed in a dynamic flux of symbols and actions.

It is appropriate that Robert Coover's fictional tribute to Angela Carter, "Entering Ghost Town," should be prefaced by his headnote statement that he and Carter encountered one another in the "landscape of the tale" (242). Both he and Carter are, in Coover's words, "intransigent realist[s]" (242), committed to the tale because of its refusal, as Carter puts it, to "betray its readers into a false knowledge of everyday experience" (242). Both Coover and Carter deal in landscapes of the fictional/metafictional kind, traversing a geography of the imagination that, again in Carter's words, can "help to transform reality itself" (242). The specific landscape Coover addresses in his piece is that of the mythic Old West, previously carved into a cultural institution by literary, journalistic, and cinematic treatments but which Coover both grits up and defuses into a tale that offers no comfort in nostalgia. The mythical elements of the lonesome stranger who rides up to others' campfires and meets with a requisite showdown involving suspicious questions about his identity, origin, and destination, all become, under Coover's pen, a telling interrogation not only of the mythic Old West—a consolatory nonsense inhabited by American ghosts, Carter might say—but also of self-comforting American millennialist assumptions about a heroic past.[14]

For writer Marina Warner, reading Carter's *The Bloody Chamber* "turned the key" (250), opening the door to a "hidden room" (250) of women's sexuality and desire, which, Warner recognized, opened up the possibility for herself and other women authors to "improvise . . . from what [they] already knew and liked" (252). Warner's story, "Ballerina: The Belled Girl Sends a Tape to an Impresario," does just that by retelling the Grimms' fairy tale "The Maiden without Hands" in a contemporary setting. The story plays on the intersection of two different institutions, the psychiatric hospital and the media, in which women (in the stereotypes of the madwoman and the star) have acquired notoriety or fame. Being the center of spectacle has always been the name of the game for Warner's protagonist. Within that game, she has been objectified and mutilated—*belle* (the traditional Beauty) turned into a woman with bells for hands—and yet she is eager to use herself as an instrument of music once again because this is her only ticket to being loved or valued. The protagonist Phoebe Jones is, like the folktale maiden, a child-victim of those she trusts, and also a resilient improviser and performer.

In preparing the special issue of *Marvels & Tales* as well as the present volume, we have become increasingly aware of how much interest there is all over the world in Angela Carter's work. We could include only some of this scholarship, and only when written in English. However, we have retained both British and American spellings to mark the conversation between two traditions of Carter criticism that have often been exclusive of one another, and we have attempted to represent a more broadly European perspective as well. We look forward to the publication of more globally diversified scholarship on Carter and the fairy tale.

We wish to thank all the contributors for their careful and patient cooperation during the editing process. Special thanks to Robert Coover, Corinna Sargood, and Marina Warner for offering their pieces as a tribute to Angela Carter; to Donald Haase for inviting us to edit the special issue; to John Rieder, Craig Howes, Alison Regan, and John Zuern for providing friendly encouragement and editorial or word-processing assistance when we assembled the special issue; to Arthur Evans for contributing his support in bringing this volume to fruition; and to Kristin Harpster for her attention to this Wayne State University Press project.

Notes

1. Carter's relationship to other traditions, which are not treated here, includes that of Orientalism—the European imaginative construction of the Middle East as evidenced, for example, in adaptations and borrowings from *The Thousand and One Nights*—and that of British folklore. As part of the latter, in the introduction to her first fairy-tale collection, *The Old Wives' Fairy Tale Book*, Carter writes of her indebtedness to British folklorist Andrew Lang: "[This] collection has been consciously modeled on those anthologies compiled by Andrew Lang at the turn of the century that once gave me so much joy" (xiv). For a particularly useful transnational collection of fairy tales from a variety of traditions, including commentary, see Tatar's *Classic Fairy Tales*.
2. For example, the first English translation of Madame d'Aulnoy's collection of French fairy tales was published as *The Tales of the Fairies in Three Parts, Compleat* in 1707.
3. Within folkloristics, there has been much debate but little consensus as to what constitutes a fairy tale. One specific term is *Zaubermärchen*, which designates "the tale of magic." *The Types of the Folk-Tale* lists tale types and motifs of the magic tale under nos. 300–749.
4. Carter's second fairy-tale collection appeared under the title *Strange Things Sometimes Still Happen.*
5. Carter's stories and tales are given in *Burning Your Boats: The Collected Short Stories.* All page numbers are to this edition.
6. An additional topic for criticism was Louis XIV's reign—his heavy taxes, his costly wars of territorial acquisition, his absolutist rule, and the deteriorating social conditions that had developed as a result of these events.
7. Perrault published the fairy tales *Donkey Skin* and *The Foolish Wishes* in 1694, followed by eight more tales in *Histoires ou contes du temps passé* in 1697. In their brevity, their more straightforward plot lines, and the way they downplay *précieux* style, Perrault's fairy tales were not representative of the majority of tales written during this period.
8. In addition to French criticism, the Grimms, prompted by their romantic belief in the simplicity of *Märchen*, praised Perrault at the expense of the French women. In their introduction to the first edition of the *Kinder- und Hausmärchen* (1812), they even assert (erroneously) that the women's work is derivative of Perrault: "France must surely have more [tales] than those given us by Charles Perrault, who alone treated them as children's tales (not so his inferior imitators, d'Aulnoy, Murat); he gives us only nine, certainly the best known and also among the most beautiful" (qtd. in Harries 152).
9. The vogue of salon fairy tales in France was followed by that of Oriental tales. This was marked most significantly by the efforts of male authors, particularly Antoine Galland's *Les Mille et Une Nuits* (1704–17). Zipes identifies a third phase, that of the "Comic and Conventional Fairy Tale" (beginning around 1720), as emphasizing "standard notions of propriety and morality that reinforced the socialization process in France" (*Beauties* 10). Mme. Leprince de Beaumont's "Beauty and the Beast" (1757) is of this period. Anny Crunelle-Vanrigh (this volume) reads Carter's tale "The Courtship of Mr Lyon" in light of Beaumont's story.
10. Another women's salon tradition—that of the *Kaffeterkreis* in Germany—also deserves attention. Founded in 1843 and essentially defunct by 1851, this association

encouraged the discussion of art and aesthetics as well as the rewriting of fairy tales, which its members presented orally or rendered in short plays. In Shawn Jarvis's words, these fairy tales presented female protagonists who "found happiness in being educated and single rather than married and brain dead" (106).

11. Alternatively, Carter can localize fairy godmothers yet keep them otherworldly by presenting them as spirits, specifically those of the three deceased mothers of Carter's "Ashputtle or the Mother's Ghost."

12. The earliest literary version of "Puss-in-Boots" is that of the sixteenth-century Italian, Straparola. In it, the cat, who is a fairy in disguise, assists the male hero in gaining his princess by duping a king, a lord, and many commoners. His version is essentially the one offered by Perrault, though in the latter's retelling the cat is male, not a fairy, and acquires a pair of boots from his human master.

13. Signor Panteleone, nicknamed Pantaloon in Carter's story, recalls a stock character of the same name in the Commedia dell'Arte who was typically depicted as an old man in slippers. The name Pantalone was originally a nickname for a Venetian, after Pantaleone, a saint popular in Venice. Thus, we can construct the image of a slippered, miserly, and self-righteous Panteleone—or foolish *leone*: a "lion" cat—who is bested by Carter's robust, ethically shady, and booted ginger tom.

14. The intended references here are to the title of Carter's last collection of tales, *American Ghosts & Old World Wonders,* and to her attitude toward myth as evidenced, for example, in *The Sadeian Woman.*

Works Cited

Bottigheimer, Ruth B. "From Gold to Guilt: The Forces Which Reshaped *Grimms' Tales.*" McGlathery, 192–204.

Canepa, Nancy L. "Quanto 'nc'è da ccà a lo luoco dove aggio da ire?": Giambattista Basile's Quest for the Literary Fairy Tale." Canepa 37–80.

———, ed. *Out of the Woods: Origins of the Literary Fairy Tale in Italy and France.* Detroit: Wayne State UP, 1997.

Carter, Angela. *American Ghosts & Old World Wonders.* London: Chatto & Windus, 1993.

———. "Angela Carter." *The Writer's Imagination: Interviews with Major International Women Novelists.* By Olga Kenyon. Bradford: U of Bradford Print Unit, 1992. 23–33.

———. *Burning Your Boats: The Collected Short Stories.* New York: Henry Holt and Company, 1995.

———. *The Sadeian Woman and the Ideology of Pornography.* New York: Pantheon Books, 1978.

———, ed. *The Old Wives' Fairy Tale Book.* New York: Pantheon Books, 1990.

———, ed. *Strange Things Sometimes Still Happen.* Boston: Faber and Faber, 1992.

Dégh, Linda. "What Did the Grimm Brothers Give to and Take from the Folk?" McGlathery 66–90.

Duncker, Patricia. "Re-Imagining the Fairy Tale: Angela Carter's Bloody Chambers." *Literature and History* 10 (1984): 3–14.

Gamble, Sarah. *Angela Carter: Writing from the Front Line.* Edinburgh: Edinburgh UP, 1997.

Goldberg, Christine. "Märchen." *Encyclopedia of Folklore and Literature.* Ed. Mary Ellen Brown and Bruce A. Rosenberg. Santa Barbara, CA: ABC-CLIO, 1998. 407–08.

Haase, Donald, ed. *The Reception of Grimms' Fairy Tales: Responses, Reactions, Revisions.* Detroit: Wayne State UP, 1993.

Harries, Elizabeth W. "Fairy Tales about Fairy Tales: Notes on Canon Formation." Canepa 152–75.

Jarvis, Shawn. "Trivial Pursuit? Women Deconstructing the Grimmian Model in the *Kaffeterkreis.*" Haase 102–26.

Köhler-Zülch, Ines. "Heinrich Pröhle: A Successor to the Brothers Grimm." Haase 41–58.

Lappas, Catherine. " 'Seeing Is Believing, but Touching Is the Truth': Female Spectatorship and Sexuality in *The Company of Wolves.*" *Women's Studies* 25 (1996): 115–35.

Makinen, Merja. "Angela Carter's *The Bloody Chamber* and the Decolonization of Feminine Sexuality." *Feminist Review* 42 (1992): 2–15.

McGlathery, James M., ed. *The Brothers Grimm and Folktale.* Urbana: U of Illinois P, 1988.

Penzer, N. M., ed. *The Pentamerone of Giambattista Basile.* London: John Lane, 1932.

Scherf, Walter. "Jacob and Wilhelm Grimm: A Few Small Corrections to a Commonly Held Image." McGlathery 178–91.

Seifert, Lewis C. *Fairy Tales, Sexuality, and Gender in France, 1690–1715: Nostalgic Utopias.* Cambridge: Cambridge UP, 1996.

Tatar, Maria, ed. *The Classic Fairy Tales: Texts, Criticism.* New York: W. W. Norton, 1999.

———. *Off with Their Heads! Fairy Tales and the Culture of Childhood.* Princeton: Princeton UP, 1992.

Thompson, Stith, and Antti Aarne. *The Types of the Folk-Tale: A Classification and Bibliography.* Folklore Fellows Communication 184. Helsinki: Academia Scientiarum Fennica, 1964.

Zipes, Jack. *Fairy Tale as Myth. Myth as Fairy Tale.* Lexington: UP of Kentucky, 1994.

———. *Happily Ever After: Fairy Tales, Children, and the Culture Industry.* New York: Routledge, 1994.

———, trans. *Beauties, Beasts and Enchantment: Classic French Fairy Tales.* New York: Meridian Books, 1989.

———, ed. and trans. *The Complete Fairy Tales of the Brothers Grimm.* New York: Bantam Books, 1987.

Jacques Barchilon

Remembering Angela Carter

Remembering Angela Carter is bittersweet for me. I first came across her writings when looking for a good modern translation of Charles Perrault's tales. After reading Marianne Moore's inaccurate version of "La Belle au bois dormant," I was delighted to find Angela Carter's beautiful 1977 rendition. I quickly saw that—unlike Marianne Moore and others—she had not stumbled over Perrault's French. When Sleeping Beauty awakens, she engages in a lively conversation with her rescuer, who is far less articulate than the princess. The French text explains that his "discours furent mal rangés: ils en plurent davantage . . ." (102); however, "plurent davantage" is hardly Moore's "they shed some tears as well" (23).[1] In contrast, Angela Carter effectively interpreted: " . . . and though he stumbled over the words, that made her very happy, because he showed so much feeling" (66). Obviously the author of *The Bloody Chamber* understood French well enough to translate Perrault with accuracy and imagination.

It was in that 1979 collection that I next read Carter's retellings, or modern adaptations, of Perrault's tales. In general I don't like retellings of famous fairy tales. I did not approach her stories with pleasant anticipation. But I was immediately "taken in" by the magic of her style. Her version of "Bluebeard" or "The Bloody Chamber" (this first story giving its title to the collection) is both modern and elegantly French—rooted in a luxurious, gloomy castle in early twentieth-century Brittany, with a protagonist who wears gowns by Poiret, the great Parisian couturier, and is possessed of a wry humor. Told in the first person by the young wife, the story unfolds with many echoes of Perrault. Of course, the protagonist enters the forbidden chamber and finds the bodies of previous wives; of course, she drops the key and "burst[s] into a tumult of sobbing that

Marvels & Tales: Journal of Fairy-Tale Studies, Vol. 12, No. 1 (1998), pp. 19–22. Copyright © 1998 by Wayne State University Press, Detroit, MI 48201.

contain[s] both pity for his other victims and also a dreadful anguish to know [she], too, was one of them" (29). As expected, and in spite of the protection of the blind piano-tuner (this character an addition to Perrault's original tale), she is nearly decapitated. The originality of Carter's ending lies in its uncanny magical humor: because the telephone lines to the outside world are dead, the poor wife cannot call her mother (rather than her brothers as in Perrault) to the rescue. But the mother does appear in the nick of time and, wielding a "service revolver: . . . without a moment's hesitation, she raised my [late] father's gun, took aim and put a single, irreproachable bullet through my husband's head" (40). How did the mother know her daughter was in danger? In the author's own words: "I can only bless the—what shall I call it?—the *maternal telepathy* that sent my mother running headlong . . ." (40).

In the other stories of *The Bloody Chamber,* Carter displays her unabashed eroticism. Using the feminist language of today, one could say her style is "gendered," but in which sex? She intuitively identifies with male and female heroes. This is clear in her beautiful "Snow Child," a succinct (seven paragraphs, barely one or two pages of print) version of a widespread folkloric tale type (AT 408), "The Three Oranges."

If I may be forgiven, I am now repeating something I published a few years ago ("Angela Carter, a Tribute," in the May 1992 issue of *Merveilles & Contes*). In "The Snow Child," the father, known as the Count, magically has "the child of his desire," who is born from a hole filled with blood in the snow, without the participation of his wife, who immediately becomes jealous. The child is beautiful: white as snow, red as blood, with hair black as a raven's feathers. While in the traditional folktale versions the white, red, and black erotic fixation expresses the wish for a woman lover, here it marks a fixation for a child, a pre-pubescent girl: " . . . naked; she is the child of his desire and the Countess hated her. The Count lifted her up and sat her in front of him on his saddle, but the Countess had only one thought: How shall I be rid of her?" (91).

Nothing can mitigate the horror and erotic poetry of the ending. The child, obeying her "stepmother's" command to pick up a rose, pricks herself, falls, and begins to bleed to death. In this desperate moment the father tries not mouth-to-mouth breathing, but something stronger and erotically surreal: "Weeping, the Count got off his horse, unfastened his breeches and thrust his virile member into the dead girl. . . . [H]e was soon finished" (92). This father's behavior makes the story peculiarly Carter's own. Such desperate life-giving action does not save the Count's child: she not only bleeds to death, but also melts, since she is made of snow ("white as snow"). What happens in that story, I have argued, is not child rape—how can one rape a child made of snow?—but an event in the artistic realm of the supernatural.

At that moment of my acquaintance with Carter's writings (1985–86), I felt I had to connect personally with the author of such beautiful literary echoes of classical folktales. As luck would have it, I found out she was in the United States, teaching a course in creative writing at the University of Iowa. I wrote to her, sending her an essay full of praise for her stories. I was to present that essay at the International Colloquium on the Marvelous at Oslo University (June 1986). She immediately answered, telling me that my own writings on the fairy tale were familiar to her, and thanked me for my sensitive appreciation of her stories. A sporadic correspondence followed. We even talked on the telephone. I invited her with husband and child to be my house guests in Boulder. I tried to arrange for her to come to the University of Colorado to give a lecture. I regret to say that she did not come, through no fault of hers, or mine.

I treasure the few letters I received from Angela Carter, especially since she told me that she hated to write letters. A sort of friendship, based on a mutual appreciation of each other's writings, evolved. As a member of the Editorial Board of *Merveilles & Contes,* she agreed to advise me in my role as editor of the journal. She sent me her beautiful prose poem, "Ashputtle," for publication in the journal. I will not go into other aspects of our correspondence, concentrating rather more on the personal aspect of our long-distance friendship.

One of the nicest letters I received from her came with the gift of her fine anthology of folktales in which women are the primary and strong heroines, *The Virago Book of Fairy Tales* (1990): "Herewith a book I have assembled . . . according to a highly personal, possibly idiosyncratic set of prescriptions."

In another letter I found out why she did not write very often: she was very ill with lung cancer and easily tired, and she apologized for "not having been in touch . . . sorry to have missed contributing to the Perrault [special issue of *Merveilles & Contes*] . . . had in fact a story all planned but it never got written; we've had rather a bad summer . . . lung cancer, which is pretty annoying since I stopped smoking 8 years ago. . . . But I do not mean to tug your heart strings. I am getting back to work. . . . So I am more irritated, & indeed, offended, or affronted, by my tumour than anything else—please don't be distressed! I'll keep in touch—yours, Angela" (letter of 9 September 1991).

I have always thought that the most seductive aspect of Angela Carter's talent was her happy blend of erotic evocation, bi-sexual gendering, and a sort of surreal imagination. I am thinking of her early stories in *Fireworks* (1974) as tales that pointed the way to her later works. In that collection I liked especially "The Loves of Lady Purple," in which a Japanese puppet master falls in love with one of his giant marionettes, Lady Purple, even taking her to bed with him every night, until she becomes alive: " . . . now manifestly a woman, young and extravagantly beautiful, the leprous whiteness of her face gave her the appearance of a corpse animated solely by demonic will" (39). She is truly demonic, as she kills her master, like a vampire: "She sank her teeth into his throat and drained him" (38). In her "Afterword" to *Fireworks,* Angela Carter states her aesthetics of the tale genre in a few sentences that seem applicable to all her subsequent stories: " . . . fabulous narratives that deal directly with the imagery of the unconscious—mirrors; the externalized self; forsaken castles; haunted forests; forbidden sexual objects. . . . [T]he tale differs from the short story in that it makes few pretenses at the imitation of life. . . . The tale has relations with subliterary forms of pornography, ballad and dream, and it has not been dealt with kindly by literati" (132–33).

I still like her work very much, as does one of the great writers of our times, Salman Rushdie, also one of her friends. In an obituary a few weeks after her passing, he wrote: "[I]n spite of her worldwide reputation, here in Britain she somehow never quite had her due" (5). And yet, since her death, she has become quite popular in England. This special issue of a scholarly journal she loved is one of the best things we can do to critically appreciate and remember her, internationally.

Note

1. Marianne Moore confused the verb "plaire" (to please, be pleasing, in the past tense) with the verb "pleurer" (to cry).

Works Cited

Barchilon, Jacques. "Angela Carter, A Tribute." *Merveilles & Contes* 6.1 (May 1992): 1–4.
Carter, Angela. *The Bloody Chamber.* 1979. London and New York: Penguin Books, 1981.
———, trans. *The Fairy Tales of Charles Perrault.* 1977. Illus. Martin Ware. New York: Avon, 1979.
———. *Fireworks: Nine Stories in Various Disguises.* 1974. New York: Harper & Row, 1981.
Moore, Marianne. *Puss in Boots, The Sleeping Beauty, and Cinderella: A Retelling of Three Classic Fairy Tales Based on the French of Charles Perrault.* Illus. Eugene Karlin. New York: Macmillan, 1963.
Perrault, Charles. *Contes de Charles Perrault.* Ed. Gilbert Rouger. Paris: Garnier, 1967.
Rushdie, Salman. "Angela Carter, 1940–92: A Very Good Wizard, a Very Dear Friend." *New York Times Book Review* 8 Mar. 1992: 5.

Stephen Benson

Angela Carter and the
Literary Märchen:
A Review Essay

It is perhaps fitting, given Angela Carter's interest in all aspects of folklore, that her work has itself become the subject of a modern legend, albeit one whose truth is very much ascertainable. This is the legend of the "Carter effect," identified by The British Academy Humanities Research Board, which distributes postgraduate studentships. Lorna Sage states the facts, as reported by the President of the Academy: in the year 1992–93, "there were more than forty applicants wanting to do doctorates on Carter, making her by far the most fashionable twentieth-century topic" (*Flesh and the Mirror* 3). Paul Barker, editor of the magazine *New Society*, which published the bulk of Carter's essays from the late 1960s to the early 1980s, recounts a more detailed version, given at an academic conference devoted to Carter's work: the Academy received "[f]orty proposals for doctorates on her writing in 1992–93 . . . more than for the entire eighteenth century."[1] Barker thus nominates Carter as "the most read contemporary author on English university campuses" (14), an assumption made in similar fashion by Jan Dalley, who, after rehearsing the facts, canonizes "St Angela of the Campus" (29); and finally, in Tom Shippey's further expanded version, we have the makings of a genuinely legendary aura: more English students are writing theses on Carter "than on any author or area from anywhere in the seventeenth or eighteenth century"; or so "it is said." Like Barker and Dalley, Shippey can thus extrapolate: postmodernism "wouldn't make sense without her" (20).

Marvels & Tales: Journal of Fairy-Tale Studies, Vol. 12, No. 1 (1998), pp. 23–51. Copyright © 1998 by Wayne State University Press, Detroit, MI 48201.

Whichever way you choose to tell it, Carter's work appears ensconced in the pantheon of the contemporary, indicative of all things modern, or postmodern (albeit for the seemingly contradictory reasons of being both symptomatic [Bayley, "Fighting for the Crown"], and prescient [Barker; Sage, *Flesh and the Mirror* 1]). Essential to this fixing is the extraction of a quintessence, a central facet or facets, that can pass into common circulation. Hence the legend of the "Carter effect," which can be invoked to fix Carter's work as academically correct, having given rise to "[t]he burgeoning academic industry of Carterology" (Barker 16). Critics refer to "[t]ypical Carter territory";[2] an English pop singer is described as "covering the territory of Angela Carter's *Company of Wolves*";[3] and, as I write, a newspaper article on the use among female columnists of details from friends' personal lives is titled "The Company of Wolves."

As these non-academic examples suggest, the facet of Carter's work that seems to have made the transition into the mainstream is its association with the fairy tale, which runs as a seam through her output from the early novels to one of her last published volumes, *The Second Virago Book of Fairy Tales*. The majority of her work as editor and translator revolved around the fairy tale, and the two film adaptations of her writing are based on her own fairy-tale inventions. As Merja Makinen points out, the obituaries that followed Carter's death already proved the extent to which the author had been indelibly marked by this association (3); indeed, the mythologizing of a "benevolent witch-queen" (Rushdie, "Angela Carter" 5), the "Faerie Queene" (Warner, Introduction xii) whose life reads like a "fairy-tale" (Barker 14), has itself already been the subject of demythologizing comment (Makinen 2–3; Lee 311). Nevertheless, there is a strong case for upholding this popular conception of Carter as an author to whom the fairy tale and, more broadly, folklore were pivotal: literally, if we concur with Lorna Sage's periodization of Carter's output in terms of "Beginnings," "Middles" and "Ends," whereby *The Bloody Chamber* acts as the pivot between the works of the middle and late periods (*Angela Carter*), or if we follow Makinen in seeing *The Bloody Chamber* as pivoting "between the disquietingly savage analyses of patriarchy of the 1960s and 1970s . . . and the exuberant novels of the 1980s and early 1990s" (3; compare Palmer, "From 'Coded Mannequin' to Bird Woman" 196). Carmen Callil nominates *The Bloody Chamber* as "the first of her [Carter's] masterpieces" (6), while Salman Rushdie refers to it as her "masterwork . . . the most likely of her works to endure" (Introduction xi); even Dalley, disagreeing with Rushdie, believes the title story of the collection to be "perhaps the one that most fiercely polarizes the reactions of Carter's readers" (29). If we accept that Carter is, in whatever sense, a quintessential contemporary writer, it would thus appear that her relationship with the fairy tale lies at the core of her contemporaneity.

The purpose of this essay is to review the various ways in which Carter's use of the fairy tale has been read in English-language criticism, and I have chosen to preface this survey with the above thumbnail sketch of more general assessments, not in order to justify the endeavour but rather to pose a series of questions based on these assessments. In what ways do the many critical readings of Carter's fairy tales affirm or contest their status, within her work and as defining texts of postmodernity? What are suggested as the characteristics of these texts, including their relation to their source material, and how do they affect our notions of the contemporary, of the literary canon, and of conceptions of authorship? And have these texts been neutralized in the process of being defined as representative or do they retain a distance from their categorization?

In part, it is via the various narratives or methodologies that readers have brought to the subject that we can locate its contemporaneity, and a reading of this criticism provides a snapshot of the most prominent critical debates of the past twenty years, given that gender and feminism have played a large part in defining these debates, albeit at times antagonistically, in a manner analogous to the definition of Carter's writing in terms of the fairy tale. Yet this question of definition should not be taken as suggestive of singularity, despite the journalistic need for quick fixes that is one of the pitfalls of crossover recognition. The publication of *The Bloody Chamber* as a collection in 1979 was contemporaneous with that of two influential but contentious essays which, in their different ways, argue for a pluralist feminism: Julia Kristeva's "Le temps de femmes" ("Women's Time") and Annette Kolodny's "Dancing Through the Minefield." While the former theorizes a third stage of feminism in which a variety of feminist projects co-exist, the latter argues for a plurality of feminist literary theories and readings rather than a single, overarching hermeneutic model, the possibility of which was much discussed at the time. Given that readings of *The Bloody Chamber* can be partly contextualized in terms of these contemporaneous speculative essays, and while there is undoubtedly a broadly definable critical consensus regarding the collection, critical writing about *The Bloody Chamber* and about questions relating to its narrative models demonstrates a multiplicity of approaches that would seem to affirm Kristeva's and Kolodny's suggestions, in terms of the variety of critical methods and the range of ways in which Carter's relation to the fairy tale is made to signify.[4] It is my hope that a thematic review of the literature will not overly tame this heterogeneity.[5]

Reviews

Continuing to use journalistic accounts as a means of entry, and as a first indication of conflicting opinions, we can turn back to look at reviews of the Carter works in question. These reviews reveal an interesting divergence between those readers for whom *The Bloody Chamber* is complex and those for whom it is transparent: a split between a reading of the collection as "elaborate and fanciful . . . too rich and heady for casual consumption" (Craig, "Gory" 762;[6] compare Kennedy), and a weary recognition that we are "too far along in history, too knowing nowadays, for the old fairy tale *frisson*" (Friedman 15; in direct contradiction, Selina Hastings sees *The Bloody Chamber* as a collection of "beautiful and ornate" fairy tales, "the introduction of modernity [into which] gives an extra frisson" [15]). One reviewer comments that "it's not always easy to tell when she's [Carter's] giving new meaning to her basic theme of sexual potency, or merely embroidering on it" (Bannon 55), and this seemingly contradictory sense of innovation and strangeness versus mere repetition continues in more recent reviews—of the collected edition of Carter's stories, for example—which have the added benefit of hindsight. The most notorious instance of a reviewer's reading of Carter is that by John Bayley, for whom her various fairy-tale narratives are patently self-explanatory, "wholly explicit"; he believes Carter's fairy tales "lack the secret style of independence": "[t]old by Grimm [sic] or Perrault, or even Andrew Lang in his 'Fairy Books,' blue, green, and red, these old tales remain free and enigmatic. Retold by Angela Carter . . . they become committed to the preoccupations and to the fashions of our moment" ("Fighting for the Crown" 10–11). Like Friedman before him, Bayley thus sees Carter's fairy tales as predicated on "an art of mutual knowingness" ("Stand the Baby on its Head" 19).[7] Yet contrary to this seeming transparency of intent—Dalley plays devil's advocate in suggesting that the "40-odd over-scented pages [of "The Bloody Chamber"] are scarcely worth the single, feminist, final twist" (29)—Shippey and Hastings see the elusive nature of fairy tales retained in Carter's versions in the feeling they evoke of "deep meaning forever receding just out of reach" (Shippey 20) and, in direct opposition to Bayley, in their "lightness of touch": "[T]here remains the distancing effect of a vision. . . . For it is magic, it is strange . . . the characters are not of this world" (Hastings 15).

What appears from scanning the reviews is a general desire to contextualize Carter's writing and the centrality to that writing of her concern for the fairy tale as a particular narrative model, with conflicting opinions arising out of the extent to which the texts are seen to be of, or ahead of, their variously conceived historical moment. Bayley thus grants Carter's importance for the same reason that Friedman is bored by her (or at least by some of her work), and this dialectic of prescience and datedness can serve as a bridge to the academic critiques that seek to explicate *The Bloody Chamber,* in which the charge of enthrallment to old models is countered by what others see as essentially speculative, with Carter actively renewing Peter and Iona Opie's definition of fairy tales as "the space fiction of the past" (18).

"The Bloody Chamber" and Intertextuality

Critics of any of Carter's works are faced with the issue of intertextuality, and with the fact that these intertexts are always "already read"; thus, another reason for viewing *The Bloody Chamber* as paradigmatic is that it stages the processes of intertextuality in distilled form. Readings of the narratives must be based, albeit implicitly, on an attitude to the folk- and fairy-tale source material, which can act either as the main focus of attention, as in Cristina Bacchilega's several pieces on the collection, and in essays by Donald Haase and Mary Kaiser; as a summarized "given" which acts as merely one aspect, as in readings of "The Bloody Chamber" by Lisa Jacobson and Kari Lokke; or as a productive absence, giving rise to readings which deliberately concentrate their attention elsewhere, as in Becky McLaughlin's Lacanian reading of the title story, Lucie Armitt's tendentious concentration on *The Bloody Chamber*'s navigation of the spaces and frames of the Gothic, and Harriet Kramer Linkin's detailed account of "The Erl-King" in terms of its recasting of some of the literary tropes of English Romantic poetry. Indeed, the possibility of readings such as these last three demonstrates the extent to which the folk- and fairy-tale material in Carter's work has nearly always passed through a series of filters, making a folkloristic account of the narratives, of the "detective" kind that at one time characterized folklorically-oriented readings of literary texts, problematic at best. However, folkloristically naive readings, as opposed to those which productively look elsewhere, are liable to be less successful, and I will return below to the question of the easy seductiveness of this form of intertextuality.

Referred to by Mary Kaiser as "the paradigmatic story of the collection" (31), the title story in *The Bloody Chamber* is fittingly placed and has certainly engendered the most critical comment.[8] For Rushdie it acts as the "overture" (Introduction xi), announcing the thematic material to be played out in what follows (although in not quite as mannered a fashion as this description might suggest), while both Bacchilega and Elaine Jordan see a deliberate ploy at work in the placing of an extended narrative which frames the more thematically concise tales that follow, serving as both context (Bacchilega, *Postmodern Fairy Tales* 183n39) and justification (Jordan, "Dangers" 127–28).

Bacchilega's reading of "The Bloody Chamber," as part of her *Postmodern Fairy Tales,* is by far the most aware of folkloric intertexts. This book-length study, which includes a reading of tales from *The Bloody Chamber* in each of its chapters, represents the first and so far only large-scale attempt to approach the collection via an informed assessment and understanding of the tale types which lie behind Carter's rewritings. Carter's own work on this source material is ample justification, if it were needed, for such an approach, and Bacchilega successfully uses folk narratives as the starting point from which to navigate what she terms

Carter's "metafolkloric or archeological project" (124). Each of the chapters in the book is concerned with a specific tale type, with the readings of literary texts prefaced by a wide-ranging survey of recorded versions. In terms of "The Bloody Chamber," this approach allows for a reading, which draws on related work by Maria Tatar and Catherine Velay-Vallantin, that demonstrates the literary origins of views of "Bluebeard" as primarily concerned with female culpability and waywardness, as opposed to a folklorically sanctioned reading which sees rather the positive aspects of curiosity and "a process of initiation which *requires* entering the forbidden chamber" (107).[9] In addition, the contentious depiction of the venal heroine in "The Bloody Chamber" can be read as a deliberate avoidance of the far more cunning models offered by the tale types related to "Bluebeard" (AT 311 and AT 955), allusions to which appear in Carter's narrative: thus, for Bacchilega, "*not* using them is symptomatic of Carter's strategic focus on the victim role, pointing to a 'lack' in the resolution of 'The Bloody Chamber' itself" (185n43).

While this depth of awareness of folkloric intertexts is largely absent from other readings of "The Bloody Chamber," Robin Ann Sheets offers a thorough overview of literary versions of "Bluebeard" (including the popularity of the tale in decadent and symbolist literature, which certainly provides much of the material for Carter's narrative), similarly drawing on Tatar to indicate the historical provenance of the sanctioned moral of the tale; while Patricia Duncker ("Re-Imagining") and Mary Kaiser introduce their readings by drawing on the work of Jack Zipes, with summaries of the history of the fairy tale as a literary narrative which appropriates folkloric material for quite specific purposes. Duncker, Sheets and Kaiser each makes much of the more overt changes introduced by Carter as part of her adaptation, namely the complex depiction of the heroine-narrator and the characters of Jean-Yves and the avenging mother. While Jordan is rightly critical of readings which overly concentrate on these more explicit pivot points—"[t]o stop short at particular sensational instances is to reproduce the titillating censoriousness of newspapers" ("Dangers" 130)—this focus nevertheless serves my purpose in introducing the theme of intertextuality, to the extent that those readings which are less concerned to go beyond the more obvious Perrault/Bettelheim avenue of folkloristic inquiry tend to view these changes as both wholly original and wholly successful. Jacobson identifies the three changes listed above with an "alternative, matriarchal, world view" (83), while Lokke believes Carter's tale "ends as a feminist fairy tale should, with the rescue of the daughter by her strong and heroic mother" (10).

While these readings raise interesting topics—Jacobson's references to the Freudian "uncanny" and Lokke's interest in the Bakhtinian "grotesque"—the unquestioned acceptance of these elements of the tale as wholly Carteresque illustrates how a lack of folkloristic insight can lead to readings which are prone to rather general judgements of Carter's source material. By locating the primary focus of the narrative at these points, such readings play into the hands of the likes of Bayley, for whom Carter's retellings are little more than waves of a feminist magic wand, and are thus liable to give rise to a conception of these narratives as paradigmatic because reflective of their historical moment—which is, of course, only one step away from datedness. As Bacchilega comments with reference to the tale types closely related to "Bluebeard," "[o]nly readers who believe that fairy-tale heroines are hopelessly entangled in patriarchal values will be surprised that the mother's eccentricity is the key to her success" (*Postmodern Fairy Tales* 127). Thus Kaiser, who is concerned with the intrinsic intertextuality of the fairy tale as a literary genre, sees "The Bloody Chamber" as a retelling of "Bluebeard" deliberately staged in a *fin de siècle* environment which historically contextualizes Carter's depiction of the "woman-as-victim" and "woman-as-avenger" (31–33), while both Jordan ("Dangers" 122) and McLaughlin (412), from very different perspectives, are willing to see the blind piano-tuner as an ambivalent figure rather than a wholesale alternative to male sadism: "pretty dull fare," to quote McLaughlin.[10]

It is not a question of "deep" as opposed to "surface" readings but rather of how we approach Carter's intertextual strategies. Jordan and McLaughlin do not make their judgements in the light of folklorically-informed insight alone (McLaughlin largely ignores this aspect) but rather through close attention to the symbolic and intertextual economy of the narrative—a close attention which may seem at odds with a popular conception of postmodernist fictions as actively seeking to prevent such dissection as well as with contemporary critical practice, but which in fact demonstrates the extent to which Carter's work exemplifies one particular mode of feminist textual strategy. Yet running counter to this is the possibility of a negative judgement of Carter's reliance on folkloric intertexts which are indicative, indeed constitutive, of a traditional conception of gender as the fixed relation between aggressive masculinity and passive princesses. This is to introduce what constitutes the second major strand in readings of this seam of Carter's work—the issue of pornography and its relation to conceptions of female sexuality—and at the risk of shifting away from a survey of the theorizing of intertextuality within criticism of Carter and the fairy tale, to which I will return, it is necessary to admit this parallel theme.

Pornography and the Fairy Tale

Although I refer above to the usefulness of a knowledge of folk and fairy tales as a means of avoiding unmediated readings of the more overt elements of Carter's rewritings, Duncker views this tradition as inherently and insuperably restrictive, a structural "strait-jacket" confining Carter to a depiction of gender relations which mimics the set pieces of the pornographic encounter: "The realities of male desire, aggression, force; the reality of women, compliant and submissive" ("Re-Imagining" 8).[11] While Duncker's reading is strangely contradictory—aware of historical continuities and discontinuities within the history of folkloric material but unwilling to admit Carter's negotiation of the strands of tradition—its repeated reference to Andrea Dworkin, including the latter's scathing critique of the fairy tale in *Woman Hating,* represents how *The Bloody Chamber* has been contextualized, to varying effect, within the debate surrounding pornography.

It was around this subject that conflicting camps of feminist thought arranged themselves in the late 1970s and 1980s, as part of a debate that crystallized broader issues relating to types of feminist politics and the question of the status of representation. In short, while it was accepted that pornography reflected a sort of distilled essence of the entrenched binaries of patriarchal gender relations, the conflict revolved around the extent to which pornographic representations could be appropriated as a critique of the status quo and as a medium for the speculative imagining of alternatives. Thus the debate was, and to an extent still is, a test case for a conception of feminism and feminist cultural production, and, given that fairy tales underwent a concerted feminist critique in the 1970s, the parallels are self-evident: can fairy tales as, traditionally, miniature carriers of a conservative ideology of gender be appropriated to critique, and imagine alternatives to, traditional conceptions of gender and its construction, given the history of their role in the installation of these very traditions?

It was Angela Carter's direct intervention in this debate, with the publication of *The Sadeian Woman* in the same year as *The Bloody Chamber,* that sealed the link between her conception of fairy tales and of pornography, a link which constitutes the prime historical and critical context within which the tale collection has subsequently been read. *The Sadeian Woman* refers to the genre of the fairy tale on several occasions—*Justine* is described as "a black, inverted fairy-tale" (39), and Carter characterizes the writings of de Sade as directly related to "the black and white ethical world of fairy tale and fable" (82)—and has been used by critics as a parallel text, or polemical preface, to *The Bloody Chamber.* Margaret Atwood thus reads the latter as "a 'writing against' de Sade, a talking-back to him": the collection "can be understood much better as an exploration of the narrative possibilities of de Sade's lamb-and-tiger dichotomy than as a 'standard' work of early seventies to-the-barricades feminism" (120–21). Atwood goes on to provide her own summary of the main conflicting camps in the feminist debate, a summary which is given in much more detail, and with further reference to the specific dynamics of the issues raised by pornography, in the essays by Sheets and Michele Grossman, each of whom reads "The Bloody Chamber" via this historical and conceptual context (an interpretative relationship which is reversed by Sally Keenan, who uses *The Bloody Chamber* as one means of approach to *The Sadeian Woman*, referring to the two texts as "contrasting sides of the same genre" [136]). Sheets's is an impressive and invaluably detailed overview of the dynamics of the debate, beginning in the late seventies with the anti-pornography movement, which characterized pornography as the eroticization of male dominance, encouraging sadomasochism "by placing the male viewer/reader in the sadist's active position while assigning the masochist's passive role to the female viewer/reader" (339). This was countered by those groups for whom sadomasochism was reflective of the unavoidable role of power in sexual relations and thus a route to the exploration of an eroticism untainted by the proscriptions of (heterosexual) ideology (340–41).

Duncker's critique of *The Bloody Chamber* is predicated on a disagreement with Carter as to the possibility of a constructive use of pornography—she describes Carter's notion of the "moral pornographer" as "utter nonsense"— and a reading of Carter's putative exploration and deconstruction of the subject positions of sadist and masochist as merely a reproduction of pornographic archetypes: "Carter envisages women's sensuality simply as a response to male arousal. She has no conception of women's sexuality as autonomous desire" ("Re-Imagining" 7). Hence the reconceived transformations that are described in "The Tiger's Bride" and "The Company of Wolves" merely replay the "meeting of sexual aggression and the cliché of female erotic ingenuity" alongside a vision of female sexuality as merely "the mirror image of his [the wolf's] feline predatory sexuality" ("Re-Imagining" 7). As one of the first published essays devoted to *The Bloody Chamber,* Duncker's has been an influential reading, acting as a reference point for those who are made similarly uneasy by what is taken as a tautological amalgamation of fairy tale and the structures of pornography. Thus Avis Lewallen, although more open to the play of irony in Carter's narratives, is disturbed by what she sees as a vision of female sexuality still operating within a Sadeian framework, still responding only within prescribed encounters; and a similar judgement is made by Robert Clark, for whom "The Company of Wolves" offers only "the standard patriarchal opposition between the feral domineering male and the gentle submissive female" (149).

To an extent, narratives such as "The Tiger's Bride" and "The Company of Wolves" present readers with an either/or scenario: either we see the representation of some form of alternative to or merely the replication of traditionally sanctioned roles. Thus Sylvia Bryant reads "The Tiger's Bride" as ultimately utopian, offering "an alternative model for the female subject's desire," in which the heroine's refusal to be objectified leads to a "reciprocal relationship of desire and trust" (448–50), and Melinda Fowl reads "a narrative where a sense of 'strangeness' or 'otherness' shapes experiences of fear, desire and self-understanding in a mutually preserving relationship" (76). Yet in the same way that it is possible to read the more overt interpolations Carter introduces into "The Bloody Chamber" as constructively ambivalent, so it is that readings which opt to *explore* the either/or scenario, rather than wholeheartedly espouse one side of the equation, tend to find a more complex depiction of the pornographic encounter.

Although largely negative, Lewallen's reading does grant that in some of the tales at least, Carter is depicting the social and economic underpinnings of sexual relations, "the historically determined nature of desire" (156), and it is this sense of an active grappling with gender roles as they have been played-out in history that characterizes the readings of Grossman, Sheets and Bacchilega. Sheets is one of the few critics to differentiate between Carter's attitude to pornography in *The Sadeian Woman* and *The Bloody Chamber,* rather than to take the argument of the former as directly enacted in the latter, for better or worse. Thus "The Bloody Chamber" "continues—but also qualifies" *The Sadeian Woman,* more critical of pornography than the latter in its detailed depiction of " 'aesthetic sado-masochism' " (347, Sheets quoting Linda Williams) but equally concerned to represent, in the ambivalent figure of the narrator-heroine, the fact that "complicated economic, social, and psychological forces contribute to the objectification, fetishization, and violation of women" (357). Along the same lines, Bacchilega reads the narrator's "double-voiced confessional mode" (*Postmodern Fairy Tales* 126) as fluctuating between "the religiously sanctioned subject position of 'virtuous victim,' " which not only "fosters her passivity . . . but also lets the narrator justify that passivity" (125), and "a painful recognition from within of masochism's presence in sexual and economic exploitation" (123).

These attempts at a more supple reading of the subject positions of sado-masochism as depicted by Carter are of a piece with the frequent reference to feminist film theory in readings of these narratives, an obvious route of inquiry given the stress on vision in Carter's most prominent fairy tale sources— "Bluebeard," "Beauty and the Beast," "Red Riding Hood"—and, of course, given the film of *The Company of Wolves.* Sheets provides an overview of the theory and criticism that arose, at least in part, as a direct response to the shift in the anti-pornography movement towards a more general critique of "the pornography of representation" (to quote the title of a book by Susanne Kappeler), a pornography predicated on a rigid conception of the "male gaze"— a shift which exacerbated an already "generalized and ahistorical" bias shaping work in this area (341–42). The response involved, on the one hand, a study of specific representations and the possibility of "multiple and fluid cross-gender identification" (342) and, on the other, a theorizing of possible alternatives that would relativize the primacy accorded to vision in philosophical and psychoanalytic accounts of the subject and of subjectivity. The influence, both general and specific, of this field of inquiry is evident in a range of criticism on *The Bloody Chamber* and related texts by Carter, three particular instances of which I have chosen to highlight.

In the first case, an attention to the shifting play of looks in Carter's narratives—the looks that pass between the Marquis and his wife, the tiger and his bride, and the multiple encounters of wolf and young girl—allows for an avoidance of dichotomous critical judgements which wholly espouse or censure the basic tenor of the narrative. One of the pitfalls of such judgements is demonstrated in Bryant's reading of the denouement of "The Tiger's Bride," where a recognition of the "inherently voyeuristic" nature of "Beauty and the Beast" leads her to resolve the transformation by positing a "primal and natural state" for the girl's desires, "one that is pre-Oedipal, almost pre-ideological" (448). Such utopianism is problematic, not the least because it replays the historically potent association of female sexuality with timelessness and nature, against which Carter writes elsewhere. Rather than seeking to do away with voyeurism, it is possible to read "The Tiger's Bride" as an exploration, on several levels, of the gaze, as Bacchilega demonstrates by concentrating on the narratological concept of focalization (*Postmodern Fairy Tales* 95–102). Read against "The Courtship of Mr Lyon" which uses "shifting focalization" to chart the process by which Beauty's view of herself is constructed and naturalized (90–95), "The Tiger's Bride," like "The Bloody Chamber," presents "the heroine's confused perception": "an external, but not impartial or 'natural' focalization, the humanistic, patriarchal gaze, conditions her responses, even though she realizes that this order victimizes her" (98). While we are witness to the heroine's ultimate refusal to comply with a conditioning that requires the tiger's look to be read as pornographic objectification, it is precisely this "visual-education component" that undercuts the "somewhat Marcusean liberation of the pleasure principle" (100). Focalization is used to highlight and frame the workings of the transformation, thus "mak[ing] its own enchantment suspect by constructing it so conspicuously" (101).

In accounts of the film adaptation of *The Company of Wolves,* the more supple reading of the gaze demonstrated by Bacchilega has also been allied to readings concerned with how the fairy tale can provide a critique of, and allow for speculation about alternatives to, the primacy accorded to vision in psychoanalytic accounts of the subject and related theories of individuation. Both Catherine Lappas and Donald Haase follow the path of "seeing" as it figures in the film and as it is gradually challenged by the possibility of a relationship based on touch. By concentrating closely on the use of proverbial language in the speech of particular characters, namely Rosaleen's father and her Granny, Haase demonstrates how a web of references is used, not, as in the Grimms' tales, to "suggest the language and atmosphere of the fairy tale" but conversely to "demystify its [the fairy tale's] proverbial language and the conventional wisdom that it expounds" (91). Following in the spirit of her mother, whose speech is largely proverb-free, Rosaleen questions popular, received wisdom, including her father's assertion that "[s]eeing is believing" to which she responds with the question: "What about touching?" Haase identifies the proverb "Seeing is believing" as a "leitmotif that marks for us the progress of Rosaleen's maturation," and the possibility that "*touching* might reveal truths unknown to those limited by seeing (such as her bespectacled grandmother)" (95).

This attention to and critique of seeing not only connects with what Guido Almansi identifies as Carter's "specific curiosity about the functioning and range of our five senses" (217), and with Sheet's speculation regarding the role of Jean-Yves in "The Bloody Chamber"—"[p]erhaps if Carter were to continue the story, she would develop a male sexuality centred on smell, touch, and sound" (357);[12] it also ties in with attempts by feminist theorists to reconceptualize the successful relationship of daughter and mother in terms not based on renunciation. Alongside the nascent alternative to aggressive male sexuality conceived as objectification that is hinted at in the figure of Jean-Yves, Sheets views the representation of the mother in "The Bloody Chamber" as "challenging Oedipal models of development which privilege separation over dependence," and thus as concurring with theorists such as Jessica Benjamin and E. Ann Kaplan regarding the possibility that "recognizing the mother as sexual subject might provide a solution to the representation of desire" (356). This view is shared in part by Bacchilega within the context of her comments on the folkloric antecedents of the mother character (*Postmodern Fairy Tales* 127). Similarly, Ellen Cronan Rose, despite beginning by concurring with Bettelheim's orthodox Freudianism, concludes her reading of *The Bloody Chamber* by commenting that one purpose of the feminist retelling of fairy tales lies in the possibility of an account of "female development . . . grounded in the mother-daughter matrix" (227).

Intertextuality Revisited

Such readings and contextualizations of Carter's fairy-tale narratives, which suggest links with the writings of, among others, Nancy Chodorow and Hélène Cixous, need to be treated with care, given the tendency to mythologize in considerations of the maternal body—a tendency which Carter is at pains to avoid in *The Sadeian Woman* and in *The Passion of New Eve*. One of the problems of reading Carter's work in this way is that she is rarely wholly speculative at the expense of a representation of the social and cultural realities within which her characters function, and this is perhaps the root cause of discontent for those who find in her fiction merely a reproduction of fairy-tale sanctioned norms; as Rose comments, comparing *The Bloody Chamber* to the work of two of Carter's fellow rewriters: "Sexton is an analyst of fairy tales and their cultural implications, while Broumas is an improviser, using the tales as a base for imaginative speculation. Carter is both" (222).

Yet it is exactly this sense of simultaneity, of narratives unwilling whole-heartedly to accept *or* evade the discourses they represent, that allows me to reconnect with my temporarily diverted review of readings of Carter's inter-textual strategies. One notable instance of a more flexible conceptualization of spectatorship in particular film genres (specifically the "paranoid Gothic films" of the 1940s) occurs in the work of Mary Ann Doane, which acts as a reference point in the essays by McLaughlin (406–08), Lappas (118; 129), and Sheets (342; 354), and in a reading of *Nights at the Circus* by Sally Robinson (118–32).[13] While Sheets draws a parallel between the heroine of "The Bloody Chamber" and the heroines of the gothic films Doane discusses, in terms of how their " 'active investigating gaze' " undermines rigid theories of viewer identification and of woman as passive spectacle (342; thus concurring with Mulvey's speculative attempt to appropriate the trope of female curiosity ["Pandora"]), Lappas and Robinson focus on Doane's notion of the masquerade, which is conceptually related to Judith Butler's notion of gender as performance and Luce Irigaray's theorizing of female mimicry. In short, and at the risk of my simplifying her argument, what Doane suggests is a theory of the self-conscious enactment of femininity as a means of deconstructing its traditional status as self-evident image; by actively simulating this normative image, the masquerade " 'holds it at a distance,' " thus denaturalizing it: "If one can both take it and leave it, then gender becomes a performance rather than an essence" (Robinson 119–20).[14]

Lappas uses this notion to explain the representation of Rosaleen in *The Company of Wolves* (129), and in so doing her account represents one of the ways in which Carter's relation to the folkloric material she uses has been read in terms of a variously conceived postmodernist intertextuality. Carter is a materialist, concerned with the efficacy within history of particular representations, including those of the fairy tale, and it is via the simultaneous inscription and subversion of these representations in her work that she depicts history as process, both determining our conceptions of ourselves and allowing for the possibility of change. Hence we find Sage's reluctance to label Carter as "postmodern," in the sense of an implied "terminal reflexiveness," preferring instead Linda Hutcheon's concept of "historiographic metafiction" and Christine Brooke-Rose's "palimpsest history," "since they put the time dimension back in" (*Angela Carter* 58).

Anne Cranny-Francis discusses the manner in which feminist revisions of the fairy tale present "the text on the page and its absent referent" (89), with the difference between the two revealing "the discourses encoded in the traditional tales, which are shown as ideologically determined" (94). Taking this a step further, Makinen continues to avoid the either/or scenario by positing the play of an "ironic deconstructive technique"—"an oscillation that is itself deconstructive"—within the narratives of *The Bloody Chamber*: "Carter's tales do not simply 'rewrite' the old tales by fixing roles of active sexuality for their female protagonists—they 're-write' them by playing with and upon (if not preying upon) the earlier misogynistic version" (5). Makinen is responding to Duncker's reading of *The Bloody Chamber* as a doomed project based on intractable material, a criticism which is developed in Robert Clark's sustained attack on Carter's alleged inability to provide an account of, or see beyond, the social structures she ostensibly critiques. For Clark, part of the problem is what he sees as Carter's "transvestite style": "her primary allegiance . . . to a postmodern aesthetics" which precludes the possibility of "feminist definitions based upon a radical deconstruction and reconstruction of women's history" (158). Yet it is exactly this play of deconstruction and reconstruction that lies at the heart of Carter's project as it is interpreted by, among others, Lappas, who finds in *The Company of Wolves* a "call for a feminist irony which simultaneously rejects misogynist assumptions *and* inscribes a new set of assumptions" (119), and Danielle Roemer, for whom the tales in *The Bloody Chamber* "both embrace the past and scrutinize its claims to authority" (9) by using a "doubled voice" via which "[t]he past is referenced, reframed, and rethought" (2).[15] Again, responding directly to Duncker and Clark, Bacchilega conceives of the rewriting of fairy tales as precisely a "two-fold" process, "seeking to expose, make visible, the fairy tale's complicity with 'exhausted' narrative and gender ideologies, and, by working from the fairy tale's multiple visions, seeking to expose, bring out, what the institutionalization of such tales for children has forgotten or left unexploited" (*Postmodern Fairy Tales* 50; in her introduction Bacchilega specifically discusses the "performative" in relation to postmodern fairy tales as "meta-folklore" [19–24]).

This process of institutionalization has drained the fairy tale of its history, allowing it to appear as self-apparent truth, and part of the effect of the intertextual strategies of *The Bloody Chamber* is to denaturalize the mythic pretensions of its source texts. McLaughlin's Freudian reading of this act of repetition with a difference—a circular "renunciation of the old narrative" that finds its meaning in the "uncanny return" of what has been repressed in the original (419–20)—can thus be placed alongside those readings in which what has been repressed is precisely identified as history, or histories.[16] Kaiser draws on the work of Julia Kristeva to characterize the "embedded" intertextuality of the fairy tale as a narrative form with a history (an introductory point also made by Geoffroy-Menoux [249–50]), but rather than turn away from this history, as in Duncker's critique, Kaiser identifies Carter's reaffirmation or "heightening" of it as a means of exploring the "culturally determined" nature of its representations: a use of intertextuality which "moves the tales from the mythic timelessness of the fairy tale to specific cultural moments, each of which presents a different problem in gender relations and sexuality" (31). Hence "The Bloody Chamber" acts as "a symbolist version of the battle of the sexes," a decadent version of "Bluebeard" which "brings the sadomasochistic subtext of the original to the foreground by giving its murderous episodes the lush refinement of Beardsley's illustrations of *Salome*" (32), and likewise "The Snow Child" can be seen, at least in part, as a portrayal of "the sexual consequences of a feudal system of absolute power" (34).[17] Similarly, Robert Rawdon Wilson finds "The Lady of the House of Love" to be indicative of tales "powerful in their historicity" (115), and he reads it against the grain of a postmodernism viewed as decontextualized pastiche. For Wilson, the tale offers a layered depiction of decaying traditions on the brink of collapse, set during the uneasy calm of summer 1914, while Geoffroy-Menoux, as well as suggesting a host of folkloric parallels for this narrative, reads it primarily as a struggle between "[t]he automaton of Eternity" and "the puppet of History" (258). To slightly different effect, Grossman reads the various forms of allusion that Carter builds around her source tale in "The Bloody Chamber" as part of a negotiation "between the mythologically suggestive and the historically conditioned"; a deliberate fusion of the "familiar and magical, tangible and indecipherable," to suggest that "it is precisely such overlapping which can obscure the historical particulars that shape and sustain a culture's knowledge of itself" (153–54).

The "historical particulars" that litter *The Bloody Chamber* include the multiple intertexts that Carter places alongside her fairy-tale narratives, through and against which the reader experiences the at least partly familiar story. To acknowledge the fairy tale's inherent intertextuality is to acknowledge the variety of its literariness—the distinctive style of Perrault, de Beaumont or Lang—and part of Carter's continuation of the "unnatural" style of literary tale-telling lies precisely in the literature she brings to her renditions, the "*mixing of modes*" which disrupts any suggestion of generic purity (Fowl 71).[18] Hence Elaine Jordan, demonstrating that Carter's tales "offer three for the price of one" ("Enthralment" 24), reads "The Bloody Chamber" as, in part, a sustained "quarrel" with the fiction and biography of Colette concerning "the ways in which women can be complicit with what captivates and victimizes them" ("Dangers" 130).

Jordan uses her retrospective identification of this intertext as an example of the need for close readings of Carter's work—"you have to go through it, and along the line of Carter's narrative arguments to evaluate them properly" ("Dangers" 130)—a fact recognized by the author herself as stemming from an interest in medieval allegorical literature (Interview, *Novelists in Interview* 86).

One sustained and extremely impressive example of such a close reading is Linkin's account of "The Erl-King" as "a reimagining of the subject's position in Romantic poetics and ideology" (306). Drawing on a carefully identified range of "canonical nineteenth-century lyric poetry" (307), Linkin follows the twists and turns of a narrative voice aware of itself as coded to enact the part of silent muse or embodiment of nature, indeed partly seduced by this role, but who uses language "to perform a sort of verbal exorcism" (317; Jordan refers to "[t]he shifting of tense and of grammatical subject" in "The Erl-King" as "twistings and turnings" which seek "to escape the transparent, unambiguous world of experience" ["Dangers" 126]). The narrator's intertextually dense versions of her story, which Linkin suggests can in one sense be read as self-justifying, posit several outcomes, but "lacking a cultural model," the narrator, as an "increasingly resistant reader," succeeds only in "substitut[ing] female for male in the constituent master plot of nineteenth-century lyric poetry" (16): a plot which requires "the subjugation of the other" as part of "an epistemology that insists on the culturally gendered dualism of subject/object or presence/absence distinctions" (17).

Carter and Folktale Traditions

We are thus back in the thick of the "structural strait-jacket" debate, but rather than read this as a failure on Carter's part to imagine a genuine alternative, Linkin draws attention to the status of "The Erl-King" as one tale within a collection: while its companion narratives may offer "alternate solutions to the problematic nature of desire . . . none offers so self-conscious an analysis of the problematics of high Romantic aesthetic theory and nineteenth-century ideology for both men and women" (322). This raises two points. Firstly, the proliferation of intertexts throughout *The Bloody Chamber* can be read as a deliberately excessive strategy that serves both to heighten the implicit constructedness of the fairy tale as a literary genre and to draw attention to the particularity of each retelling as requiring inspection on its own terms. For Jordan, part of the problem with the critiques of Clark and Duncker lies in their attempt to "lay a grid across her [Carter's] work and read off meanings from it, according to a law of the same" ("Dangers" 122; in saying "the law of the same," Jordan seems to allude to monolithic definitions of the fairy tale and of femininity) rather than attending to the interactive manner in which the web of meaningful allusions draws the reader in—or, in Bacchilega's words, acts as "an explosive charge which will go off at different points for different readers upon one or more readings" (*Postmodern Fairy Tales* 184n40).[19] As Makinen suggests, this "space for the reader's activity" may tacitly posit a reader at least capable of realizing some of the clues (6), but, again, the myth of universality is not one to which Carter's fiction subscribes.

Secondly, this notion of discrete narratives intersecting within, and beyond the confines of, a collection can be conceived as one of the ways in which *The Bloody Chamber* relates to the folkloric tradition of which its source material is a part: a tradition of versions and variants which play off and against one another, despite the implicit or deliberate attempts of literary tellers and collectors to fix authoritative texts. Speaking of her own fictions, Carter commented that "they're never really finished" (Interview, by Goldsworthy 7). Her constructive avoidance of closure is attested in what can be recognized as her adoption of the model of folkloric narration as an ongoing process.[20] Thus Makinen discusses the manner in which each tale in *The Bloody Chamber* "takes up the theme of the earlier one and comments on a different aspect of it, to present a complex variation of female desire and sexuality" (10); Fowl considers the "structural" aspect of the collection as "a shared reservoir of signs," whereby each tale "mixes and meshes with the other tales" (72), while Bacchilega writes of the tales' "talking back at each other," a process in which "the masks peeled off in one scenario are refracted differently in another" (*Postmodern Fairy Tales* 141); similarly, Armitt, although not concerned with folkloric parallels, discusses "the narrative form of the collection" in terms of a "kaleidoscope," with its "ever-shifting, compulsive repetitions of interconnecting images" (98).

While the majority of criticism on *The Bloody Chamber* and its related texts is primarily concerned with the multiple ways in which Carter questions and provokes her fairy-tale sources, the collection, along with Carter's fiction as a whole, can thus also be read as constructively related, in general terms, to the folk tradition. Sage comments on how, during the 1970s, Carter became "more explicitly and systematically interested in narrative models that pre-date the novel: fairy tales, folk tales, and other forms that develop by accretion and retelling" ("Angela Carter" 173), and while this interest formed part of a broader fascination on Carter's part with non-canonical modes of writing (and can thus be viewed within the context of those feminist studies published contemporaneously with *The Bloody Chamber* which sought to establish alternative histories of women's writing, based around genre), the specific import of the folk tradition is twofold.[21]

Just as this tradition can be read as providing Carter with a model of serial narration—as well as with the store of less famous narrative materials that lies beyond the strictly limited canon of the literary fairy tale (as discussed in Bacchilega's book)—so Sage discusses it as offering a conception of the role of the author markedly at odds with the historically determined "modern" Western version: "She could experiment with her own writer's role, ally herself in imagination with the countless, anonymous narrators who stood behind literary redactors like Perrault or . . . the brothers Grimm" (*Angela Carter* 40). Sage places such experimentation within the context of "the old 1960s utopian dream of 'The Death of the Author,' " and while making this link avoids a reading of Carter's interest in the anonymous narrator in terms of some form of primitive ideal, Sage herself is also quick to distance it from any suggestion of avant-gardism (*Angela Carter* 43).[22] Carter had a highly personal "nostalgia for anonymity, for the archaic powers of the narrator whose authority rests precisely on *disclaiming* individual authority" (Sage, *Flesh and the Mirror* 2), which included a profound dismissal of Romantic notions of the writer as an isolated, individual genius. Carter's semi-adoption of the role of the oral narrator was exactly that: a deliberate performance, staged in part to deflate the myth of paternal authority, hence her own repeated reference to mainstream European literature as "a kind of folklore . . . a folklore of the intelligentsia" (Interview, *Novelists in Interview* 82).

If the adoption of the role of Mother Goose was in part a deliberate siding with the non-Bloomian territories of literature (and with a distinctly un-Bloomian conception of literary tradition and influence) and, concomitantly, with a performative, even pantomimic notion of authorship, it was also an unequivocally feminist strategy, demonstrated in Carter's editing of the two Virago books of fairy tales (in a glintingly provocative sideswipe, she once commented, regarding the first Virago volume: "That sorted out the men from the boys. Can you see Martin Amis allowing himself to be observed leafing through something called *The Virago Book of Fairy Tales*? He'd rather be seen reading *Guns and Ammunition*" ["Angela Carter Interviewed by Lorna Sage" 187]).[23] Marina Warner argues for the identification of a shift in Carter's "sensibility" from the early works, including *The Bloody Chamber,* to *Nights at the Circus:* a shift "bound up with her change of attitude to fairy tales," which was influenced by Zipes's work (a fact which reminds us that the latter's first major book on the fairy tale was published in the same year as *The Bloody Chamber*). For Warner, the outcome of this shift can be seen in Carter's introduction to the first Virago collection ("Angela Carter" 244). In short, "[f]airy tales came to represent the literature of the illiterate: the divine Marquis yielded pride of place to the illiterate peasant" ("Angela Carter" 245), and while Warner charts this influence in Carter's fictions in terms of their increasing concern for Walter Benjamin's "cunning and high spirits," it also signals the seriously tendentious nature of her editorship. Amply aware, like Warner, of the impossibility of identifying a purely female narrative tradition lying behind the figure of Mother Goose and of the use of just such a putative tradition as a means of dismissing particular types of storytelling (Carter, *Virago Book of Fairy Tales* xi), Carter nevertheless set about documenting "the richness and diversity with which femininity, in practice, is represented in 'unofficial' culture: its strategies, its plots, its hard work" (Carter, *Virago Book of Fairy Tales* xiv). Reviewing the second volume of Virago tales, Warner comments that while Carter has "sifted" the tales "from a variety of folklorists and ethnographers . . . her choice bears throughout the stamp of her mind" ("That Which is Spoken" 21). Unlike the seemingly contradictory fusion of homogenization and authenticity aimed at by previous transcribers and editors, Carter takes her tales, wholly and without alteration, from existing written collections. As Bacchilega says, Carter "overtly participates in the chain of transmission by explicitly making her selection on the basis of specific class and gender considerations," presenting fairy tales as the carriers of "unofficial, cross-culturally varied, and entertaining knowledge" (*Postmodern Fairy Tales* 20–21; see also Philip, "Unvarnished Tales"). This tendentiousness has a productively double-edged relation to tradition, to the extent that while Carter returns to the lesser known regions of folkloric narratives, she also continues the tradition of didacticism that was taken up so energetically by literary fairy-tale tellers and commentators, albeit to different effect than their anonymous sources. Carter's chosen tales, like her own versions and like her work in general, have a job, or jobs, to do (Sage, *Angela Carter* 37).

As the latter paragraphs of this review demonstrated, Carter's fairy tales are divisive, demanding that the reader have an opinion, take a side, and the simple fact that this essay is being written within the context of a volume devoted to *Angela Carter and the Fairy Tale* makes the tenor of my particular bias virtually unavoidable.[24] Yet, to an extent, this reflects another aspect of the critical literature. The folkloric intertextuality of Carter's tales makes them superficially "easy" to write about, provides an obvious means of approach, but one the very obviousness of which has led not only to a degree of repetition in the criticism—"Carter rewrites fairy tales from a feminist perspective"—but also to a degree of misinterpretation (for want of a less prescriptive word): for example, a distinction between "oral" and "literary" versions of "Bluebeard" which is really a distinction between folkloric tale types (Jacobson); readings, already mentioned, which identify the denouement of "The Bloody Chamber" as "strongly feminist," despite the many folktales that offer instances of just such female agency; and a judgement of "Beauty and the Beast" which bizarrely refers to the "trite, story-book ending" as "perhaps the most unsatisfying and unrealistic aspect of this, and any, fairy tale" (Bryant 445). Moreover, some readings suffer from a failure to distinguish between Carter's narrative and its primary folkloric intertext, giving rise to comment on the former which could equally be read as wholly concerned with the latter (a potentially revealing critical stance, but one which, to be constructive, needs to be explicitly or implicitly acknowledged and worked through). Grossman and McLaughlin, both of whom largely ignore the fairy tale element, are prone to this misalignment, despite the undoubted efficacy of their readings. Indeed, McLaughlin's Lacanian account of "The Bloody Chamber," like Linkin's reading of "The Erl-King," stands out from the main body of criticism by dint of its singular focus, although it does offer another demonstration of the sheer interpretability of these narratives. While Lacan overtakes "Bluebeard" as the primary intertext in McLaughlin's essay, the discussion of a clinically perverted Marquis and a paranoid heroine nevertheless relates directly and illuminatingly to the mainstreams of criticism on this tale. However, if readings of Carter's tales can suffer from a lack of attention to the folkloric aspect—and from the tendency to be redundant which is an ever-present possibility in writing about such metafictional texts (Sage, *Flesh and the Mirror* 19)—it is equally true that purely folkloristic readings will suffer from their own drawbacks. It is ultimately the dialectical relationship between the fairy tale and *The Bloody Chamber* that helps to keep both sides of the equation fermenting.

To an interesting degree, Carter has colonized the conception of the fairy tale among a large number of Western readers. Indeed, if the reading of fairy tales among children is on the wane, the circulation of tales in academic papers represents one alternative avenue of continued dissemination. Yet part of this broadly benign colonization has involved the espousal of a pluralist, heterogeneous conception of the tradition, both literary and folkloric: an espousal of impurity, and the basic fact that, as Carter herself wrote, a tale's "whole meaning is altered now that *I* am telling it to *you*" (*Virago Book of Fairy Tales* xiv). Thus what Carter's fairy-tale narratives still require is a reading of their timeliness in all its aspects: a detailed contextual overview or genealogy, along the lines of Sheets's account of the pornography debate, of the role of *The Bloody Chamber* in the renaissance of interest in the fairy tale that has occurred over the past three decades, a genealogy which could include the fiction of Robert Coover, Tanith Lee, and Margaret Atwood, as well as the critical work of Zipes, Alison Lurie, Kay Stone, and work on the Grimms' tales by Ruth B. Bottigheimer and Maria Tatar (to choose merely a selection of the most prominent names). Beyond this, other possibilities include a consideration of folk and fairy tales as they figure in the novels, a starting point for which could be Carter's repeated recourse to the "Sleeping Beauty" tale type, from *The Magic Toyshop* and *The Infernal Desire Machines of Doctor Hoffman* through to *Nights at the Circus;* an extended discussion of the role of the folkloric in Carter's work, following Warner's identification of a shift in the author's attitude to folklore over her writing career; and a reading of the reconceptualization of the techniques and ideological significance of fantasy in the contemporaneous work of writers influenced, to various effect, by folk narrative, which would place Carter alongside Rushdie, Calvino, and Coover. The possibilities are manifold.[25]

Warner writes of how easy it is "in the case of a great writer . . . to lose sight of the pleasure they give, as critics search for meaning and value, influence and importance" (Introduction xvi), and this is particularly apposite in the case of

Carter and the fairy tale. While criticism on such knowing material can appear redundant, even repetitively "celebratory" (Britzolakis 44), it also runs the risk of obfuscation in the face of the enticingly uncluttered surfaces of the fairy tale. None of the critical methodologies or contextualizations can hope fully to account for the relationship or for the seeping of one into the other—fairy tale into Carter and Carter into fairy tale—which is one reason why *The Bloody Chamber* has not been swamped beneath the weight of critical comment it has generated.[26] As Shippey speculates, regarding the sense of thematic variation that pervades *The Bloody Chamber,* "[I]f one could decide what the theme was, and how it varied from the master- or mistress-theme of the traditional tales in which these tales are rooted, well, one would then know a good deal about contemporary literature, contemporary gender and contemporary society" (20). Yet while such a possibility may be true in theory, it is specious in practice, and it is the taking part, not the critical "winning," that is important in seeking to account for Carter's idiosyncratic blend of tradition and (post)modernity.

Notes

1. Essays based on papers given at the conference referred to by Barker—held at the University of York, England, in 1994—have now been published as *The Infernal Desires of Angela Carter: Fiction, Femininity, Feminism,* edited by Joseph Bristow and Trev Lynn Broughton.
2. From a review of *The Company of Wolves* in the *Guardian,* quoted in Anwell (76).
3. The singer described is Kate Bush, who, according to Michael Bracewell, "was covering the territory of Angela Carter's *Company of Wolves* in the guise of a Pre-Raphaelite raised on *Jackie*: folkloric fable and disturbed dreams, focusing on the rites of passage between girlishness and womanhood" (160–61).
4. For readings of Carter's work which espouse this notion of critical pluralism, see Elaine Jordan ("Enthralment" 37), Laura Mulvey ("Pandora" 70–71), and Cristina Bacchilega ("Folk and Literary Narrative" 303).
5. It is nevertheless expedient, in reviewing a body of critical literature of this size, for individual nuances to be sacrificed in order amply to address the main thematic strands, for which I apologize in advance.
6. It is strange, given Patricia Craig's initial reaction to *The Bloody Chamber,* that in a more recent review of other works by Carter she refers to the collection as "simply mak[ing] explicit the harsh or carnal import of certain folk tales" ("Angela and the Beast" 24).
7. For a rejoinder to Bayley's faint praise, see Lee.
8. That the collection has become somehow synonymous with an essential Carter is indicated by the number of times the title story has been used as a shorthand index of all things Carteresque: thus Robert Coover ends his short remembrance by praising Carter as "a true witness of her times, an artist in the here and now of both life and art, Bloody Chamber though it may be" (10), while Gina Wisker feels that "[r]eading a new Angela Carter novel resembles the experience of Bluebeard's wife in 'The Bloody Chamber'" ("Winged Woman and Werewolves" 89).
9. This fits with Mulvey's highly suggestive reading of the trope of female curiosity,

in which she draws on the Freudian account of woman as enigma, along with the myth of Pandora, to recast what becomes "a self-reflexive desire to investigate femininity itself"—a femininity culturally constructed as a variously threatening riddle. While Mulvey only mentions "The Bloody Chamber" in passing, in terms of its awareness of the Pandora analogue, her suggestion of a "transformed and deciphered" motif corresponds with the readings of Tatar and Bacchilega (Mulvey, "Pandora" 64–66); Peter Brooks concurs with Mulvey regarding "the plot of female curiosity," which he discusses with reference to "The Bloody Chamber," as part of a reading of *Daniel Deronda* (250–52).

10. According to Jordan, Carter gave "seven explanations" for the significance of this character, a fact which certainly calls Bayley's easy categorizations into question ("The Dangerous Edge" 334n17).

11. Ironically, it is this intransigent conception of the history of the fairy tale that leads to Duncker's approval of Carter's portrayal of the mother in "The Bloody Chamber" as one of the only ideologically "significant" elements ("Re-Imagining" 11–12); a constructive account of this character *within* the fairy-tale genre is impossible given Duncker's reading of the tradition. In a more recent survey of other feminist rewritings, however, Duncker appears to have become more amenable to the possibilities offered by this material, praising Margaret Atwood and Tanith Lee in particular, for re-imagining, "in radical literary ways, characters and themes which are already central concerns in the traditional stories" ("Fables, Myths, Mythologies" 156).

12. Bacchilega refers to the three "women-in-the-company-of-wolves" stories in *The Bloody Chamber* as "imag(in)ing a different kind of self-reflexivity, one pouring out of touch, voice, and blood" (*Postmodern Fairy Tales* 66). The idea of music, in this case of the voice, as the basis for an alternative relationship of mutuality is explored further in the depiction of Mignon and the Princess in *Nights at the Circus.*

13. Full references to the work of Mary Ann Doane, along with the various other feminist theorists I have alluded to, are included in Sheets and Lappas.

14. As my passing allusion to Butler and Irigaray suggests, the various notions of the performative in relation to gender constitute a major strand in recent feminist theory, confronting and unpicking Freud's literally puzzling allusions to femininity. Given Carter's interest in the various connotations of theatricality, it is not surprising that a number of readings of her work draw on Butler and Irigaray: indeed, Bristow and Broughton refer to an "after-the-fact 'Butlerification' of Carter," with the caveat that, at least as far as the theories of Butler are concerned, Carter's texts are anticipatory (19); Jordan concurs on this point, suggesting that Carter's work "could just as well be used to explicate Butler" (Afterword 219). For readings of Carter which concentrate specifically on this area, including its potential shortcomings, see Britzolakis, Palmer ("Gender as Performance"), and Fernihough, each of whom cite Joan Riviere's seminal 1929 essay, "Womanliness as Masquerade"; in addition, Paul Magrs offers a highly suggestive account of the performance of masculinity in Carter, including, of course, "The Bloody Chamber."

15. This reference to a "doubled voice"—which need not imply a secret, "true" story, but rather an oscillation between narratives—has several analogues in feminist literary criticism and theory from the late 1970s and 1980s, including Elaine Showalter's suggestion that "women's fiction can be read as a double-voiced discourse, containing a 'dominant' and a 'muted' story" (266).

16. The conclusion of Robinson's chapter on Carter can be appropriated here as a rejoinder to Clark's accusations: "To assume the doubled perspective of feminist theory, simultaneously inside and outside gender as ideological representation, means to question the construction of Woman without ignoring the cultural productions of women, or the material effects of that representation" (133); for a direct response to Clark, see Jordan ("Enthralment").

17. Similarly, Bacchilega refers to "The Werewolf" as "a quasi-ethnographic sketch of early modern upland peasant life" (*Postmodern Fairy Tales* 60). Carter herself spoke of how she "reinvented" specific localities in certain of *The Bloody Chamber* tales (Interview, by Katsavos 14), although she tacitly warned off any future biographical detection by also suggesting that the source of such "cold, wintry stories" lay in the fact of their having been composed in Sheffield (Interview, *Novelists in Interview* 84).

18. Lappas remarks that Carter is "troubled by remaining within the strictures of any one genre, for narrative determinism has *its* potential dangers" (128). Taking this idea a step further, we can see the tales within *The Bloody Chamber* as deliberately troubling the genre of the fairy tale on two fronts: via the rash of literary intertexts that jostle for attention throughout, and, in a post-structuralist mode, precisely by proclaiming excessively their status as fairy tales: in the knowing allusions, in the intratextual cross-references, and in their use of analogous folkloric tale types. For Armitt, arguing from a different but related standpoint, attempts to define *The Bloody Chamber* in terms of its possible fairy-tale source material are not only restrictive—"[W]e must start to loosen our grip on the formulaic fairy-tale structures and open this collection up to the vagaries of narrative free play"— but also misleading: "Quite clearly, rather than being fairy tales which contain a few Gothic elements, these are actually Gothic tales that prey upon the restrictive enclosures of fairy-story formulae . . ." (89–90; compare Wisker on Carter and horror writing in "At Home All Was Blood and Feathers" and "Revenge of the Living Doll"). Nevertheless, it is Carter's awareness of the "layered" nature of fictional genres—the fact that generic norms develop by accretion over time—that generates the allusive density of her narratives, along with their historicism; in Carter, modes are always already mixed. On the subject of Carter's negotiation of generic strands, in this case those of the popular romance, see Benson.

19. As Jordan illustrates with reference to the character of Jean-Yves in "The Bloody Chamber," an acceptance of Carter's narratives as localized projects avoids the sometimes tortuous attempts to read individual elements as aesthetic or sexual manifestos rather than as being "produced by the needs of the story's argument" ("Dangers" 122).

20. Another example of Carter's interest in narrative versions is her work in other media, the majority of which involves stories from *The Bloody Chamber*. Along with Neil Jordan's film of *The Company of Wolves* (1984), the radio play *Vampirella* (1976) was significantly altered to form "The Lady of the House of Love," a shift of format reversed in the case of the stories "Puss-in-Boots" and "The Company of Wolves," the radio-play versions of which, first broadcast in 1980 and 1982 respectively, Carter referred to as "reformulations" (Carter, Preface to *Come unto These Yellow Sands, The Curious Room* 500).

21. Discussing Italo Calvino, another writer heavily influenced by the folktale, Carter herself commented on how "[h]is fairy tale book had a transformational effect on his

entire career . . . made him write and think in a completely different way" ("Angela Carter Interviewed by Lorna Sage" 187).

22. Carter's interest in radio and film has also been interpreted in terms of a preoccupation with oral culture: Sage quotes Carter's reference to the radio dramatist as retaining "some of the authority of the most antique tellers of tales" (Carter, Preface to *Come unto These Yellow Sands*, *The Curious Room* 502), a conception picked up by Almansi (225–26), while Mulvey, drawing on Marina Warner's argument for film as "essentially an oral medium," discusses Carter's relationship with the cinema as drawing on subterranean links between film and oral narration ("Cinema Magic and Old Monsters").

23. Warner writes about Carter in terms of the link between Mother Goose and pantomime, and of the themes of the masquerade of identity and a distinctly English transvestism—themes which connect with the more recherché theories of gender as performance discussed above ("Angela Carter"). Warner has also written at length on the history of the Mother Goose figure and the elusive possibility of a tradition of "ancient female narrative" ("Speaking with Double Tongue").

24. For an account of *The Bloody Chamber* which explicitly seeks to work against, and move away from, those readings which concentrate on fairy-tale sources, and which can thus be offered as the dissenting voice in this review, see Armitt.

25. Other suggestions for future avenues of inquiry, not directly related to the fairy tale, are made by Jordan (Afterword), while Bristow and Broughton speculate on the possibility of "the emergence of a 'queer' (as distinct from a feminist) Carter," given "current theoretical traffic between feminism and queer politics" (18). While Carter's fairy-tale narratives deal with heterosexual relations—leading Duncker to comment that Carter "still leaves the central taboos unspoken. . . . She could never imagine Cinderella in bed with the Fairy Godmother" ("Re-Imagining" 8; for a response to this charge, see Jordan ["Dangers" 127–29])—it would be interesting, in the light of Bristow and Broughton's suggestion, to consider *The Bloody Chamber* in relation to lesbian rewritings such as those by Olga Broumas, Suniti Namjoshi, and Emma Donoghue.

26. I have not focused on those few tales written by Carter that have appeared elsewhere than in *The Bloody Chamber*, for example "Peter and the Wolf" and, most notably, "Ashputtle *or* the Mother's Ghost: Three Versions of One Story." For a reading of the former, see Wyatt, and for discussion of the latter, see Atwood (132–35) and Bacchilega (*Postmodern Fairy Tales* 142–43).

Bibliography

Carter and the Fairy Tale

Alexander, Flora. "Myths, Dreams and Nightmares." *Contemporary Women Novelists*. London: Edward Arnold, 1990. 61–75.

Almansi, Guido. "In the Alchemist's Cave: Radio Plays." Sage, *Flesh and the Mirror* 216–29.

"Angela Carter." *The Times* 17 Feb. 1992: 15.

Anwell, Maggie. "Lolita Meets the Werewolf: *The Company of Wolves*." *The Female Gaze: Women as Viewers of Popular Literature*. Ed. Lorraine Gamman and Margaret Marshment. Seattle: Real Comet, 1989. 76–85.

Armitt, Lucie. "The Fragile Frames of *The Bloody Chamber*." Bristow and Broughton 88–99.

Atwood, Margaret. "Running with the Tigers." Sage, *Flesh and the Mirror* 117–35.

Bacchilega, Cristina. "Cracking the Mirror: Three Re-Visions of 'Snow White.' " *boundary 2* 15.3 (Spring/Fall 1988): 1–25.

———. "Folk and Literary Narrative in a Postmodern Context: The Case of the *Märchen*." *Fabula* 26 (1988): 302–16.

———. *Postmodern Fairy Tales: Gender and Narrative Strategies.* Philadelphia: U of Pennsylvania P, 1997.

Bannon, Barbara A. Rev. of *The Bloody Chamber,* by Angela Carter. *Publisher's Weekly* 10 (Dec. 1979): 55.

Barker, Paul. "The Return of the Magic Story-Teller." *Independent on Sunday* 8 Jan. 1995, Sunday Review: 14–16.

Bayley, John. "Fighting for the Crown." Rev. of several books by Angela Carter. *New York Review of Books* 23 Apr. 1992: 9–11.

———. "Stand the Baby on Its Head." Rev. of *The Second Virago Book of Fairy Tales,* ed. Angela Carter. *London Review of Books* 22 July 1993: 19–20.

Benson, Stephen. "Stories of Love and Death: Reading and Writing the Fairy Tale Romance." *Image and Power: Women in Fiction in the Twentieth Century.* Ed. Sarah Sceats and Gail Cunningham. London: Longman, 1996. 103–13.

Blackburn, H.J. "Modern Fantasy." *The Fable as Literature.* London: Athlone, 1985. 168–74.

Bradfield, Scott. "Remembering Angela Carter." *Review of Contemporary Fiction* 14.3 (1994): 90–93.

Bristow, Joseph, and Trev Lynn Broughton, eds. *The Infernal Desires of Angela Carter: Fiction, Femininity, Feminism.* Studies in Twentieth-Century Literature. London: Longman, 1997.

Brooks, Peter. *Body Work: Objects of Desire in Modern Narrative.* Cambridge, MA: Harvard UP, 1993.

Bryant, Sylvia. "Re-Constructing Oedipus Through 'Beauty and the Beast.' " *Criticism* 31 (1989): 439–53.

Callil, Carmen. "Flying Jewellery." *Sunday Times* 23 Feb. 1992, sec. 8: 6.

Carter, Angela. "Angela Carter Interviewed by Lorna Sage." *New Writing.* Ed. Malcolm Bradbury and Judy Cooke. London: Minerva, 1992. 185–93.

———. *The Bloody Chamber and Other Stories.* London: Gollancz, 1979. Harmondsworth: Penguin, 1981.

———. *Burning Your Boats: Collected Short Stories.* Introd. Salman Rushdie. London: Chatto & Windus, 1995.

———. *The Curious Room: Plays, Film Scripts and an Opera.* Ed. with Production Notes by Mark Bell. Introd. Susannah Clapp. London: Chatto & Windus, 1996.

———. *Expletives Deleted: Selected Writings.* London: Chatto & Windus, 1992. London: Vintage, 1993.

———, trans. and fwd. *The Fairy Tales of Charles Perrault.* London: Gollancz, 1977.

———. Interview. By Kerryn Goldsworthy. *meanjin* 44.1 (1985): 4–13.

———. Interview. By Anna Katsavos. *Review of Contemporary Fiction* 14.3 (1994): 11–17.

———. Interview. *Novelists in Interview.* By John Haffenden. London: Methuen, 1985. 76–96.

———. Interview. "Pulp Novels and Television Soaps Are Today's Fairy Tales." By Paul Mansfield. *Guardian* 25 Oct. 1990: 32.

————. *Nothing Sacred: Selected Writings*. Rev. ed. London: Virago, 1992.

————. *The Sadeian Woman: An Exercise in Cultural History.* London: Virago, 1979. London: Virago, 1993.

————, ed. *The Second Virago Book of Fairy Tales*. London: Virago, 1992.

————, ed. and trans. *Sleeping Beauty and Other Favourite Fairy Tales*. London: Gollancz, 1982.

————, ed. *The Virago Book of Fairy Tales*. London: Virago, 1990.

Christensen, Peter. "The Hoffman Connection: Demystification in Angela Carter's *The Infernal Desire Machines of Doctor Hoffman.*" *Review of Contemporary Fiction* 14.3 (1994): 63–70.

Clapp, Susannah. "On Madness, Men and Fairy-Tales." *Independent on Sunday* 9 June 1991, Sunday Review: 26.

Clark, Robert. "Angela Carter's Desire Machine." *Women's Studies* 14 (1987) 147–61.

Collick, John. "Wolves through the Window: Writing Dreams/Dreaming Films/Filming Dreams." *Critical Survey* 3 (1991): 283–89.

Coover, Robert. "A Passionate Remembrance." *Review of Contemporary Fiction* 14.3 (1994): 9–10.

Craig, Patricia. "Angela and the Beast." Rev. of *Black Venus* and *Come unto These Yellow Sands: Four Radio Plays,* by Angela Carter. *London Review of Books* 5 Dec. 1985: 24.

————. "Gory." Rev. of *The Bloody Chamber,* by Angela Carter. *New Statesman* 25 May 1979: 762.

Cranny-Francis, Anne. "Fairy-Tale Reworked." *Feminist Fictions: Feminist Uses of Generic Fiction.* London: Polity, 1990. 85–94.

Dalley, Jan. "A Saint More Beastly than Beautiful." Rev. of *Burning Your Boats: Collected Short Stories,* by Angela Carter. *Independent on Sunday* 30 July 1995, Sunday Review: 29.

Duncker, Patricia. "Re-Imagining the Fairy Tale: Angela Carter's Bloody Chambers." *Literature and History* 10 (1984): 3–14.

Fowl, Melinda G. "Angela Carter's *The Bloody Chamber* Revisited." *Critical Survey* 3.1 (1991): 71–79.

Friedman, Alan. "Pleasure and Pain." Rev. of *The Bloody Chamber,* by Angela Carter. *New York Times Book Review* 17 Feb. 1980: 14–15.

Geoffroy-Menoux, Sophie. "Angela Carter's *The Bloody Chamber*: Twice Harnessed Folk-Tales." *Para.doxa* 2 (1996): 249–62.

Grossman, Michele. " 'Born to Bleed': Myth, Pornography and Romance in Angela Carter's 'The Bloody Chamber.' " *Minnesota Review* 30/31 (1988): 148–60.

Haase, Donald P. "Is Seeing Believing? Proverbs and the Film Adaptation of a Fairy Tale." *Proverbium* 7 (1990): 89–104.

Hastings, Selina. "Recent Fiction." Rev. of *The Bloody Chamber,* by Angela Carter. *The Times* 14 June 1979: 15.

Jacobson, Lisa. "Tales of Violence and Desire: Angela Carter's 'The Bloody Chamber.' " *Antithesis* 6.2 (1993): 81–90.

Jordan, Elaine. "The Dangerous Edge." Sage, *Flesh and the Mirror* 189–215.

————. "The Dangers of Angela Carter." *New Feminist Discourses: Critical Essays on Theories and Texts.* Ed. Isobel Armstrong. London: Routledge, 1992. 119–31.

————. "Enthralment: Angela Carter's Speculative Fictions." *Plotting Change: Contemporary Women's Fiction.* Ed. Linda Anderson. London: Edward Arnold, 1990. 19–40.

Kaiser, Mary. "Fairy Tale as Sexual Allegory: Intertextuality in Angela Carter's *The Bloody Chamber*." *Review of Contemporary Fiction* 14.3 (1994): 30–36.

Keenan, Sally. "Angela Carter's *The Sadeian Woman*: Feminism as Treason." Bristow and Broughton 132–48.

Kennedy, Susan. "Man and Beast." Rev. of *The Bloody Chamber*, by Angela Carter. *Times Literary Supplement* 8 Feb. 1980: 146.

Krailsheimer, A.J. "Red Riding Hood Rides Again." Rev. of *The Fairy Tales of Charles Perrault*, trans. Angela Carter. *Times Literary Supplement* 28 Oct. 1977: 1273.

Lappas, Catherine. " 'Seeing is believing, but touching is the truth': Female Spectatorship and Sexuality in *The Company of Wolves*." *Women's Studies* 25 (1996): 115–35.

Lee, Hermione. " 'A Room of One's Own, or a Bloody Chamber?': Angela Carter and Political Correctness." Sage, *Flesh and the Mirror* 308–20.

Lewallen, Avis. "Wayward Girls but Wicked Women? Female Sexuality in Angela Carter's *The Bloody Chamber*." *Perspectives on Pornography: Sexuality in Film and Literature.* Ed. Gary Day and Clive Bloom. New York: St. Martin's, 1988. 144–57.

Linkin, Harriet Kramer. "Isn't It Romantic? Angela Carter's Bloody Revision of the Romantic Aesthetic in 'The Erl-King.'" *Contemporary Literature* 35 (1994): 305–23.

Lokke, Kari E. "*Bluebeard* and *The Bloody Chamber*: The Grotesque of Self-Parody and Self-Assertion." *Frontiers* 10 (1988): 7–12.

McLaughlin, Becky. "Perverse Pleasure and Fetishized Text: The Deathly Erotics of Carter's 'The Bloody Chamber.'" *Style* 29 (1995): 404–22.

Magrs, Paul. "Boys Keep Swinging: Angela Carter and the Subject of Men." Bristow and Broughton 184–97.

Makinen, Merja. "Angela Carter's *The Bloody Chamber* and the Decolonization of Feminine Sexuality." *Feminist Review* 42 (1992): 2–15.

Mulvey, Laura. "Cinema Magic and the Old Monsters: Angela Carter's Cinema." Sage, *Flesh and the Mirror* 230–42.

———. "Pandora: Topographies of the Mask and Curiosity." *Sexuality and Space.* Ed. Beatriz Colomina. Princeton Papers on Architecture. New York: Princeton Architectural P, 1992. 53–71.

Palmer, Paulina. "From 'Coded Mannequin' to Bird Woman: Angela Carter's Magic Flight." *Women Reading Women's Writing.* Ed. Sue Roe. Brighton: Harvester, 1987. 179–205.

Perrick, Penny. "Men Beware Women." Rev. of *The Virago Book of Fairy Tales*, ed. Angela Carter. *Sunday Times* 2 Dec. 1990, sec. 8: 4.

Philip, Neil. "Fantastic Images." Rev. of *The Second Virago Book of Fairy Tales*, ed. Angela Carter. *Times Educational Supplement* 27 Aug. 1993: 17.

———. "Unvarnished Tales." Rev. of *The Virago Book of Fairy Tales*, ed. Angela Carter. *Times Educational Supplement* 9 Nov. 1990, Reviews section: 3.

Roemer, Danielle M. "Angela Carter's 'The Bloody Chamber': Liminality and Reflexivity." Unpublished paper. American Folklore Society Meeting, Jacksonville, Florida. Oct. 1992.

Rose, Ellen Cronan. "Through the Looking Glass: When Women Tell Fairy Tales." *The Voyage In: Fictions of Female Development.* Ed. Elizabeth Abel, Marianne Hirsch, and Elizabeth Langland. Hanover, NH: UP of New England, 1983. 209–27.

Rushdie, Salman. "Angela Carter, 1940–92: A Very Good Wizard, a Very Dear Friend." *New York Times Book Review* 8 Mar. 1992: 5.

———. Introduction. *Burning Your Boats: Collected Short Stories.* By Angela Carter. London: Chatto & Windus, 1995. ix–xiv.

Sage, Lorna. *Angela Carter.* Writers and their Work. Plymouth: Northcote House in association with The British Council, 1994.

———. "Angela Carter." *Women in the House of Fiction: Post-War Women Novelists.* Basingstoke: Macmillan, 1992. 168–77.

———, ed. *Flesh and the Mirror: Essays on the Art of Angela Carter.* London: Virago, 1994.

———. "The Savage Sideshow: A Profile of Angela Carter." *New Review* 4.39/40 (1977): 51–57.

———. "The Soaring Imagination." *Guardian* 17 Feb. 1992: 37.

Sheets, Robin Ann. "Pornography, Fairy Tales, and Feminism: Angela Carter's 'The Bloody Chamber.'" *Journal of the History of Sexuality* 1 (1991): 633–57. Rpt. in *Forbidden History: The State, Society, and the Regulation of Sexuality in Modern Europe: Essays from the "Journal of the History of Sexuality."* Ed. John C. Fout. Chicago: U of Chicago P, 1992. 335–59.

Shippey, Tom. "Tales for the Literati." Rev. of *Burning Your Boats: Collected Short Stories,* by Angela Carter. *Times Literary Supplement* 4 Aug. 1995: 20.

Warner, Marina. "Angela Carter: Bottle Blonde, Double Drag." Sage, *Flesh and the Mirror* 243–56.

———. *From the Beast to the Blonde: On Fairy Tales and Their Tellers.* London: Chatto & Windus, 1994.

———. Introduction. Carter, *The Second Virago Book of Fairy Tales* ix–xvii.

———. "That Which is Spoken." Rev. of *The Virago Book of Fairy Tales,* ed. Angela Carter. *London Review of Books* 8 Nov. 1990: 21–22.

Wilson, Robert Rawdon. "SLIP PAGE: Angela Carter, In/Out/In the Post-Modern Nexus." *Past the Last Post: Theorizing Post-Colonialism and Post-Modernism.* Ed. Ian Adam and Helen Tiffin. Hertfordshire: Harvester, 1993. 109–23.

Wisker, Gina. "At Home All Was Blood and Feathers: The Werewolf in the Kitchen— Angela Carter and Horror." *Creepers: British Horror and Fantasy in the Twentieth Century.* Ed. Clive Bloom. London: Pluto, 1993. 161–75.

———. "Revenge of the Living Doll: Angela Carter's Horror Writing." Bristow and Broughton 116–31.

———. "Winged Woman and Werewolves: How Do We Read Angela Carter?" *Ideas and Production* 4 (1985): 87–98.

Wyatt, Jean. "The Violence of Gendering: Castration Images in Angela Carter's *The Magic Toyshop, The Passion of New Eve,* and 'Peter and the Wolf.'" *Women's Studies* 25 (1996): 549–70.

Zipes, Jack, ed. *Don't Bet on the Prince: Contemporary Feminist Fairy Tales in North America and England.* New York: Methuen, 1986. Aldershot: Scolar, 1993.

Other Aspects of Carter's Writing: Selected Works

Britzolakis, Christina. "Angela Carter's Fetishism." *Textual Practice* 9 (1995): 459–76. Rpt. in Bristow and Broughton 43–58.

Fernihough, Anne. "'Is she fact or fiction?': Angela Carter and the Enigma of Woman." *Textual Practice* 11 (1997): 89–107.

Jordan, Elaine. Afterword. Bristow and Broughton 216–20.

Kendrick, Walter. "The Real Magic of Angela Carter." *Contemporary British Women Writers: Texts and Strategies.* Ed. Robert E. Hosmer Jr. London: Macmillan, 1993. 66–84.

Lee, Alison. *Angela Carter.* Twayne English Authors Ser. 540. New York: Twayne, 1997.

Palmer, Paulina. "Gender as Performance in the Fiction of Angela Carter and Margaret Atwood." Bristow and Broughton 24–42.

Robinson, Sally. "Angela Carter and the Circus of Theory: Writing Woman and Women's Writing." *Engendering the Subject: Gender and Self-Representation in Contemporary Women's Fiction.* Albany: State U of New York P, 1991. 77–134.

Schmidt, Ricarda. "The Journey of the Subject in Angela Carter's Fiction." *Textual Practice* 3 (1989): 56–75.

Suleiman, Susan Rubin. "The Politics and Poetics of Female Eroticism." *Subversive Intent: Gender, Politics, and the Avant-Garde.* Cambridge, Mass.: Harvard UP, 1990. 119–40.

Other Relevant Works Cited

Bracewell, Michael. *England is Mine: Pop Life in Albion from Wilde to Goldie.* London: HarperCollins, 1997.

Duncker, Patricia. "Fables, Myths, Mythologies." *Sisters and Strangers: An Introduction to Contemporary Feminist Fiction.* Oxford: Blackwell, 1992. 133–66.

Kolodny, Annette. "Dancing Through the Minefield: Some Observations on the Theory, Practice, and Politics of a Feminist Literary Criticism." 1980. Showalter, *The New Feminist Criticism* 144–67.

Kristeva, Julia. "Women's Time." 1979. Trans. Alice Jardine and Harry Blake. *The Kristeva Reader.* Ed. Toril Moi. 1986. Oxford: Blackwell, 1992. 187–213.

Opie, Iona, and Peter Opie, eds. *The Classic Fairy Tales.* 1974. London: Paladin, 1980.

Showalter, Elaine. "Feminist Criticism in the Wilderness." 1979. Showalter, *The New Feminist Criticism* 125–43.

———, ed. *The New Feminist Literary Criticism: Essays on Women, Literature, and Theory.* 1985. London: Virago, 1992.

Warner, Marina. "Speaking with Double Tongue: Mother Goose and the Old Wives' Tale." *Myths of the English.* Ed. Roy Porter. Cambridge: Polity, 1992. 33–67.

STEPHEN BENSON

Addendum

"Of course, it's a world of appearances. I call this materialism" (Sage 55). So said Carter of her own fictional landscapes in 1977. A full materialist reading of her work would of necessity include a consideration of its various physical forms, what Jerome McGann refers to as the "bibliographical codes" of the literary work, partners in the production of meaning with the more commonly studied "linguistic codes" (for an example see Makinen). Such materialist considerations are applicable not only to Carter's work itself—to reprints of the novels, and now to the collected editions of the stories, dramatic works, and essays—but also to the critical volumes that take the work and its author as their subject. I say the work *and its author* because Carter herself, or rather her biography, is very much in evidence in the monographs that have recently begun to appear, several of which use on their cover one of the late photographs of the author, thus furthering the iconic status of these now familiar images. Of those studies that are a little more pictorially imaginative—more Carteresque—Aidan Day's is notable for its use of the most famous of Goya's etchings from the *Los Caprichos* series, *El sueño de la razon produce monstruos* (1797–98).

Day's choice of image is reflective of his thesis, which is that Carter's fiction offers a sustained critique of Enlightenment rationality, not in order to argue in favour of some form of anti-Enlightenment postmodernism but rather to expose the construction of, and flaws in, the Enlightenment project (however one might choose to define it)—to overhaul its exclusive and exclusionary practices in the pursuit of an egalitarian realization of its principles. Carter offers a "rationalist feminism," a "metaphysical materialism" defined by "her empiricism and her passion for reason" (Day 12). Day's view of the fairy tale is thus of an Enlightenment narrative tradition that potently embodies hegemonic definitions of gender and sexuality, definitions which Carter's tales in *The Bloody*

Chamber expose and undercut, suggesting "different representations, different models" (134) in the process. Given the body of criticism that has grown up around *The Bloody Chamber*, it can only be said that Day's reading toes the line; or rather, by siding with the likes of Merja Makinen and Elaine Jordan against Patricia Duncker and Robert Clark, toes one of the two prominent lines of interpretation, conceiving of the volume as having "successfully inscrib[ed] an old form with a new set of assumptions" (145). Day sets out by stating that the readings he offers are not concerned with Carter's many-layered allusions nor with the related question of her style, and so it is understandable that his account of *The Bloody Chamber* is little interested in the specificities of the tale traditions with which Carter sets up a dialogue, or in the intertextual and contextual wealth she lavishes on her own tales. While this leads to the familiar mistake of a reading of the *coup de théâtre* with which "The Bloody Chamber" concludes as "a radical modification of the original story" (156), it also raises more far-reaching questions regarding critical attitudes to Carter's fairy-tale narratives.

What tends to get lost in the overarching thesis required of the single-author study is a recognition of intertextual particularities. This is especially true in the case of the chronological overview—the structure adopted by Day and by Linden Peach—whereby similarity overrides difference, and where the fairy tale, together with the other folk-narrative traditions that Carter knowledgeably utilizes, tends to be viewed as no more or less than one item in a lineup of usual suspects waiting patiently for trial by demythology. It should be stressed that my saying this is in no way a prescriptive call for a solely folkloristically informed criticism, although the avenues of inquiry opened up for the nonfolklorist by Carter's work in this area are very much of a piece with her dismantling of canonical literary traditions and conceptions of narrative and the author. Rather, it is to agree with Lucie Armitt in seeing a need for a treatment of *The Bloody Chamber* (and of Carter's oeuvre viewed in the light of this volume) which matches up to its multiplicity rather than tames it with the label of "rewriting," or sidesteps it as another instance of rationalist critique; that is, to "open this collection up to the vagaries of narrative free play" (Armitt 90).[1] To pick one instance, Peach states that "The fact that she [Carter] edited fairy stories is particularly important to an appreciation of her fiction" (2), one reason being that she was interested in "blurring the boundaries" between forms of writing, "challenging our perceptions of what we mean, for example, by a short story or a novel" (3). It thus seems odd that Peach should leave Carter's stories out of his survey in order to concentrate on her "contribution to the development of the novel" (3).[2] Generic boundaries remain, a missed opportunity given Peach's reading of *The Magic Toyshop*—a novel he sees as anticipating *The Bloody Chamber*—in terms of Jack Zipes's work on fairy tales and the Freudian notion of the uncanny (78–79). And also because Peach is particularly alive to the ramifications of Carter's irreducible intertextuality, conceived as an ironically undermining mark of authorial authenticity and, increasingly as her writing career progressed, as "a boldly thematized part of her work, in which her own culture is rendered as 'foreign' " (4).

While explicitly aiming for the student-oriented overview, Sarah Gamble's monograph is more inclusive and less strictly chronological than Day's or Peach's work, and it offers interpretative rather than merely supportive readings of Carter's copious non-fiction (thus shaking the posts of at least one boundary distinction). Broadly speaking, Gamble concurs with Day on the subject of Carter's strategic negotiation of fantastic and realist modes, and thus on a view of her fiction as stopping well short of a fully textualized conception of history and of the real; and Gamble concurs with Peach on the importance for criticism of a historicist dimension, a recognition of the contexts within and against which Carter produced particular works at particular times. However, it is the attention Gamble pays to the nonfiction which leads to a more focused consideration of the fairy-tale texts and of the far-from-unrelated implications of the models and traditions upon which they draw: traditions of oral narration, of unfixed, fluid stories that have a particular historical resonance for the female author (130–31). In addition, Gamble highlights the role of *The Bloody Chamber* as "a gleeful, subversive, commentary on her [Carter's] earlier work" (131); as a fictional working through of the polemical positions outlined in *The Sadeian Woman*; and as a volume of interconnected narratives, "compulsively circling and reworking" images and scenarios (132). At the risk of seeming as if I am seeking justification for a focus on Carter and the fairy tale, there does seem to be something emblematic about the bond between the two. For Gamble, the connection is interestingly ambivalent. On the one hand, "what fairytale did was to offer Carter a way to be *more herself*" (138; emphasis in original); conversely, the fairy tale was also attractive given the appeal for Carter of camp as a form "innately performative and deliciously aware of its own fictitiousness" (66–67). As Gamble's readings of the autobiographical essays demonstrate, Carter was ever aware of her own construction of herself and of her writing persona. Nevertheless, in line with a withdrawal from the frontline of poststructuralist conceptions of subjecthood, the fairy tale, unlike the possibly elitist, conservative subtexts of camp, offers recoverable, gender- and class-specific histories of storytelling, reflected for example in *The Bloody Chamber's* "preoccupation . . . with community and connectedness" (191). For Gamble, this democratizing tendency is borne out by the fact that Carter's fairy-tale influenced texts are "her most accessible, and hence most widely read" (68).

This last interpretative move on Gamble's part is an instance of the manner in which criticism in this area can benefit from the speculative connection, the tendentiously tangential critical gambit (easier to accomplish in the essay than in the monograph, of course). In the afterword to an impressive collection of Carter criticism, Elaine Jordan identifies among its contributors a tendency to relegate a consideration of "Carter's particular poetics" (217) in favour of an elaboration of the politics of the content, often accompanied approvingly by extracts from prominent critical theorists. Important work, no doubt, but the risk of redundancy and repetition is high. Concentrating on the place of the fairy tale in Carter's work, the most stimulating moments of the three studies under consideration often occur on the byways of the interpretative route: in Day's thoughts on the manner of narration in "The Bloody Chamber" (162), on "Wolf-Alice" as "an allegorical dream of the unbitten apple" (164), and more centrally, in his detailed introductory comments—implicitly related to the fairy tale—on the role of fantasy in Carter (4–9). On the subject of the latter, Day works through but ultimately rejects theoretical positions offered by Tzvetan Todorov and Rosemary Jackson, in favour of a qualified view of Carter as allegorist, to whom fantasy acts in a constitutive fashion in the construction of personal and national identities (Day draws here on Jacqueline Rose's *States of Fantasy*).

In his own introduction, Peach stresses the formative influence of the changing climate of Britain in the 1950s and 1960s on Carter, as post-imperialist and post-industrial realities began to dawn (13–16). These realities, Peach suggests, underpin the melancholic sense of loss that echoes through Carter's early works. More broadly, they offer a historical gloss on Carter's strategic use of intertextuality as a means of rendering her own culture as " 'foreign' " (4). Peach's contextualization bears an interesting relation to Gamble's use of the notion of "marginality," a concept developed in post-colonial studies, in the work of Sneja Gunew in particular (Gamble 4–6).[3] While Gamble is concerned with thinking through the construction of Carter and her work as marginal—a characterization fostered not least by the author herself—the suggestion of the work as following and caught up in the wake of empire is productive not only because it offers the possibility of a reading of Carter's use of folk materials but also because it links Carter's work with her much professed attitude to European high art as "a folklore of the intelligentsia" (Haffenden 82), as related to the strategies employed by a number of post-colonial writers similarly engaged in the exploration of marginality.[4] As Jordan comments about the collection she surveys, "there is not much consideration of how Carter's writing intersects with that of her more-or-less contemporary peers in both 'serious' and 'popular' fiction" (216)—an interpretative route that would certainly open what can appear as the rather foregone conclusions of the more holistic, explicitly political accounts. Turning to Andrew Sanders's *Short Oxford History of English Literature*, we find Carter situated alongside discussions of Doris Lessing's *The Four-Gated City* and Jean Rhys's *Wide Sargasso Sea* (admittedly, and mischievously, separated by the less obviously relevant Barbara Pym), which places Carter's work in a line of technically innovative, canonically disruptive women's fiction, in which elements of fantasy play a defining role (614–17).

If all we find in Carter is some form of confirmation, then we run the risk of seconding reductive views of the writing as merely fashionable. In part, this is to suggest the possibility of a less corroborative, more antagonistic relation between Carter's texts and their contextualization in criticism. As such, it is illuminating to return to the shock of the old offered by the etchings that compose Goya's *Los Caprichos*: technically innovative, politically challenging in both their outspoken satire and their disquieting fantasy, generically hybrid, discrete yet variously interconnected, and expressive as much of Enlightenment ideals as of disruptive counter-Enlightenment energies. It is no New Critical fetishization of the artwork to suggest that Goya's series still retains its edge, its difference, and that the best we can hope for Carter's fairy-tale texts is a similar critical fate.[5]

Notes

1. On the subject of Carter's generic transgressions, see Lidia Curti's book *Female Stories, Female Bodies: Narrative, Identity and Representation*.
2. The exclusion of the story collections does not seem to be a result of the position of Peach's study in a series devoted to modern novelists: The parallel volume on Joyce, for instance, includes a chapter on *Dubliners*.
3. See for example Gunew's "Distinguishing the Textual Politics of the Marginal Voice," *Southern Review* 18 (1985): 142–56 and *Framing Marginality: Multicultural Literary Studies* (Carlton, Victoria: Melbourne UP, 1994).
4. For a brief example of Carter on colonialism and patriarchy, see her conference presentation in the collection *Critical Fictions*, in which she appears alongside Ama Ata Aidoo and Nawal El Saadawi, among others.
5. For examples of book-length studies of Carter other than those reviewed here, see the items by Anja Muller and Yvonne Martinsson in the list of works cited.

Works Cited

Armitt, Lucie. "The Fragile Frames of *The Bloody Chamber*." Bristow and Broughton 88–99.

Bristow, Joseph, and Trev Lynn Broughton, eds. *The Infernal Desires of Angela Carter: Fiction, Femininity, Feminism*. Studies in Twentieth-Century Literature. London: Longman, 1997.

Carter, Angela. Conference presentation. *Critical Fictions: The Politics of Imaginative Writing*. Ed. Philomena Mariani. Dia Center for the Arts Discussions in Contemporary Culture 7. Seattle: Bay Press, 1991.

———. Interview. *Novelists in Interview*. By John Haffenden. London: Methuen, 1985. 76–96.

Clark, Robert. "Angela Carter's Desire Machine." *Women's Studies* 14 (1987): 147–61.

Curti, Lidia. *Female Stories, Female Bodies: Narrative, Identity and Representation*. New York: New York UP, 1998.

Day, Aidan. *Angela Carter: The Rational Glass*. Manchester: Manchester UP, 1998.

Duncker, Patricia. "Re-Imagining the Fairy Tale: Angela Carter's Bloody Chambers." *Literature and History* 10 (1984): 3–14.

Gamble, Sarah. *Angela Carter: Writing From the Front Line*. Edinburgh: Edinburgh UP, 1997.

Jordan, Elaine. Afterword. Bristow and Broughton 216–20.

Makinen, Merja. "Angela Carter's *The Bloody Chamber* and the Decolonization of Feminine Sexuality." *Feminist Review* 42 (1992): 2–15.

Martinsson, Yvonne. *Eroticism, Ethics and Reading: Angela Carter in Dialogue with Roland Barthes*. Stockholm Studies in English 86. Stockholm: Almqvist and Wiksell, 1996.

McGann, Jerome. "What Is Critical Editing?" *Text* 5 (1991): 15–30.

Muller, Anja. *Angela Carter: Identity Constructed/Deconstructed*. Heidelberg: Winter, 1997.

Peach, Linden. *Angela Carter*. Macmillan Modern Novelists. London: Macmillan, 1998.

Sage, Lorna. "The Savage Sideshow: A Profile of Angela Carter." *New Review* 4 (1977): 51–57.

Sanders, Andrew. *The Short Oxford History of English Literature*. Rev. ed. Oxford: Clarendon, 1996.

Angela Carter: The Fairy Tale

You mention folk culture and people immediately assume you're
going to talk about porridge and clog-dancing. . . .
　　　　　　　　　　　　　—Angela Carter, 1991

Nineteen seventy-nine was Angela Carter's *annus mirabilis* as a writer, the hinge-moment or turning point when she invented for herself a new authorial persona, and began for the first time to be read widely and *collusively,* by readers who identified with her as a reader and re-writer. New wine in old bottles was already one of her most serviceable slogans for her practice as a novelist, but now she gave roots and a rationale to her habitual vein of fantasy, parody and pastiche. In the two slim books she published that year, *The Bloody Chamber* and *The Sadeian Woman,* she explained herself, unpacked her gifts, played her own fairy godmother. She had already published seven novels and a book of stories. In fact, she would produce only two more novels, one more collection of short fiction and another of journalism before she died in 1992. But the really magical thing about the books of 1979 was this: they not only heralded her carnival transformation in *Nights at the Circus* (1984) and *Wise Children* (1991), but they gave back her earlier work to herself and her readers, the re-writer re-read and canonised. She had started out as a member of the 1960s counterculture—"the savage sideshow" as she wryly called it—but twenty years on she no longer looked marginal at all.[1] The present essay sets out to explore some of the implications of this story, and the role fairy tales played in it.

Marina Warner, herself much affected and influenced by the post-1979 Carter—Warner described *From the Beast to the Blonde: On Fairy Tales and Their Tellers* (1994) as "inspired by the writing of Angela Carter" (in Sage, *Flesh and the Mirror* 344)—saw Carter's relation to this genre as an affair of the heart: "Fairy tales explore the mysteries of love. . . . Angela Carter's quest for Eros,

Marvels & Tales: Journal of Fairy-Tale Studies, Vol. 12, No. 1 (1998), pp. 52–68. Copyright © 1998 by Wayne State University Press, Detroit, MI 48201.

her attempt to ensnare its nature in her imagery . . . drew her to fairy tales as a form . . ." (Warner 243). But it was just as much an affair of the head, motivated by what Carter called in a 1989 review of Pavic's *Dictionary of the Khazars* "the cerebral pleasure of the recognition of patterning afforded by formalism" (Carter, *Expletives Deleted* 9). In her work, she valued and sought abstraction as an antidote to the climate of foggy realism in which she'd grown up. And in this she resembled, as she herself saw, such writers as Italo Calvino, whose story also highlighted the transformative effects of his rediscovery of fairy tales and folktales (Carter, "Angela Carter Interviewed by Lorna Sage" 187–88).[2]

"When I began my career, the categorical imperative of every young writer was to represent his own time, . . ." Calvino wrote, looking instead to time past and to the future, in *Six Memos for the Next Millennium* (3). The 1956 collection of Italian folktales he edited (and re-wrote out of their various dialects into Italian) had seeped into the structure and texture of his own work, and given him the clue to a different dialogic relation to readers (most obviously in the fragmentary, permutable *Invisible Cities* in 1972 and in *If on A Winter's Night a Traveller* in 1979). "If . . . I was attracted by folktales and fairy tales, this was not the result of loyalty to an ethnic tradition . . . nor the result of nostalgia for things I read as a child," he explained in his lecture on the narrative virtue of "Quickness": "It was rather because of my interest in style and structure" (35). He was in rebellion against the postwar socialist-realist orthodoxy, which preached that the artist could only connect himself with "the people" if he wrote naturalistically. The folktale suggested a different way of thinking about this: the craft of storytelling as practised by people themselves had been once upon a time on the side of fantasy and recursive patterns. Choosing to evade "the weight, the inertia, the opacity of the world" (Calvino 4) wasn't escapist or decadent, and quite the opposite of an addiction to Art for Art's sake:

> I am accustomed to consider literature as a search for knowledge . . . as extended to anthropology and ethnology and mythology. Faced with the precarious existence of tribal life—drought, sickness, evil influence—the shaman responded by ridding his body of weight and flying to another world. In centuries and civilizations closer to us, in villages where the women bore most of the weight of a constricted life, witches flew by night on broomsticks, or even on lighter vehicles such as ears of wheat or pieces of straw. Before being codified by the Inquisition, these images were part of the folk imagination. . . . (Calvino 26–27)

This tale about the origin of "Lightness," a tale about the pretexts of tales, resembles Carter's own position on the matter; in the Preface to the first of the two collections of fairy tales she edited for Virago, she wrote that fairy tales and folktales represent "the most vital connection we have with the imaginations of the ordinary men and women whose labour created our world . . ." (Carter, *Virago* ix). In *The Sadeian Woman,* more peremptorily, she said: "If nobody, including the artist, acknowledges art as a means of *knowing* the world, then art is relegated to a kind of rumpus room of the mind" (13). Like pornography, the fairy tale was practical fantasy, in this view, and it worked by narrative levitation—abstraction, patterning, getting above yourself. . . .

Well, up to a point, and depending on who you were. Calvino, who had spent the boom years of structuralist theory in Paris, refers us to Propp's *Morphology of the Folktale* (1968): "[I]n folktales a flight to another world is a common occurrence. Among the 'functions' catalogued by Vladimir Propp . . . it is one of the methods of 'transference of the hero,' defined as follows: 'Usually the object sought is in "another" or "different" realm that may be situated far away horizontally, or else at a great vertical depth or height' " (27). You can see how this schema would have appealed to Calvino, since he has already described his cast of mind in the 1940s—"the adventurous, picaresque rhythm that prompted me to write"—at the time he set out on his own anti-realist quest for identity as a writer (Calvino 3). But for the female reader/writer, surely the case is altered? Most of Propp's examples, as Jack Zipes points out in *Don't Bet on the Prince* (1986), contain a very different pattern of signification for girls and women: "What is praiseworthy in males . . . is rejected in females; the counterpart of the energetic, aspiring boy is the scheming, ambitious woman. . . . Women who are powerful and good are never human . . ." (187). Zipes, a scholar of the fairy tale, is also a self-confessed fan of Carter's work; and indeed the cheerful confidence of his tone here owes a lot to her arguments and example. Carter, of course, hadn't put her money on the prince. The hero of transference almost never I think appears in her own fairy tales, except possibly in the guise of Puss-in-Boots, an agile, resourceful tom who scales rococo and neoclassical facades with great panache; and just possibly as the cyclist hero of "The Lady of the House of Love," whose bicycle replaces seven-league boots. In the novels, he's represented by Desiderio in *The Infernal Desire Machines of Dr. Hoffman* (1972) and by Walser (in *Nights at the Circus,* 1984)—especially the latter, who is apprenticed to a shaman on his fumbling way to becoming a fit mate for the winged heroine Fevvers, who is indeed powerful and good and not exactly human.[3]

During the 1970s, Carter had been re-reading fairy tales and Sade in tandem, and bleakly contemplating the fate of good, powerless girls, the Red Riding Hoods and Sleeping Beauties of the world. She practiced a deliberate and reductionist habit of interpretation. In *The Sadeian Woman,* there are many occasions when she refers to "bankrupt enchantments" and "fraudulent magic":

To be the *object* of desire is to be defined in the passive case.

To exist in the passive case is to die in the passive case—that is, to be killed.

This is the moral of the fairy tale about the perfect woman. (77)

You could argue that she's here merely using the term "fairy tale" in its colloquial sense: a sugar-coated lie; or more grandly, a "myth," a cultural construct naturalised as a timeless truth. But the profile of the passive heroine is too close to too many fairy-tale characters to sustain the distinction. Sade, Carter argues, has this to be said for him: that in the person of his long-suffering heroine Justine he "contrived to isolate the dilemma of an emergent type of woman. Justine, daughter of a banker, becomes the prototype of two centuries of women who find the world was not, as they had been promised, made for them. . . . These self-consciously blameless ones suffer and suffer until it becomes second nature . . ." (*The Sadeian Woman* 57).[4] You can find this woman in conduct books, novels, psychoanalysis, and suburbia as well as in pornography. And the fairy tale too has come to serve this post-romantic-agony culture that is modern and masochistic at once. Carter had always played with other "genres"—the Gothic, science fiction—which belong to this Sadeian moment. Women writers (for example, Ann Radcliffe and Mary Shelley) are hugely inventive in these genres, but they don't afford the formal distance of the fairy tale, which has a longer and larger history.

So fairy tale has here a two-faced character. Its promiscuity—the stories are anybody's—means that you do have to understand it historically, as drawn into the sensibility of the times, more often than not as a supporting strand in a realist or sentimental bourgeois narrative. But you can tease out the sub-text; and in any case older, sparer tales, and alternative tellings, surviving ghettoised in the nursery or in folklore collections alongside their assimilated versions, contrive (like Sade's repetitive and obscene narratives) to isolate their elements for cruelly lucid contemplation. The one thing you mustn't do is mistake the endless recurrence of these characters and these plots for evidence of the universal cultural passivity of women in the past.[5] In fairy tales once upon a time people *could* see the wood for the trees. And so Carter, while registering with grim humour and clarity the awful legacy of "the fairytale about the perfect woman," still sees in the genre a means by which a writing woman may take flight. Gender-politics don't undo the formal appeal of the fairy tale, though they do mean you have to take a longer detour through cultural history to arrive at lightness.

In 1978, in her radio play *Come unto These Yellow Sands,* Carter has one of the products of Victorian fairyland, Oberon (as characterised by Shakespeare-as-seen-by-painter-Richard Dadd), give an indignant revisionist lecture (to an audience of goblins, elves, and other disenfranchised figments) about the history of "fairy subjects." Oberon's line is a post-Marxist one: the ascendant middle-classes lived off the imaginative labour of the poor, just as they lived off their physical labour:

> The primitive superstitions of the countryside, the ancient lore born on the wrong side of the blanket to religious faith, could not survive in the smoke, the stench, the human degradation . . . of the great cities. . . . Here the poor were stripped of everything, even of their irrational dreads, and the external symbols of their dreams and fears . . . were utilized to provide their masters with a decorative margin of the "quaint," the "fanciful" and the "charming." . . . This realm of faery served as a kitsch repository for fancies too savage, too dark, too voluptuous, fancies that were forbidden the light of common Victorian day *as such.* (*Yellow Sands* 23–24)

The phrase "kitsch repository" anticipates *The Sadeian Woman's* "rumpus room of the mind." But that is indeed where you have to rummage if you want to retrieve art as "a way of *knowing* the world." This didactic radio-play Oberon is a very apposite (and funny) exponent of the revisionist analysis of fairy tale as a means of knowledge and of *self-knowledge.* When he describes Victorian fairyland as "a kind of pornography of the imagination," he is pointing to its last link with reality, its saving gracelessness.

In this sense, "genre" retains its own separate power: like pornography, fairy tale relies on repeated motifs, multiple versions and inversions, the hole in the text where the readers insert themselves. Its availability to interpretation, its *potential* poverty, bareness, lightness, represent the possibility of rendering the obsessive matter of cruelty, desire and suffering (which is mainstream fiction's fantastical and Gothic underside) profane and provisional. In his 1979 book *Breaking the Magic Spell,* Jack Zipes wrote that "the best of folk and fairy tales chart ways for us to become masters of history . . . they transform time into relative elements" (18–19). They are an antidote to eternity, in other words, "born on the wrong side of the blanket from religious faith." And in this as in other ways, re-reading them is an *Enlightenment* project. In a 1978 interview, Carter said, about Sade, "He's sent me back to the Enlightenment, where I am very happy. They mutter the age of reason is over, but I don't see how it ever began so one might as well start again, now. I also revere and emulate Sade's rigorous atheism . . ." (Interview 1–2). Carter habitually associated the prestige and glamour of passivity with the cult of Christianity and Father Gods in general, and was also deeply unsympathetic to the idea of their replacement with Mothers: "If women allow themselves to be consoled for their culturally determined lack of access to the modes of intellectual production by the invocation of hypothetical great goddesses, they are simply flattering themselves into submission. . . . Mother goddesses are just as silly a notion as father gods" (*The Sadeian Woman* 5).

One of the reasons she so valued fairy tale—and one that is obscured by a too-exclusive focus on gender-politics—is that she associated it with a world where our dreads and desires were personified in beings that were not-human without being divine. Kurt Vonnegut used to make the same point in his oft-delivered vaudeville routine about writing an anthropology dissertation for his MA (rejected), drawing graphs of the story-lines of our western myths and favourite legends. He discovers that the Bible story produces the same pattern as "Cinderella," with the risen Christ as Prince Charming:

> The steps . . . are all the presents the fairy godmother gave to Cinderella, the ball gown, the slippers, the carriage, and so on. The sudden drop is the stroke of midnight. All the presents have been repossessed. But then the prince finds her and marries her, and she is infinitely happy ever after. She gets all the stuff back and *then* some. A lot of people think this story is trash, and, on graph paper, it certainly looks like trash. . . . But . . . then I saw that the rise to bliss at the end was identical with the expectation of redemption. . . . The tales were identical. (Vonnegut 315)[6]

Sade and *The Bloody Chamber* combined provided Carter with a potted history of "fantasy"; and also with a new vantage point on her own marginality, a new way of understanding it as not the position of a *literary* victim or decadent. Nineteen seventy-nine was the year of Gilbert and Gubar's hugely influential *The Madwoman in the Attic,* we should not forget, and the specific issue of pornography was dividing feminists. The critic most diametrically opposed to Carter's use of Sade—and, by implication, to her ironic, "light" re-reading of the fairy tale about the perfect woman—was Susanne Kappeler in *The Pornography of Representation:*

> Carter, the potential feminist critic, has withdrawn into the literary sanctuary, has become literary critic. . . . Like good modern literary critics, we move from the author/writer to the oeuvre/text which by literary convention bears his name. . . . Sade's pornographic assault on one particular patriarchal representation of woman—the Mother— renders him, in the eyes of Carter, a provider of a service to women. . . . Women, of course, neither produced nor sanctified the mothering aspect of their patriarchal representation, but it is doubtful whether they would thank Sade for replacing the myth of the Mother with that of the victim or the inverted sadist. . . . (134)

Kappeler is deliberately reading Carter reductively, rather in her own spirit; and she is wrong to suggest that Carter's Sade *replaces* Mother with her suffering and sadist daughters Justine and Juliette. All three, Carter argues, belong to the same mythology (which Sade extrapolates, rather than invents): it's Mother who makes her daughters this way, though this whole family of women is of course also formed by patriarchal society. What is at stake is the meaning of the "literary": for Carter genres like pornography, romance, fairy tale and science fiction are not at all hedged with piety in the way Kappeler assumes. They are already desecrating "the literary sanctuary." This does not mean that they are to be claimed automatically as "transgressive" or "subversive," only that their currency and their craft (as opposed to high art, except insofar as they contaminate it, which they most often do) lends itself to both or all parties. For Carter does not agree with Kappeler that "Women . . . neither produced nor sanctified the mothering aspect of their patriarchal representation"; her reading of Sade, and of fairy tales, is precisely an attack on this version of women as blameless, as having no part in the construction of their world, and of themselves: "Justine marks the start of a kind of self-regarding female masochism, a woman with no place in the world, no status, the core of whose resistence has been eaten away by self-pity" (*The Sadeian Woman* 57).

Kappeler thinks that "representation" *in itself* is powerfully impure and voyeuristic, and therefore cannot be safely distinguished from pornography. Carter agrees. But this is where their paths diverge, for Kappeler is a fundamentalist and an iconoclast, who wants to do away with literariness, to destroy the images, and to have people speak for themselves without artifice in the name of truth. In contrast, Carter wants to turn out the mind's rumpus room and vindicate women's creative role, past and present. The blameless woman is for Carter also the unimaginative woman. So *The Sadeian Woman* and the fairy tales were a way of asserting the value of her vocation as a writer in the face of radical puritanism (compare, again, Calvino and the postwar pressure from the Party left). Not because art is autonomous: "genre" is a site where the literary and the extra-literary confront each other and converse. Still, Carter was giving a formal, fictive and "untruthful" answer to a political question, and that meant that, at the time, she was frequently convicted of heresy.

In the years since, the development of different emphases in gender studies has produced a theoretical frame that fits Carter so much better that it seems set to canonise her. I'm thinking, for example, of Judith Butler, with her description of bodies that "wear" our "cultural history"—"the body is a *field of interpretive possibilities*, the locus of a dialectical process of interpreting anew a historical set of interpretations which have become imprinted on the flesh" ("Sex and Gender" 45). Butler—like Carter, though from a different angle—is spreading the act of creation around the culture at large, highlighting the symbolic importance of disguise, cross-dressing, various perverse "carnival" tactics, as images of the not especially decadent or bohemian, but actually often *homely*, practice of making up gender as you go along. Butler's 1993 gloss on the theoretical and creative position implied in "performativity" is a good description of Carter's procedures in *The Sadeian Woman:* "Performativity describes this relation of being implicated in that which one opposes, this turning power against itself to produce alternative modalities of power" (*Bodies* 241). Fairy tales too use this tactic.

Density of allusion, quotation, and bricolage were already hallmarks of Carter's writing in 1979. Some of the earlier novels are, as Elaine Jordan says, "stories of a crucial change in some young person"s life . . . closer to realist fictions of experience and development" (196–97). Others are more obviously fantastical and speculative, and by the 1970s this second kind had taken over. But they shared a repertoire. Plots, for instance, tend to divide into the cabinet-of-curiosities or mausoleum shape, not quite always death-bound (*Several Perceptions* in 1968 is an open-ended exception) but essentially static; and into the more picaresque frame, with Gothic and science-fiction overtones. The girl we can recognise in retrospect as the Justine or Sleeping-Beauty type of heroine recurs again and again—murdered Ghislaine in her first novel *Shadow Dance* in 1965 and suicidal Annabel in the 1971 *Love,* but the distinction between self-murder and murder is less significant than it might seem, for this heroine lives in the passive case. In Carter's work the realist "rite of passage" plot about the young person's entry into the world is turned ironically back on itself: this heroine's refusal to grow up is clearly for Carter the most honest and telling thing about her.

Tristessa, the Hollywood icon of *The Passion of New Eve,* is the perfection of this woman-as-idea: "Tristessa's speciality had been suffering. Suffering was her vocation. She suffered exquisitely" (*Passion* 8). Her name itself, we're told, "whispered rumours of inexpressible sadness; the lingering sibilants whispered like the doomed petticoats of a young girl who is dying" (122). That s/he is a transvestite makes perfect sense; indeed several of the martyred heroines are daddy's girls, his creatures. Ghislaine in *Shadow Dance,* for instance: " 'You know her father's a clergyman? . . . She wrote to me that it was a spiritual defloration when I knifed her' " (124). And Albertina in *The Infernal Desire Machines of Doctor Hoffman,* though she has many disguises, is the agent of her mad scientist father, who keeps her dead mother's body embalmed in his castle. All of these figures and more are summed up in *The Bloody Chamber* in "The Lady of the House of Love," her strings pulled by her vampire ancestors, who sleeps all day in her coffin and sleep-walks so reluctantly through her carnivorous nights. Like her predecessors, she is "in voluntary exile from the historic world, in its historic time that is counted out minute by minute" (*The Sadeian Woman* 106).[7] And that is why the prince will kill her when he wakes her up: death, though, is the one thing she's right about. The stinking red rose our hero takes from her Sleeping-Beauty's overgrown garden to remember her by will bloom all the way from her Transylvanian fastness to the trenches of the War in France, historic time's bloodbath.

The other implication of this story's title—the House of Love as brothel (indeed it reminds its chaste hero of a necrophiliac tableau in a brothel in Paris)—alludes shorthand-style to the bargain involved in marriage and/or prostitution. The title story "The Bloody Chamber" refers to this, and so do the Beauty-and-the Beast stories. *The Sadeian Woman* has a savage aphorism on the subject: "[T]he free expression of desire is as alien to pornography as it is to marriage" (13). This helps to explain why the heroines who survive their rite of passage are cruelly calculating, like Marianne in *Heroes and Villains,* who finds her true vocation as a widow, taking over the master's mantle—" 'I'll be the tiger lady and rule them with a rod of iron' " (*Heroes* 150). The Little Red Riding Hood of "The Werewolf" in *The Bloody Chamber,* who arranges for her Grandmother's murder and inherits her cottage, is in a similar mould, and so is the bride of the title story—where it's Mother who does the dirty work. In fact, these figures are now revealed as imperfect avatars of Justine's sister, Sade's Juliette:

> a model for women, in some ways. She is rationality personified and leaves no single cell of her brain unused. She will never obey the fallacious promptings of her heart. Her mind functions like a computer programmed to produce two results for herself—financial profit and libidinal gratification. By the use of her reason, an intellectual apparatus women themselves are still inclined to undervalue, she rids herself of the more crippling aspects of femininity; but she is the New Woman in the mode of irony. (*The Sadeian Woman* 79)

New Women had been on the margins of Carter's picture since the beginning: there's a minor character, Emily, who walks away unscathed from the murderous mess at the end of *Shadow Dance,* and she does it because she's already an adept; she knows the story in advance:

> "I found this key in one of his trouser pockets, see, and I thought, you know, of Bluebeard."
> "Bluebeard?"
> "Bluebeard. And the locked room. I don't know him very well, you know. And Sister Anne, Sister Anne, what do you see . . ." (*Shadow Dance* 103–04)

But this early character was halfway out of the book, just looking in. Carter would later in 1979 be unlocking Bluebeard's chamber from the inside.

Fairy tales, in their multiple reflections on each other, and their individual and internal layerings of interpretations, exemplify *and unravel* something of the process by which meanings get written on bodies. You can see the decorative patina—the vampire tale written over the Sleeping Beauty story, itself easily pared down to a tale as bleak and brief as "The Snow Child" where the daughter is dreamed up and destroyed in a moment, "nothing left of her but a feather a bird might have dropped; a bloodstain, like the trace of a fox's kill on the snow; and the rose . . ." (*The Bloody Chamber* 92). And in the same process, you can see *through,* see the figures and moves stripped of the weight of finality. There's no core, or point of origin, or ur-story "underneath," just a continuous interweaving of texts. Still, there's a sense of simplification at work. You can see that mothers and stepmothers have a good deal in common; just as in Sade's text Justine and Juliette "mutually reflect and complement one another, like a pair of mirrors" (*The Sadeian Woman* 119).

Doubling and redoubling these daughters, these mothers, Carter arrives, on the far side of *The Bloody Chamber,* at the virtuoso 1987 Cinderella story "Ashputtle *or* The Mother's Ghost," three versions for the price of one. The first, "The Mutilated Girls," reflects dryly on how easy it is, if you think about the stepmother's cruel urgency to marry her daughters off to the prince, to make this a tale "about cutting bits off women, so that they will *fit in*" (*American Ghosts* 110), but that's to miss the agency of the (good) dead mother. Then again, Carter's narrator toys with the idea of going back into the past, where perhaps the father was already involved with the stepmother. Perhaps her daughters, too, are his? That would explain his speedy remarriage, the way that the step-family are dead set on replacing the first family, and the dead mother's refusal to lie down. But such a soap-opera plot "would transform 'Ashputtle' from the bare necessity of fairy tale, with its characteristic copula formula, 'and then,' to the emotional and technical complexity of bourgeois realism" (*American Ghosts* 113). Instead the mothers converge: the ghost coming back to send her daughter to the ball, the stepmother hacking her daughters' feet to get them into the slipper, which after all will only fit "Ashputtle's foot, the size of the bound foot of a Chinese woman, a stump. Almost an amputee already. . . ." The ghostly mother (who's taken the form of a turtle dove) coos triumphantly, " 'See how well I look after you, my darling!' " (*American Ghosts* 116). Version number two, "The Burned Child," is brief: here, there's no prince and no stepsisters, only a bare peasant drama. The ghost possesses in turn a cow, a cat, and a bird and, through them, feeds her orphaned daughter, and grooms and dresses her so that she can take the man the stepmother wants: "He gave her a house and money. She did all right" (*American Ghosts* 119). And mother rests in peace. The third version, "Travelling Clothes," is the shortest of all. The cruel stepmother burns the child's face; the dead mother kisses her better, gives her a red dress—" 'I had it when I was your age' "—and worms from her eyesockets that turn into a diamond ring (" 'I had it when I was your age' "); the mother invites her to step into her coffin. The girl at first recoils, but the pattern is set, the formula from the past is sprung like a trap (" 'I stepped into *my* mother's coffin when I was your age' "): "The girl stepped into the coffin although she thought it would be the death of her. It turned into a coach and horses. The horses stamped, eager to be gone. 'Go and seek your fortune, darling' " (*American Ghosts* 119–20).

The barer and more elliptical these stories become, however, the more they imply. We don't go back into the past realist-style to supply depth and motive; but we do go back to link the mother to *her* mother, the clothes and jewels and coach-and-horses to puberty, marriage and early death, and to link happy endings to sad ones, all of these interpretations imprinted on the flesh, here unwound like a shroud. The Lady of the House of Love wears "a hoop-skirted dress of white satin draped here and there with lace. . . . [She is] a girl with the fragility of the skeleton of a moth, so thin, so frail that her dress seemed to him to hang suspended, as if untenanted in the dark air, a fabulous lending, a self-articulated garment in which she lived like a ghost in a machine" (*The Bloody Chamber* 100). Carter's heroines in the earlier fiction had repeatedly tried on dead women's wedding dresses, stepped into mother's shoes. They were at the same time, these stories suggest, finding out something about the nature of their skins, that those too could come off.[8]

The ghost's valediction (" 'Go and seek your fortune' ") has a double meaning, then. Either "go and repeat the story," or "go and *don't* repeat the story" (if you've seen the shape of mother's legacy, thanks to the story). Looking back to her novel *Love* in 1987 (itself a rewriting of her first book), Carter called it in a jokey revisionist Afterword "Annabel's coffin" (*Love* 114); she herself would not repeat that structure again, though some of her characters would still act out (in freak shows, for money) the fairy tale of the perfect, suffering woman. The young person's rite-of-passage story (which fairy tale and realist fiction have conspired together to tell since the eighteenth century) is to be shed and discarded like an old skin. Or, in a different but related image—"he gave her a house and money"—the house is burned, ruined, abandoned. Carter's characters had been burning down houses almost since the start of her writing career, and now she had worked out more exactly why: "When mother is dead, all the life goes out of the old house. The shop in *The Magic Toyshop* gets burned down, the old dark house, and adult life begins . . ." (Carter, "Angela Carter Interviewed by Lorna Sage" 190).

This is her farewell to "realist fictions of experience and development," which in any case had only ever been containers for her characters' vagrant lives. She'd jettisoned a whole "great tradition," gladly. To measure the sense of vertigo and freedom involved, you need to think back to what that tradition had meant, especially for women. Antonia Byatt, a contemporary who wants—by contrast—to salvage continuity, has described very exactly, in *Imagining Characters: Six Conversations about Women Writers,* how realist fictional structures and habits of reading work to domesticate the world: "[T]he other thing that happens in all novels is that because you read a novel by yourself in a room, inner space in your mind and outer space in novels become somehow equivalent, images of each other. . . . There's a way in which the whole landscape is inside in a novel, even if it's said to be outside" (37).[9] The quickness and lightness of the fairy tale and the "performative" sense of cultural history as travelling clothes all serve to undo this sense of accommodating interiority that belongs to the novel "proper." For Carter, outside stays out. When she moved on, post-*Bloody Chamber,* she looked to radio, film, the stage, oral and/or performance-oriented media, taking her clue from the fairy tales that cast the writer in the role of re-teller of tales.

But what is "outside"? "Note the absence of the husband/father" in these Cinderella stories, says the didactic narrator of "Ashputtle": "[T]he father is unacknowledged but all the same is predicated by both textual and biological necessity. In the drama between two female families in opposition to each other because of their rivalry over men (husband/father, husband/son), the men seem no more than passive victims of their fancy, yet their significance is absolute because it is ('a rich man,' 'a king's son') economic" (*American Ghosts* 110–11). Carter's fictional landscapes had always been artificial (parks, gardens, the "wilderness" itself) so that nature for her was always "second nature," landscape history. This was father's domain. Viewed romantically, the decaying houses, cottages and castles of her novels seem to be being eaten up by nature but, if you look more closely, this nature is ready-dishevelled and stylised (by romantics and their Victorian followers). The rose from the vampire Lady's bower can travel to France in 1914 and bloom there because historic time and fairy-tale time are linked by Father Time. In *The Infernal Desire Machines of Doctor Hoffman* (1972), the last novel with a father-magus who manipulates appearances, creating and uncreating the world, there is a minor episode with yet another doomed Sleeping Beauty, this time a waif in the landscape:

> the roses had quite overrun the garden and formed dense, forbidding hedges . . . sprayed out fanged, blossoming whips. Those within the house were already at the capricious mercy of nature. . . . As I drew nearer . . . I heard, over the pounding of the blood in my ears, notes of music falling. . . . She played with extraordinary sensitivity. The room was full of a poignant, nostalgic anguish . . . her hair and dress were stuck all over with twigs and petals from the garden. She looked like drowning Ophelia. I thought so immediately, though I could not know how soon she would really drown, for she was so forlorn and

desperate. A chilling and restrained passivity made her desperation all the more pathetic. (*Infernal Desire* 50–53)

For nature, read Shakespeare. When it comes to the world of outside, Carter tracks Shakespeare everywhere, for in literary terms, he is the father, and drowning Ophelia is his great kitsch contribution to the pantheon of passive heroines.[10] This reached its apogee with Victorian Sir John Everett Millais's painting of Ophelia drifting on the water, borne up by her clothes, wreathed with flowers and weeds. Carter's character Oberon in *Come unto These Yellow Sands* is meant to be lecturing on Richard Dadd's paintings inspired by *A Midsummer Night's Dream,* but cannot resist an allusion to Ophelia, for she so exactly fits his theme:

> The richly sexual symbolism of aspects of the mythology of the "wee folk" was buried so deeply beneath the muffling layers of repression and the oppression of women. . . . It might be said of these fairy painters, as Hamlet says of Ophelia:
>> Death and affliction, even hell itself,
>> She turns to favour and to prettiness. (*Yellow Sands* 24)[11]

Dadd's paintings (done in mental hospital after he cut his father's throat) caught, for Carter, the paralysing effects of "burying" symbolism. Titania steps out of one of them to describe "Dew, dew everywhere . . . the dew drips like tears that have dropped from a crystal eye, heavy, solid, mineral, glittering, unnatural" (*Yellow Sands* 42).[12]

These landscapes of psychohistory are for Carter, like the "bankrupt enchantments" of fairy tales about women's passivity, true lies. That is, they can be persuaded to reveal how myths of timelessness are made and disseminated. Her 1982 story "Overture and Incidental Music for *A Midsummer Night's Dream,"* first published in the magazine *Interzone,* goes behind the scenes of Shakespeare's text in order to draw it and him into a present-tense revisionist perspective: "This wood is, of course, nowhere near Athens; the script is a positive maze of false leads. The wood is really located somewhere in the English midlands, possibly near Bletchley, where the great decoding machine was sited. Correction . . . oak, ash and thorn were chopped down to make room for a motorway a few years ago. However, since the wood existed only as a structure of the imagination, in the first place, it will remain" (*Black Venus* 67). Dense layers of interpretation over time constitute this landscape, and beyond it stretch realms of pre-literary history that serve also to put it in its place—"nothing like the dark necromantic forest in which the Northern European imagination begins and ends, where its dead and witches live, and Baba-yaga stalks about in her house with chicken's feet looking for children in order to eat them" (*Black Venus* 67). In the process of this narrative, Shakespeare's wood, "*the* English wood," is stripped of its nostalgic weight and universality, becomes readable and rewritable: "there is always a way out of a maze. . . . A maze is a construct of the human mind, and not unlike it. . . . But to be lost in the forest is to be lost to *this* world . . ." (*Black Venus* 68). Shakespeare, for Carter, looks two ways; his stage was a threshold between worlds, where folk culture was made over into high culture, but never completely. In a late interview Carter observes, "intellectuals . . . are still reluctant to treat him as popular culture. . . . Shakespeare . . . is one of the great hinge-figures that sum up the past—one of the great Janus-figures that sum up the past as well as opening all the doors to the future. . . . I like *A Midsummer Night's Dream* almost beyond reason, because it is beautiful and funny and camp—and glamorous and cynical. . . ." ("Angela Carter Interviewed by Lorna Sage" 186–87). Here she addresses in passing this question of the "outside." Shakespeare, through his connections with the pre-literary past and with popular culture past and future, points outside the very world his theatre helped construct—"almost *beyond reason.*"

It is time to admit that, for all Carter's deconstructive and demythologising inventiveness, Marina Warner is after all right to say that her relation to fairy tales is a love-affair. It's no accident that the most popular of her tales—"The Tiger's Bride," "The Company of Wolves" and "Wolf-Alice"—are those which step beyond the knowable maze. In the *Midsummer Night's Dream* story, she writes that to be lost in the forest is "to be committed against your will—or, worse, of your own desire—to a perpetual absence from humanity, an existential catastrophe, for the forest is as infinitely boundless as the human heart" (*Black Venus* 68). The girls in the stories who abandon their human separateness, of their own desire (or who, like Wolf-Alice, are only now discovering it), are lovers of this mutant kind. In *The Sadeian Woman,* Carter ends with a praise of love: "[O]nly the possibility of love could awaken the libertine to perfect, immaculate terror. It is in this holy terror of love that we find, in both men and women themselves, the source of all opposition to the emancipation of women" (150). One could argue, I think, that the title *The Bloody Chamber* itself, alludes in the last analysis not to Bluebeard's meat-locker, nor even to the womb/tomb, but to the human heart.

My argument for fairy tales as a means of simplification and abstraction still stands, however, though I suppose it is *soul* that Carter finds so marvellously and instructively missing in them, not heart. Calvino in his essay on "Lightness" has a phrase that applies here—"anthropocentric parochialism" (Calvino 22)— the "holy" difference between ourselves and the substance of the world. This "ancient lore born on the wrong side of the blanket from religion" returns us to a world still unknown, our *profane* interiority.

Less portentously, her fairy tales returned Carter to the picaresque, time-travelling exuberance of her last two large novels, with their historical travesties, tableaus and confidence tricks which are both staged and debunked: "The notion of a universality of human experience is a confidence trick and the notion of a universality of female experience is a clever confidence trick" (*The Sadeian Woman* 12). Elaine Jordan has described the double move involved here most accurately: "Judgements of [Carter's] work have often been made from limited perspectives which ignore the extent to which she entwines the local with the global, and sees universality as something to be challenged when it's assumed as given, and constructively struggled for when it's not. . . ." (Jordan 210). The fairy tale enabled Carter to locate and explore the processes of interpretation that make us seem ineluctably continuous with ourselves. It supplied her with an (anti-) myth of origins, a recipe for transformations, a trunkful of travelling clothes and a happy ending. Except that, as she would have been the first to object, there's no such thing, unalloyed. Her own fairy tales are exercises in the suspension of *belief,* but a glance at the snapshot of our *fin de siècle* cultural moment presented by, for example, Elaine Showalter in *Hystories* (1997), will serve to reveal that Sleeping Beauty lives on in her dream of blamelessness.[13] Indeed, it may well be that some of the strength of Carter's present reputation is due to credulous misreading. She sometimes suspected as much: "I become mildly irritated when people . . . ask me about the 'mythic' quality of work I've written lately" (she wrote in 1983): "I'm in the demythologising business. I'm interested in myths . . . just because they are extraordinary lies designed to make people unfree" ("Notes" 71). Fairy tales are less-than-myths, however. They are volatile, anybody's—"This is how *I* make potato soup" (Carter, *Virago* x). It's hard to deny for long that they are part of the historic world, and Carter's example has made it harder.

Notes

1. See "The Savage Sideshow" for a profile by Lorna Sage. In the United Kingdom (and in Europe more generally) Carter's works are currently set texts at school and university, and the subject of a great many graduate dissertations. In 1997 she was the only contemporary British writer to be the subject of a separate seminar at the annual conference of the European Society for the Study of English (ESSE), where a large proportion of the papers focused on the fairy tales. Carter's first real fairy-tale book was her translation, *The Fairy Tales of Charles Perrault;* in 1982 she edited a collection, *Sleeping Beauty and Other Favourite Fairy Tales; The Virago Book of Fairy Tales,* which she edited, was published in 1990; *The Second Virago Book of Fairy Tales* in 1992, the year of her death.

2. If Calvino had not at some point read Vladimir Propp he would not have written *Invisible Cities,* Carter says there of Calvino ("Angela Carter Interviewed by Lorna Sage" 187).

3. Fevvers, the heavy-weight trapeze artiste and Winged Victory of *Nights at the Circus* combines the characteristics of many ready-made symbolic and allegorical figures of the turn of the nineteenth century, and is subject inside the text to endless

interpretation and re-interpretation. Carter and her illustrator Martin Ware had already sketched her out in 1977 in the "Lilac Fairy" who looks a lot like Mae West with wings in *The Fairy Tales of Charles Perrault* (155).

4. In this same passage Carter refers to Justine as "the ancestress of a generation of women in popular fiction who find themselves in the same predicament, such as the heart-struck, tearful heroines of Jean Rhys, Edna O'Brien and Joan Didion who remain grumblingly acquiescent in a fate over which they believe they have no control" (*The Sadeian Woman* 56).

5. See Jack Zipes's essay " 'Little Red Riding Hood' as Male Creation and Projection."

6. Literature's profanity was important to Carter: "We think blasphemy is silly," she wrote in a 1979 review of Bataille's *Story of the Eye,* but we're wrong (*Expletives Deleted* 37). Salman Rushdie's predicament drew her deepest sympathy.

7. It may seem a bit hard to call this heroine's exile "voluntary," though in a sense she proves it is when she abandons it, joins the world and dies.

8. In "Donkey Skin" (*The Fairy Tales of Charles Perrault*), Carter had found a missing link for this story in the figure of the fairy godmother who sends the daughter's beautiful clothes after her: " 'Wherever you may be, your trunk, with all your clothes and jewels in it, will speed after you under the ground' " (140).

9. Byatt's "postmodern" fictions, starting from *Possession* (1990), are actually a knowing re-creation of Victorian literary values, demystificatory neither in intent nor effect.

10. Kate Chedgzoy, in *Shakespeare's Queer Children: Sexual Politics and Contemporary Culture,* is impressed by the carnival takeover by "illegitimate theatre" in Carter's *Wise Children,* but concentrates, for the sake of linking postcolonial themes with gay gender politics, on *The Tempest.*

11. Carter's Oberon was misquoting from memory. It is Laertes who speaks these lines, and they actually go: "Thought and affliction, passion, hell itself . . ." (*Hamlet,* Act IV, scene 5, lines 86–87).

12. *Wise Children* (1991) stages the comic extremity of this petrified scene, on the set of the 1930s film of *A Midsummer Night's Dream,* where "all was twice as large as life. Larger. Daisies big as your head and white as spooks, foxgloves as tall as the tower of Pisa . . . hanging in mid-air as if they'd just rolled off a wild rose or out of a cowslip, imitation dewdrops, that is, big *faux* pearls, suspended on threads. And clockwork birds, as well . . ." (124). In this novel Tiffany, who's thought to have drowned herself but turns up alive and angry, is a New Ophelia.

13. See especially the sections on "Recovered Memory" and "Multiple Personality Syndrome," where Showalter, who is of course a literary critic as well as a cultural historian, finds herself describing "stories" that have obvious fictional connections and strategies, but whose tellers absolutely refuse any suggestion that they are making them up, and indeed often "recover" them only under hypnosis or drugs or both.

Works Cited

Byatt, A.S., and Ignes Sodre. *Imagining Characters: Six Conversations about Women Writers.* London: Chatto & Windus, 1995.

Butler, Judith. *Bodies That Matter,* New York and London: Routledge, 1993.

———. "Sex and Gender in Simone de Beauvoir's *Second Sex." Yale French Studies* 72 (1986): 35–50.

Calvino, Italo. *Six Memos for the Next Millennium.* Cambridge, MA: Harvard UP, 1988.

Carter, Angela. *American Ghosts and Old World Wonders.* 1993. London: Vintage 1994.

———. "Angela Carter Interviewed by Lorna Sage." *New Writing.* Ed. Malcolm Bradbury and Judy Cooke. London: Minerva, 1992. 185–93.

———. *Black Venus.* London: Chatto & Windus, 1985.

———. *The Bloody Chamber.* 1979. London: Vintage, 1995.

———. *Come unto These Yellow Sands: Four Radio Plays.* Newcastle on Tyne: Bloodaxe, 1985.

———. *Expletives Deleted: Selected Writings.* 1992. London: Vintage, 1993.

———. *The Fairy Tales of Charles Perrault.* London: Gollancz, 1977.

———. *Heroes and Villains.* 1979. Harmondsworth: Penguin, 1981.

———. *The Infernal Desire Machines of Doctor Hoffman.* 1972. Rpt. *The War of Dreams.* New York: Bard/Avon Books, 1977; Harmondsworth: Penguin, 1982.

———. Interview. By William Bedford. *New Yorkshire Writing* 3 (Winter 1978): 1–2.

———. *Love.* 1971. Rev. ed. London: Chatto & Windus, 1987.

———. "Notes from the Front Line." *Gender and Writing.* Ed. Michelene Wandor. London: Pandora, 1983. 69–77.

———. *The Passion of New Eve.* 1977. London: Virago, 1982.

———. *The Sadeian Woman: An Exercise in Cultural History.* London: Virago, 1979.

———, ed. *The Second Virago Book of Fairy Tales.* London: Virago, 1992.

———. *Shadow Dance.* 1965. London: Virago, 1994.

———, ed. *Sleeping Beauty and other Favourite Fairy Tales.* London: Gollancz, 1982.

———. *The Virago Book of Fairy Tales.* London: Virago, 1990.

———. *Wise Children.* London: Chatto & Windus, 1991.

Chedgzoy, Kate. *Shakespeare's Queer Children: Sexual Politics and Contemporary Culture.* Manchester: Manchester UP, 1995.

Dundes, Alan, ed. *Little Red Riding Hood: A Casebook.* Madison: U of Wisconsin P, 1989.

Jordan, Elaine. "The Dangerous Edge." Sage, *Flesh and the Mirror* 189–215.

Kappeler, Susanne. *The Pornography of Representation.* Oxford: Polity, 1986.

Sage, Lorna, ed. *Flesh and the Mirror: Essays on the Art of Angela Carter.* London: Virago, 1994.

———. "The Savage Sideshow." *New Review* 4.39–40 (July 1977): 51–57.

Showalter, Elaine. *Hystories.* London: Picador, 1997.

Vonnegut, Kurt. *Palm Sunday.* London: Jonathan Cape, 1981.

Warner, Marina. "Anglea Carter: Bottle Blonde, Double Drag." Sage, *Flesh and the Mirror* 243–56.

Zipes, Jack. *Breaking the Magic Spell: Radical Theories of Folk and Fairy Tales.* London: Heinemann, 1979.

———, ed. *Don't Bet on the Prince.* New York: Methuen, 1986.

———. " 'Little Red Riding Hood' as Male Creation and Projection." Dundes 121–28.

"The Bloody Chamber" by Corinna Sargood. Copyright © Corinna Sargood. Reproduced with permission.

KATHLEEN E.B. MANLEY

The Woman in Process in Angela Carter's "The Bloody Chamber"

Readers of "The Bloody Chamber," Angela Carter's version of the tale known to folklorists as AT 312 ("Bluebeard"), often see the protagonist as doing little, for the most part, to avoid the fate her husband has planned for her (Bacchilega 126; Sanchez). She is not always passive, however, but rather oscillates between being insecure and feeling sure of herself. She is a woman in process, someone who is exploring her subject position and beginning to tell her own story.

Cristina Bacchilega recognizes the narrator's oscillation "between naive expectations of sex and knowing descriptions of economics" (123) as well as Carter's use of varying distances of viewpoint in "The Bloody Chamber" (121). In addition to these techniques, Carter engages ideas that appear in Susan Gubar's essay on Isak Dinesen's "The Blank Page"; uses mirrors to show the dawning of the protagonist's sense of subjectivity; and also engages ideas from Richard Wagner's opera *Tristan and Isolde*. The comments Carter has her protagonist make when she has finished telling about her marriage and rescue also show that the protagonist is still struggling to establish her subjectivity; though less influenced by others' opinions than she was, she is still conscious of them and has been attempting to expiate, through her story, the shame she feels about her history.

In her analysis of Isak Dinesen's short story "The Blank Page," Susan Gubar provides a perspective on women's difficulties in telling their own stories, treating Dinesen's story as a study of narrative creativity among women. Though

Marvels & Tales: Journal of Fairy-Tale Studies, Vol. 12, No. 1 (1998), pp. 71–81. Copyright © 1998 by Wayne State University Press, Detroit, MI 48201.

it applies to some extent to the narrative dynamics of "The Bloody Chamber," Gubar's essay is not entirely satisfactory in explaining the story, nor does it completely explain female storytelling. Carter's protagonist *appears* to be the blank page upon which her husband will inscribe his story of her. Nevertheless, partly because her mother's life story serves as a model for her and because her mother has provided her with the opportunity to have a career, the protagonist is not a blank page, and she escapes the story the Marquis planned for her.

Dinesen's "The Blank Page" concerns the special linen sheets nuns in a Portuguese convent traditionally wove for the marriage beds of Portuguese princesses. Displayed the morning after the wedding night, the bloody sheets told the story of each bride's (loss of) virginity. In return for their excellent work, the nuns used to receive "that central piece of the snow-white sheet which bore witness to the honor of a royal bride" (Gilbert and Gubar 1421); and they displayed these pieces, framed and with the appropriate princess's name on each, in a gallery at the convent. Of most interest to visitors, however, is one piece of linen which is a blank page: no blood appears on it and no name appears on the frame. Many stories of this piece of linen are thus possible, and, in her essay, Gubar discusses this blank page as a symbol of these possibilities rather than as a symbol of the patriarchal definition of woman as "a tabula rasa, a lack, a negation, an absence" (89). In contrast, Gubar argues, the bloody sheets symbolize the necessity for those women to use their own bodies to tell "their" story (78–79), and that story is the one patriarchy wants to hear: that is, women's willingness to be "objects of exchange" (84). These women are not, then, telling their own stories.

In discussing the piece of linen with no blood on it, Gubar writes that the woman who tells the overall tale of the convent, the linen, and the display of sheets "also praises the blank sheet because it is the 'material' out of which 'art' is produced. Women's creativity, in other words, is prior to literacy: the sisterhood produces the blank sheets needed to accomplish writing" (89). Carter's "The Bloody Chamber," like Gubar's and Dinesen's texts, explores the "material" with which her protagonist has been provided—the material that allows her to begin narrating her own story. Significantly, women figure in providing the material for both Carter's protagonist and the Portuguese princesses.

At least three passages in Carter's "The Bloody Chamber" indicate engagement with ideas that also occur in Dinesen's "The Blank Page." First, the Marquis mentions the custom, no longer followed in what he rather smugly calls "these civilized times," of hanging the bloody bridal sheets out the window to prove the bride's virginity (17). Second, the bride appears to be a "blank page"; she was, she says, a mere seventeen, a girl who knew "nothing of the world" when she married (5). She also, later, calls herself "only a baby" when her husband entrusts her with his keys (19). Third, following the tale patriarchy wants to read in the bloody sheets, the protagonist's husband clearly considers her an object of exchange and plans to inscribe upon her his continuing tale of punishment for wives' disobedience; the ruby choker he has her wear when he deflowers her (15) prefigures, as he later says, the decapitation he has planned as the end of her story (40). As Robin Ann Sheets points out, the Marquis "has arranged the setting, written the script, and set the plot in motion" (647).

While her youth and view of herself as innocent indicate a correspondence between the protagonist and the blank page, Carter's protagonist is not an entirely blank page. Gubar would say the bride as blank page has possibilities for telling her own story and a choice of whether to allow the patriarchal story of herself as an object of exchange to occur. But Carter indicates that female storytellers actually may have more to draw upon than the possibilities of a completely blank page. Fibers like those in the warp or weft of the linen the nuns weave already exist for Carter's protagonist to use in beginning to tell her own story: she has material to draw upon both from her mother's life story and from the opportunity her mother has offered her to have a career and thus be financially independent. Before she can make use of this material, however, she must start a journey toward establishing herself as a subject; this journey involves consciously seeing herself as others (and particularly the Marquis) see her.

In illustrating the bride's journey toward recognizing herself as subject, Carter places her protagonist in several scenes involving mirrors. The mirrors, by providing opportunities to see herself as others see her, allow the protagonist to begin to have a more complete sense of herself as subject. They also reinforce her in-process situation by indicating her wish to see herself as innocent and yet capable of recognizing the Marquis's wish to dictate her story.

The first group of mirrors in Carter's tale, at a performance of *Tristan and Isolde* the night before her wedding, causes the protagonist to recognize and acknowledge her fiancé's view of her; she sees him look at her with "sheer carnal avarice." Seeing in the mirror a child in a flimsy white dress with his wedding gift of a collar of rubies around her neck, she feels "a potentiality for corruption" within her that shocks her (7). This glimpse of herself provides not only the beginnings of subjectivity but also some honesty; she admits she previously might not have *acknowledged* her fiancé's lust, though she has already as much as admitted to her mother that she does not love the Marquis (2). At the same time, however, the mirrors at the opera encourage her acquiescence in the story the Marquis wishes to write of her, for the dichotomy Carter sets up and that the Marquis favors is a dichotomy between innocence and debauchery, not innocence and experience. Later, after the wedding's consummation, the bride "realize[s], with a shock of surprise, how it must have been my innocence that captivated him" (17); and slightly later, telling his bride about his gallery of paintings, the Marquis breaks off to say, "Your thin white face, cherie. . . .

Your thin white face, with its promise of debauchery only a connoisseur could detect." Her interior response to this remark is: "I was not afraid of him, but of myself. I seemed reborn in his unreflective eyes, reborn in unfamiliar shapes. I hardly recognized myself from his descriptions of me and yet—and yet, might there not be a grain of beastly truth in them? And in the red firelight, I blushed again, unnoticed, to think he might have chosen me because, in my innocence, he sensed a rare talent for corruption" (19).

This passage emphasizes the bride's uncertainty and also underscores once more the Marquis's attempt to write his bride's story: not only a story of wives' disobedience, but in her case the story of the virgin-or-whore choice for women. The bride's innocence, to him, signifies the possibility of guilt; she believes this story of her could be true. Had her sense of self been stronger she might have questioned this view and perhaps seen herself simply as having the capacity to enjoy her sexuality.

Carter confirms the bride's lack of knowledge of herself in several other mirror scenes, using them also to show the beginnings of her realization of subjectivity. For example, in the bedroom mirrors, she becomes a multitude of identical girls just before her husband disrobes his "bargain," and she realizes once again his objectification of her. He even says that he has acquired a "whole harem" for himself (11–12). When he deflowers her, "a dozen husbands impaled a dozen brides" in the mirrors. Her experience of her loss of virginity is painful; she calls it a "one-sided struggle" (15). That evening, however, she still takes refuge in thinking that her naiveté gives him pleasure (17). At this point in her story, she accepts the stereotypical patriarchal view of a young girl in relationship to an experienced man; he is to initiate her and to enjoy his conquest. Many hours later, after she has visited the forbidden room and he returns from his supposed business trip to confront her disobedience, she sees herself again in the bedroom mirrors. This time, however, she does not think of herself as she did when her husband disrobed her and she felt a kinship with the woman objectified in a Rops etching—one he had shown her during their engagement (12). Instead, she nearly succeeds in seducing him, and she now thinks herself capable of changing his determination of her story: "I saw myself, pale, pliant as a plant that begs to be trampled underfoot, a dozen vulnerable, appealing girls reflected in as many mirrors, and I saw how he almost failed to resist me. If he had come to me in bed, I would have strangled him then" (38). She is no longer naive about her situation, though she may be naive about her courage and ability to kill her husband. Not long after this statement, however, she despairs when Jean-Yves compares her to Eve, a woman often considered the first victim of curiosity. The bride feels as Eve did when God ordered her and Adam out of the Garden of Eden: she must obey (42). Once again, she oscillates between extremes: insecurity and uncertainty on the one hand and growing confidence on the other.

Carter's mirrors in "The Bloody Chamber," then, indicate not only the protagonist's dependence on her sense of innocence but also her lack of a sense of herself as subject. Mirrors also help her to see herself as others see her and provide the beginnings of that sense. At the same time, the mirror scenes establish the protagonist as oscillating between girlhood and womanhood, between a patriarchal view and her own definition of herself.

As she gains and admits to the view others, and particularly her husband, have of her, the bride becomes aware of and begins to use the material in her character provided by her mother. Her mother's story helps give the protagonist courage, and her mother's having provided her with the opportunity to study music ultimately gives her daughter both courage and stability.

The protagonist is well aware of her mother's story. She says she bragged to other music students about her mother's adventures: during her girlhood on a tea plantation in Indochina, the mother "had outfaced a junkful of Chinese pirates, nursed a village through a visitation of the plague, [and] shot a man-eating tiger with her own hand." In addition, she "had gladly, scandalously, defiantly beggared herself for love" (2). It is partly this model that enables the protagonist to look into the story her husband wishes to inscribe upon her; she walks toward the forbidden room "as firmly as I had done in my mother's house," without hesitation or fear (28). When she sees the contents of the torture chamber, for the first time she realizes she has "inherited nerves and a will from the mother who had defied the yellow outlaws of Indochina. My mother's spirit drove me on, into that dreadful place, in a cold ecstasy to know the very worst" (29). The knowledge the protagonist gains in following her mother's spirit helps her to try to tell her own story rather than her husband's story of her, and her first step, as we have seen, is to attempt to seduce her husband—in spite of her fear and disgust—hoping to delay his discovery of her disobedience (38). Later she does lose courage as she and Jean-Yves await her husband's summons to her execution, relapsing into passivity and despair; but then again she feels bold enough, when Jean-Yves hears the hoofbeat of her mother's horse, to delay her descent to the courtyard as much as she dares (42–43). Finally, she takes advantage of the Marquis's momentary confusion at her mother's noisy arrival to leap up from her position at the block and help her lover unbar the castle gate to their rescuer (44). She does not move in a straight line toward changing her passive behavior but rather gains ground, loses it, and then gains it again. Although she appeared to be a blank page to her husband and even to herself, the fiber within her—a result of her mother's story having provided a strong model—helps prevent the Marquis from continuing his tale of punishment of wives' disobedience and assists the bride, finally, in establishing a subject position from which to determine her own story.

Although Carter does not explicitly mention curiosity as a trait the mother has and might have modeled, the mother's active, devil-may-care life indicates she may possess this trait. Certainly her daughter is extremely curious, and her curiosity actually helps her in her process toward womanhood; she is not only curious about the locked room, but she is also curious about marriage—she calls it an "unguessable country" (1)—and about sex. "Had he not hinted to me, in his flesh as in his speech and looks, of the thousand thousand baroque intersections of flesh upon flesh?" (21). In a persuasive essay on masks, spaces, and women's bodies in film, Laura Mulvey cites Carter's version of the "Bluebeard" story as an example of the connection Mulvey sees between spaces such as rooms or boxes and the "mystery and threat" of female sexuality (64, 66), a threat belied by the woman's appearance (58–59). Using the Greek myth of Pandora as a central image and the topography of outside/inside and its relationship to masculine/feminine (54–56, 58), Mulvey argues that one can interpret woman's curiosity about such spaces as actually being curiosity about the nature of being female, including the nature of female sexuality (66). Carter's bride, then, marries partly because she is curious about sex; Mulvey sees her curiosity about the locked room as a symbol for curiosity about female sexuality. The knowledge the protagonist gains from the forbidden room is thus knowledge of herself; it encourages her to see herself as subject and to attempt to fashion her own story. Curiosity per se seems rewarded at the end of the text, too, when the protagonist describes her husband's death as if the action were like that of a mechanical toy: "And then it was as though a curious child pushed his centime into the slot and set all in motion" (45).

In addition to the fiber provided by her mother as model, the protagonist also, as she gradually determines to write her own story, draws upon another gift from her mother: the opportunity to be a musician. The mother "had sold all her jewelry, even her wedding ring, to pay the fees at the Conservatoire" (10). Since the daughter played in a salon—"hired out of charity"—her music is the reason the Marquis notices her (9), and it is at least partly responsible for her idealism about love and marriage; but it is also a solace after she has discovered the Marquis's intentions for her (33), and it ultimately provides her with a career. In addition, her sense of herself as a musician allows her to assert herself in a field in which she is more knowledgeable than her husband: when she finds that her bridal-gift piano is slightly out of tune, her perfect pitch prevents her from practicing (13) because the note she would hear internally as middle C, for example, is not the note that comes from her piano. This musical discrimination, "a blessing," according to the bride, causes her to demand that her husband add a piano-tuner to the staff (13).

In presenting her protagonist as a musician, Carter has the young woman refer to several specific musical texts and engage one in particular. Twice during the course of her story, the bride mentions having seen Wagner's *Tristan and Isolde;* she saw the opera first as a child and second with the Marquis on the evening before her wedding. With its lush, romantic music and story, the opera might well have had a profound effect on an impressionable, musical child and again, later, on a young bride who envisions herself a princess travelling to a fairy castle (3, 9). The castle, like the Irish princess Isolde's, is near the sea, and the bride might have still another reason to compare herself to Isolde: her husband's first wife sang the part the first time the protagonist heard the opera (5). The bride makes a passing reference to King Mark, too, in her description of her husband's enormous dining table (25); in the opera King Mark is King of Cornwall, Tristan's lord, to whom Tristan is bringing Isolde as bride. Tristan and Isolde betray the king as a result of the love potion, drunk on the voyage to Cornwall, that forces them to declare their already-existing love (Negus 19). In spite of essentially admitting she does not love the Marquis (2), the young bride appears to wish for and certainly is curious about the kind of passion released by the love potion of the opera: it is a passion so powerful that one lover cannot live without the other (Krehbiel 265), a passion that goes beyond physical fulfillment to metaphysics (Rose 11). Certainly when she sees the opera the night before her wedding, the music affects the bride-to-be strongly enough to make her feel, during the *Liebestod* at the end of the last act, that she must "truly love" the Marquis (6). She also indicates her desire to *know* her husband (perhaps wanting to love him) as she wonders about the mask his face seems to her (3–4, 15); searches through his office to find out something personal about him (24–27); and thinks, on her way to the forbidden chamber, that she may find a bit of his soul there (28). In addition, she dislikes reminders of his previous wives (4–5), wishing to be his only love. Her girlish romanticism appears, too, in her desire for a cheap novel (a romance?) (14) as she waits "until my husband beds me" (13). Unlike Isolde, who would rather die with Tristan than wed King Mark and be near Tristan without the latter's love (Wagner 54), this young bride comes to see that if she truly desires the kind of romantic, obsessive passion with her husband that the opera portrays, she will continue to play out his script for her (39). Though her youthful, romantic self may think she wants the kind of love portrayed in *Tristan,* the protagonist takes a step toward adulthood when she realizes what this kind of relationship would mean for her. "The revelation that she, like the other women, has chosen death shocks the protagonist into life" (Sheets 652). In contrast, Isolde, victim of the love *potion* administered by her well-intentioned maid Brangäne (Wagner 57–63) as well as of love itself, has no choice.

In the opera, Isolde wishes death for herself and Tristan if he does not require her love. Carter's Marquis, however, desires death not for a beloved, but for a woman whose story he wishes to control. At the end of Carter's text, the bride compares her escape to an imagined scene of the Marquis's "beloved" Tristan's suddenly becoming a completely different character, one with an agenda of life and happiness (44–45).

A further connection to the opera exists in Jean-Yves, who in part resembles Wagner's Tristan. His blindness is a reminder of the opera's "true lovers," who long for the night (and metaphorically, death) to release them from pain and allow them ecstasy (again, more metaphysical than physical) (Negus 22–23; Swales and McFarland 36). Though Jean-Yves's love is apparently not the passionate one about which the young, romantic protagonist was once curious, like Tristan he is loyal, devoted, and a lover who "sees me clearly with his heart" (46).

Additional dialogue between Carter's story and the opera appears in the latter's connection to Schopenhauer's vision of the world: humans are but small individuals trying to find release in a world controlled by the Will,

> either in a return to the primal matter of the Will, or in an escape from the Will's clutches. In Wagner's *Tristan* the lovers seek both: submersion and transcendence. Moreover, for Schopenhauer music expressed the very groundswell of the Will itself. Listening to Wagner's score, one has some idea of what Schopenhauer meant: against the ceaseless current of the orchestral writing the human voice and its medium— language—function as the individuated part of this extraordinary symphonic texture. (Swales and McFarland 36)

This aspect of *Tristan and Isolde* is clearly relevant to a story in which a protagonist is in the process of finding her subjectivity and her voice.

Another musical text that, like *Tristan and Isolde,* provides symbolic clues to the protagonist's views and emotions is Bach's *The Well-Tempered Clavier.* The bride plays this music, "for the sake of the harmonious rationality of its sublime mathematics," after she has discovered the Marquis's intentions for her. She says that perhaps she thought she "could create a pentacle out of music that would keep me from harm" and that would return her, literally and figuratively, to her virgin state (33). Her desire to play the piano may arise from the correspondence between her thoughts about her virgin state and her having devoted herself to her music when in that state, but subconsciously she may also recognize her music as an alternative to her position as object in someone else's script; her music can (and ultimately does) provide her with an income and independence. At first she can play only exercises, but after she has managed these, she sets up a bargain for herself; if she can play Bach's *The Well-Tempered Clavier* through without a mistake, she will be a virgin once again in the morning (33). Her desire to create a pentacle, a symbol used in magic, to protect herself shows once again her youthful romanticism and the influence upon her of *Tristan and Isolde* and its magic. This particular musical choice of *The Well-Tempered Clavier*, however, is significant in that it functions symbolically as an antidote to her romanticism and as part of a negotiation between her romantic self and the woman she is struggling to become. Bach's work is an orderly, rational series of pieces that provides strong contrast to the music of *Tristan;* even in the prelude the opera expresses "an ardent longing, a consuming hunger, . . . a desire that cannot be quenched, yet will not despair" (Krehbiel 253). As she plays Bach, a noise outside the music room causes the bride to think her husband has returned, and she stops playing. Although she has not completed the task she set herself and no one grants her wish for a magical return to her virgin state, her "pentacle" of music has nonetheless helped her in a manner she had not foreseen; she finds within herself the courage to respond to the noise defiantly (33). The nature of her response suggests that she has shed some of her romantic ideas.

Also related to music is one of the Marquis's wedding gifts to his bride, a Flemish painting of Saint Cecilia (11). The bride links herself with Cecilia; looking at the painting, she says, "I saw myself as I could have wished to be" (11). *Could*—if she had not chosen marriage or were more self-confident about her music? Again, the bride appears unsure of herself. Saint Cecilia is the patron saint of music, and the protagonist's wish to be like her shows her seriousness about her music, a seriousness that also appears in her annoyance at finding her piano out of tune (13) and in her three hours of practice, later, after the piano tuner has tuned it (22). Saint Cecilia dedicated herself to a "career" of modeling celibate Christianity; the protagonist considers herself a musician but has not entirely committed herself to a career. Ultimately Saint Cecilia was martyred because of her dedication to being a celibate Christian, and later the protagonist wonders about the nature of the saint's martyrdom (32), which, like the Marquis's plan for his bride, was decapitation (de Voragine 323).

As Carter's protagonist tells her story, then, "material" from her mother— courage and the opportunity to study music—as well as the narrator's focus on mirrors and on particular musical texts show that the protagonist is far from a blank page. She only gradually, however, develops a sufficiently strong subject position from which to attempt to tell her own story. Significantly, the last word in the story she tells is *shame*, an emotion she tries to expiate by making a story-sacrifice to replace the sacrifice the Marquis wished to make of her person. Her feeling of shame appears in her somewhat defensive "I felt I had a right to retain sufficient funds . . ." (46), and she emphasizes the quiet life she, her mother, and Jean-Yves lead; part of her shame lies in her having been seduced by wealth. "Sometimes we can even afford to go to the Opéra, though never to sit in a box, of course" (46). That the events she experienced are recent is clear from her discussion of her inheritance: "we *have given* most of it away" (45; my emphasis) rather than the more distant "we *gave*." Widowed at seventeen, she seems not far from that age, still fashioning her story both verbally and by living with her mother as well as Jean-Yves (46). In significant contrast to the earlier scene at the opera when she is so conscious of people's whispering and looking at her (6), the protagonist's stronger sense of her subjectivity now allows her increased freedom from caring about what other people think; she says (still, however, with a remnant of her naiveté), "We know we are the source of many whisperings and much gossip, but the three of us know the truth of it and mere chatter can never harm us" (46).

This ending to "The Bloody Chamber," in which the protagonist is continuing to determine her story and her subject position, underscores the importance of understanding that story as one of a woman in process. Carter indicates her awareness of this kind of situation in "Notes from the Front Line," in which she comments on herself as in process; she is looking back on her days as a young writer (71). Her protagonist in "The Bloody Chamber" is a young woman still trying to make sense of her role in the events about which she tells; and she oscillates between insecurity and growing certainty, both in the story itself and after she has told it. Thanks to her mother's life story as model and to the opportunity her mother gave her to study music, this woman escapes the tale patriarchy wished to tell of her and instead tells her own story, but she is not finished. Carter's use of mirrors, of the mother's legacy, and of music supports her vision of the protagonist as impossible to classify as girl *or* woman, wife *or* career woman, guilty *or* innocent. At the end, it is clear that the protagonist, though less concerned with others' opinions than before, is still sufficiently concerned about them to be telling her story as a way of expiating shame. She is a woman in process, one still establishing subjectivity.

Note

This essay is dedicated to my mother, Kathleen B. (Kay) Manley, whose love and performance of music inspired my own.

Works Cited

Bacchilega, Cristina. *Postmodern Fairy Tales: Gender and Narrative Strategies.* Philadelphia: U of Pennsylvania P, 1997.

Carter, Angela. *The Bloody Chamber and Other Adult Tales.* New York: Harper & Row, 1979.

———. "Notes from the Front Line." *On Gender and Writing.* Ed. Michelene Wandor. London: Pandora, 1983. 69–77.

de Voragine, Jacobus. *The Golden Legend.* Trans. William Granger Ryan. Vol. 2. Princeton: Princeton UP, 1993.

Dinesen, Isak. "The Blank Page." Gilbert and Gubar 1418–23.

Gilbert, Sandra M., and Susan Gubar, eds. *The Norton Anthology of Literature by Women.* New York: W. W. Norton, 1986.

Gubar, Susan. " 'The Blank Page' and the Issues of Female Creativity." *Writing and Sexual Difference.* Ed. Elizabeth Abel. Chicago: U of Chicago P, 1982. 73–93.

John, Nicholas, series ed. *Tristan and Isolde: Richard Wagner.* English National Opera Guides. Vol. 6. London: John Calder, 1981.

Krehbiel, Henry Edward. *A Book of Operas.* New York: Garden City, 1917.

Mulvey, Laura. "Pandora: Topographies of the Mask and Curiosity." *Sexuality and Space.* Ed. Beatriz Colomina. Princeton Papers on Architecture. New York: Princeton Architectural P, 1992. 52–71.

Negus, Anthony. "A Musical Commentary." John 17–28.

Rose, John Luke. "A Landmark in Musical History." John 9–16.

Sanchez, Victoria. "Beauties and Beasts: Literary Fairy Tale in *The Bloody Chamber.*" American Folklore Society Meeting, Pittsburgh, Pennsylvania. Oct. 1996.

Sheets, Robin Ann. "Pornography, Fairy Tales, and Feminism: Angela Carter's 'The Bloody Chamber.' " *Journal of the History of Sexuality* 1 (1991): 633–57.

Swales, Martin, and Timothy McFarland. "An Introduction to the German Text." John 36–37.

Wagner, Richard. "Tristan and Isolde." Trans. Andrew Porter. John 45–92.

CHERYL RENFROE

Initiation and Disobedience: Liminal Experience in Angela Carter's "The Bloody Chamber"

Angela Carter's "The Bloody Chamber," when read as a young woman's initiatory quest for knowledge rather than as the story of an overly curious girl who makes a disastrous marriage, provides its readership with a woman-centered perspective that both reflects and allows for social change through individual liminal experience. In its form, plot, characterizations, and mythic parallels, Carter's rewriting of "Bluebeard," more than most other versions, is permeated with images of the liminal. Its marked intertextuality, a characteristic that in itself implies a transitional quality, is not shared by Perrault's "Bluebeard," the well-known version upon which "The Bloody Chamber" is based. Nor does Perrault's plotting of the tale portray the heroine's ordeal at the hands of her husband as specifically informing her subsequent life values and choices. The effect of Carter's postmodern telling, with its plot sequence analogous to a rite of passage, unconventional characterization, and strong associations with the biblical story of the temptation of Eve, is to induce a complex, layered experience of reader-initiation via sympathetic identification with its heroine. The reader may find herself experiencing the unfolding of knowledge along with the girl in the story and then reframing the long-standing condemnation of Eve. Consequently, the way is opened for individual revision of traditional attitudes toward women rooted in Judeo/Christian creation mythology and in the story of

Marvels & Tales: Journal of Fairy-Tale Studies, Vol. 12, No. 1 (1998), pp. 82–94. Copyright © 1998 by Wayne State University Press, Detroit, MI 48201.

the fall. By positing a strong female subjectivity and offering usually unavailable possibilities for positive reader-identification with Eve within the standard (Perrault's) misogynistic tale frame, Carter's literary revision of "Bluebeard" undercuts the Christian doctrine of original sin. Her heroine's agonizing ordeal, so similar to Eve's, is portrayed as a necessary and bold initiation into self- and worldly knowledge rather than as an act of foolish disobedience. Because of Carter's subversion of Perrault's dominant casting of the tale, complacent thought on marriage and ingrained attitudes about the character of women based on the story of the fall and subsequent New Testament teachings are likely to be deeply disturbed. Hence, a visit to "The Bloody Chamber" can become, for the reader, an opportunity to pluck her own forbidden fruit.

Expanding on Arnold van Gennep's theories, Victor Turner's *The Ritual Process* (1969) specifically identifies a kind of liminal experience undergone by audience/participants when engaged in the brief liminality provided by carnival, drama, and film.[1] Turner describes these aesthetic forms as representing "the reflexivity of the social process, wherein society becomes at once the subject and the direct object" (vii). It follows then that story in general and, as will be shown, the literary *Märchen* in particular hold the capacity to provide liminal spaces for scrutinizing social process through the reader's exposure to new information contained within the narrative. Thus, the act of reading a story can become a small initiation, a movement away from old patterns of thinking into new and, ideally, better ones.

As a literary elaboration on an oral tale, "The Bloody Chamber" retains the initiatory plot basic to most fairy tales. Typically, a fairy tale revolves around the protagonist's journey outward beyond the limen, or threshold, of her hearth and home, outside geographical, emotional, and cognitive boundaries. Besides this basic initiatory premise, the literary *Märchen,* or the written version of a fairy tale, as Danielle Roemer has noted, encompasses a further liminal dimension. Roemer sees the particular intertextuality inherent in the narrative form of the literary *Märchen* as necessarily liminal. Drawing as it does on the well-known traditional versions of oral tales while simultaneously voicing the contemporary and personal mores of its author, the literary *Märchen* juxtaposes both sets of values in the mind of the reader, enabling her to traverse the ideological territory between the two. This bridging of the traditional and the visionary, or radical, offers the opportunity for sharp comparisons and the possibility of transitions to new modes of thinking.

Carter's version of "Bluebeard," like all literary *Märchen* by definition intertextual, is a transformation of Perrault's literary version of "Bluebeard," which in turn is based on collected oral versions with other referents, less obvious but still influential, mixed in. One of Carter's expressed purposes in writing is to "precipitate changes in the way people feel about themselves," especially through reassessment of "the social fictions that regulate [their] lives." Her often quoted analogy of the literary fairy tale to "new wine in old bottles" ("Notes" 76, 70, 69), in view of the textual indeterminacy of her work, is particularly well suited to any discussion of the liminal experience of "The Bloody Chamber."[2] Adding to its complexity, Carter's tale is told by its heroine in retrospect so that the narrator, as the post-liminal voice of the girl, and the reader, through familiarity with the traditional tale, are all along privy to several layers of knowledge about the Marquis's motivations, the contents of the chamber, and the outcome for the protagonist.

In the Perrault version of "Bluebeard," a young girl weds a rich and mysterious older man, who takes her away to his palatial estate. Directly after they arrive, the husband contrives to leave for a period of time, bestowing on the girl the keys to all the rooms of the castle and instructing her to enter and explore all but one of them. Constantly entertaining friends and finally running out of diversions, the girl is consumed by curiosity, succumbs to temptation, and enters the forbidden chamber. Inside she discovers the remains of her husband's many former wives, each with her throat cut, and is abruptly faced with the horrifying truth about her own situation. In the telling, it is made clear that she is a frivolous girl who, in spite of strict and distinct instructions, chooses to defy the man who is her lord and master. Though she is badly frightened, there is no indication that Perrault's heroine gains perspective or wisdom through her experience. Perrault's version, like most other ones, does not portray a particularly strong liminal event. Bruno Bettelheim emphasizes that in this particular tale type, "most of all, no development toward higher humanity is projected. At the end, the protagonists, both Bluebeard and his wife, are exactly the same persons they were before. Earth-shaking events have taken place in the story and nobody is the better for them . . ." (302–03). Carter's story, however, belies Bettelheim's general analysis of the tale type. Her version of "Bluebeard" relates an individual woman's initiation experience that changes her irrevocably.

Unlike Perrault's heroine, Carter's protagonist is painfully isolated and there is no mistaking her motivation to explore the chamber as frivolous; rather, she is driven to face both internal and external demons by entering the forbidden room. Her pre-liminal situation has centered around her mother and her doting childhood nurse, their state of poverty, and her potential career as a pianist. After a richly elaborate but too hasty courtship and marriage, she embarks on a train journey with her new husband, leaving behind her past values, her musical ambitions, and the security her capable, fiercely independent mother provides. Isolated in a castle on a strand, she expects that her sexual initiation will bring her from childhood to womanhood, from innocence to full sexuality, from unknowing to knowing. The girl is both apprehensive and anticipatory about the ordeal she must pass through—the loss of her virginity to an older, very experienced man—believing that this sexual rite will establish her as a respectable married woman of high-ranking position. Though she is bothered by her response to the Marquis's corrupt sexuality and the lure of his wealth, she is completely unaware that her true initiation is not first intercourse, but the ordeal of the bloody chamber. The girl believes she is moving toward sexual knowledge, wealth, power, and new status, but in the liminal phase, all alone in the castle, she has soul-searching experiences which cause her to redefine in unexpected ways who she is and what she wants. The girl's fear, which before the ordeal of the chamber is only intuitive, is inarticulately communicated in a phone call to her mother, prompting her eventual rescue. All along the girl has quelled guilty uneasiness in order to flirt with the promise of her husband's obscene wealth and sexual debauchery. Indeed, her mother realizes before the girl does just how cruel and deadly the fulfillment of that promise might be. She resolves to check on her daughter, and so the rescue is set in motion before the girl has grappled with the truth the key unlocks. Yet it is not the girl's rescue, but her daring and disobedient exploration of the forbidden chamber that actually changes her, develops her, and allows her to see her husband, and more importantly herself, from a more knowledgeable perspective. Her eyes are opened to her own mistakes as well as to the reality of her desperate situation, and though the knowledge she gains by defying her husband and entering the chamber does not directly save her, it is crucial to the fulfilling future life she eventually chooses for herself. Through her participation in this particular rite of initiation, she faces her husband's true nature and is forced to acknowledge what her intuition and her guilty self-doubt have told her all along. The gripping sense of shame she must finally own is not born of her disobedience to her husband, but of her own susceptibility to the corruption he represents. Later, after the acute danger is past, the girl returns home ready to embrace the marriage values of her mother, or perhaps even to carry her mother's defiant refusal to marry for money a step further by not marrying at all. Like her mother, she is now content to live modestly employing her own talents, choosing integrity over wealth and status, and enjoying the love of a man who "sees" and loves her for who she is.

Though the evolving characterization of the girl is a study in the effect of initiatory experience, Carter puts a spin on the usual pattern of separation, transition, and return by marking the girl's mother, as a role model for her daughter, as one who has clearly operated outside the normal status quo of community expectations. Earlier in her life, the mother married for love, not money, and has, as an adult, shown more than the socially accepted level of daring and self-reliance. Presumably, the mother's own past initiatory experiences have caused her to reject certain of society's long-standing edicts for women. The girl's changing attitude toward wealth, sexuality, and marriage then, while signaling progress in her own personal value system and a return to many of her mother's ideals is, at the same time, a reversal of the expectations held for her by society at large. The marriage of wealth and power, standard goal for fairy-tale heroines, is rejected. She has been allowed, through her initiation in the chamber, to understand and survive the deadly peril that kind of marriage holds for her. By positioning the girl and her mother in this way, yet simultaneously moving them through a plot sequence parallel to that of Perrault's version, Carter exposes her reading audience to a radical view on fairy-tale marriage. By portraying the husband as a fabulously wealthy nobleman who lives in a castle but also showing that in the privacy of his home he wields total, brutal power over his wife, Carter allows the reader to observe and so participate vicariously in the initiation of the girl while successfully subverting the well-established imperative for women to marry "well"—or indeed to marry at all. Perrault's version has the young widow marry "a worthy gentleman" shortly after her rescue, using Bluebeard's fortune as dowry; but through the liminal experience provided the reader by Carter's version, marriage to a prince, or possibly the institution of marriage itself, has become suspect, no longer the foolproof path to "happily ever after." The humble, blind piano tuner, a person whose abilities and interests dovetail with the girl's, and who requires no fortune to engage his loyalty, but who can promise little or nothing in the way of financial contribution or enhanced social status, is shown to be incomparably preferable to the evil Marquis. Although at the end of the story she and her mother set up housekeeping with him, it is not clear that the girl ever marries the piano tuner. The girl makes a post-liminal determination—to choose her life partner on the basis of love and to fend for herself if need be—that is similar to, and perhaps even more radical than, her mother's defiant choice a generation earlier.

Aside from its plot-driven liminality, "The Bloody Chamber," in its simultaneous presentation of traditional and emergent ideologies, invites readers to critique long-held assumptions about the character of women assigned by conventional interpretations of the biblical Eve, thus encouraging an awareness that Eve's disobedience was perhaps not motivated by lust, greed, or frivolous curiosity, and that it did not, in fact, bring disaster upon the world. Instead, Eve's action in the garden can be interpreted as an ordeal of initiation resulting in the very first instance of the exercise of free will intended to fulfill human beings and set them apart from beasts and plants. Anthropologist Bruce Lincoln, in a 1981 study on women's initiation rituals, *Emerging from the Chrysalis,* argues that identification with a mythic heroine or goddess is an essential component for the success of women's initiations. According to Lincoln, temporarily assuming the personality of the mythic or archetypal heroine exposes the initiand to an elevated state of being that further prepares her for her higher, post-liminal role.[3] Clearly, the mythic heroine with whom Carter's protagonist identifies and is identified, is Eve. And it is in her *positive* identification with Eve that the process of a liminal reframing of the character of women can be charted. Furthermore, the positive reframing that occurs for the character in a sympathetic identification with Eve can occur for the reader as well. And it is this individual reader-initiation that holds propensity for social change in the tangible world, beyond the liminality experienced by the characters in Carter's story.

Marina Warner, Maria Tatar, and Lisa Jacobson are among several contemporary critics who have noted and commented on the link between Eve and the forbidden tree, and the heroine of "Bluebeard" and the forbidden chamber. Warner illustrates certain "Bluebeard" passages in her book, *From the Beast to the Blonde,* with an 1874 engraving of Bluebeard's wife that "shows the heroine against a wall painting of the Temptation in the Garden of Eden, making a direct analogy with Eve, and thus disclosing the inner structure of the fable: Bluebeard acts like God the Father, prohibiting knowledge—the forbidden chamber is the tree of the knowledge of good and evil—and Fatima [the 'Bluebeard' heroine] is Eve, the woman who disobeys and, through curiosity, endangers her life" (244). Significantly, Tatar sees the Perrault version, containing early illustrations clearly alluding to Eve and the fall, as having influenced most extant commentary found on "Bluebeard." She cites the prevalence of the Eve/"Bluebeard" association and the frequency with which the heroine's act of exploring the chamber is considered to be the cause of all the trouble in spite of the husband's heinous crimes: "Nearly every nineteenth-century printed version of 'Bluebeard' singles out the heroine's curiosity as an especially undesirable trait" (158). Jacobson also points out important similarities between Perrault's Bluebeard heroine and Eve and makes the relevant observation that "in Perrault's version of the tale, the only way in which she may be absolved from these transgressions is by performing, like Eve, the very rituals expected of a sinner—forgiveness and prayer" (85). Perrault's attached moral, with its innuendo of dire sin for the sake of illicit knowledge, represents what each of these critics has recognized as the typical take on the story's meaning: "Ladies, you should never pry,— / You'll repent it by and by! / 'Tis the silliest of sins; / Trouble in a trice begins. / There are, surely—more's the woe— / Lots of things you need not know . . ." (43). Perrault's encapsulation clearly places the sin of transgression on the woman, evidencing a blatant blame-the-victim mentality (Tatar 159); it also downplays the importance of knowledge for women—even knowledge crucial to survival! Not unexpectedly, the common view of Eve is consistent with the condemnation accorded Bluebeard's wife.

In the New Testament, Paul's often-quoted instructions to the early church, based upon the premise of Eve's disobedience, manifest the misogynistic effects of the dominant view of the story of the fall. The writer of 1 Timothy, who might or not have been Paul, in a moralizing manner similar to Perrault's, delivers the standard judgment on Eve: "I give no permission for a woman to teach or to have authority over a man. A woman ought to be quiet, because Adam was formed first and Eve afterwards, and it was not Adam who was led astray but the woman who was led astray and fell into sin" (1 Tim. 2.11–14). Though these famous assumptions have been challenged by feminist theologians such as Phyllis Trible (see *God and the Rhetoric of Sexuality,* chapter 4) and critics such as Mieke Bal in her astute application of the principles of narratology to early "Genesis" (*Lethal Love,* chapter 5), the story of Eve is still widely held to be the story of the end of paradise, and not the beginning of human ability and advancement through the trial and error of free will.[4] But, despite "Paul's" dictates in 1 Timothy, Eve has not been universally condemned by Christian interpreters. Elaine Pagels in her 1988 discussion of the fall, *Adam, Eve, and the Serpent,* presents in detail the views of gnostic Christians, members of an early sect branded heretical by orthodox apologists, that did not hold with the concept of original sin through the disobedience of Eve. Pagels describes the loose, symbolic interpretations of some of the more radical gnostics: "Many gnostics read the story of Adam and Eve . . . as an account of what takes place within a person who is engaged in the process of spiritual self-discovery" (66). She goes on to outline the gnostic approach to the first woman's disobedient act: "[I]nstead of blaming the human desire for knowledge as the root of all sin, they did the opposite and sought redemption through gnosis. And whereas the orthodox often blamed Eve for the fall and pointed to women's submission as appropriate punishment, gnostics often depicted Eve—or the feminine spiritual power she represented—as the source of spiritual awakening" (68). Nevertheless alternate, positive interpretations have remained suppressed while, according to Mieke Bal, "there has been in Christian, Western culture a continuous line toward . . . 'the dominant reading': a monolithically misogynist view of those biblical stories wherein female characters play a role . . ." (2). Bal makes a startling and convincing case for feminist content in those few but important verses in Genesis by employing a detailed narratological approach to the story of the fall that specifically includes the concept of initiation.[5] She asserts that what is at stake for Eve in the garden "is knowledge, including sexual knowledge with its consequence for life; in 3:3 the idea of death as the other side of life is mentioned; in 3:11 sheer disobedience or, in another sense, emancipation from blind command provides the passage from one to the other: once sexuality is accepted, humanity can do without impossible immortality" (122). Bal's connection of disobedience and initiation provides a way to see Eve's action as a fulfillment of the reason and independence granted at the moment of her creation. Because Christian orthodoxy has suppressed sympathetic interpretations of Eve's disobedient act, and has instead built case after case against all women on the basis of it, opportunities for women to identify proudly with their mythic ancestral past have been diminished. The loss of such opportunities may make it more difficult for women to successfully transact liminal situations in their lives.

In "The Bloody Chamber," Carter strongly acknowledges the mythic parallels between "Bluebeard" and Genesis, but, facilitated by the intertextual nature of the *Märchen* form, casts her own feminist perspective on the heroine's actions. The girl's conversation with the piano tuner reveals her connection with Eve, but also highlights her refusal to accept blame for wrong-doing in entering the forbidden chamber. Both the girl and the piano tuner acknowledge that the visit to the chamber has been deliberately set up by the Marquis, an all-powerful being with a desire to punish. The girl and the piano tuner give voice to their understanding of her husband's similarity to the God of Genesis:

> "Who can say what I deserve or no? . . . I've done nothing; but that may be sufficient reason for condemning me."
> "You disobeyed him," he said. "That is sufficient reason for him to punish you."
> "I only did what he knew I would."
> "Like Eve," he said. (37–38)

In this identification with Eve and in the subtle acknowledgment that the patriarchal God, not woman, is acting as the malignant force,[6] Carter's attempt at social change through the liminality of the literary fairy tale is most potently at work. Her subversion of Perrault's "Bluebeard," like Bal's narratological vindication of Eve, offers an alternative to established paradigms on women's character. Both Perrault's and Carter's stories, like most versions of "Bluebeard," can and have been seen from two opposing perspectives, each presenting a judgment on an archetypal representation of women.[7] Cristina Bacchilega has noted and called specific attention to this "doubling" aspect of the Bluebeard story, explaining it in terms of central motifs and dual subjectivity. In her 1997 book, *Postmodern Fairy Tales,* Bacchilega presents options for reading the tale based upon which motif is considered central. "If the 'Forbidden Chamber' rather than the 'Bloody Key' is treated as the tale's central motif, then 'Bluebeard' is no longer primarily about the consequences of failing a test—will the heroine be able to control her curiosity?—but about a process of initiation which *requires* entering the forbidden chamber" (107). The two conceivable central motifs (the key versus the chamber, or, disobedience versus initiation) evoke an awareness of what Bacchilega calls "double subjectivity," that is, the possibility of reading "Bluebeard" from the point of view of either the husband or the young wife. Carter tells her version of the tale from the young girl's point of view using the girl's own narrative voice, placing the initiatory emphasis on the girl's metamorphosis through daringly gained knowledge. Yet, there is still a definite *dual* motivation and consciousness surrounding the act of disobedience since both the husband and the girl herself are independent actors in the initiation proceedings. In "The Bloody Chamber," since the heroine's exploration of the chamber is overtly desired by both the husband and the girl for *different* reasons and with the hope of *different* outcomes, the tale becomes at once a depiction of the oppressive sexual initiation of a young girl at the hands of a powerful older man as well as a tale of self-initiation and survival undertaken willingly by a member of a community of women.

The husband purposefully plans the girl's exposure to graphic pornography, to painful and sadistic sexual intercourse, and finally to the chamber of horrors, with the specific goal of terrorizing and corrupting her for his own pleasure. He wants her to experience the chamber, but his ultimate goal for her is to suffer a punishment he will relish inflicting. He does not intend her new knowledge to free her physically or intellectually. Since he obviously sees her as incapable of obedience or self-control, he must consider her failure to avoid his trap inevitable. He believes that should she manage to obey him the first time, he has only to heighten the atmosphere of boredom within the castle walls and bait her once more for her natural "weakness" to win out. Once he has initiated her in the chamber, her terror will make his predatory pleasure complete.

In contrast, within the community of women, the mother's decision to allow the girl to marry the Marquis against her intuitive sensibilities implies her awareness of the girl's need and readiness to participate in the liminal experience of marriage. Though the mother has herself refused to marry for wealth, she recognizes her daughter's right to choose her own path. The girl's decision to explore the world and her options away from home, and to experience sexuality with the partner of her choice, are established early on as her own. Both mother and daughter override personal hesitations in response to the girl's need to attain adult status through exposure to the adult knowledge the union will bring, though neither woman guesses the nature of the ordeal in store. In this sense, the girl's exploration of the bloody chamber, occurring after the loss of her virginity, becomes a determined move toward facing the frightening peril she senses in order to overcome it; and once she does, the full realization of her husband's purposes rises to her consciousness, effectively changing her perspective on life and marriage.

Lincoln's study confirms the possibility of two different agents in the performance of women's initiations, each with a different purpose in mind. He poses the important question of who performs the rites upon the female initiand, and with what intention:

> Who is it that initiates young women when they come of age? . . . For
> if men initiate women, then female initiation must be seen as an act
> imposed on women from outside, an indoctrination, a subjugation, an
> assault. If it is men who are the effective agents, then initiands must
> be understood as the victims of their initiators, passive objects who
> are remade according to the tastes and desires of people quite dif-
> ferent from themselves. Under such circumstances initiation becomes
> a rite of oppression. . . . Conversely, if women initiate women, . . .
> [i]t becomes a rite of solidarity. . . . Rather than an act of oppression,
> initiation becomes an act of unity, of resistance, of commiseration. (92)

If Lincoln's distinction between male and female initiators is applied to women's
rites of passage in nontribal cultures, it may be seen that Perrault's interpretation
of "Bluebeard" and those of many of his successors have depicted an oppressive
initiatory testing performed "on" women by men—in effect, an assault meant to
subjugate. Likewise, statements like the one in 1 Timothy show that dominant
readings of Eve's story have also had the effect of an assault on the character
of women with the directly stated purpose of silencing and subjugating them.
But with renewed insistence on Eve's disobedience as the beginning of a liminal
journey into the uncharted territory of free will, perhaps a successful rite of
passage can finally be completed for women in our culture. As the indelible
mark of the bloody key is pressed upon the young girl's forehead in Carter's tale,
shame has been pressed upon women by the dominant interpretations given
a few verses in Genesis. By entering, through "The Bloody Chamber," into an
ideological re-exploration of the old texts and of the old interpretations that have
confined us, we enter into a liminal experience that offers the erasure of shame.

Western culture has often seen men's disobedience as a virtue. In contesting
civil injustice or in resisting tyranny, the rebel's disobedient methods are called
revolutionary and courageous; but woman's disobedience, forever colored by
traditional interpretations of the first biblical instance of it, is seldom admired.
Through the medium of Carter's literary *Märchen,* Eve's disobedient act, a young
wife's flouting of her husband's authority, a woman writer's usurpation of a
misogynous tale, a feminist's reinterpretation of Genesis, all, are vindicated. The
girl, by way of her mother's rescue, has broken free from the castle prison and,
through her own daring exploration of the forbidden unknown, has attained a
future life of independence and self-respect. Likewise, Eve's disobedience and
her willful pursuit of forbidden knowledge have promoted the human race to
a higher plane of freedom and enhanced human existence. The reader, in her
encounter with "The Bloody Chamber," has possibly been initiated into new
ways of seeing her own mythic past. Like one of van Gennep's initiands, she
has been taken to a far-off intellectual island and exposed to Carter's unique

intertextual blend of ideas and ideology, with the hope of enlightening results. Through the rite of passage that can occur by reading "The Bloody Chamber," she has been granted license to reinterpret for herself the most authoritative and enduring story ever told about her: that of Eve and the fall of humankind.

Notes

1. The rite of initiation, as outlined in Arnold van Gennep's authoritative anthropological study, *The Rites of Passage* (1909), consists of three distinct phases. First, the initiand is separated from quotidian tribal life by removal to a place of seclusion; next, he undergoes an ordeal that exposes him to new or sacred information; and finally, he returns to society with changed perspective and enhanced status. The liminal phase, according to van Gennep, is the indeterminate middle phase during which the initiand is subjected, usually alone, to a trial by ordeal. This liminal space is the corridor through which one must pass to leave one social stage behind and gain entry into another.

2. The scope of Carter's intertextual range in this particular story has been commented on effectively by Elaine Jordan and is also aptly exemplified in Cristina Bacchilega's article "Sex Slaves and Saints? Resisting Masochism in Angela Carter's 'The Bloody Chamber.'" Bacchilega notes that, besides significant allusions to the martyred Saint Cecilia, Carter's story is nuanced by an artistic field extending "from 'Genesis' to Colette's novels, from Baudelaire to the gothic, from opera to Redon's charcoal drawings" (77–78). The inherently intertextual narrative form, purposefully amplified by Carter, encourages the reader to make constant mental comparisons between traditionally held social values and the new ones the girl is being propelled toward, and then to draw personal conclusions from the experience.

3. In light of research on tribal women's initiation rites and on misogynist interpretations of biblical stories, the lack of admirable mythic heroines must have had an adverse effect on the spiritual and social progress of women. Lincoln lists four specific types of action typically present during the liminal phase in women's tribal initiation rituals, including body mutation (tattooing, scarification, etc.), journeying or seclusion, involvement in a play of opposites, and most significant, identification with a mythic heroine or goddess. Carter's heroine neatly fulfills all of Lincoln's criteria. She undergoes body mutation both in the loss of her virginity and in the permanent red mark of the bloody key left on her forehead—a mark of her changed outlook. The train journey away from home and her seclusion in the sea-bound castle place her in a different space far from the expectations of home and outside the protective laws of society. The play of opposites is continually present in differences between the girl and her husband: age/youth; corruption/innocence; wealth/poverty; power/helplessness; male/female. The mythic woman she identifies herself with is, of course, Eve.

4. Trible asserts that the traditional interpretation of the narrative in Genesis "proclaims male superiority and female inferiority as the will of God. It portrays woman as 'temptress' and troublemaker who is dependent upon and dominated by her husband. Over the centuries, this misogynous reading has acquired a status of canonicity so that those who deplore and those who applaud the story both agree upon its meaning" (73). She lists eleven specific ideas supposedly drawn from the text as support for misogyny that she subsequently argues violate the rhetoric of

the story. Her premise is that a "literary study of Genesis 2–3 may offer insights that traditional perspectives dream not of" (74).

5. Mieke Bal builds on Trible's narratological approach. Bal calls the story of Eve's disobedience "the one that has been the most generally abused, presented as evidence that it was the woman who began it all, that hers is all the guilt; in short, the story is widely adduced as a justification for misogyny" (104). She acknowledges that " 'Paul's' view of women, as it is expressed in a well-known passage (1 Tim. 2.11–14), is not basically different from, say, common Christian morality" (104). By applying a narratological reading strategy to the Genesis material, she produces a possible reading that undercuts the paradigmatic one "in order to show the functioning of the retrospective fallacy as a major factor in the production of the sexist myth of 'Eve,' the derivation of which from this text is far from inevitable" (109).

6. In fact, if Eve's disobedience is interpreted as humanity's initiation into free will, then an all-powerful God might well be considered the benevolent overseer and main agent of the successful proceedings.

7. As with Eve, positive, sympathetic portrayals of Bluebeard's wife do exist. Many versions of the tale, in fact, applaud the girl's wiliness and courage. For example the great number of English folk ballads which tell a similar story generally portray the heroine as an innocent victim who, through her own intelligence and strength, overcomes the wicked husband without the aid of a male rescuer. The English ballad equivalent to "Bluebeard" is "Lady Isabel and the Elf Knight," which has perhaps, according to Francis Child, attained the widest circulation of any of the ballad types. The earliest versions have a lady, a king's daughter, lured into the wood by a knight from the south, the north, or some other foreign realm, who plays an alluring (elfin) horn, or entreats her to follow him in some other irresistible way. When she arrives at the isolated place, she sees that he has slain seven king's (or miller's) daughters and is informed that she shall be the eighth. She stalls, persuades him to lay his head in her lap, and then stabs him with his own dagger. Or, the girl arrives at a well, lake or place by the sea where the knight has drowned some number of king's daughters, and she will be next. She either asks him for a kiss and while he obliges her she pitches him in and drowns him, or, as he has insisted she undress, she asks him to turn his head and then pushes him in. In these early ballad versions the girl rescues herself by killing the knight.

Works Cited

Bacchilega, Cristina. *Postmodern Fairy Tales: Gender and Narrative Strategies*. Philadelphia: U of Pennsylvania P, 1997.

———. "Sex Slaves and Saints? Resisting Masochism in Angela Carter's 'The Bloody Chamber.'" *Across the Oceans*. Ed. Irmengard Rauch and Cornelia Moore. Honolulu: U of Hawaii P, 1995. 77–86.

Bal, Mieke. *Lethal Love*. Indianapolis: Indiana UP, 1987.

Bettelheim, Bruno. *The Uses of Enchantment: The Meaning and Importance of Fairy Tales*. 1976. New York: Vintage, 1989.

Carter, Angela. *The Bloody Chamber*. New York: Penguin, 1979.

———. "Notes From the Front Line." *On Gender and Writing*. Ed. Michelene Wandor. London: Pandora, 1983. 69–77.

Gennep, Arnold van. *The Rites of Passage*. Trans. Monika B. Vizedom and Gabrielle L. Cafee. Chicago: U of Chicago P, 1960.

Jacobson, Lisa. "Tales of Violence and Desire: Angela Carter's 'The Bloody Chamber.'" *Antithesis* 6.2 (1993): 81–90.

Lincoln, Bruce. *Emerging From the Chrysalis: Studies in Rituals of Women's Initiation*. Cambridge: Harvard UP, 1981.

The New Jerusalem Bible. Rev. ed. New York: Doubleday, 1985.

Pagels, Elaine. *Adam, Eve, and the Serpent*. New York: Vintage, 1988.

Perrault, Charles. *Perrault's Fairy Tales*. Trans. A. E. Johnson. New York: Dover, 1969.

Roemer, Danielle. "Angela Carter's 'The Bloody Chamber': Liminality and Reflexivity." Unpublished paper. American Folklore Society Meeting, Jacksonville, Florida. Oct. 1992.

Tatar, Maria. *The Hard Facts of the Grimms' Fairy Tales*. Princeton: Princeton UP, 1987.

Trible, Phyllis. *God and the Rhetoric of Sexuality*. Philadelphia: Fortress, 1978.

Turner, Victor. *The Ritual Process*. Ithaca: Cornell UP, 1969.

Warner, Marina. *From the Beast to the Blonde: On Fairy Tales and Their Tellers*. London: Chatto & Windus, 1994.

DANIELLE M. ROEMER

The Contextualization of the Marquis in Angela Carter's "The Bloody Chamber"

Angela Carter is not only an author but also a tale teller: someone who understands well the dynamics of story as a metonymic phenomenon.[1] To be sure, stories can be considered narrational units; however, they are also sites of opening, thresholds on to other tales which themselves provide entry into others. Carter as a tale teller recognizes this—that indeed no story is ever the whole story. My essay borrows this perspective in exploring the associative capacity of allusion in Carter's tale "The Bloody Chamber," her contribution to the oral/literary repertoire of "Bluebeard" stories. Acknowledging the tendency of previous tellers to depict the "Bluebeard" antagonist as an Oriental despot, I consider Carter's Marquis within an alluded-to gallery of "Oriental" tyrants—the fourteenth-century warlord Timur/Marlowe's Tamburlaine, the sixteenth-century Persian Shah Abbās, and the early twentieth-century Parisian couturier Paul Poiret. My purpose is to open up the character of the Marquis, to investigate some of his motivations, strategies, and goals, by considering his place within a pantheon of tyrants.

Allusion

Reader-activated allusion operates within the context of an appreciation of curiosity. A sensed uncomfortableness with the status quo mixed with a desire

Marvels & Tales: Journal of Fairy-Tale Studies, Vol. 12, No. 1 (1998), pp. 95–115. Copyright © 1998 by Wayne State University Press, Detroit, MI 48201.

for associations that extend beyond the given, curiosity motivates the allusive enterprise. Carter has linked associativeness with the exploration of possibility which, in turn, can constitute a move toward freedom: "What do exist are images or objects that are enigmatic, marvelous, erotic—or juxtapositions of objects, or people, or ideas that arbitrarily extend our notion of the connections it is possible to make. In this way, the beautiful is put at the service of liberty" ("Alchemy" 73). The act of intervening in the authoritatively sanctioned with the intent of reframing it within an emotionally and politically responsible iconoclasm is a crucial dynamic of Carter's project of demythologizing—that is, her self-conscious lobbying against cultural discourses that function "to make people unfree" ("Notes" 71). Her commitment to exploring possibility is illustrated in various ways within her storytelling economy: those I am interested in here involve allusive relations.

Lorna Sage has explained Carter's notion of a "narrative Utopia" as a "dialogue with the reader" (*Angela* 50). One opportunity for this dialogue is in the arena of intertextuality. By providing stories that can be read as echoing one another, such as her "Beauty and the Beast" tales in *The Bloody Chamber* collection, Carter prompts readers to view a particular type of situation from a variety of perspectives (Atwood; Crunelle-Vanrigh). By encouraging them to construct perceptually such story sets and thereby to place the constituent tales in conversation with one another, Carter sets into motion the literary version of an important dynamic of oral narration: the spinning of tales from other tales (Benson). Allusion offers another opportunity for dialogue that can operate in ways similar to those of intertextuality.

Rather than serving as seemingly simple and, therefore, presumably dismissable ornament, Carterian allusions can function as invitations to alterity. Allowing her own prose to stand as the given, Carter's use of reference invites the reader to traverse thresholds of interpretive experience from the manifest into the supplement and back again, thus intervening in the romantic notion of author and supplied text as repositories of truth. Indeed, exploring the kinetics of Carterian allusions typically involves opening doors onto alternative story rooms, an appropriate activity for engaging "The Bloody Chamber," not only as the initial story of the published collection but also as a tale that serves as a version of "Bluebeard."

In exploring some of Carter's allusions in what might be called an other-directed way, I foreground information that might otherwise appear as mere background within her story. My principal foci, frankly, derive from story references to a few carpets and a white muslin dress. Not obviously crucial fare, I admit. However, my investigating of the socio-political-historical contexts of those carpets and that dress has led me to three "Oriental" tyrants, two of whom are not even mentioned in the story and all three of whom are not Bluebeard figures per se. However, by analogically mirroring the Marquis, each of these figures provides an interpretive frame of reference for him. Also, each plus the Marquis can be read as representative of patriarchal agendas traditionally practiced in both the East and the West but which, in their more extreme form, are attributed by the West to the stereotypical Oriental despot. The dialogue that can be established among Timur/Tamburlaine, Shah Abbās, Paul Poiret, and the Marquis suggests more similitude than substantial difference in Eastern and Western tyrants of patriarchy.

The Orient

If we apply the familiar epithet of "the cradle of civilization" to the general region of the Middle East, we are reminded that this area—known for centuries in Europe as the Orient—was an historical source point for some of Western civilization's basic systems of order (e.g., the Phoenician alphabet, the practice of coining money).[2] Conversely, the Orient has also served as a context of origin for some of Europe's more potent images of disorder: those of both wonder and terror. Described by Edward Said as "one of the deepest and most recurring images of the Other" (1) and by Lisa Lowe as a "powerfully consuming unknown, a forbidden erotic figure, a grotesquely uncivilized world of violence, and a site of incomprehensible difference" (78n3), the idea of the Orient has long proved useful in Europe's definition of itself.

For the West, daydreams of Eastern plentitude have operated in tension with images of Oriental tyrants who stood as threshold guardians of those riches. The daydreams date back at least to the ancient world's perception of the Lydian king Croesus (c. 560–546 BCE) whose territorial acquisitions reputedly brought him so much booty that his wealth became proverbial. If Croesus was one of the first Oriental emperors of luxury to capture the Western imagination, then the far eastern potentates whom Marco Polo described a millennium and a half later intensified even further Europe's desire to delight in tales of the East and eventually to co-opt its splendor literally. As a result, for example, Polo's travel journal—originally circulated as *Description of the World* (1298)—so impressed explorer Christopher Columbus that he carried a copy of it, marked copiously with marginalia, on his first voyage to discover a Western sea route to India (Hart 146). On the other hand, of course, Oriental rulers did not volunteer their wealth for European control and, moreover, could hold territorial ambitions of their own. From the late Middle Ages on, Eastern opposition to European perceptions of security came, in turn, from the Muslim "dogs" who defended the Holy Land between the eleventh and thirteenth centuries, the Mongul "hordes" that swept across Asia and into Central Europe in the thirteenth century, and, from the sixteenth into the eighteenth centuries, the Empire of the Ottoman Turks, which chose strategically to extend its borders westward rather than to threaten its brother Muslim countries to the east. In the eighteenth and nineteenth centuries, however, Western perceptions of Eastern threat progressively modified, and it is no coincidence that these centuries saw an intensification of the capitalistic "marketing" of Orientalia for European elitist consumption.[3]

As one aspect of this, Europe increasingly played back to itself an image of the East as an appropriate site for the inscription of its myth of the man of action: that is, a man (e.g., adventurer, entrepreneur, soldier, colonizer) who, in the name of Western superiority, could impose his will upon Oriental forces and/or resources and thereby gain fame and fortune for himself and his home country. As Elleke Boehmer explains, Europe developed the story of this imposition through a variety of discourses, among them the nineteenth-century literature of empire. In the standard romantic versions of this literature, the protagonist is male, and his ultimate achievement of the object of desire defines the story's successful conclusion (60–97).[4] What is judged crucial to the hero's success is initiative: the direct translation of will into effective enterprise. As historian of colonialism Raymond Betts puts it: "The magic word was 'action' " (41).

On first glance, the Orient may not seem to be a particularly useful context for an interpretation of "The Bloody Chamber." Obvious allusions are present in the story, but they are not numerous. There is, of course, the fact of Carter's luxurious and sensual prose, reminiscent in an Orientalist context of the rich colors and profuse designs of a Persian carpet. And, here and there, the story's narrator does reference some Oriental images: among these, she compares the Marquis's great wealth to that of Croesus, and she quotes her husband as saying that he has "acquired a whole harem for [himself]" in the mirrors that line her bedroom (14). Once we set Carter's story within the tradition of other "Bluebeard" tales (and illustrations) though, its links to the Orient become more apparent.

Marina Warner suggests that the very fact of Bluebeard's beard, as the character is described in Perrault's 1697 version, indicates "an outsider, a libertine, and a ruffian," based on the fact that facial hair was out of fashion in the court of Louis XIV. Of equal significance, Warner continues, the phonological similarity of the French word *barbe* (beard) with *barbare* (barbarian) may have contributed, in the woodcuts of Perrault's first edition and continuing into the watercolors of Arthur Rackham and others, to depictions of Bluebeard as an "Oriental, a Turk in pantaloons and turban, who rides an elephant, and grasps his wife by the hair when he prepares to behead her with his scimitar" (242).[5] For her part, Maria Tatar sees if not a source for "Bluebeard," then a significant parallel to him in King Schahriyar, from *The Thousand and One Nights,* who beheads "one wife after another because of the discovery of his [first] wife's sexual curiosity." In light of this "Oriental legacy," Tatar continues, "it becomes all the less remarkable that examples of female curiosity are repeatedly accompanied by moral glosses in fairy tales, while instances of male curiosity stand as gateways to the world of high adventure" (167–68).

To be sure, recent commentary on "The Bloody Chamber" has explored various relationships between the story's female protagonist and Western myths of female passivity (Bacchilega; Jordan; Renfroe). Here, as I've indicated, I take an alternate track, investigating strongly negative mirror images of the wife's curiosity—her husband's and other despots' pronounced and sometimes rapacious extension of their will into the world around them.

Bloody Carpets

In considering the patriarchal myth of the man of action with respect to "The Bloody Chamber," we need first to recognize that European literature did not restrict its depiction of this character type to European exemplars. In addition, it occasionally processed images of the male Other—including that of the Oriental tyrant—to serve in the definition of European male hegemony. Included in this group is the fourteenth-century Tartar warlord Timur, whom late sixteenth-century English playwright Christopher Marlowe (1564–93) transformed into the hero of his first and very successful play *Tamburlaine, the Great* (composed 1587).[6] By considering selected aspects of the historical Timur and his avatar, the literary Tamburlaine, we can gain productive slants on the obsessive "appetites" of Carter's Marquis as a version of the man of action and will.

The historical Timur (1336–1405) led a remarkable and admirable life—admirable, that is, if one values positively the exploits of conquerors. Born into the Central Asian nomadic pastoral/warrior culture of the Western Tartars, by his thirty-third year Timur had achieved a kingdom in the area east of the Caspian Sea. From there, he conquered Northern India (his descendants established the Mogul Empire), Anatolia, and Persia. In 1402, Timur's forces defeated the Turks and were proceeding against the southern Chinese empire when he died in 1405. Summarizing Timur's character traits as reported in relatively contemporary Arab, Persian, Syrian, and European documents, Una Ellis-Fermor finds the man to have been marked by contradictions: "a strange balance of heroic virtues and savagery, of ungoverned passions and supreme military discipline, of opulence and austerity, of cruelty and [a] love of art and philosophy" (22).

Depicted in Ellis-Fermor's summary as a man of "flaming will and illimitable aspiration" (22) who had "dared everything possible to his imagination and never faltered" (21), the figure of Timur had already been processed through various European histories and tale collections by the 1500s. And given his reputation as a man of unstoppable force, it is not difficult to see why Timur captured the imagination of the young, adventuresome Christopher Marlowe, who, in the late 1500s, was then in his mid-twenties.[7] Building on his fascination with this warrior-king, Marlowe depicts Timur's extension of his empire, a topic that appealed strongly to the pro-expansion, pro-mercantile, and pro-adventure factions of Marlowe's late Elizabethan audience.[8]

Referencing the historical Timur's career-long fierceness as a warrior, Marlowe is quite clear on the fact of his character Tamburlaine's bloodletting. In writing of the play, Susan Richards characterizes its hero as devoted to "the art of death" (299). Indeed, Richards continues, Marlowe presents Tamburlaine and/or those he conquers as "swimming in blood, bathing in blood, marching under bloody flags, [and] dyeing the ocean red with blood" (303), thus turning Central Asia itself into a kind of bloody chamber. And with this point, we can note Timur/Tamburlaine's credentials as a figure relevant to Carter's tale.

As Carter's female protagonist is exploring her husband's library, she remarks that the "rugs on the floor, deep pulsing blues of heaven and red of the heart's dearest blood, come from Isfahan and Bokhara" (16). Along with his capital of Samarqand, Bokhara has been said to be the historical Timur's favorite city (Irving 140).[9] Over the several hundred years prior to Timur's reign as well as during it, Bokhara had become a center for, among other artistic pursuits, the pre-eminent weaving of marvelous carpets and textiles; it was as well a center for literature, learning, and commerce. By the tenth century, these accomplishments had earned Bokhara the epithet of the "dome of Islam in the east," judged the equal of the western city of Baghdad (Frye 43). Bokhara, then, was the city that Timur acquired and elaborated upon, and it is one of the cities whose history lies encapsulated on the floor of the Marquis's library. Like the city of Bokhara, the Marquis's library is ostensibly a chamber devoted to the celebration of literature and the arts, splendid and sensuous in its appointments; yet, beneath its ornamentation, it is a chamber marked (as the Marquis's crypt is itself stained) with the bloodthirstiness of its master—a bloodlust that is as red as the "heart's dearest blood" (16).

Passing "over the face of Asia like a consuming fire or a whirlwind, [and] driven by a fanatical lust for dominion" (Ellis-Fermor 21), Marlowe's Tamburlaine speaks often of his consuming ambition, his quest to achieve beyond the limits of the commonly thought possible. One of his more famous monologues describes this ambition in terms of sensations of appetite: it is the "thirst of reign and sweetness of a crown" (part 1, act 2, scene 7, line 1) that pushes him onward until he reaches the "ripest fruit of all," which is the "sweet fruition of an earthly crown" (lines 27–29). Tamburlaine is so impressed with the accomplishments of his appetite that he even rates monarchical achievement (particularly his own) over the deeds of the gods. He asserts that a "god is not so glorious as a king" because the gods' pleasure "[c]annot compare with kingly joys in earth" (part 1, act 2, scene 5, lines 57–59). Unlike ancient Greek heroes who paid for their hubris, Tamburlaine's arrogant snub of the gods—perhaps akin to the Marquis's treading on the "deep pulsing blues of heaven" (16) that are captured in his carpets—does not earn him any punishment. Indeed, as he lies on his deathbed (succumbing to illness and old age but, legend says, never to military defeat), Tamburlaine has the audacity to call for a map of the world so that he can see, with regret, how much of the world there is still left for him to conquer (part 2, act 5, scene 3, lines 123–25). Analogous appetites and a similar arrogance characterize Carter's Marquis.

To be sure, Marlowe depicts Tamburlaine as having risen from the status of a Scythian shepherd in a "poor boy makes good" story while the Marquis lays claim to an eight-hundred-year-old aristocratic lineage, which has contributed to his aura of "monstrous presence, heavy as if he had been gifted at birth with a more specific *gravity* than the rest of us" (20; emphasis in the original). In terms of similarities, however, both Timur/Tamburlaine and the Marquis distinguish themselves by the bloody ways in which they stretch the limits of the possible. And if we should take Tamburlaine's arrogance as indicative of the Marquis's, we can understand better the profound shock and rage the Marquis feels at the story's climax when his wife's execution is disrupted: "The Marquis stood transfixed, utterly dazed, at a loss. . . . The puppet master, open-mouthed, wide-eyed, impotent at the last, saw his dolls, break free of their strings. . . . [Then the] heavy bearded figure roared out aloud, braying with fury, and, wielding the honourable sword as if it were a matter of death or glory, charged us, all three" (39–40). Significantly, even just moments before his death, Carter references the Marquis's beard: that sign of the barbarian whose heritage is heavy with bloodlust.

As Lorna Sage comments, as part of her demythologizing project Carter is concerned to "unrave[l] . . . romance" ("Angela Carter Interviewed" 185). Although it might seem unimaginable that anyone could admire Carter's Marquis, he does possess attributes that, over the centuries, patriarchal culture has promoted: power, wealth, and either an aristocratic name or a social sophistication, of use in facilitating social intercourse and thus power plays when at least the veneer of respectability matters. Historically, unethical men who have possessed these traits have enjoyed a certain protection from moral blame or other consequences of their actions.[10] This certainly has been the case in the patriarchally-oriented reception of male murderer tales such as "Bluebeard" where, historically, literary retellers have roundly blamed the young wife for her curiosity but neglected to condemn Bluebeard for his serial killings (Bacchilega 104–38; Tatar 156–70). Carter, however, tries to strip away this protection: given the mythic promotion of figures who, like Tamburlaine, believe they hold "the Fates bound fast in iron chains, / And with [their] hand turn Fortune's wheel about" (part 1, act 1, scene 2, lines 173–74), she attempts to expose the "omnivorous egocentrism" (*Sadeian Woman* 32) beneath the mask.

Although Marlowe buys into the patriarchal myth and Carter does not, both choose the metaphor of appetite to describe the rapacity of the tyrants they deal with. Both also extend that metaphor—Carter does so at length—such that the tyrant is presented as an arrogant predator, one who whets his appetite by toying with his prey before devouring it. In Marlowe's play, after defeating Bajazeth, Emperor of the Turks, Tamburlaine imprisons him in a cage and subjects him to various humiliations, including at one point using him as a human footstool (part 1, act 4, scene 2). For his part, the Marquis objectifies and humiliates his new wife, treating her like a mannequin during the "formal disrobing of the bride" scene, a degrading interaction that nonetheless prompts her sexual stirring. Then, without satisfying her needs in any way, he objectifies her further, closing her legs "like a book" and announcing that he must leave to tend to business (15). The wife's "bewildered senses" (16) point to the Marquis's behavior as a cat-and-mouse game, a fact that Carter anticipates subtly in earlier references to the "leonine shape of [the Marquis's] head" (8) and to the wife's "mouse-coloured hair" (10).

On the surface, the Marquis's appetites are varied: they are perversely sexual ("[H]ad he not hinted that he was a connoisseur of such things?" [16]), economic ("bankrupt[ing] a small businessman in Amsterdam" [25]), criminal (he was "engaged in some business in Laos that must . . . be to do with opium" [25]), elitist ("My husband liked me to wear my opal over my kid glove, a showy, theatrical trick" [13]), literary (in his library, "[r]ow upon row of calf-bound volumes" [16]), artistic ("the picture gallery, a treasure house filled by five centuries of avid collectors" [20]) as well as sensual and mortuary, among others. Essentially, though, the Marquis's appetites are one: they derive from an obsessive and sadistic desire to consume that which surrounds him, particularly the emotional responses and talents of others. Carter most fully develops this appetite metaphor in terms of cuisine.

The underlying dynamic of the cuisine metaphor is quite basic: there are those who eat, and there are those who are eaten. For example, in remembering the Marquis's assessment of her at the opera the night before their wedding, the protagonist describes the Marquis's dehumanizing regard as akin to that of "a housewife in the market, inspecting cuts on the slab" (11). Later, during the "disrobing" scene, the Marquis strips the wife, "gourmand that he was, as if he were stripping the leaves off an artichoke" (15). In spite of the reputed properties of the artichoke as an aphrodisiac, she notices that he "approached his familiar treat [artichokes? herself? any given new bride?] with a weary appetite" (15).[11] Later, though, he does become sexually aroused when, with "mockery and relish," he feeds off her "painful, furious bewilderment" (17) and vulnerability at finding the sadomasochistic pictures in the volume *The Adventures of Eulalie at the Harem of the Grand Turk*. And there are other instances of the cuisine metaphor's use.

The Marquis's predatory hunger—his compulsion to devour the dignity, integrity, individuality, and ultimately the life of others in the exercise of his "omnivorous egocentricity"—suggests the sterile void within him. Committed to the basest of social materialisms and thus to an external definition of self, the Marquis constructs himself through the deconstruction and reconstruction of others. Whereas Marlowe's Tamburlaine "collects crowns as a philatelist collects stamps and remains unsatisfied" (Daiches 330), the Marquis acquires wives whose erasure of self and life brings him much pleasure. Thus, as he ascertains his present wife's (unwitting) cooperation in her own impending death by her discovery of the burial chamber, his attitude is marked by a "sombre delirium . . . compounded of a ghastly, yes, shame but also of a terrible, guilty joy" (36). In other words, the Marquis marries to subjugate and then to lose wives. Describing the burial chamber as his "den"—the protected place to which a lion might haul a carcass for devouring—he explains: "There I can go, you understand, to savour the rare pleasure of imagining myself wifeless" (21). Note that he does not refer to himself as a widower or as a bachelor (although the present wife assumes that the latter was his meaning). Rather, he chooses an identity—"wifeless"—based on the explicit naming of the exterminated Other. What remains to him then after the presumably delicious joy of intentional loss are corpses which, in the exercise of a physically asexual but "artistic" necrophilia, he can fill unobstructed with his own meaning. Both protecting and abhorring the vacuum within, the Marquis "feeds" that moral void by acts of creating absence, which then lead to his own particular mode of creating substance.

Strategic Display

Given Carter's emphasis on the Marquis's appetites, it is not surprising that she also stresses sensory experience. Her rich prose calls attention to a variety of reported sights and tastes as well as smells, textures, and sounds. The actual descriptions, of course, are presented as those of the female protagonist. Her emotional and sensuous sensitivities give her the capacity to appreciate and to respond in deeply felt ways to the world around her, particularly through her music. Offering a treasure of sensory stimuli and social hierarchical privileges, the Marquis has tried to exploit his wife's sensitivities and her naiveté concerning them. Attempting to convince her that he can recognize her inner and true self, he suggests that she holds within a "promise of debauchery" (20) towards which her sensitivities should be directed. He, the connoisseur, will help her develop those hidden talents. In his strategic providing of sensory experience for another's attention and his own gain, the Marquis can be compared to another indirectly allusive figure of the story, Shah Abbās (I), the Great (1571–1629) of Persia, whose former capital of Isfahan is the other primary source for the carpets in the Marquis's library.

Selecting (rather than inheriting) Isfahan as his capital, Abbās strategically refashioned the city into an "emblem of [his] power" (Irving 147).[12] As the Marquis's family has done with their castle over the centuries, Abbās turned Isfahan into an "advertisement, a beacon of one man's energy, imagination and ego" (148). He achieved this not only by making the city into a center of learning, commerce, and foreign diplomacy but also by fashioning it into a pre-eminent showplace of the visual arts (carpet and textile weaving, the arts of the book, and the manufacture of glazed polychrome and mosaic architectural tiles [Savory 74]). Abbās's usefulness as an analogue to Carter's Marquis, then, stems primarily from the fact of the Shah's understanding of visual display as a tool of power. However, we can also link him to the Marquis in terms of habits of bloodletting. Like the Marquis, Abbās engaged in gendered domestic murder; however, the Shah focused on male targets, sending to their deaths several stepbrothers and one son (as well as blinding two other sons). And like the Marquis, Abbās is alleged to have been a sexually-oriented sadist: legend says that he preferred to personally geld the male slaves of his household (Irving 160). Ironically apropos of our noticing similarities in brutality between the Shah and the Marquis, the seventeenth-century English adventurer Sir Anthony Sherley, who entered Abbās's service, observed: "[T]here was not a Gentleman there but the King: the rest were shadows which moved with his body" (qtd. in Irving 161).

For his part, the Marquis's manipulation of his fiancée/new wife extends sensuous display into the realm of seduction; his is a strategic operation concocted of glamor and glamour. As Cristina Bacchilega has pointed out, in order to have been attracted to the Marquis, the young wife must have had some affinity with him to begin with (112). That affinity is grounded in the two characters' sensual and desiring response to experience. Although their ethics and intensity of desire differ, the Marquis tries to convince the wife that her wants complement his own. Vulnerable to her own desires and to others' manipulation of them, the young wife is susceptible to a variety of temptations. The Marquis's social standing and great wealth are obvious lures for they allow her to regain (many times over, in fact) what was lost to her by her mother's rebellious decision to marry out of her social class. Thus, the young wife—this former working girl—is given the keys to the kingdom and unlimited access to a "jinn's treasury" (24). Further, the wife's access to the castle's riches is essentially unimpeded: the "slick Yale lock" (26)—perhaps it had been recently oiled—that closes her husband's office is easily sprung, and the "new lock" on the crypt's door opens "as easily as a hot knife in butter" (27): no fumbling with rusty mechanisms required. And still further, the young wife is provided the leisure to explore: "Henceforth, a maid would deal with everything" (14).

In addition, the Marquis's wealth allows him to offer his new wife the means not only to satisfy desire but also to acquire—or at least to approach—contexts of origin. Thus, the Marquis can take an "orphan, [once] hired out of charity to give [a princess and her guests] their digestive of music" (13), and give her one of the very best of musical instruments for her own private use: the Bechstein piano she receives as a wedding present. Further, since her previous socio-economic status and education would have provided her with much secondary but little primary elite experience, the wife is vulnerable to the original fine art in her husband's picture gallery ("[A]h, he foresaw I would spend hours there" [20]) as well as to the "rare collector's pieces" (17) and fine editions from "over-exquisite private press[es]" (16) in his library. Like Abbās's city of Isfahan, the Marquis's castle appears to offer the dream made real. But it is the person of the Marquis himself that *seems* to provide the young wife with the most satisfying hope of approaching a lost context of origin: the Marquis as a potential emotional substitute for the wife's deceased father. Considerably older than she is, the Marquis reminds the wife of her father in several ways, among them, by scent: the Marquis's cigar produces "a remembered fragrance that made [her] think of [her] father, how he would hug [her] in a warm fug of Havana, when [she] was a little girl, before he kissed [her] and left [her] and died" (12). Further, to remind her intentionally of her father as well as to appeal to her expectations of romantic love, the Marquis takes his fiancée to a performance of the opera Tristan and Isolde, Richard Wagner's tribute to partially coerced, partially self-induced destructive passion. And the experience does indeed prompt memories of her father's sympathetic touch when he took her as a child to a performance of *Tristan*: her "father, still alive (oh, so long ago), [as he] took hold of [her] sticky little hand, to comfort [her], in the last act" (10). Although throughout her narrative the protagonist's tone berates her former self for selling herself to the Marquis as in a "brothel" (15) for "a handful of coloured stones and the pelts of dead beasts" (18), her motives were not as petty as her guilty conscience would make them. Even though the Marquis has not sensed accurately the wife's potential for corruption, he has appraised correctly her strong emotional need to recuperate the loss of her father. The Marquis, who loses wives intentionally, recognizes (but certainly cannot empathize with) his wife's painful vulnerability, and he exploits that as part of his seduction strategy.

However, if we attend to Carter's politics of ornamentation, even at the level of seeming triviality, we can see that some of the Marquis's more sensuous material possessions can be read as tell-tale signs of his deceptive character. So read, they suggest the façade of the "exquisite tact" (8) and "tenderness" (18) the protagonist once thought the Marquis showed as well as the life of cruelty and containment that he is actually offering. There are, for example, the "lush, insolent incense" (18) of his hot-house (i.e., forced to flower) arum lilies, which, under natural conditions, bloom in the late spring, not in November; the "grand, hereditary, matrimonial bed" (14) of ebony: a rare but decorative material sliced from the heartwood of its trees; the Marquis's trousseau gift to the wife of a fur "wrap" (12) of ermine and sable: a luxurious containment whose nomenclature signals the conventions of aristocratic heraldry but which was made possible, originally, only through bloodletting; and, finally, a "cloisonné cupboard" (18), an appropriate cubicle for the telephone in this castle of isolation for *cloisonné* derives from the Latin *clausiō* for "enclosure" and, in French, is known as the art of partitioning, of separation.

Just as Shah Abbās's commitment to visually exquisite public splendor can be interpreted in stark relief to his privately brutal conduct, so too do the sensuous riches of the Marquis's castle contrast sharply with his involvement in degradation, deprecation, and death. And the narrator eventually realizes this contrast. Although she has linked the Marquis to her beloved father through positive olfactory memory, she later perceives her husband as reeking of death and decay as if the "Russian leather of his scent were reverting to the elements of flayed hide and excrement of which it was composed" (35). Looking back on events, she realizes further that the passionate swells of Wagner's opera, which had previously enticed her, had served merely as an aural veil over the "silent music . . . of [her] unknowingness" (19). She also becomes aware that that music was eventually superceded by the Marquis's "cold metal" (19) carillon of lock keys, a ring of keys which at one point she leaves on her music stool in unwitting mimicry (parody?) of the Marquis's plans to entomb her gift of music in his memory and her own ivory-colored bones in his burial chamber. Her previous sense of leisure soon turns into a feeling of boredom, which she compares to that of wealth-colored fish confined in a tank (23). And that sense of boredom, in turn, changes to a sense of entrapment when she realizes that the castle's servants, who presumably are there to answer her every need, are all her husband's "creatures" (30). In addition, the promises of the treasure house with which she has supposedly been gifted separate from reality just as, when she lights each candle around the first wife's catafalque, a "garment of that innocence of [hers] for which [her husband] had lusted fell away" (28). Indeed, by the time the wife rests her head on the execution block, all the material and sensory accoutrements of her newly enhanced status—save for the ruby necklace that prefigures her decapitation—have been stripped away. Once dressed as a richly appointed wildflower (12), by the climax of the tale, she is reduced to the level—metaphorically, to the status—of a "little green moss, growing in the crevices of the mounting block" (39), feeling as dismissable and as interstitial as the moss.

A White Muslin Dress

From the bloody territorialism of Timur/Tamburlaine and the strategic splendor of Shah Abbās as analogues of the Marquis and as figures of access to the story, we can turn finally to an early twentieth-century "sultan" who was not of the Orient but rather operated as an entrepreneur of Orientalism. Carter's narrator reports the Marquis's continuing interest in one particular trousseau item: "a sinuous shift of white muslin tied with a string under the breasts" (11). This dress was designed by the alluded-to Paul Poiret (1879–1943), who in history was arguably the most fashionable Parisian couturier of his day.

Poiret's own statement concerning the role of the couturier is a useful place to begin for it echoes aspects of the myth of the man of action that I sketched above. The couturier, Poiret explained, is called to "live his dream, excite the imagination of the public, . . . acquire art objects, inspire emulation by painters, . . . open new paths of research for 'spices and unknown savors' even in the exotic, [and] collect documents about and authenticate samples of adornment that are inaccessible to everyday people, and cultivate public taste for them" (qtd. in White 351–53). Here, then, we find yet another version of the familiar patriarchal story: a tale of the ideal man who can control his own destiny, who can move in elite and thus powerful circles as a patron of the arts and of literature, but who, beneath the veneer, manipulates others, strategically manages sensory experience, and exploits hierarchy.

Dubbed "le Magnifique" by the French press during his heyday (from about 1907 to 1914), early in his career Poiret worked at the house of Worth et Bolbergh but was soon fired. Incapable of operating in terms other than his own (or, in mythic language, operating as a man of will), Poiret was committed to the display of opulence in fashion. To be sure, his designs maintained a simple line, but the ones for which he ultimately became most famous—those capitalizing on Orientalist motifs—suggested an exotic luxuriousness in their use of rich and oftentimes dazzling fabrics and decorative appointments.[13] Not surprisingly, given the Marquis's own interest in visual display, Carter's protagonist acquired some of these gowns in her supplied trousseau. However, she is well aware of their flamboyance. After her husband leaves her to (supposedly) take care of business, a maid asks if the wife will dress for dinner. Remembering that at the time she laughed at the idea, the narrator comments: "But, imagine—to dress up in one of my Poiret extravaganzas, with the jewelled turban and aigrette on my head, roped with pearl to the navel, to sit down all alone in the baronial dining hall" (25).

Like Timur/Tamburlaine, Poiret launched a successful career on the bodies of others—for Poiret, on that of his wife, dressing her as the primary display mannequin of his artistic vision. Analogous to the Marquis's believing that he could sense the "promise of debauchery" (20) within his own fiancée, Poiret saw Denise as possessing an untapped plentitude of "hidden graces" (28) and "secret desires" (29) which only he, with the "eye of an artist" (White 28), could recognize and develop. On the other hand, as the reverse side to his commitment to luxurious display, Poiret, like the Marquis and to some extent like Shah Abbās, felt compelled to create a sense of absence in those he controlled. For Poiret, this meant fostering and managing a modern-day harem of women clients who were willing to be transformed by deletion; as Poiret put it: "In dressing Madame Poiret, I strive for omission, not addition" (White 39). For her part, Denise was quite willing to cooperate, writing in her diary three years after her transformation had begun, "My taste is becoming more and more refined at present. That is to say, I am removing every thing on me and around me that is not consistent" (39)—not consistent, we can infer, as defined by her husband's artistic vision. What appears to have mattered most to Poiret was a woman's textile skin, designed by Poiret; her individuality could be suppressed.

Through his relatively brief tenure as a successful couturier, Poiret's art of deletion manifested itself in various ways.[14] He dealt a death blow to the corset and significantly reduced the number of clothing layers the fashionable woman was expected to wear.[15] In addition, in pursuing his fascination with omission, he seems to have been struck with the concomitant idea that if a woman can be reconstructed at a man's will, then a couturier might as well dress her as an object to begin with. And this Poiret occasionally did, although most of these designs were for the stage. He dressed chorus girls in revues as lavishly packaged bottles of perfume, chess pieces, playing cards, and dice. And, for a 1913 play with an Oriental theme, he costumed the female lead as a minaret. Another design, intended as an evening gown and not as a stage costume, was dubbed by the press as the lampshade tunic. It consisted of a hoop-skirted tunic worn over harem pantaloons (White 89, 100–01). To be sure, dressing actors in ways congruent with a given stage production is one of the conventions of the theater. However, since Poiret saw little to no distinction between theater and life, the designs mentioned above point to patriarchal assumptions applicable to the everyday—for example, that a woman is not the light of a man's life; she is simply the lampshade. Or that women are ornamental objects useful in stimulating a man's senses, that they are convenient pawns in men's games, or that they are beautifully constructed steps by means of which a man might elevate himself above others. Or, to carry this trope further, as I do below, that women are pieces of sculpture, created and crafted by the male artist.

Poiret's much touted "arrival" in the Parisian fashion scene in 1907–08 was marked by his first signature design: the simply-lined, high-waisted, sheath-like dresses of his "Hellenic" style, an evening gown example of which, as I have mentioned, appears repeatedly in "The Bloody Chamber." Understanding that fashion design involved "three-dimensional construction" that transformed "dressmaking into sculpture" (de Marly 40), Poiret freely admitted that he had studied ancient Greek sculpture for inspiration, intending his Hellenic columnar look to evoke the styles of classical antiquity (White 31). To my eye, the white muslin dress of Carter's protagonist is reminiscent of the *peploi* gowns worn by ancient Greek *korai*, most famously the Caryatids sculpted to support the south porch roof of the Erechtheion on the Acropolis.[16] Tall, stately, a bit heavier in proportion than Carter's slender protagonist but beautiful, the Caryatids (again, to my eye) represent women placed into stasis almost at the moment of action. The seeming serenity they suggest, contributing as it does to the myth of the arrested and thus ideal woman, attracted Poiret as a textile artist: "I feel satisfied with my creations," Poiret commented, "only when they give an impression of simple charm, of calm perfection comparable to that which is felt when standing before an antique statue" (qtd. in White 39).

Like Poiret, the Marquis also takes pleasure in regarding "his" women as sculpted objects. Indeed, during the course of the story, the Marquis has the protagonist wear the white muslin dress whenever he has a special need to objectify and thus to dehumanize her. In addition, like Shah Abbās and Paul Poiret, the Marquis is well aware of how spectacle can be used as a tool of social power. The narrator first dons the gown when the Marquis puts her on display at the opera. A strategically costumed sign of her fiancé's wealth and status, the protagonist's primary public value is to serve as a focus of others' desire as well as a marker of their exclusion. As an embodied designer dress label, that material sign of elite membership, the begowned wife is used to emphasize her own and her fiancé's privileged separation from the commonplace ("On his arm, all eyes were upon me. The whispering crowd parted like the Red Sea to let us through" [10]). In addition, given the French press's touting of the design as *empire,* we can also read the dress as suggesting the hegemonic domination and exploitation of the Other.[17] In this sense, the white dress is indicative of the Marquis's planned treatment of the protagonist once they are married.

The Marquis next has the wife wear the white gown when he bestows on her the keys of the castle. Traditionally, in having charge of the keys, a chatelaine would operate at an elevated level of status and power within the castle community. However, in Carter's story, the young wife's repeated experiences with the servants' disdain points to her subordinate status. Later, she discovers more directly her actual role: that of a mannequin, a constructed object, in service to the Marquis's obsessions. Thus, an alternate meaning of chatelaine becomes relevant: not that of the person who controls the keys but rather that of an artifact/receptacle for receiving them. If at the climax of the story the wife is reduced metaphorically to the status of stone moss, by accepting the castle keys she is reduced to the metaphorical status of a key-bob as well as of the keys on it. The target of a cruel and potentially lethal joke—yet another of the Marquis's cat-and-mouse games—the wife as an embodied key is supposed to unlock her way through the castle until, by opening the final door, she seals her fate.[18] What she must learn for her own survival is that she is the one on the chain as well as the chain itself. Prior to discovering the crypt, the young wife senses that her isolation at the castle makes her somewhat resemble a chained prisoner ("this lovely prison of which I was both the inmate and the mistress" [24]). After discovering the burial chamber, she understands all too well that, as a result of cooperating in her husband's manipulations, she has been wound like a chain on a "spool of inexorability" (29) toward a "destiny as oppressive and omnipotent as [her husband] himself" (34).

The third and final time the Marquis requires the wife to wear the white dress is at her decreed execution. It is on this occasion that the Marquis plans to transform her from a sculpted body (i.e., one bedecked in a supplied trousseau) into a body preserved as sculpture—in other words, into an artifact for his "museum of . . . perversity" (28).[19] If successful, the Marquis would extend his own art of deletion, recalling that of Poiret, into the act of eliminating life itself. When the wife discovers the museum of death, the fact that it contains "statues" is not lost on her, although her immediate impression is of the torture machines therein: "Wheel, rack and Iron Maiden were, I saw, displayed as grandly as if they were items of statuary and I was almost consoled" (28). Then, of course, she finds the previous wives whose bodies have been oh so artfully arranged. Fittingly, Carter ironically inverts the metaphor of statuary at the story's climax when the tables are turned on the Marquis. There, as the narrator's mother charges in on horseback, it is the Marquis who is made to stand "stock-still, as if [the mother] had been Medusa" (40) and had turned him to stone. And in the next moment, this statue of the Marquis is miniaturized, reduced to a figurine under glass: "[T]he sword still raised over [the Marquis's] head as in those clockwork tableaux of Bluebeard that you see in glass cases at fairs" (40).

Within a patriarchal framework viewed through an Orientalist lens, the paradigmatic case of the collection is the harem. In his essay on collecting, Jean Baudrillard comments: "Surrounded by the objects he possesses, the collector is pre-eminently the sultan of a secret seraglio. Ordinary human relationships, which are the site of the unique and the conflictual, never permit such a fusion of absolute singularity and indefinite seriality" (10). Odalisques and ornaments, the women of the harem are expected to reflect the wishes and desires of their sultan-master for, as Baudrillard says, "it is invariably *oneself* that one collects" (12; emphasis in the original). What of himself then has the Marquis collected in his set of female artifacts? As one answer, we can turn again to Baudrillard: because both desire and seriality are open-ended, he argues, "the collection deflects the menace of death" (18); insofar as "we truly possess it," Baudrillard continues, "the object stands for our own death, symbolically transcended" (17). By killing in series and then crafting a souvenir of each murder, the Marquis—who embodies the consuming void—can pretend to himself that he transcends even himself. Each woman in the museum offers the Marquis an illusion of triumph over death by virtue of the fact that he has been the agent who called death into being.

A second question: What aspects of himself—actual or desired—does the Marquis collect by gathering together the individual corpses of his previous wives? Each of the previous wives was acquired, among whatever other reasons, because she possessed some specific talent; each was murdered or is displayed in a way reminiscent of that talent. The opera singer was strangled, vocal chords crushed by a man who, though not a musician, is drawn to music. The model's face, with its beautiful, "sheer planes" (29) of bone, is flayed and suspended in mid-air by a man whose own (in the protagonist's opinion) unappealing, "white, broad," "heavy, [and] almost waxen" (8) face seems to hover "disembodied . . . like a grotesque carnival head" (12). And the Countess, who styled herself a "descendant of Dracula" (26) and perhaps believed/hoped that she was immortal, has herself been pierced in a phallic-studded, iron gown by a man who, with his own "enigmatic, self-sustaining carapace" (26), seeks to conquer death. Whether the Marquis truly believes he can take on the qualities of those he kills by the very fact of having killed them is probably a moot question. Rather, it can be said that by acquiring a specially talented wife, the Marquis "gains" possession of that talent—not as a generating capacity within himself but rather as a memory whose corporeal mnemonic (the wife's corpse) only he owns. Whether any given wife is living or dead, whether she is demonstrating her talent in actuality or in her husband's recollection, the Marquis can call forth and recycle that demonstration at will. In addition to whatever else they are, these acts of recycling serve as rituals conducted to intervene in the linearity of time.

What then of the most recent wife? What does this seventeen year old have to offer to the Marquis's collection? Among the possibilities: as the supposedly naive and therefore especially corruptible "little girl" (18) or even "Baby" (17), the protagonist appeals to the father-pretender pedophile in the Marquis. As the ingenue, she is a fitting subject for the Marquis's reverse Pygmalionism in which a malleable young woman is first managed and then turned into a statue. As a sensitive who interacts strongly with the world through all the senses, she is a potential voluptuary, available to the Marquis's appetites. And if the corpses of the singer, the model, and the Countess represent flesh, bone, and blood, respectively, then the newest wife represents spirit—the spirit of curiosity that motivates exploration. The daughter of two adventurers—a code-defying mother and an experience-seeking soldier—the wife journeys with the "delicious ecstasy of excitement" into the "unguessable country of marriage" (7).

She feels the "exhilaration of the explorer" (24) when she realizes that she has scarcely seen most of the castle that is now her home. And it is her inheritance of the nerves, will, and spirit of her adventuresome mother that drives her on (28) once she enters the crypt, the "kingdom of the unimaginable" (36). As one who revels in the transgression of boundaries, the Marquis is attracted to the exploratory spirit he senses in the protagonist, but he also plans on using it to destroy her. What he does not count on, of course, is the independent spirit of a fiercely protective mother.

A final question: given all this, what makes the young wife's motivation to explore beyond the given qualitatively different from that of Timur/Tamburlaine, Shah Abbās, Paul Poiret, and the Marquis? Among the relevant factors, there is the crucial and stark contrast between the tyrant's commitment to territorialism, sensory exploitation, the dehumanization of others, and omnivorous egocentricity, on the one hand, and journeying beyond the status quo with committed respect for oneself and for others, on the other. Given Carter's reluctance in her tales to offer simple answers to complicated questions, though, I am sure there is more to the matter than just that. But, as with the adventurings of allusion, that as they say is another story.

Notes

1. I thank Ulrich Marzolph and Mackenzie Osborne for their generosity with reference materials concerning Shah Abbās and the Caryatids, respectively. Any errors in the present essay are my own.
2. Generally speaking, for centuries Europe sensed only vaguely the location of the Far East—Cathay (northern China)—until adventurers and traders progressively opened the area to the West in the seventeenth through the nineteenth centuries.
3. As an early example of the marketability of the Oriental Other, a published version of the *Arabian Nights* was introduced to Europe at the turn of the eighteenth century in Antoine Galland's French translation *Les Mille et Une Nuits, contes arabes traduits en français* (1704–12). It appeared a few years after Charles Perrault's *Histoires ou contes du temps passé* (1697), which contained "La Barbe-Bleue."
4. For a discussion of "The Bloody Chamber" as treating a woman protagonist's rite of passage, see Manley; and Bacchilega 104–38.
5. Michael Foreman, illustrator of Carter's *Sleeping Beauty & Other Favourite Fairy Tales,* depicts Bluebeard as a literally blue-bearded sultan who waves a scimitar. For a discussion of Bluebeard figures in folk and written literature, see Bacchilega 104–38. An historical Oriental brigand with an unusual beard was Khayr ad-Dīn (d. 1546), by-named Barbarossa (Redbeard). A Turkish Barbary pirate and later admiral of the Ottoman fleet, his ships ravaged Mediterranean coastal areas and set into motion a piracy that lasted for three centuries after his death.
6. Marlowe originally intended to write only Part 1 of *Tamburlaine;* however, its popularity prompted him to compose Part 2 in 1598.
7. Possibly involved now and then in government secret service, occasionally getting into trouble with city authorities for his disreputable behavior, and allegedly

professing atheism for which a writ of arrest was written against him by England's Privy Council, the twenty-nine-year-old Marlowe was killed in a tavern brawl.

8. *Tamburlaine* was first offered to audiences only two years after the English had defeated the Spanish Armada, a patriotism-inspiring event that confirmed England's status as a major European power and as mistress of the seaways.

9. Modern-day Bukhara (Bokhara; 1990 population 228,000) is located in western Uzbekistan.

10. Up until the climax of "The Bloody Chamber," the Marquis had apparently enjoyed such protection. When the young wife describes the "room, the rack, the skull, the corpses, [and] the blood," the piano-tuner replies in wonder: "I can scarcely believe it. . . . That man . . . so rich; so well-born" (32).

11. Legend reports that the artichoke, with its alleged aphrodisiac properties, was a favorite food of Catherine de Medici (1519–89) (Root 14), queen consort of Henry II of France and the named source of the Marquis's "sultry, witchy" (13) fire-opal ring. In addition to supposedly possessing the stereotypically male despotic trait of rampant sexuality, Catherine, through history, has also been labeled a social predator, being identified as the principal planner of the St. Bartholomew's Day Massacre (23–24 August 1572) in which several thousand French Huguenots were killed.

12. Modern-day Esfahan (Isfahan; 1985 population 1,121,200) is located in west central Iran.

13. Although Orientalist motifs had appeared sporadically in haute couture since the turn of the century, the 1909 arrival in Paris of the Ballets Russes had a major impact on that city's theatrical and social tastes: the Ballets Russes "was a burst of fireworks, an explosion of brilliant colour and torrid tones into a world accustomed to subdued shades and understated clothing. . . . Suddenly the barbaric East was in fashion" (de Marly 85).

14. After serving in the French military during World War I, Poiret returned to a much changed fashion scene. Orientalist designs were not only considered passé but were also associated with the "old order's" privileging of elitist values; many saw the fact of such privileging as having contributed to the causes of the Great War. Because Poiret could not adapt to the more practical clothing desired by young, postwar, working women, in the early 1920s sales of his designs fell rapidly. Adding to his financial problems were his habits of making unwise investments and of throwing lavish parties. By the end of the decade, his business had failed and his wife had divorced him. Poiret died almost penniless in 1943 (White).

15. Although the demise of the corset was a medical boon to women, Poiret replaced it with the mid-body girdle, a "thin, lightweight rubber garment that fitted like a skin" (White 31)—thus continuing the patriarchal assumption that a woman's body (and, by extension, women themselves) should be restricted. However, in reviewing David Kunzle's book *Fashion and Fetishisms,* Carter refers to various forms of "body sculpture"—such as stiletto-heeled shoes and the "tight-lacing" of corsets—as "voluntary self-mutilations" that women collude in as ways of acquiring and maintaining social power within a patriarchal system ("David" 173–74).

16. A *kore* (pl. *korai*) is a carved, draped, standing female figure. The *peplos* (pl. *peploi*) was a sleeveless, one-piece gown that hung from the shoulders and was worn belted (Pedley 171).

17. The press's term *empire* recalled a similar fashion popularized around the turn of

the nineteenth century by Josephine, wife of Napoleon Bonaparte. By so naming it, the press, however (un)intentionally, linked the style not with democracy (as "Hellenic" suggests) but with political empire.

18. I am reminded here of Tamburlaine's humiliating and objectifying of the Emperor of the Turks by using him as a human footstool.

19. Using human bodies—actually body parts—to construct ego-proclaiming monuments was a traditional—or, at least, a legendary—practice among Oriental despots. Reportedly, the Persian Shah Tahmasp (1524–76) punished a rebellious Isfahan by erecting a pillar there composed of the heads of 30,000 of its slain residents. For his part, Timur was said to have built three towers of heads, taken from those killed when he captured the city of Damascus (Herbert 136).

Works Cited

Atwood, Margaret. "Running with the Tigers." *Flesh and the Mirror: Essays on the Art of Angela Carter.* Ed. Lorna Sage. London: Virago, 1994. 117–35.

Bacchilega, Cristina. *Postmodern Fairy Tales: Gender and Narrative Strategies.* Philadelphia: U of Pennsylvania P, 1997.

Baudrillard, Jean. "The System of Collecting." Trans. Roger Cardinal. *The Cultures of Collecting.* Ed. John Elsner and Roger Cardinal. Cambridge: Harvard UP, 1994. 7–24.

Benson, Stephen. "Angela Carter and the Literary *Märchen:* A Review Essay." *Angela Carter and the Fairy Tale.* Ed. Danielle M. Roemer and Cristina Bacchilega. Detroit: Wayne State UP, 2001. 30–58.

Betts, Raymond. *Tricouleur: The French Overseas Empire.* London: Gordon & Cremones, 1978.

Boehmer, Elleke. *Colonial & Postcolonial Literature.* Oxford: Oxford UP, 1995.

Carter, Angela. "The Alchemy of the Word." *Expletives Deleted: Selected Writings.* London: Chatto & Windus, 1992. 67–73.

———. "The Bloody Chamber." *The Bloody Chamber and Other Stories.* London: Penguin, 1979. 7–41.

———. "David Kunzle: *Fashion and Fetishisms.*" *Expletives Deleted: Selected Writings.* London: Chatto & Windus, 1992. 173–76.

———. "Notes from the Front Line." *On Gender and Writing.* Ed. Michelene Wandor. London: Pandora, 1983. 69–77.

———. *The Sadeian Woman and the Ideology of Pornography.* New York: Pantheon, 1979.

———, trans. *Sleeping Beauty & Other Favourite Fairy Tales.* Illus. Michael Foreman. 1982. Boston: Otter, 1991.

Crunelle-Vanrigh, Anny. "The Logic of the Same and *Différance:* 'The Courtship of Mr Lyon.'" *Angela Carter and the Fairy Tale.* Ed. Danielle M. Roemer and Cristina Bacchilega. Detroit: Wayne State UP, 2001. 128–44.

Daiches, David. "Language and Action in Marlowe's *Tamburlaine.*" *Christopher Marlowe's Tamburlaine, Part One and Part Two.* Ed. Irving Ribner. Indianapolis: Odyssey, 1974. 133–62.

de Marly, Diana. *The History of Haute Couture, 1850–1950.* New York: Holmes & Meier, 1980.

Ellis-Fermor, U[na] M. Introduction. Marlowe, *Tamburlaine the Great in Two Parts* 1–62.

Frye, Richard N. *Bukhara: The Medieval Achievement.* Norman: U of Oklahoma P, 1965.

Hart, Henry H. *Marco Polo: Venetian Adventurer.* Norman: U of Oklahoma P, 1967.

Herbert, Thomas. *Travels in Persia, 1627–1629.* 1929. Ed. Sir William Foster. New York: Books for Libraries, 1972.

Irving, Clive. *Crossroads of Civilization: 3000 Years of Persian History.* New York: Barnes & Noble, 1979.

Jordan, Elaine. "The Dangers of Angela Carter." *New Feminist Discourses.* Ed. Isobel Armstrong. London and New York: Routledge, 1992. 119–31.

Lowe, Lisa. *Critical Terrains: French and British Orientalisms.* Ithaca: Cornell UP, 1991.

Manley, Kathleen E.B. "The Woman in Process in Angela Carter's 'The Bloody Chamber.' " *Angela Carter and the Fairy Tale.* Ed. Danielle M. Roemer and Cristina Bacchilega. Detroit: Wayne State UP, 2001. 83–93.

Marlowe, Christopher. *Tamburlaine the Great in Two Parts.* 1930. Ed. U[na] M. Ellis-Fermor. New York: Gordian, 1966.

Pedley, John Griffiths. *Greek Art and Archaeology.* Englewood Cliffs, NJ: Prentice Hall, 1993.

Renfroe, Cheryl. "Initiation and Disobedience: Liminal Experience in Angela Carter's 'The Bloody Chamber.' " *Angela Carter and the Fairy Tale.* Ed. Danielle M. Roemer and Cristina Bacchilega. Detroit: Wayne State UP, 2001. 94–106.

Richards, Susan. "Marlowe's Tamburlaine II: A Drama of Death." *Christopher Marlowe's Tamburlaine, Part One and Part Two.* Ed. Irving Ribner. Indianapolis: Odyssey, 1974. 298–311.

Root, Waverly. *Food: An Authoritative and Visual History and Dictionary of the Foods of the World.* New York: Konecky & Konecky, 1980.

Sage, Lorna. *Angela Carter.* Writers and their Work. Plymouth: Northcote House in association with The British Council, 1994.

———. "Angela Carter Interviewed by Lorna Sage." *New Writing.* Ed. Malcolm Bradbury and Judy Cooke. London: Minerva, 1992. 185–93.

Said, Edward W. *Orientalism.* New York: Vintage, 1978.

Savory, R. M. "Abbās I." *Encyclopaedia Iranica.* Ed. Ehsan Yarshater. London: Routledge & Kegan Paul, 1985. 71–75.

Tatar, Maria. *The Hard Facts of the Grimms' Fairy Tales.* Princeton: Princeton UP, 1987.

Warner, Marina. *From the Beast to the Blonde: On Fairy Tales and Their Tellers.* New York: Farrar, Straus and Giroux, 1994.

White, Palmer. *Poiret.* New York: Clarkson N. Potter, 1973.

Anny Crunelle-Vanrigh

The Logic of the
Same and Différance:
"The Courtship of Mr Lyon"

In his introduction to the collection of Angela Carter's short stories, Salman Rushdie notes how, in *The Bloody Chamber*, "the fable of Beauty and the Beast [is made] a metaphor for all the myriad yearnings and dangers of sexual relations."[1] Of all the stories in *The Bloody Chamber*, "The Courtship of Mr Lyon" is the least unsettling, one dealing with the "yearnings" more than the "dangers" of sex, if only because, closely following the plot of Madame Leprince de Beaumont's story, Carter also seems to endorse this eighteenth-century writer's moral point. "Courtship" is a tale about the harmonious passage from oedipal attachment to mature love marked by the metamorphosis of the Beast into a man. It holds a special place in the collection, referring back to the best-known version of "Beauty and the Beast" and preceding "The Tiger's Bride," its dark twin-piece. The quiet domesticity of the final image in "Courtship" makes it—with a good measure of irony—a socializing tale, quite unlike Carter's "Bride" or "The Werewolf," which disclose the animal at the heart of the human, the Beast *always already* within Beauty.

Carter chooses the tale, the genre *par excellence* of iteration (re-telling), for her game of replication (re-writing). The double status of "Courtship" as fairy tale and as hypertext thus places repetition and difference at the core of her enterprise.[2] A similar tension is to be felt between closure and indeterminacy. Fairy tales are informed by closure, a movement from change to permanence. Their plots move from an initial, pernicious metamorphosis to a stable identity

Marvels & Tales: Journal of Fairy-Tale Studies, Vol. 12, No. 1 (1998), pp. 116–32. Copyright © 1998 by Wayne State University Press, Detroit, MI 48201.

that must and will be reached or recaptured. Carter, however, stubbornly moves the other way round, from stability to instability, undermining the closed binary logic of fairy tale and eventually substituting *différance* for *différence* or difference. She takes her reader along the paths of indeterminacy, revelling in a state of never-ending metamorphosis, as she disseminates her stories through *The Bloody Chamber.*

Starting from repetition as the structuring principle of "The Courtship of Mr Lyon" and as a common denominator for its interpretation, whether in terms of narratology, genre, gender, or psychoanalysis, I shall attempt to trace how Carter challenges every one of these perspectives, the better to deconstruct them as all her work is a statement about Otherness and Difference.

"Le plagiat est la base de toutes les littératures, excepté la première, qui d'ailleurs nous est inconnue": All literature originates in plagiarism—all except the very first text, which anyway remains an unknown quantity. Carter's rewriting of popular tales in *The Bloody Chamber* is an exemplar of Jean Giraudoux's classic aphorism. Giraudoux, an adept at adapting stories from Greek mythology *(La Guerre de Troie n'aura pas lieu, Amphitryon 38, Electre),* addressed the questions of adaptation, imitation, re-writing—that is, more generally, hypertextuality. Implicit in his statement is the idea that the "pleasure of the text" is to be derived as much from the text itself as from the reader's identification of it as an instance of *bricolage* or palimpsest. The co-presence—and possible clash—of hypo- and hypertext, is what gives the experience of "palimpsestuous" reading its particular spice and pungency, with two texts superimposed, the original showing through.[3] Though any hypertext, even Joyce's *Ulysses,* can be enjoyed per se, failing to identify it as a hypertext undermines the significance and aesthetic value underlying re-presentation.

"The Courtship of Mr Lyon" moves to Beaumont's tale and back, emphasizing its presence as a hypotext to Carter's hypertext. Carter thus creates a double textuality, relying on imitation *and* insistent differentiation. Her text depends on intertextuality and pastiche to proclaim its sense of belonging *and* simultaneously on anachronism and travesty to advertise its difference. Rewriting is an interplay of repetition, imitation and difference, which, as I hope to show, far exceeds the limits of a brilliant "writing game" for *cognoscenti.*

"The Courtship of Mr Lyon" is overwhelmingly intertextual, like all of Carter's work. Its specific connection with the fairy tale as a genre is proclaimed through quotations and allusions complementing the overt hypertextuality of the narrative.[4] The opening paragraph combines references to "Snow White" and "Cinderella": "Outside her kitchen window, the hedgerow glistened as if the snow possessed a light of its own. . . . This lovely girl, whose skin possesses that same, inner light so you would have thought she, too, was made all of snow, pauses in her chores in the mean kitchen to look out at the country road" (144). A brief echo of *Alice in Wonderland* points forward to the Beast's final metamorphosis: "On the table, a silver tray; round the neck of the whisky decanter, a silver tag with the legend: *Drink me*, while the cover of the silver dish was engraved with the exhortation: *Eat me*, in a flowing hand" (145). Embedded half-way through the narrative is Carter's acknowledgment of her source material, the "courtly and elegant French fairy tales about white cats who were transformed princesses and fairies who were birds" (148). Her portrayal of the Beast, with his agate eyes, "head of a lion," the "golden hair of [his] great paws" (147) looks like a color version of the leonine mask Cocteau designed for Jean Marais in his screen adaptation of "Beauty and the Beast." The Beast in Beaumont's version is a mere "monster," as shadowy as is Victor's Creature in Mary Shelley's *Frankenstein,* and certainly no lion. Only Cocteau's mythopoetic sense turned him into a lion. That the Beast's deal with the father in "Courtship" is triggered by the contemplation of Beauty's photograph "where the camera had captured a certain look she had" (147) and not by the mere mention of her existence, as in Beaumont, is additional evidence that Cocteau's film is part of the story's intertext. The cinematic structure of Carter's story—sequences, ellipses and abrupt cuts—points in the same direction.

"One cannot imitate a text, only a style, that is, a genre," Genette suggests (91). He defines pastiche as pure entertainment, sprightly imitation devoid of satiric intent, the intertext's most playful mode. A puckish homage to the classics, Carter's imitation relies for its visibility on what the Russian Formalists termed "stylization" and Genette "saturation," an increased frequency of the traits—thematic, stylistic and otherwise—specific to a genre. This is where the fireworks of her language most perfectly answer the needs of fairy tale. An array of "might" and "as if" takes us into a world of porphyry and lapis lazuli, dulcimers and turquoises, sometimes too much so for the purist's queasy stomach. "Some of her puddings are excessively egged," Rushdie conceded (Carter xiv). But then what of that? Is not the art of *cuisine* her most spirited metaphor for the art of writing, as demonstrated with untiring zest in "The Kitchen Child"?[5] Is not pastiche, the old Italian *pasticcio*, a tasty potpourri of ingredients and flavors? Carter's awareness of etymology may well induce the reader to see in the text's partiality to food—"sandwiches of thick-cut roast-beef" (145), "cold soufflé, cheese" (147), "eggs Benedict and grilled veal" (148), incidentally eaten while browsing through a book—some form of metatextual comment, a literalization of etymology. The Beast's final utterance: "I think I might be able to manage a little breakfast today, Beauty, if you would eat something with me" (153) sounds like an invitation to share Carter's *pasticcio,* her feast of words.

Words very much her own, however. In the tension between imitation and difference, pastiche and intertextuality speak for imitation, while textual intrusion, anachronism and reversal speak for difference. The text's (sparse) comments on its own narrative procedures jolt the reader into awareness of its fictional status. Textual intrusion acknowledges within the story the existence of a privileged space "where all the laws of the world . . . need not necessarily apply" (145). This is as good as a definition of the contract between the reader and the text, and a reminder of the text's artificiality and precariousness. Repeated anachronisms work to the same effect—telephones, a twenty-four-hour rescue service (146), a taxi (150), a slow train (151). This never-never land shot through with contemporary references works out a schizophrenic vision paralyzing the reader's willingness to suspend disbelief and forget the text's "otherness."

Ironic reversals undercut the reader's expectations. Carter's Beauty is not the bashful girl of Beaumont's story. The selflessness of Beaumont's heroine is replaced by the thoughtlessness and narcissistic egotism of Beauty, oblivious of her promise. She flings herself into a mad whirl of pleasure with her father: "a resplendent hotel; the opera, theatres; a whole new wardrobe for his darling so she could step out on his arm to parties, to receptions, to restaurants, and life was as she had never known it" (150). Beaumont's demure girl, unaware of her own beauty, spends hours in Carter's tale looking at her reflection in the mirror (151). Carter actually substitutes modern stereotypes for old ones. Though Carter's Beauty is initially made to serve coffee to the Beast on their first evening together in the best tradition of the woman doubling as servant ("to her well-disguised dismay, she found her host, seated beside the fire with a tray of coffee at his elbow from which she *must* pour" 149; my emphasis), she soon takes over as the dominant partner to a shy, awkward, inarticulate male: "He forced himself to master his shyness, which was that of a wild creature, and so she contrived to master her own—to such effect that soon she was chattering away to him as if she had known him all her life" (149). Moving from woman's traditional inarticulateness ("small talk had never, at the best of times, been Beauty's forte" 149) to (frivolous) language, she is also seen to be the mistress of the sexual game. Her initial embarrassment betrays an awareness of sex which would have been foreign to Beaumont's heroine: "these strange companions were suddenly overcome with embarrassment to find themselves together, alone, in that room in the depths of the winter's night" (149). She is quite capable of decoding similar sexual awareness in the Beast. With a compassionate sense of superiority, she passes judgment on the inadequacy of this unusual Romeo who cannot "kiss by the book": "she felt his hot breath on her fingers, the stiff bristles of his muzzle grazing her skin, the rough lapping of his tongue and then, with a flood of compassion, understood: all he is doing is kissing my hands"(149). The final stage of their courtship is—most appropriately for a modern travesty—a bed scene, the symbolism of which Madame de Beaumont would most certainly have found objectionable: "She flung herself upon him, so that the iron bedstead groaned, and covered his poor paws with kisses. . . . When her lips touched the meat-hook claws, they drew back into their pads and she saw how he had always kept his fists clenched but now, painfully, tentatively, at last began to stretch his fingers" (153).

Carter thus plays a subtle game of differences even as she acknowledges her indebtedness to a specific genre. Following her source more closely than she does in "The Bloody Chamber," she retains its system of binary oppositions up to a certain point, as is manifest in the handling of space, moving from London to the Beast's mansion and back. Yet Beaumont's system of binary oppositions is anchored not only in narratology, but also in the gender policy of her age, something Carter cannot endorse. Carter explodes it with infectious glee. She follows Beaumont the better to entrap her. The more rigid the stronghold, the greater the pleasure to blow it up.

After ascertaining the parallel existence of two worlds, Carter derails the coding and the decoding, and throws the text back into undecidability, into a space in-between, into a world of *neither/nor*. Her strategy is one of deconstruction. The two distinct worlds of Beauty and the Beast are gradually contaminated by each other, as are the protagonists themselves up until the final metamorphosis. Undecidability is emblematically put forward as programmatic in the opening paragraph where Carter moves from the symbolic boundaries between inside and outside, "here" and "there," "hedgerow" and "kitchen window," to an unmarked snowy expanse, a road that is no longer one, "white and unmarked," present and absent, between presence and absence, undecidable, a trace. The text's incipit, like its two-line excipit, brackets the text as a *parergon*, a frame.[6] Its very position, neither within nor without the narrative, both intrinsic and extrinsic, makes the text's opening yet another undecidable, blurring the limits of the text as aesthetic object: "*Outside* her kitchen window, the hedgerow glistened as if the snow possessed a light of its own. . . . This lovely girl, whose skin possesses that same, inner light so you would have thought she, too, was made all of snow, pauses in her chores in the mean kitchen to look out at the country road. Nothing has passed that way all day; the road is white and unmarked as a spilled bolt of bridal satin" (144; my emphasis). From here the text's symbolic thresholds (the mansion's wrought-iron gate, its mahogany front door, etc.) no longer usher the reader into a radically different world, but into one which is neither the same nor different. They are not so much thresholds as distorting mirrors. Spaces begin to overlap.

The required timelessness of the Beast's world is shot through with references to a "Palladian house" (144), a Queen Anne dining room (147), "a garage that advertised a twenty-four-hour rescue service" (146), anachronisms belonging to travesty, one of the burlesque modes of hypertextuality.[7] But conversely, timelessness steals its way into Beauty's world of lawyers and florists and evenings out at the opera. She forgets her promise to the Beast because her own world is more timeless than his: "since the flowers in the shops were the same all the year round, nothing in the window could tell her that winter had almost gone" (151). Carter makes a similar point with her use of the anthropomorphic motif. She plays it down in the Beast's world ("she saw, with an indescribable shock, he went on all fours," 149) but reactivates it metaphorically in Beauty's. Animality permeates the girl's human-ness. She is first a sacrificial "Miss Lamb" (148), a dish fit for a lion—a normal enough fate for the daughter of a man who first appears wrapped in a sheepskin coat. She then goes on a shopping spree for expensive *furs* (151), and Carter eventually turns her into a predatory sort of animal, a milder version of her leonine suitor: "Her face was acquiring, instead of beauty, a lacquer of the invincible prettiness that characterizes certain pampered, exquisite, expensive cats" (151). The change she undergoes here as she symbolically moves to sexual awareness is not seen in human but animal terms. She does not move from girl to adolescent but from "Miss Lamb" to "pampered cat." This transformation, though merely metaphorical, deconstructs her role as the instrument of the Beast's final metamorphosis into a man. It adumbrates the female narrator's change into a Tiger in the final line of "The Tiger's Bride." "Courtship" ends on the ambiguous image of a man "with a distant, heroic resemblance to the handsomest of all the beasts." The equivocal name of Mr and Mrs Lyon, half human, half animal, epitomizes their ambiguous nature. This final instance of undecidability takes us a long way from Beaumont's fable of virtue recompensed and humanity restored.[8] The spaniel partakes of both worlds too, as emphasized by the narrative voice: "if she had not been a dog, she would have been in tears" (151). The spaniel wears no collar, but a diamond necklace (145). A creature in-between (and female), she is the story's go-between, the embodiment of the "betweenness" that is so much part of this text.

Carter playfully goes all the way from the kind of clear-cut oppositions encapsulated in Beauty's initial *either/or* view—"a lion is a lion and a man is a man and, though lions are more beautiful by far than we are, yet they belong to a different order of beauty" (147)—to the kind of shady categories where a creature is neither a man nor a lion, both man and lion. The very genre of "Courtship" becomes undecidable. Its style and plot belong to the *Märchen,* but the magic motifs of the original—the fairy tale signature—have gone, most notably the fairy's curse. The Beast's plight is never ascribed to any magic charm to be dispelled by the virtuous love of a beautiful princess. The final metamorphosis is "psychologized" as a result.[9] It takes place in Beauty's eye much rather than in the Beast's body, as if scales fell from her eyes and her initial judgment had been the result of some form of myopia or hermeneutic confusion, a mere problem of interpretation: "How was it that she had never noticed before that his agate eyes were equipped with lids, like those of a man? Was it because she had only looked at her own face, reflected there?" (152). "Psychologization" becomes itself one of the text's undecidables and opens it up. The narrative is destabilized, and standard critical procedures break down along with the reader's assumption that s/he can master whatever is inside it. Carter imitates Beaumont the way Derrida imitates Joyce in "Ulysses Gramophone," to keep the narrative at play.

Märchen, psychoanalyst Bruno Bettelheim demonstrated in *The Uses of Enchantment,* convey overt and covert meanings. They overtly advocate moral conduct as advantageous both to the individual and to the social structure; they also covertly convey—on account of their inclusion in the larger category of myths—symbolic meanings, all operating along lines later explored and mapped out by psychoanalysis. The sort of psychologization favored by modern hypertexts, which internalizes processes so far described as external to the psyche (curse, potion or spell), similarly foregrounds analytic disclosure. Repetition has a similar impact.

Unlike poetry or the novel, but like myth or drama, *Märchen* depend on telling and re-telling, on the endless and preferably exact repetition of the same story. Familiarity, not novelty, is what matters, what *signifies.* Repetition is central to psychoanalysis as well. It is a basic phenomenon of the psyche, the manifestation of the unconscious whether in the form of the return of the repressed, the repetition compulsion, or simply transference.[10] The analytic situation tracks down the compulsion to repeat, inducing the repressed to return and be re-lived, re-presented, re-enacted (and eventually ab-reacted) in transference. Both symptom and cure are dependent on repetition. Dramatic representation is one such form of transference, and the stage a privileged place of catharsis, be it in Aristotle's or psychoanalyst André Green's sense of the word.[11] The performing arts are, Freud suggests cryptically in the final lines of *Beyond the Pleasure Principle,* the adult form of the *fort-da* game he had observed in his nephew and interpreted as an attempt to master through repetition an unpleasant situation.[12] The child's untiring (and possibly tiresome) desire to hear the same old story over and over again is part of the same process: "Soon he will indicate that a certain story has become important to him by his immediate response to it, or by his asking to be told the story over and over again. . . . Finally there will come the time when the child has gained all he can from the preferred story or the problems which made him respond to it have been replaced by others which find better expression in some other tale" (Bettelheim 18). As repetition betokens the presence of drives, it is only natural that drives should find a metaphoric expression in a genre ruled by repetition. That Carter's text is the product of re-writing and pastiche—that is again, repetition—results in a significant *mise en abyme,* particularly fitted to the mechanisms at work in the tale.

Bettelheim sees in Beaumont's "Beauty and the Beast" a harmonious passage from a previously solved oedipal attachment to mature love. In terms of Bettelheim's metaphors, the tale starts at the stage when the child has renounced sexual desire for its parent but has not yet moved to mature sexual attachment. Non-sexual attachment to the father is symbolized by the *white* rose Beauty requests from him. Yet this attachment still rules the child's life, for whom the parent remains the only love object. Beauty is willing to sacrifice herself for her father and would much rather face death for herself than let him die:

> Il ne périra point. Puisque le monstre veut bien accepter une de ses filles, je veux me livrer à toute sa furie et je me trouve fort heureuse puisqu'en mourant j'aurai la joie de sauver mon père et de lui prouver ma tendresse. (Leprince de Beaumont 21)

> (He shall not die. Since this monster is willing to accept one of his daughters in his stead, I will deliver myself unto his fearful hands and hold myself fortunate thus by my death to save my father's life and attest the love I bear him.) [my translation]

Sex at this stage is still envisaged by the child as repulsive and bestial, as a result of the repression of incestuous desires. Love has yet to be transferred from the parent to a new love object from whom all (including sexual) gratifications will from then on be derived. This is shown to be achieved in the tale when the Beast, not the father any more, holds in his hands the family's fortunes—he can take care of the child. When Beauty is magically transported back to her father's home, in an attempted regression into childhood, she finds herself provided with rich clothes. But they are a gift from her suitor, not her father who has now given up his role as sole provider for the child:

> La Belle, après les premiers transports, pensa qu'elle n'avait point d'habits pour se lever; mais la servante lui dit qu'elle venait de trouver dans la chambre voisine un grand coffre plein de robes d'or, garnies de diamants. Belle remercia la bonne Bête de ses attentions. Elle prit la moins riche de ces robes et dit à la servante de ranger les autres dont elle voulait faire présent à ses soeurs. Mais à peine eut-elle prononcé ces paroles que le coffre disparut. Son père lui dit que la Bête voulait qu'elle gardât tout pour elle, et aussitôt les robes et le coffre revinrent à la même place. (Leprince de Beaumont 35)

> (After warmly greeting her father it occurred to Beauty that she had no proper clothes to wear, but her maid told her that she had just found in the next room a large chest with intertissued robes of gold

and diamonds. Beauty was grateful to the Beast for his bounties. She chose the least expensive from amongst these robes and requested the maidservant to store away the others which she intended to give unto her sisters. But no sooner had she uttered these words than the chest vanished into thin air. Her father told her that it was the Beast's intention that she should keep them for herself, whereupon chest and robes reappeared.) [my translation]

Beauty's future is thus shown to lie with the Beast. When she acknowledges this and returns to him, accepting him as a desirable love object, sexuality ceases to appear as a source of anguish, and the monstrous Beast turns into a most eligible Prince Charming.

This is Bettelheim's account of Madame de Beaumont's tale. Not Carter's. Her careful deconstruction of form and genre affects meaning as well. As I have discussed, she pulled down the binary system structuring Beaumont's tale. This same binary system also structured that version along the gender lines of the patriarchal system in which Beaumont lived and wrote. Carter's *écriture* now plays havoc with it.

Jeanne-Marie Leprince de Beaumont published books by the dozen and lived by her pen, out of necessity more than choice. This alone does not make a woman a proto-feminist and a pioneer of *écriture féminine* in eighteenth-century France. She wrote edifying books with a moral purpose. A governess and private tutor, she was the product of her time and an instrument in the perpetuation of its values. "Beauty and the Beast" features a bourgeois family, rich, patriarchal and motherless. The whole life of the merchant's three daughters revolves around marriage, a woman's sole way to rise in class-status. The open ambition of the two "evil" daughters in the family is to marry up into the nobility. Nothing barring a duchy will do. Beauty has "greatness thrust upon her" by the sheer merit of her virtue and charity, without the taint of personal ambition. She achieves her advancement, social and matrimonial, by proving submissive, passive, self-effacing, self-sacrificing. She is a virtuous daughter with a natural instinct for domesticity and has all the qualities pertaining to a mother. In other words, she is an ideal woman, never autonomous, always dependent on a man (husband or father) for her welfare and her happiness. She depends on him for her very existence as well perhaps, as is implicitly suggested by the absence of a mother who appears tastefully to have died in childbirth, leaving the road clear for patriarchal structures to develop unimpeded. She is literally made into a self-less woman. The text is informed by the binary logic of patriarchal thinking—ambition/submissiveness, father/daughter, wife/husband, good/evil, rich/poor, active/passive—all subsumed under the masculine/feminine opposition and the hierarchy implicit in it. In such fairy tales, submission to masculinity is the be-all and end-all of her being, a bed the beginning and end of her journey, as Hélène Cixous once wrote in an analysis of "Sleeping Beauty": "Woman, if you look for her, has a strong chance of always being found in one position: in bed. In bed and asleep—'laid (out).' She is always to be found on or in a bed: Sleeping Beauty is lifted from her bed by a man because, as we all know, women don't wake up by themselves: man has to intervene, you understand. She is lifted up by the man who will lay her in her next bed so that she may be confined to bed ever after, just as the fairy tales say" ("Castration" 43). "Beauty and the Beast" follows this pattern, carrying out the law of the Father, the law of the male. It flourishes at the point where analytic discourse and patriarchal gender-policy meet. "Courtship" originates at the point where they move apart.

"Courtship" does map out sexual awakening along the traditional lines of Bettelheim's psychology. Beauty has reached "the end of her adolescence" (151)—symbolically registered as the end of winter—and is hovering on the brink of a change she both longs for and shrinks from: "She sent him flowers, white roses in return for the ones he had given her, and when she left the florist, she experienced a sudden sense of perfect freedom, as if she had just escaped from an unknown danger, had been grazed by the possibility of some change but, finally, left intact. Yet, with this exhilaration, a desolating emptiness" (151). At the first mention of spring, the text names the urge and ushers in its messenger:

> The soft wind of spring breathed in from the nearby park through the open window; she did not know why it made her want to cry.
> There was a sudden *urgent,* scrabbling sound, as of claws, at her door. (151; my emphasis)

Still Carter will not go beyond this into supporting the gender policy exemplified in Beaumont's tale. The ironic blending of old and new stereotypes of woman—Beauty serving coffee, sitting at her embroidery, Beauty gardening, Beauty socializing glamorously—punctures the underlying ideology of Beaumont's version. So does the prosaic bourgeois domesticity of the final lines, displayed as a down-to-earth, anticlimactic equivalent of the tale's formulaic ending "and they lived happily ever after." Carter in "Courtship" uses "Beauty and the Beast" as a paradigm of the phallocentrism at the core of fairy tales. She playfully erodes the illusions of a value system which presents Man as the Alpha and Omega of Creation by suggesting that the Beast's metamorphosis into a man is less than a blessing, much rather a fall from grace: "And it was no longer a lion in her arms but a man, a man with an unkempt mane of hair, and how strange, a broken nose, such as the noses of retired boxers, that gave him a distant, heroic resemblance to the handsomest of all the beasts" (153). She gives the story's "apotheosis" a distinct whiff of nostalgia with its "drift of fallen petals" (153) that takes it headlong into autumn instead of eternity. The final advent of man as the symbol and source of power conspicuously spells the end of magic in the tale. Re-writing the text with a difference, the difference brought about by feminism, Carter marks the limits of the ideology underlying "Beauty and the Beast." She starts sounding a note of her own.

Carter's text shows the disappointing victory of binary thinking, of *either/or*, but celebrates the nostalgia of a form of all-inclusiveness. The Beast was infinitely superior to his disappointingly human avatar. Beauty's metamorphosis into a full-grown woman is seen in terms of more, not less, animality. Here Carter departs entirely from the original in which man is duly redeemed from animality. In "Courtship," she builds the premises of the system developed in "The Tiger's Bride," in many ways the twin essay of "Courtship," a cruel, unsettling twin. What "Courtship" merely adumbrates, "Bride" brings to the fore. There the female narrator's father is no good old man plagued by ill-luck, but a drunkard "in the last stages of debauchery" who plays—and loses—his daughter at cards. Carter reverses the child's willingness to sacrifice everything to the loved parent into the parent's own willingness to sacrifice all, child and wife, to his mad egotism and childish pleasure-seeking. Whereas Beauty accepted, even "with a pang of dread," that her visit to the Beast should be "the price of her father's good fortune" (148), the narrator of "The Tiger's Bride" recalls how her own mother was "bartered for her dowry to such a feckless sprig of the Russian nobility that she soon died of his gaming, his whoring, his agonized repentances" (155). In "Bride," the exchange of a white rose between father and daughter grows distressingly ironic, no longer a father's love token to his beloved child, but the daughter's reluctant (and hence meaningless) sign of her forgiveness: "My tear-beslobbered father wants a rose to show that I forgive him" (158). A similar reversal is worked in the animality motif: the Beast is no longer a man with the appearance of a lion but a tiger wearing the mask of a man. Can one say more clearly that identity is an artifact?

> He throws our aspirations to the godlike sadly awry, poor fellow; only from a distance would you think The Beast not much different from any other man, although he wears a mask with a man's face painted most beautifully on it. Oh, yes, a beautiful face; but one with too much formal symmetry of feature to be entirely human: one profile of his mask is the mirror image of the other, too perfect, uncanny. He wears a wig, too, false hair tied at the nape with a bow, a wig of the kind you see in old-fashioned portraits. (156)

Beauty's kiss turning the Lion back into a man is changed to the Tiger's tongue licking his bride into his likeness, in a striking reversal (or is it a continuation?) of the transformation scene in "Courtship": "And each stroke of his tongue ripped off skin after successive skin, all the skins of a life in the world, and left behind a nascent patina of shining hairs. My earrings turned back to water and trickled down my shoulders; I shrugged the drops off my beautiful fur" (169). It is "as though her whole body were being deflowered and so metamorphosing into a new instrument of desire, allowing her admission to a new ('animal' in the sense of *spiritual* as well as *tigerish*) world," Rushdie comments (Carter xii). Here is the point of Carter's deconstruction of fairy tales. Where Beaumont starts from a recognition of the potentially dangerous polymorphousness latent in each individual and attempts to fix and channel and castrate it according to the requirements of the social structure, Carter's stories move toward polymorphousness as a desirable, excitingly perverse end. Pleasure lies in the unfixing of identity, in the recognition of its fluidity. The fairy tale moves from the margins to the center, Carter from the center to the margins. The hopelessly closed ending of "Courtship" with its couple walking for eternity in an autumn garden that looks alarmingly like a sepia photograph from an old family album is superseded in "The Tiger's Bride" by the open-endedness of a metamorphosis in the making. It celebrates the perverse desirability of indeterminacy and liminality, the erotic but dangerous fascination of multiplicity. The Golden Herm of *Wise Children* is another such figure, his androgyny the equivalent of "humanimality" in *The Bloody Chamber.*

The fixed meaning guaranteed by the extra-systemic metaphysics of (male) Presence is replaced by a game of *différance*, of volatile and unstable identity— beast or beauty, tiger or bride, wolf or girl—in which the new identity/signifier can in a sense be said to give meaning to the previous one and so on "forever after."[13] The process of deferral thus established is reflected in the very process of Carter's re-writing of Beaumont's story and in making its modern avatar part of a larger series. Not one of the stories at play in *The Bloody Chamber* can be said to signify in itself, though it can be enjoyed on its own. The meaning of "Courtship" is constructed through a process of referring to other texts. Coming from, and pointing back and forward, to other stories, it is only one signifier in the process of referring to other, absent signifiers. There is a constant interplay, a game of *différance* in which the meaning of "Beauty and the Beast," which Madame de Beaumont had intended as fixed and self-constituted, is now made volatile, permanently deferred, as we move from tale to tale of changing forms and metamorphoses, from "The Courtship of Mr Lyon" to "The Tiger's Bride," "The Snow Child" and "Wolf-Alice."[14]

Carter's deconstruction of fairy tales is part of a larger feminist statement. With a few exceptions, instability is a character of, or is granted by, the feminine. Woman, in the form of Beauty or the Wolf-girl, is the liminal figure endowed with a power to take her partner across the boundaries of *either/or* into un-decidability and the destabilization of identity ("Wolf-Alice" and "Courtship").

Or she is merely enjoying for herself the crossing of the line, the state of *in-between*. The heroine of "The Tiger's Bride" moves almost naturally from one layer of identity to the next as she divests herself of her clothes. She moves from clothes to skin to fur, helped through the last stage of her metamorphosis by the Beast's tongue ripping off "skin after successive skin, all the skins of a life in the world" until there appears this "nascent patina of shining hairs" (169). The Beast, unlike his bride, never fuses human mask and tiger's fur, never masters this *neither/nor* condition so clearly spelt out in "Wolf-Alice": "Nothing about her is human except that she is *not* a wolf; it is as if the fur she thought she wore had melted into her skin and become part of it, although it does not exist" (221). Dressing-gown, mask and wig are not part of the Beast, but a costume, "the empty house of his appearance" (168). Man or Tiger, but never both, he is a prisoner of dualism, while Alice and the Tiger's bride are representatives of another, feminine, plural economy.

Carter's extreme statement of her sexual politics appears in "Peter and the Wolf," a story featuring the encounter of the masculine and the feminine as implied in the title. Peter, whose hypotextual model is the gun-toting little boy of Prokofiev's piece, discovers sexual difference in the form of a wolf-girl. Peter's fascination with her sex is seen in terms which recall Carter's description of the Tiger's bride's transformation, an endless receding into Otherness:

> He could not take his eyes off the sight of the crevice of her girl-child's sex, that was perfectly visible to him as she sat there square on the base of her spine. . . . It was neither dark nor light indoors yet the boy could see her intimacy clearly, as if by its own phosphorescence. It exercised an absolute fascination upon him.
>
> Her lips opened up as she howled so that she offered him, without her own intention or volition, a view of a set of Chinese boxes of whorled flesh that seemed to open one upon another into herself, drawing him into an inner, secret place in which destination perpetually receded before him, his first, devastating, vertiginous intimation of infinity.
>
> She howled.
>
> And went on howling until, from the mountain, first singly, then in a complex polyphony, answered at last voices in the same language. (287–88)

Inner and outer lips, sex and voice merge. But the infinity of her sex cannot be articulated, just howled. Or sung, as the Sphinx does: "She's an animal and she sings out. She sings out because women do . . . they do utter a little, but they don't speak" (Cixous, "Castration" 49). Language is the mark of the Symbolic and she is outside the Symbolic, embedded in the Imaginary. Her language is of a different nature, not the product of the Law, like Peter's, but "a complex polyphony," beyond the reductive articulateness of male language.[15]

Just as she is outside the Symbolic, she is outside the city ("the city is man, ruled by masculine law"; Cixous, "Castration" 49) or on the other side of the river, across the boundary from where Peter watches her. Peter is momentarily tempted "to cross over to the other side to join her in her marvellous and private grace, impelled by the access of an almost visionary ecstasy" (290). He is aware that this would have to be at the cost of language, as "language crumbled into dust under the weight of her speechlessness" (290).[16] On the verge of discovering the mystery of Otherness, he looks at her. Indeterminacy and inarticulateness descend upon him: "The boy began to tremble and shake. His skin prickled. He felt he had been made of snow and now might melt. He mumbled something, or sobbed" (290). There is a moment of recognition as he is about to cross into the realm of the feminine, something like the unbelievable discovery of a common nature: the wolf-girl is acknowledged as "his cousin" (290). Otherness is knowable and "there was nothing to be afraid of" (291). *"The 'Black Continent' is neither black nor inexplorable"* (Cixous, "The Laugh" 255). The text marks Peter's initiation into Otherness with a deluge of water, both baptismal and feminine: "He burst out crying. He had not cried since his grandmother's funeral. Tears rolled down his face and splashed on the grass. He blundered forward a few steps into the river with his arms held open, intending to cross over to the other side" (290). He is on the verge of attaining knowledge of the feminine—which subsequently supersedes the quest for male knowledge which was taking him to the seminary. He very nearly steps into a realm described by Cixous as essentially fluid: "We are ourselves sea, sand, coral, sea-weed, beaches, tides, swimmers, children, waves" (Cixous, "The Laugh" 260). But Carter takes this moment away from us: "His cousin took fright at the sudden movement, wrenched her teats away from the cubs and ran off" (290). The feminine eventually remains elusive. Peter dries himself and retreats into manhood again: "When the boy recovered himself, he dried his tears on his sleeves, took off his soaked boots and dried his feet and legs on the tail of his shirt" (291). Yet he has learned something: "What would he do at the seminary now?" (291).

And so he turns his back on the wolf-girl's mountain. He crosses back into the structured space of the Symbolic, towards the town, "into a different story." What story? A man's story? Or that of a boy who once encountered the mystery of Otherness? Carter will not say. It will remain undecidable.

Carter's appropriation of the icons of culture covers an eclectic range going from Beaumont to Perrault ("Puss-in-Boots"), to Collodi ("The Loves of Lady Purple"), to major luminaries such as Poe ("The Cabinet of Edgar

Allan Poe") and Shakespeare ("Overture and Incidental Music for *A Midsummer Night's Dream,*" *Wise Children*). This makes repetition and difference the prime movers of her writing practice. Central to hypertextuality, though from a purely technical perspective, these strategies take on a different magnitude with the rewriting of *Kinder-Märchen*. Tales, like psychoanalysis, the instrument of their decipherment, rely on repetition, but repetition that is more to do with meaning than technique. Carter, a great explorer of fantasy and fantasies, takes this as an opportunity to shed some light in obscure recesses, harping again on daughters, fathers and mothers, even if it requires bringing them back from the dead as she does in "Ashputtle *or* The Mother's Ghost." She is not one for comfortable truths and middle-of-the-road notions, however. She goes for the margins—some might say for the throat. She splits open closed texts and revels in what she finds there, blood, scars, perversion. She puts her dialectic of repetition and difference at the service of a revaluation of the marginal that is the feminine, sabotaging— as she would—patriarchal structures and phallogocentrism, indulging in the fantasy of an undecidable being, the wolf-girl, both animal and woman, Carter's most mysterious representative of feminine Otherness.

Notes

1. Carter, *Burning Your Boats* xii. All references are to this edition.
2. The notions of *hypo-* and *hypertext* are discussed in Genette's *Palimpsests* (7–17). A branch of transtextuality, hypertextuality denotes any kind of connection existing between text B (which he calls *hypertext*) and text A (which he calls *hypotext*) from which B is derived. What Genette calls *hypotext,* Louis Marin calls *architext.* Here I follow Genette's terminology throughout for consistency.
3. The term "palimpsestuous" was coined by Philippe Lejeune and taken up by Genette (450).
4. I here follow Genette's restricted definition of intertextuality as the co-presence of two or more texts in the explicit form of quotations or allusions, i.e., as micro-, not macro-structures. Riffaterre's larger definition of the concept is subsumed in Genette's "transtextuality" (Genette 8–9).
5. See Crunelle-Vanrigh.
6. Derrida calls *parerga* such parts of a work of art as are attached to it but not part of its intrinsic form, e.g., a picture frame, the prologue to a play, or, as in "Courtship," the incipit, clearly standing out from the rest of the text.
7. Genette 73–74.
8. I use the world fable here because Madame Leprince de Beaumont's and Madame d'Aulnoy's works are a cross between *Märchen* and moral fables. One eventually gets the feeling that the magic is subordinated to the moral discourse or even that the moral discourse masquerades as fairy tale. It is symptomatic that Madame d'Aulnoy's "tales" conclude on a rhymed epilogue in the style of La Fontaine's fables, extolling the Christian virtues of pity, charity and the love of one's neighbour which alone can earn the heroine the ultimate recompense of "living happily ever after."
9. Genette considers psychologization a side effect of modern transposition. In Wagner's adaptation of Gottfried's early poem, for example, the passion of Tristan and

Isolde is immediate and natural, not induced by Brangäne's love potion. Modern transpositions tend to substitute an inner, natural cause, for one that was external, and supernatural. Drives are the modern face of the ancient *fatum* as in O'Neill's trilogy (Genette 375).

10. Repetition is explored in particular in *The Uncanny* (1911), *Beyond the Pleasure Principle* (1927), and *Inhibition, Symptoms and Anxiety* (1926).

11. See Green 29–35. He refuses the classic Christian definition of catharsis as a purification of emotions, but sees it as a release, i.e., Freudian abreaction.

12. The child threw a wooden piece of reel out of sight over the side of his cot, then pulled it back again into sight. For Freud this game was the child's symbolic attempt to represent the regular experience of his mother's absence and return, along with his symbolic mastery of it.

13. For Derrida, *différance* is the opposite of logocentrism. Logocentrism, "the matrix of every idealism," posits the existence of fixed meanings (absolute knowledge, original truth, determinate signification) guaranteed by an extra-systemic Presence. Derrida sees this as a mere attempt to control the proliferating play of signifiers by making them subject to a transcendental signified. Such a centered structure results in a binary system of hierarchical values on the *either/or* mode (nature/culture; speech/writing; mind/body; true/false; present/absent). He questions the idea that the world is governed by decidable categories, and defeats the oppositional logic of Western philosophy. He emphasizes instead the notion of undecidability *(neither/nor, and/and)* cutting across the oppositional logic. *Différance* is one of these *neither/nor*. A coinage bringing together the two meanings of the French *différer,* difference and deferment (and incidentally an example of the *neither/nor* mode), it sees meaning as permanently deferred. In the absence of signifieds, the signifier refers only to other signifiers. Language is in a state of endless seeding *(dissemination),* as a result of the play of signifiers. "This, strictly speaking, amounts to destroying the concept of 'sign' and its entire logic," Derrida admitted (*Of Grammatology* 7). Another casualty is the male/female category, the foundation of patriarchal thinking, which is where Cixous takes over from Derrida.

14. A similar experience in *dissemination* is carried out in "Ashputtle," where Carter offers three versions of the same story.

15. The wolf-girl's "howling" is Carter's extremest form of "Other language," the crudeness of which is to do with the specific form given to the feminine in the story. Yet even this choice is a significant statement of how *womanspeak* is "the Voice, a song before the Law, before the breath was split by the Symbolic, reappropriated into language under the authority that separates" (Cixous, *La Jeune Née* 172; trans. Moi 114).

16. The wolf-girl's speechlessness works the same effects as *womanspeak*: it "explodes all firmly established forms, figures, ideas, concepts" (Irigaray 76).

Works Cited

Bettelheim, Bruno. *The Uses of Enchantment: The Meaning and Importance of Fairy Tales.* 1976. Harmondsworth: Penguin, 1991.

Carter, Angela. *Burning Your Boats: Collected Short Stories.* Intro. Salman Rushdie. London: Vintage, 1996.

Cixous, Hélène. "Castration or Decapitation?" Trans. Annette Kuhn. *Signs* 7 (1981): 41–55. Trans. of "Le Sexe ou la tête?" *Les Cahiers du GRIF* 13 (1976): 5–15.

————. *La Jeune Née*. Paris: UGE 10/18, 1975.

————. "The Laugh of the Medusa." Trans. Keith and Paula Cohen. *New French Feminisms*. Ed. Elaine Marks and Isabelle Courtivron. Brighton: Harvester, 1981. 245–64. Trans. of "Le Rire de la Méduse." *L'Arc* 61 (1975): 39–54.

Crunelle Vanrigh, Anny. "'The Kitchen Child' ou les *Grilli* d'Angela Carter." *Lez Valenciennes* 20 (1996): 61–69.

Derrida, Jacques. *Of Grammatology*. Trans. G.C. Spivak. London: The Johns Hopkins UP, 1976. Trans. of *De la Grammatologie*. Paris: Minuit, 1967.

————. "Ulysses Gramophone: Hear Say Yes in Joyce." *Acts of Literature*. Ed. Derek Attridge. London: Routledge, 1992. 253–309. Trans. from *Ulysse gramophone: Deux mots pour Joyce*. Paris: Galilée, 1987.

————. *Writing and Difference*. Trans. Alan Bass. London: Routledge, 1978. Trans. of *L'Ecriture et la différence*. Paris: Seuil, 1967.

Freud, Sigmund. *The Standard Edition of the Complete Psychological Works*. 1953. Ed. and trans. James Strachey. 24 vols. London: Hogarth, 1940–68.

Genette, Gérard. *Palimpsestes*. Paris: Seuil, 1982.

Giraudoux, Jean. *Siegfried*. 1928. Paris: Grasset, 1958.

Green, André. *Un Oeil en trop: Le Complexe d'Oedipe dans la tragédie*. Paris: Minuit, 1969.

Irigaray, Luce. *Ce Sexe qui n'en est pas un*. Paris: Minuit, 1977. "This Sex Which Is Not One." Trans. Claudia Reeder. *New French Feminisms*. Ed. Elaine Marks and Isabelle Courtivron. Brighton: Harvester, 1981. 99–106.

Lejeune, Philippe. *Le Pacte autobiographique*. 1975. Paris: Seuil, 1996.

Leprince de Beaumont, Jeanne-Marie, and Marie-Catherine Le Jumel de Barneville, Comtesse d'Aulnoy. *La Belle et la bête et autres contes*. Paris: Hachette, 1979.

Moi, Toril. *Sexual/Textual Politics: Feminist Literary Theory*. 1985. London and New York: Routledge, 1988.

Elise Bruhl and Michael Gamer

Teaching Improprieties:
The Bloody Chamber
and the Reverent Classroom

We base our discussion of Angela Carter in a far more mundane, and in many ways more unyielding, environment than that of her fiction: the classroom. To begin: in August 1997, one of us taught *The Bloody Chamber and Other Stories* (1979) to a group of pre-freshmen at Claremont McKenna College. The session was part of a two-week introduction to college writing and reading in the humanities, an intensive course for "at risk" entering students, those less in need of remedial work than in need of practice in reading and writing across a number of disciplines. Half of the syllabus focused upon folktales, fairy tales, and rewrites of fairy tales because of the ways that these narratives invite fundamental questions across an array of disciplines. Class discussions ranged from issues concerning the relation of oral and print cultures, didactic and morally ambiguous literature, authorial intention and readerly effect to more basic questions about how we read and how stories teach us to organize and understand our surroundings. After discussing the processes by which Charles Perrault and the Brothers Grimm collected and revised their foundational collections of fairy tales, the students read no less than twenty distinct literary retellings (including those in *The Bloody Chamber*) of "Red Riding Hood," "Beauty and the Beast," and "Bluebeard" in order to establish the long-standing legitimacy of retelling and remaking tales. For us, *The Bloody Chamber* was an obvious choice for inclusion in the course, and so we took care to place Carter's tales in an environment in which they would appear as part of an

Marvels & Tales: Journal of Fairy-Tale Studies, Vol. 12, No. 1 (1998), pp. 133–45. Copyright © 1998 by Wayne State University Press, Detroit, MI 48201.

established tradition of creative retelling. The sessions, on the whole, went well and, at its conclusion, the course received positive response from students; this particular intensive program, both optional to invited students and free of charge, has never not received positive ratings. The specific responses to Carter's retellings of "Red Riding Hood" ("The Company of Wolves"), "Beauty and the Beast" ("The Tiger's Bride"), and "Bluebeard" ("The Bloody Chamber"), however, were interesting both for their extremity and their typicality. Carter's continuing ability to elicit strong and varied responses from students was again confirmed after a particularly productive classroom session and its aftermath. After the class had left the classroom, the instructor noticed that two students had left their books behind: one student had simply scribbled out Carter's photo on the back of the book; the other had drawn swastikas over the picture of Carter's face. Our assumption from the handwriting inside the books was that their owners were male, but later in the afternoon a young woman came in looking for both of the books. At present, neither of us knows whether these two responses came from young male or young female students.

Each of us has taught Carter for a variety of reasons and in a variety of contexts, from graduate courses to adult education seminars to introductory composition courses to a lawyers' informal reading group. During our years in the University of Michigan graduate program, *The Bloody Chamber* was one of the most often-taught texts not only by graduate students teaching composition, but also by full professors teaching the most difficult level of graduate seminar. Of works of fiction, only Maxine Hong Kingston's *The Woman Warrior* and Toni Morrison's *Beloved* appeared more often in course syllabi for English, American Culture, Comparative Literature, and English and Education. We have had students tell us that *The Bloody Chamber* is the most important book they have ever read, and have had students so incensed by it as to call for our resignations in their teaching evaluations; yet we found this particular event to be shocking and worth considering from a pedagogical perspective. We include it here as a telling instance of what an instructor might encounter if Carter is on the syllabus. We begin with this story, however, not because we wish to dissuade instructors from teaching Carter—particularly *The Bloody Chamber*—but because we do wish to warn instructors that they should expect a bumpy ride. Our goal in writing this essay, then, is to ask not only what it is about *The Bloody Chamber* that produces such varied and visceral responses, but also why this text already has become so central in so many different kinds of classrooms.

We share a few beliefs about Carter. First, we are both avowed fans of Carter's work: its richness and difficulty; its intimacy with literary theory, folktale, and sexual politics. We have taught Carter most often, then, as a way of getting students to think about the politics of revision, convention, translation, and appropriation. Second, we have found that in every setting in which we have taught her work, and particularly when we have taught *The Bloody Chamber,* Carter's texts have had a polarizing effect on students, often producing unmitigated praise and unabashed anger in the same classroom. We have discovered similar experiences among our colleagues, and we have found even the responses of long-standing friends to defy prediction.

In our experience, the majority of students who respond hostilely to *The Bloody Chamber* may tend to be male and aggressively anti-feminist, but neither gender nor political orientation constitutes a predictable marker of like or dislike. Perhaps the primary irony surrounding the reception of *The Bloody Chamber* is that it has generated the most controversy among feminist critics, who have attacked several stories within the collection as failed attempts to embody the "misguided" arguments of Carter's earlier *The Sadeian Woman and the Ideology of Pornography* (1979). Described by Andrea Dworkin as a "pseudofeminist," by Susanne Kappeler as an apologist fleeing to a "literary sanctuary" outside of political criticism, and by Amanda Sebestyen as the "high priestess of post-graduate porn," Carter centers her work on the very issues of desire, violence, and the body that have polarized feminists since Mary Astell and Mary Wollstonecraft.[1] In addressing this conflict, Robin Ann Sheets's article, "Pornography, Fairy Tales, and Feminism: Angela Carter's 'The Bloody Chamber,'" wryly begins by understating Carter's "place in the debates about pornography that have polarized Anglo-American feminists" as "problematic" (633). But if Carter's work has roused vocal detractors, it has attracted eloquent defenders as well. Referring to both *The Sadeian Woman* and *The Bloody Chamber,* Robin Ann Sheets has called attention to Carter's "intensely political criticism" of pornography and patriarchy even as Carter ventriloquizes expertly within both discourses; Harriet Kramer Linkin and Mary Kaiser have explored Carter's respective debts to romantic poetry and folktales; and Stephen Benson and Kari Lokke have highlighted the skill with which Carter appropriates and burlesques the genres within which she writes.

At the very least, the critical controversy that has surrounded *The Bloody Chamber* provides us with a way into understanding the problems surrounding it in the classroom. Certainly the primary hurdle that any instructor teaching Carter will have to address is one that is, frankly, *proprietary.* We use this word in both of its dominant meanings, those of ownership and of appropriateness; and both come to bear on the most-often-leveled hostile responses to Carter's tales. The crux of such reactions among students is that Carter has no business in appropriating the fairy tales of their childhood and turning them into something other—violent, ornate, and highly sexualized—than what they should be. While the concept of "owning" a particular set of folktales may seem oxymoronic to most readers with any level of theoretical expertise, the issue of ownership is the most important and in many ways the most difficult hurdle to overcome in the classroom. As our short review of the rifts in extant scholarship on *The Bloody Chamber* suggests, a similar concern over ownership has managed to work its way into critical discourses as well, since most of the conflicts over the book have focused upon the question of whether it is appropriately feminist. What we wish to suggest, however, is that this conflict—particularly if one places Carter within the larger traditions of the oral folktale and of literary revision—can be turned pedagogically into an advantage in a number of ways. First, classroom discussion of the tales as rewrites can provide students with an introduction to issues of audience and to the history of literary marketing by calling their attention to the various audiences who enjoy fairy tales and to the marketing strategies used in mass producing them. Second, one can apply the proprietary outrage felt by some students to Carter's reasons for writing *The Bloody Chamber* by focusing on issues of ownership and appropriateness within the tales themselves. These issues go beyond Carter's desire to "restore" the adult materials edited out by Perrault and the Brothers Grimm. They extend not only to Carter's tendency to focus upon heroines and upon the ownership of sexual agency, but also upon her fondness for placing old tales in new historical milieus, from the pre–World War I setting of "The Lady in the House of Love" to the mixture of Enlightenment pornography, nineteenth-century romantic music and opera, and twentieth-century transportation and business technology in "The Bloody Chamber." Our own pedagogical strategy, then, is based in an overall presentation of literary culture as already appropriative and politicized and as always subject to fairly violent change. In doing so, we do not seek to vilify the work that compilers of fairy tales have done so much as to remove the Edenic notion that these tales have somehow come to modern readers uncorrupted. Our aim is to shift student attention away from outrage over Carter's act of revision and toward asking questions about what is being revised and why.

Beyond this, however, we would like to argue that much of what makes *The Bloody Chamber* "problematic" for both student and critical audiences is the glee with which it mixes disciplines and refuses to draw recognizable battlelines. A cause of much disagreement among professional critics, for example, lies in Carter's interest in *The Sadeian Woman* in the possibility of a "moral pornography"; the representation of these same oxymoronic traits within individual characters in the tales is one of the aspects of *The Bloody Chamber* that bothers the bulk of undergraduates. And interestingly, it is not Carter's realism that they question (few college students are not acquainted on a daily level with conflicts of desire and morality) so much as the *need* to juxtapose such images at all. Teach "The Company of Wolves," for example, and even the students who applaud its sexual politics—its redefining of the terms of the imminent rape scene in "Red Riding Hood" by having its heroine turn the tables sexually on the were-wolf/woodsman by ripping his clothes off—will wonder aloud why she "had" to include the passages on picking lice out of his hair, the bestial denouement, or the entire business of the "savage marriage ceremony" (*The Bloody Chamber* 118). Or, they will understand the critique of sadomasochism in "The Bloody Chamber" but question the "necessity" of Carter's lush descriptions of the insinuating texture and feel of satin nightdresses or the smell of Bluebeard's leather articles of clothing, arguing that such passages show the heroine to be complicitous in, and undermined by, her own inappropriate and unhealthy desires (*The Bloody Chamber* 8, 12). Whether they agree with Carter's aims in rewriting specific tales or with the project of rewriting fairy tales in general, what students object to in *The Bloody Chamber* is a certain kind of complexity—an almost disruptive and violent urge in the storytelling itself—and it is the nature of this complexity that we want to investigate, and for which we ultimately wish to argue.

Within this questioning of "necessity," one finds a desire for consistency of a categorical, and therefore ultimately ideological, kind. Put another way, one of the sources of discomfort in reading Carter's fairy tales comes from her determination to keep readers uneasy by not allowing them the reassuring pleasures provided by the genre's conventions. This is not to say that she seeks to deny readerly pleasure; rather, her stories aim at precisely the opposite effect, but in doing so they call attention to the sources of pleasure in fairy tales and to the processes by which these narratives construct readerly fantasy. It is no accident that *The Bloody Chamber*'s most radical departures from its source stories come usually at the end of the stories, at the moment when fairy tales usually provide elaborate poetic justice and readerly satisfaction by resolving conflicts, eradicating evil, and rewarding good as they are defined within the narrative. This means that Carter tends to intervene most ornately at the moments at which her source fairy tales are most ideological and most conventional—and often most pleasurable to readers. Red Riding Hood's dialogue with the wolf, for example, with its building of suspense in the series of "What big [eyes, ears, arms, teeth] you have" statements followed by the wolf's final pounce, becomes in "The Company of Wolves" an even more drawn-out striptease in which the expected pounce from the wolf never comes. In the Preface to her edition of *The Fairy Tales of Charles Perrault,* Carter remembers her own experiences of being read "Red Riding Hood": "My own grandmother used to tell me the story of 'Red Riding Hood' in almost Perrault's very words, although she never spoke one single word of French in all her life. She liked, especially, to pounce on me, roaring, in personation of the wolf's pounce in Red Riding Hood [sic] at the end of the story, although she could not have known that Perrault himself suggests this acting out of the story to the narrator in a note in the margin of the manuscript" (*Fairy Tales of Charles Perrault* 13). When we combine Perrault's marginalia with the fairly lengthy moral he appends to "Red Riding Hood"—in which he warns little girls to beware not only of "real wolves with hairy pelts" but also of "wolves who seem perfectly charming . . . [yet who] are the most dangerous beasts of all" (*Fairy Tales of Charles Perrault* 28)—we get two endings to "Little Red" that work at cross purposes with one another. On the one hand, we receive fairly commonsensical advice to avoid men who are wolves; on the other, we receive the thrill of being "pounce[d] on" by a reader impersonating the wolf.

Carter's revision, then, merely makes explicit what is already implied in the Perrault and later versions of the tale that incorporate Red's being saved by a huntsman. In making the huntsman a werewolf, she takes the story's dyad of male virtue and vice and places them within the changeable body of a single character. In the story's climactic scene, which we quote here at length to provide a sense of the dynamic it constructs, rape and seduction fantasies operate side-by-side rather than at some more appropriate distance from one another:

> No trace at all of the old woman except for a tuft of white hair that had caught in the bark of an unburned log. When the girl saw that, she knew she was in danger of death.
>
> Where is my grandmother?
>
> There's nobody here but we two, my darling.
>
> Now a great howling rose up all around them, near, very near, as close as the garden, the howling of a multitude of wolves; she knew the worst wolves are hairy on the inside and she shivered, in spite of the scarlet shawl she pulled more closed round herself as if it could protect her although it was as red as the blood she must spill . . . the colour of poppies, the colour of sacrifices, the colour of her menses, and, since fear did her no good, she ceased to be afraid.
>
> What shall I do with my shawl?
>
> Throw it on the fire, dear one. You won't need it again. . . .
>
> What shall I do with my blouse?
>
> Into the fire with it, too, my pet.
>
> The thin muslin went flaring up the chimney like a magic bird and now off came her skirt, her woollen stockings, her shoes, and on to the fire they went, too, and were gone for good. The firelight shone through the edges of her skin; now she was clothed only in her untouched integument of flesh. This dazzling, naked she combed out her hair with her fingers; her hair looked white as the snow outside. Then went directly to the man with red eyes in whose unkempt mane the lice moved; she stood up on tiptoe and unbuttoned the collar of his shirt. . . .
>
> What big teeth you have!
>
> She saw how his jaw began to slaver and the room was full of the

clamour of the forest's Liebestod but the wise child never flinched, even when he answered:

All the better to eat you with.

The girl burst out laughing; she knew she was nobody's meat. She laughed at him full in the face, she ripped off his shirt for him and flung it into the fire, in the fiery wake of her own discarded clothing. (*Bloody Chamber* 117–18)

This scene, and the story, end with a celebration of the winter solstice and Carter's almost gleeful finish, "See! sweet and sound she sleeps in granny's bed, between the paws of the tender wolf" (*The Bloody Chamber* 118). How to read this final line and the passage it closes is more than just challenging for students, since to produce a clean and consistent reading requires that one ignore other parts of the same passage. It also requires a willingness to acknowledge the story's sexual humor—that "All the better to eat you with" can be read as threat, as metaphor for extreme desire, or as idealized come-on—and such openness is not always easy to come by in the classroom. Usually, most students immediately notice, as they do with the ending of the "The Bloody Chamber," that Carter has rewritten the ending so that the female heroine is not saved by a heroic man. But unlike "The Bloody Chamber," whose heroine is saved from a murdering ogre of a husband by a heroic mother, "The Company of Wolves" does not engage in the ritualistic execution of predatory masculine evil. And it is here that we begin to see the "necessity" of the story's more disgusting and horrific elements. Students begin to pick up on the story's unwillingness to engage in ideological cleansing, for example, because of the unattractive appearance of the werewolf-huntsman with whom Carter's Red Riding Hood ends the story in bed—a man who, earlier in the story, Carter introduces as "a very handsome . . . fine fellow" (*The Bloody Chamber* 114) but who now has changed into something that is all hair, eyes, lice, and saliva. Faced with the question of how any woman could not be disgusted by such a beast, others in the class will argue that Red has no choice: that, in absence of a real weapon, she must use her wits and her body to save her own skin. Then why does she not dispatch him at the story's very end, when he is asleep? And how could any woman *sleep* with such a man, let alone an intended rapist who has murdered her grandmother?

These questions, we find, at the very least urge students to a second look at this misleadingly short story. Part of Carter's project certainly is to show that sexual violence occurs in multiple incarnations and to multiple effects: that rapists can just as easily be handsome and charming fellows and that women also can engage in sexually aggressive behavior. Looking to other stories in the collection like "The Tiger's Bride," "The Erl-King," and even "The Snow Child," one sees a fairly consistent tendency in *The Bloody Chamber* to depict sexuality and its relation to power as something beyond "problematic"—as closer to something endlessly adaptable, amoral, elastic, and animal. And this might be what is most discomfiting and most potentially freeing for student readers to see in these stories—that in their insistence to expose the various misogynies and patriarchal assumptions of traditional fairy stories, and in their desire to show the various underlying power relations that govern sexual behavior and dealings, Carter's tales ultimately *reject* the notion that sex should exist comfortably within any ideological system, even one that insists on equality and civility. Sex is too much an object of obsession, madness, and appetite—too often aligned with beasts and beastliness, too often insisted upon by a body working at cross purposes with the mind—to be successfully "deprogrammed" out of the characters who people her stories. Put another way, if Carter presents her readers with glimpses of various sexual utopias in this collection, these utopias are not ones whose organizing principle is the eradication of sexuality's bond with power. Whether such an eradication is possible or desirable, moreover, is precisely the kind of discussion that will move a class out of dualistic "debate-style" discussions about correctness and into something more interesting and more challenging. As with her notion of the "moral pornographer," Carter not only treats "all sexual reality as political reality"; she also assumes that sexual realities with unexposed politics ultimately repress and limit human expression, until, like Beauty in "The Tiger's Bride," even an act as "natural" as going naked becomes painful to perform: "Then I took off my riding habit, left it where it lay on the floor. But, when I got down to my shift, my arms dropped to my sides. I was unaccustomed to nakedness. I was so unused to my own skin that to take off all my clothes involved a kind of flaying. I thought The Beast had wanted a little thing compared with what I was prepared to give him; but it is not natural for humankind to go naked, not since we hid our loins with fig leaves. He had demanded the abominable" (*The Bloody Chamber* 66). If one is to begin to gain a foothold with these texts in the classroom, one might begin with this metaphor of "stripping," since so much of Carter's agenda lies in subjecting various sexual ideologies to critique—even those of mainstream feminism.

We see one of Carter's primary methods of critique in her placing contrasting ideologies next to one another, the effects of which are to dramatize the kinds of conflicting urges that can take place within a single character and to provide multiple possibilities and choices for her characters and readers. The passage above from "The Company of Wolves," for example, presents at least three separate views of the same situation, an intentional fragmentation that holds together because of the intensity of the situation. The scene ranges from showing Red Riding Hood's awareness of her situation as life-threatening ("she knew she was in danger of death") to presenting that death as a symbolically inevitable sacrifice ("the scarlet shawl . . . red as the blood she must spill") to denying the legitimacy of that reading and her role as victim in it ("The girl burst out laughing; she knew she was nobody's meat"). In doing so, the scene embodies in just two pages strategies developed at greater length in the other stories. In "The Erl-King," for example, Carter enacts this splitting of ideologies and their inevitable clash through a subtle shift from first- to third-person narration. Given that the conflict of the story centers on the narrator's inability to free herself from a man who ultimately seeks to entrap her through seduction, the shift signals the narrator's movement from inertial stasis to action, from imagining the Erl-King's death to (possibly) performing it. "The Lady in the House of Love" and "The Bloody Chamber," similarly, stage conflicts between forces that sexually entrap and forces that sexually liberate; both dramatize the processes by which protagonists are convinced of the metaphysical rightness of their role as sacrificial victim to another's desire, and both dramatize the ritualistic destruction of that or any ideology that depends upon sexual or literal sacrifice. What "The Company of Wolves" does within its culminating scene, then, "The Bloody Chamber" does to largely the same effect through the separate viewpoints of its three female characters: the heroine at age seventeen, her heroic tiger-killing mother, and the now older heroine looking back on her seventeen-year-old self as she tells the story.

If we have argued that *The Bloody Chamber*'s presentation of multiple political viewpoints has caused much of the polarization among both professional critics and students, we'd like to place even greater importance on Carter's practice of moving among multiple viewpoints and modes of narration. We find drawing attention to this practice—Carter's determination to write across disciplines, viewpoints, ideological matrices, and historical periods—particularly useful in the classroom.

Part of Carter's project, in other words, goes beyond questioning traditional fairy stories to that of directing reader consciousness to the processes that govern narration and reading themselves. Among other things, *The Bloody Chamber* attempts to bring into view the relation between restrictive categories like gender (or any set of practices based in tradition and governed by ideas of appropriateness) and the kinds of pleasure inherent in reading highly conventional and repetitive narratives. One of the supreme pleasures of genre, after all, is the way that it constructs, threatens, and ultimately confirms reader expectations; few Gothic romances (or detective stories for that matter) would be bearable were we not assured of their ending. Genres, however, are hardly static. Even as we are reassured by a predictable and ordered universe, we know that the categories ordering that universe harden into something more intractable unless they are periodically broken up by new stories with new universes governed by new ways of seeing the world. Part of the task of Carter's "moral pornographer," for instance, is to make precisely this kind of critique by "penetrating to the heart of the contempt for women that distorts our culture," and to provide new visions "of absolute sexual license for all the genders" to take its place (*The Sadeian Woman* 18–20). Her analogous treatment of fairy tales in *The Bloody Chamber* anticipates in its assumptions critical studies like Lennard Davis's *Resisting Novels* (1987) by nearly a decade in associating the ritual retelling of specific tales with ideological coping mechanisms. In Davis's study, the pleasure that comes from reading fiction has an innately ideological effect, particularly when the fiction presents coherent characters under a developing, sustained, and unified narration, because it attaches pleasure to a way of seeing the world, and invites us to ignore the world's "fragmentation and isolation" (Davis 12). Carter's own viewpoint, if we are to judge from the narrative technique of several stories in *The Bloody Chamber,* is similar if less histrionic. Tales like "The Company of Wolves," for example, suppose different cultural functions for oral and printed fairy tales, and therefore seek to recreate orality through anecdotal, circular narration and through matter-of-fact representation of violence and witchcraft. In contrast, part of Bluebeard's power in "The Bloody Chamber" is his seeming omniscience. His ability to provide a unified and omniscient account of his young wife's actions and motivations constitutes the source of his power over her, and half of the reason that she so passively assumes the role of sacrificial victim lies in the persuasiveness of his narrative—that in predicting her actions his narrative gains the right to determine her ending. What this tale exposes, then, is the power of any morality or fairy tale to format—and therefore limit—our choices.

Much of the pedagogical use of Carter's more multi-perspective narration in a story like "The Company of Wolves," then, comes from its ability to make students aware of their own readerly habits and expectations. The story accomplishes this in part by disrupting (and thereby calling attention to)'the traditional pleasures that come with reading traditional fairy tales, and in part by providing other materials and pleasures not usually associated with them. Getting to that point of student awareness, however, is another story. Although literary critics may revel in the multifaceted nature of Carter's project,[2] we note that even a relatively well-trained, well-educated non-student audience will be reluctant to join in a process of reading that is also a process of self-questioning. We recently attended a law clerks' reading group in which *The Bloody Chamber* was discussed, and found responses similar to those of entering university students—this in spite of the fact that this group was comprised of lawyers from national law schools who had graduated in the top quarter of their class. A number of the readers responded to Carter's work in a hostile manner, noting that her stories were "not linear," "too difficult," and even "too rich." While expecting the kinds of proprietary feelings that students have toward hallowed texts, we had not expected that a group of people who do a form of close reading for a living would balk at the shifting perspectives and testimonies that characterize *The Bloody Chamber*. Such responses were all the more striking in an audience trained to interpret and apply precedential legal cases to discrete sets of facts, especially given that *The Bloody Chamber* could be described as a series of case studies on familiar themes. Some of this hostility may have resulted from the discussants' legal training; law students are taught not to "fight the hypothetical" but to work within a closed system of analytical thought through the Socratic method.[3] While lawyers may want to throw off such thinking when not on the job, they no doubt have trouble—as we all do—actually doing so; giving up "issue spotting" (the technique necessary to take law school exams) when reading a work of ambiguous, intricate fiction may be too much to ask. Conversely, the story in the collection that the group had found most successful was "Puss-in-Boots," which sets forth a linear narrative of psychologically traceable, cohesive (and masculine) character development and course of action. We mention this example not as an exercise in lawyer-bashing, tempting though that might be, but as a means of illustrating just how deep-seeded these assumptions about readerly pleasure are, and how effective *The Bloody Chamber* can be in raising these issues to the forefront of discussion.

Although much of this essay has focused on the disruption and discomfort that Carter can cause her readers, that discomfort need not be a negative phenomenon for instructors, particularly if they are willing to place Carter within a series of readings that establish the long-standing legitimacy of her revisionary practices. This kind of discomfort, we find, is in fact useful—especially useful for instructors who can tolerate intense emotions in their own classrooms, or who do not panic when faced with a classroom silence. Such silences, we believe, are infinitely more difficult for students to bear than instructors. And those moments when classrooms clam up are worth calling attention to openly. Such moments can become a means of reminding students that they have seen stories like this before, that Disney's *Beauty and the Beast* is an equally profound rewrite of the tale yet somehow gets classified as "entertainment" while Carter's less acceptable "Tiger's Bride" gets dismissed as "feminist." They become opportunities for instructors to ask students to jettison these and similar categories that stop conversation dead and to look again at how it is that these texts actually *work*. And in doing so, these moments of discomfort ultimately guide students into a more nuanced approach to how they write and think about literary texts in general.

Perhaps more importantly, the disruptive mix that Carter offers gives us a means to address some of the more frustrating tendencies in student writing. We have noticed that the bulk of our students appear to have had two forms of instruction: one uses literature as a means by which students may feel emboldened to feel good about themselves or to make general commentary about "society"; the other, a particularized *explication de texte* approach, defines close reading as a wholly New Critical endeavor. Students from the first school often resist any attempt to think outside of their feelings and have difficulty imagining viewpoints outside their own; students from the second approach are often reluctant to generalize beyond particular formal elements of the text and their relation to whether the text is "good" or "bad." With *The Bloody Chamber,* however, instructors can show fairly easily the ways in which "society" is not encompassed by an individual's reading. Similarly we can show students concretely that focusing on a single viewpoint set forth in one story simply is not enough, since so many of the stories in the collection have a variety of viewpoints. The fact that Carter has altered a form that students are certain they have fully encompassed as children is in and of itself a means of addressing the limitations of particular approaches to reading—that individual experiences do not suffice, and other bodies of information and approaches must be called into play to read Carter's work and to write about it.

Further, the same subversiveness that so unsettles students may also prove a means to demonstrate to them the centrality that appropriation plays in formulating critical arguments. This, in fact, may be the way in which *The Bloody Chamber* can most change student thinking about critical writing. Students unaccustomed to imagining their relation to source texts as any other than secondary—who assume that their only job is to explicate the text in the text's terms—will be faced with a body of writing that is both an appropriation *and* a critique, and that yet still exhibits considerable reverence and even "appreciation" for its source texts. We say this because we have found students to be surprisingly reverent so far as "literature" is concerned; rather than decry such feelings altogether, we would rather expand our students' notions of what con-stitutes reverence by offering a model that includes appropriation and critique. Students may often voice initial disapproval of *The Bloody Chamber* because they feel that Carter is doing violence to the texts of their childhood, yet at the same time voice confusion at how lovingly she reconstructs these traditional narratives. If Carter offers a means by which student reverence can be turned on its head, then we can, by the same process, show students that *explication de texte* is only a part of the critical process. And if explication becomes only part of what is required within any critical act, we may begin to cease receiving the kinds of canned literary analyses and performed appreciations that our students think we want. In other words, Carter's own technique of simultaneous appropriation and critique may help us to get our students to stop writing exclusively *about* the text—where they see their primary task as one of serving and explicating it—and instead to use their analyses of source texts as a means to making their own arguments. As such, Carter offers students an example of what a thoughtful revision and critique of received truth can look like, and thus within the classroom she provides students with an example of how to develop one's own process of critical argumentation. We find, therefore, that the benefits of teaching *The Bloody Chamber* far outweigh the burdens, particularly given our suspicion that the author herself would prefer a discomfited, thinking discussion to a reverential and ultimately boring one.

Notes

1. See Dworkin 84; Kappeler 134; and Amanda Sebestyen as qtd. in Lewallen 146. For a full treatment of Carter's place within feminist debates about pornography, see Robin Ann Sheets 633–57.
2. See, for example, Linkin: "As much about the act of storytelling as it is the subversive undoing of old stories and sexual politics, *The Bloody Chamber* ultimately recodes literary history to sanction the feminist writer who comes to embrace her own desire" (307). Or see Lokke: "*The Bloody Chamber* is a contemporary transformation of that quintessentially grotesque motif, the dance of death and the maiden, a modern feminist transformation in which for once the maiden is victorious over death itself. In fact, it is the interpenetration of death with such richly positive facets of life—wealth, beauty, youth, and sexuality—that gives the symbolism of this novella its grotesque and uncanny power" (9–10).
3. For a useful and readable discussion and critique of the Socratic method and some of the recent conflicts that have occurred in legal education, see Harrington 41–68.

Works Cited

Benson, Stephen. "Stories of Love and Death: Reading and Writing the Fairy Tale Romance." *Image and Power: Women in Fiction in the Twentieth Century.* Ed. Sarah Sceats and Gail Cunningham. London: Longman, 1996. 103–13.

Carter, Angela. *The Bloody Chamber and Other Stories.* London: Gollancz, 1979; Penguin, 1981.

———, ed. *The Fairy Tales of Charles Perrault.* London: Gollancz, 1977.

———. *The Sadeian Woman and the Ideology of Pornography.* New York: Pantheon, 1979.

Davis, Lennard. *Resisting Novels: Ideology and Fiction.* New York and London: Methuen, 1987.

Dworkin, Andrea. *Pornography: Men Possessing Women.* New York: Perigee, 1981.

Harrington, Mona. *Women Lawyers, Rewriting the Rules.* New York: Plume/Penguin, 1993.

Kaiser, Mary. "Fairy Tale as Sexual Allegory: Intertextuality in Angela Carter's *The Bloody Chamber.*" *The Review of Contemporary Fiction* 14.3 (Fall 1994): 30–36.

Kappeler, Susanne. *The Pornography of Representation.* Minneapolis: U of Minnesota P, 1986.

Lewallen, Avis. "Wayward Girls But Wicked Women? Female Sexuality in Angela Carter's *The Bloody Chamber.*" *Perspectives on Pornography: Sexuality in Film and Literature.* Ed. Gary Day and Clive Bloom. New York: St. Martin's, 1988. 144–57.

Linkin, Harriet Kramer. "Isn't It Romantic?: Angela Carter's Bloody Revision of the Romantic Aesthetic in 'The Erl-King.'" *Contemporary Literature* 35.2 (1994): 305–23.

Lokke, Kari E. "*Bluebeard* and *The Bloody Chamber:* The Grotesque of Self-Parody and Self-Assertion." *Frontiers* 10.1 (1988): 7–12.

Sheets, Robin Ann. "Pornography, Fairy Tales, and Feminism: Angela Carter's 'The Bloody Chamber.'" *Journal of the History of Sexuality* 1.4 (1991): 633–57.

"M Frog" by Corinna Sargood. Copyright © Corinna Sargood. Reproduced with permission.

JACK ZIPES

Crossing Boundaries with Wise Girls: Angela Carter's Fairy Tales for Children

Long before Angela Carter had conceived the tales for her remarkable collection *The Bloody Chamber and Other Stories* (1979), she had begun experimenting with the fairy-tale genre in two highly sophisticated picture books for children, *Miss Z, the Dark Young Lady* (1970) and *The Donkey Prince* (1970), both illustrated by Eros Keith. Neglected by critics and unknown to most readers, these two tales actually laid the groundwork for Carter's future work and reveal some of her basic concepts with regard to the revisionist fairy-tale tradition. All this makes Carter's stories worth reconsidering. But even more than shedding light on her development as an innovative fairy-tale writer, they also indicate how much she esteemed children, and how much the child in her gave expression to a mischievous humor that stamps the "postmodern" quality of her fairy tales.

Carter was a sly writer in the best sense of the word. Perhaps cunning might be an even more apt description, and she passed on this cunning quality to the heroines in her two fairy tales for children. Since these narratives are not well known, I want to briefly summarize their plots before analyzing how they prefigured her later fairy tales for adults.

In *Miss Z, the Dark Young Lady,* we are told that Miss Z lives in a Parrot Jungle on a farm with her father, who is greatly annoyed by the parrots because they make such a racket with their comic songs. He uses a catapult to chase them away, and the King Parrot decides to kill him but is killed instead. Miss Z,

Marvels & Tales: Journal of Fairy-Tale Studies, Vol. 12, No. 1 (1998), pp. 147–54. Copyright © 1998 by Wayne State University Press, Detroit, MI 48201.

who has been busy making a magic dress, is convinced that her father acted too rashly, and sure enough, once the parrots depart for an unknown land, everything goes haywire because of a magic spell the revengeful parrots have cast: "Miss Z returned to her sewing machine. But the needle refused to go in and out of the fabric, and she had to finish the magic dress by hand. And the well refused to give water; the cow refused to give milk; the plow refused to turn the soil; and the fire refused to light. Even the rocking chair refused to rock" (7–8).

Miss Z's father is remorseful and promises that he would laugh at the antics of the parrots if they returned. He would even give them marmalade. So, Miss Z goes to a wise woman, who informs her that the parrots have gone to the place where the green lions live, and they plan to return with the lions to force Miss Z and her father off their farm and back to Human Town. Since her father has become sick from eating poison fruit, Miss Z decides to go to the country of the green lions by herself to undermine the parrots' plan. She takes her magic dress and a paper bag full of cheese sandwiches. Along the way she meets a small hairless and toothless animal with a red moustache named Odd, a dragon named Sandworm, and a vain unicorn, who help her find the land of the green lions. Once there she discovers that the lions are irked by the parrots who mock them with songs about their cowardice. When Miss Z tells the Lion Prince that her father is very sorry for killing the Parrot King and that they love the Parrot Jungle because "the air is so sweet and the earth is so rich" (28), the parrots decide to return in a flying rainbow to the jungle and lift the magic spell off the farm. Miss Z follows them by foot, and when she arrives, she finds her father well and listening to the sweet music of the parrots with Odd sucking barley sugar at his feet. Odd promises to scare mice to death if Miss Z will only feed him cheese sandwiches to mumble and chumble. The narrative concludes with Miss Z agreeing to this good bargain and very glad to be home.

Carter's other fairy tale, *The Donkey Prince*, concerns a queen who was given a magic apple as a wedding present by her father. This powerful king told his daughter to keep the apple safe and she would never lose her beautiful looks or fall ill. When she comes across a donkey, who asks for the apple, she tells him that she cannot give away such a valuable gift, but she would be willing to give him as much fruit as he wants at her castle. He is saddened by this reply and explains to the queen why he is so distressed: "Madam, though you see us in the shapes of donkeys, my company and I are, in fact, Brown Men of the Hills. Your father transformed us into this shape by a cruel enchantment after my son accidentally transfixed him with an arrow while he was out hunting. If you had given your father's apple to me of your own free will, because of my need, we should have returned to our natural forms at the very first bite I took from it" (9).

The queen regrets her act and learns that the only way she can help the Brown Men turned donkeys is by adopting a foal named Bruno and raising it as her son. She agrees, and Bruno is raised as a prince. When he is full grown, the queen loses her magic apple and becomes gravely ill. It turns out that a Wild Man from the Savage Mountain had found it and taken it with him. Bruno bravely decides to go off by himself to recover the magic apple so that his mother will recover from her illness. Along the way he meets Daisy, a young working girl, who knows a trick or two, and it is this working girl who now becomes the major protagonist of the story. She guides the donkey to the Savage Mountain, where they encounter an enormous Wild Man named Hlajki, who befriends them and tells them that the magic apple is in the possession of Terror, the leader of the Wild Men, who would rather kill them than return the apple to Bruno. Thereupon the practical Daisy responds: "We shall have to acquire the apple by guile. . . . I shall think of a way. A working girl knows how to use her wits" (26). So, she takes Bruno's golden saddle cloth and decorates herself so that she looks like a beautiful princess. Then she enters the village of the Wild Men with Bruno and Hlajki and tells Terror that she is a magician. At first, Terror is not impressed by her magic tricks, and he tells her that he will give her anything if she manages to really astonish him. So Daisy charms him and the Wild People with music from a little wooden whistle. Terror gives her the magic apple, but then tries to kill her and her companions as they descend the mountain. They all go through fire and water to save each other and the apple, and they themselves are rescued by the King of the West, who started everything in the first place, and he allows them to see their future in a magic mirror. Bruno is changed back into a prince, and Daisy's resourcefulness is rewarded. She and Bruno marry, and the Brown Men, also transformed, return to their native hills where they take up market gardening instead of hunting. From then on they always treat donkeys, the beasts of burden, as their equals. Meanwhile, there is a revolution on the Savage Mountain, and Terror is chased away. "Hlajki became their new leader, and under his influence, they became gentler by degrees, built themselves houses of wood and thatch, and started eating with knives and forks, which they had never done before. But all this happened long ago, in another country, and nothing is the same now, of course" (40).

Carter wrote both these ironic fairy tales in 1969–70, just as the feminist movement was about to gather storm and just as she was about to embark for Japan and claim more autonomy for herself. It was almost as if the tales were prefiguring her own life. Certainly, they anticipate the fairy tales that she was going to write in *The Bloody Chamber* (1979) and to collect later in her two anthologies *The Virago Book of Fairy Tales* (1990) and *The Second Virago Book of Fairy Tales* (1992). Marina Warner has remarked that "Carter liked the solid common sense of folk tales, the straightforward aims of their protagonists, the simple moral distinctions, and the wily stratagems they suggest. They're tales of the underdog, about cunning and high spirits winning through in the end; they're practical, and they're not high flown" (xi). In *Miss Z* and *The Donkey Prince,* Carter not only captures the down-to-earth quality of the oral folktale tradition, she endows the tales with a sophisticated understanding of the world, a strategy for survival, that was in keeping with her radical and feminist viewpoint.

Miss Z has a kafkaesque quality to it, but unlike Kafka's fables and fairy tales, this narrative is optimistic. It begins: "A dark young lady named Miss Z lived in a Parrot Jungle" (5). Immediately, this simple statement strikes our attention because of the strange situation. Like the Kafka protagonists, Joseph K. and K., Miss Z lives in a bizarre world and is thrown into an absurd situation. Her world is turned upside down by her father's misdeed, and she must seek to set it right so that "paradise" can be restored. But who is Miss Z? Why is she called dark? What is the Parrot Jungle? Perhaps Carter chose Z because this young woman is the last of her kind. Since she can make magic dresses and is associated with darkness, she may be the last of the mysterious witches. She is never described. Her actions, however, lead us to see a resourceful, clever, and persistent young woman. No matter how strange the characters are that she meets on her journey to the green lions and no matter how threatening the situation, Miss Z remains calm. In fact, she seems to like incongruities, just as Carter is fond of inserting modern objects into archaic settings and mixing the quaint folk narrative style with contemporary jargon and references. There are no logical and causal connections in Carter's narrative, and each scene has its hilarious aspect. For instance, when Miss Z goes to the wise woman for some advice, Carter describes the scene as follows: "The wise woman sat in a shed made of cardboard boxes and played solitaire. She wore a little snake with red eyes around her wrist instead of a bracelet; this snake told her secrets, so she knew where the parrots had gone" (8–9).

Gone is the traditional topos of the old omniscient woman, who is generally cooking or inventing something in a hut in the woods. Nor does she seem particularly wise herself, but her advice is practical: Miss Z had better catch the green lions before they catch her. And the practicality of this advice is what Miss Z comes to represent as she goes off on a journey that has aspects of *Alice in Wonderland* and *The Wonderful Wizard of Oz.* Miss Z never questions the fantastic and weird characters that she meets. Like Alice and Dorothy, she strides forth to create her own home, for home can only be reached through struggle and realizing one's talents.

The traditional fairy-tale quest in which the protagonist is aided by magical gifts and friendly animals is embellished by the incongruous language and situations. What is most significant in Carter's tale is that Miss Z keeps her wits about her and her integrity as she brings about a reconciliation between her father and the parrots. Her goal is *not* marriage, nor is there closure to the story. She simply wants to stay in the Parrot Jungle because the earth is rich and the air is so sweet. Implicit in such a statement is that Human Town cannot provide this kind of environment, and though the Parrot Jungle is not described as a perfect paradise, it is different from civilization. Difference is important to Carter, and Miss Z, whoever she is, takes a stand for difference, is different, and is intended to incite readers, young and old, to claim their difference.

In *The Donkey Prince,* Daisy, too, is representative of difference, and she, too, is a wily young woman, who takes charge of a quest and brings it to a successful end. When Bruno first meets her on the road, Carter describes the encounter as follows: "The child bit on a straw and stared, but not rudely, only out of curiosity. Bruno realized that he was no common sight, with his hairy ears and coat of cloth of gold, so he did not take offense. It was a girl child, but she was so dirty and her rags so nondescript that it was difficult, at first, to tell" (16). In this narrative Carter recalls the beast-bridegroom tradition of folktales. She may have read Apuleius's *The Golden Ass,* which is the forerunner to "Beauty and the Beast," or any other number of folktales in which men have been turned into pigs, hedgehogs, lions, or bears and must be saved by women. She is surely alluding to Perrault's "Donkey Skin," a tale which she later translated, one in which a young woman must disguise herself and appear besmirched and disheveled to escape the incestuous desires of her father. Daisy is also somewhat like Cinderella, albeit much more rebellious and independent. The folk- and fairy-tale motifs are ample in Carter's narrative, but it is her portrayal of the working girl Daisy that livens up this story and gives it a contemporary flavor. Daisy runs away from an old woman who exploits her. It is her common sense that continually saves the day for Bruno and Hlajki. Her goal is not to marry Bruno, but to assist him. It is Carter's emphasis on mutual respect, cooperation, and fortitude that transforms the traditional beast-bridegroom tale from one that focuses on marriage and the restitution of male power into a narrative that celebrates difference and harmonious co-existence of difference. Daisy the working girl, Bruno the donkey, and Hlajki the wild man depend on one another and seek to help one another, not because there will be some personal gain, but because Bruno's mother is dying. As in *Miss Z,* the protagonists want to cure a "sick" situation and restore harmony to a world out of joint. Here, too, Carter keeps the end open by suggesting that the "utopian" resolution happened long ago and in another country, and "nothing is the same now, of course" (40).

Cynical? No, that was not Carter's style. Provocative? Of course. Carter's fairy tales were always intended, from the very first, to compel readers to change their minds and feelings and to transform the very nature of the fairy tales themselves. Miss Z and Daisy become the models for some of her most memorable heroines in *The Bloody Chamber,* and their force of will (not unlike

Carter's herself) alters the narrative structure and outcomes of many a traditional story. The best example is "The Company of Wolves." Carter's initial description of the heroine is most striking and indicative:

> Children do not stay young for long in this savage country. There are no toys for them to play with so they work hard and grow wise but this one, so pretty and the youngest of her family, a little late-comer, had been indulged by her mother and the grandmother who'd knitted her the red shawl that, today, has the ominous if brilliant look of blood on snow. Her breasts have just begun to swell; her hair is like lint, so fair it hardly makes a shadow on her pale forehead; her cheeks are an emblematic scarlet and white and she has just started her woman's bleeding, the clock inside that will strike, henceforward, once a month. (147)

This wise young girl is about to take charge of her sexuality. She has her own knife and is afraid of nothing. She charts her own way through the woods without a compass, and in the end she tames the wolf. Carter's fairy tales are filled with women like this: fearless, erotic, cunning, hilarious, and with a gargantuan capacity for taking delight in all aspects of life. Even in the haunting rendition of the fable "Peter and the Wolf," Carter depicted a young girl as wild and savage, at home in the mountains with other wolves. The girl is not like the composite Jungian heroine of Clarissa Pinkola Estés's *Women Who Run with the Wolves* (1993). Carter never dabbled in ethereal archetypes, nor was she didactic in her feminism. Her heroines are not all strong and courageous. Many succumb to the wiles of men or to their own passions. But for the most part they do resemble the protagonist in "The Wise Little Girl" in her collection *The Virago Book of Fairy Tales*.

Marina Warner said that this tale was Carter's most favorite, and indeed, "its heroine is an essential Carter figure, never abashed, nothing daunted, sharp-eared as a vixen and possessed of a dry good sense" (xi). Certainly, if we recall Miss Z and Daisy, these are the heroines that Carter preferred and set in different plots to see how they might survive. It is thus in cultivating her narrative strategies that she appeals to the wisdom and humor of young readers in her two tales written specifically for children. Moreover, she demonstrates her respect for children by playing with the traditional plot of fairy tales and with language that calls for careful attention to detail. Critical of the way that fairy tales were dumbed down for children, Carter's writing exhorts young readers to free themselves of the traditional luggage of outdated fairy tales, the hackneyed motifs of passive princess and daring prince, and to see the world differently, to blend colors and characters in exciting original ways, much in the same way that she did for adult readers.

In this regard, *Miss Z* and *The Donkey Prince* can be considered "crossover" tales. In a recent special issue of *Children's Literature,* U.C. Knoepflmacher and Mitzi Meyers introduce the term "cross-writing," which is linked to what I mean by crossover: "We believe that a dialogic mix of older and younger voices occurs in texts too often read as univocal. Authors who write for children inevitably create a colloquy between past and present selves. Yet such conversations are neither unconscious nor necessarily riven by strife" (vii). Knoepflmacher and Meyers stress the manner in which certain narrators of children's literature bring about a cooperation and integration of conflicting voices that appeal to both children and adult readers, and certainly their point is well taken. Carter accomplishes this fusion in her two fairy tales for children. Yet, I would argue that she does even more with a postmodern technique of crossing over.

If we begin with the premise that children's literature has never really been written for children but primarily for the author herself or himself and then for adult editors with children as implicit readers, the notion of crossing over can be better grasped. The best writers of children's literature seek to bring out the child in themselves, to cross back and forth in memory and emotion and to regain what they imagine childhood was and is. Crossing boundaries of time and sound to achieve a mix of voice and style, writers do not set limits on who their audience will be. Nor do they designate audiences. Their writings cross over market categories that are socially constructed. Crossover tales such as Carter's expose false differentiation: they break down accepted definitions, norms, values, types, and forms to create an open space in which the child and adult reader can wander to reflect upon the representations of the author and to make sense of those representations in ways that will be new to the reader and unknown to the author.

In her book, *Postmodern Fairy Tales,* Cristina Bacchilega makes the following point related to my notion of Carter's "crossover tales": "In its multiple retellings, the fairy tale is that variable and 'in-between' image where folklore and literature, community and individual, consensus and enterprise, children and adults, Woman and women, face and reflect (on) each other. As I see it, the tale of magic's controlling metaphor is the *magic* mirror, because it conflates mimesis (reflection), refraction (varying desires), and framing (artifice)" (10). As Bacchilega suggests, reading Carter's tales is like holding up a mirror to our faces, but it is a magic mirror in which everything is cross-dressed. Of course, it is dangerous to generalize about Carter's tales, that is, to maintain that she continually used the same techniques and sought the same effects in all her fairy tales.

Miss Z and *The Donkey Prince* stand at the beginning of Carter's fairy-tale production. They do not have the density and complexity of her later tales. They do not have the stunning metaphors and lust for sexual imagery. But these tales are zestful because they initiate "crossing over" into new realms for her female protagonists, exploring dangerous territory, and returning home fully confident in their abilities. Carter combined the simple folk style, baroque elements of the literary fairy tale, and contemporary jargon to create unorthodox narratives that suggest the potential of women and men to change their destinies and to take full control of their lives. These tales ran counter to traditional expectations. These tales were harbingers of even more radical fairy tales to come from Carter's pen. Her last novel was fittingly titled *Wise Children* (1991), and her fascinatingly zany heroine Dora Chance is certainly related to Miss Z and Daisy. She is the wise girl grown up, not straight, but like Carter preferred, prodigiously crooked on the wrong side of the tracks and all the more admirable in her frank and cunning approach to life.

Works Cited

Bacchilega, Cristina. *Postmodern Fairy Tales: Gender and Narrative Strategies.* Philadelphia: U of Pennsylvania P, 1997.

Carter, Angela. *The Bloody Chamber and Other Stories.* London: Gollancz, 1979.

———. *The Donkey Prince.* Illus. Eros Keith. New York: Simon & Schuster, 1970.

———. *Miss Z, the Dark Young Lady.* Illus. Eros Keith. New York: Simon & Schuster, 1970.

———, ed. *The Second Virago Book of Fairy Tales.* Illus. Corinna Sargood. London: Virago, 1992. Rpt. as *Strange Things Sometimes Still Happen: Fairy Tales from Around the World.* Boston and London: Faber and Faber, 1993.

———, ed. *The Virago Book of Fairy Tales.* Illus. Corinna Sargood. London: Virago, 1990. Rpt. as *The Old Wives' Fairy Tale Book.* New York: Pantheon, 1990.

———. *Wise Children.* London: Chatto & Windus, 1991.

Knoepflmacher, U.C., and Mitzi Meyers. " 'Cross-Writing' and the Reconceptualizing of Children's Literary Studies." *Children's Literature* 25 (1997): vii–xvii.

Warner, Marina. Introduction. Carter, *Strange Things Sometimes Still Happen* ix–xvii.

Kai Mikkonen

The Hoffman(n) Effect and the Sleeping Prince: Fairy Tales in Angela Carter's The Infernal Desire Machines of Doctor Hoffman

Fairy tales play an important part as one of the interlocking circles of intertexts in Angela Carter's novel *The Infernal Desire Machines of Doctor Hoffman* (1972), while the novel also prompts the reader to pay *critical* attention to certain formal patterns and thematic aspects of the literary *Märchen*. The literary devices of polygenetic intertextuality and parody as well as the deployment of an unreliable narrator and the treatment of characters as figures of speech problematize the reading of the fairy tales evoked in this novel. The fairy-tale conventions most tested and resisted in *Infernal Desire Machines* include character construction, plot development, narrative perspective and the figure of the sleeping princess. References to E.T.A. Hoffmann's tales and to the rewriting of "The Sleeping Beauty" are especially important in this respect. Carter's treatment of the literary *Märchen* provokes questions about the representation and structural inscription of time, gender and desire, while it also thematizes the act of enunciation and renders ambiguous the narrative point of view of the tales as well as of the novel itself.

Drosselmeier and Characters as Figures of Speech

In Carter's *Infernal Desire Machines* (hereafter referred to as *IDM*), the nineteenth-century German writer E.T.A. Hoffmann is most obviously present in the name

Marvels & Tales: Journal of Fairy-Tale Studies, Vol. 12, No. 1 (1998), pp. 155–74. Copyright © 1998 by Wayne State University Press, Detroit, MI 48201.

of the character Dr. Hoffman—with only one letter, "n," dropped from his referent's name. As Peter Christensen proposes (64), Hoffman's name is most likely to evoke the dangerous, irrational, mad-scientist figures of E.T.A. Hoffmann's works. Dr. Hoffman's teutonic heritage (*IDM* 196), the fact that his great-grandfather arrived from Germany in the late nineteenth century (*IDM* 26), and that he built himself a Wagnerian castle (*IDM* 196) further emphasize the connection to the famous romantic writer and his literary characters and scenes.

Christensen argues that the most central E.T.A. Hoffmann intertext in *IDM* may be "The Nutcracker and the King of Mice," a tale which also includes an embedded story, "The Tale of the Hard Nut." Much of Christensen's analysis centers on the name Drosselmeier since this source of horror and wonder in E.T.A. Hoffmann's tale serves as a side character, another mad scientist type, in Carter's novel.[1] Christensen's reading of Drosselmeier in Hoffmann's tale and his need to be everywhere in various incarnations, and in control of every situation, shows that Drosselmeier is (1) the children's godfather, Christian Elias; (2) a mechanical figure, Nutcracker, in the toy castle Drosselmeier has made; (3) the courtier who appears in the embedded story as an inventor of ingenuous little machines; (4) the courtier's cousin Zacharias; and (5) Zacharias's son, also named Christian Elias, who turns into the Nutcracker (Christensen 66). For Christensen, the Drosselmeier character also bridges the author E.T.A. Hoffmann's and the character Doctor Hoffman's investigation of four themes: loss of freedom, the battle between the conscious and the unconscious, desire, and regression (66).

One can develop Christensen's reading by arguing that the "Nutcracker" story also generates a sense of continuity between its characters by creating a kind of a metonymic continuum from person to person. The girl Marie remarks on the peculiar likeness between Nutcracker and Drosselmeier (Hoffmann, *Best Tales* 137), and Godfather Drosselmeier moves once as if he were a puppet (148). This metonymic shifting among and combination of characters, typical to E.T.A. Hoffmann, can be found among Carter's mad scientists Dr. Drosselmeier, Dr. Hoffman, Mendoza, and the peep-show proprietor (and even their opponent the Minister through his final association with the Doctor)—and it culminates in the actual metamorphoses of Albertina, the loved one and the dream image of the protagonist Desiderio.

Yet Carter's treatment of characters as puppets, automata and interchangeable figures of speech in her novel adds another dimension to E.T.A. Hoffmann's interest in redefining the limits of a literary character. Carter's text lays bare the device of characterization by way of literalizing and realizing tropes. Albertina is a series of marvelous shapes, an image in Desiderio's mind (*IDM* 13); the Minister is not a man but a theorem; the women of the river people are described as benign automata; and the nine Moroccan acrobats negate physicality and look entirely artificial. While being captured by the centaurs, Desiderio feels a sudden, strange awe:

> I felt myself dwindle and diminish. Soon I was nothing but a misshapen doll clumsily balanced on two stunted pins, so ill-designed and badly functioning a puff of wind would knock me over, so graceless I walked as though with an audible grinding of rusty inner gears, so slow of foot our hosts could run me down in a flash for I might even be stupid enough to try to escape. And when I looked at Albertina, I saw that though she was still beautiful, she also had become a doll; a doll of wax, half melted at the lower part. (*IDM* 176)

Furthermore, the prostitutes in the House of Anonymity are circumscribed as rhetorical figures, reduced by the rigorous discipline of their vocation to the undifferentiated essence of the idea of the female (*IDM* 132–33). These women are fantastic creatures, part animals and part automata: "all, without exception, passed beyond or did not enter the realm of simple humanity. They were sinister, abominable, inverted mutations, part clockwork, part vegetable and part brute" (*IDM* 132). Here, the text openly shows the representation of women as figures of rhetoric, machines of male pleasure.[2]

Although Christensen misses the significant contexts of surrealism and the quest narrative in his reading of Carter's novel through its E.T.A. Hoffmann connection, he rightly claims that to link Carter with E.T.A. Hoffmann means more than acknowledging their mutual interest in puppets, images of seeing, and the grotesque. What Carter writes, argues Christensen, is not mere parody or pastiche but rather a critical inscription in a literary tradition (69). One might add, however, that the ambiguous sense of simultaneous admiration for the skill of automata and horror at their inhumanness, which one finds in E.T.A. Hoffmann's stories, is reiterated and elaborated in Carter's treatment of literary characters as tropes. The horror of the possibility of mistaking an automaton for a human being or the horror at the life-likeness of literary characters, although they are made of language and figures of speech, is explored deeply in *IDM*. Carter's characters are treated like artificial linguistic constructions, like tropes, which may be produced through the imagination (or in dreams and hallucinations) while they still, like any literary character, pose as human beings. Furthermore, the dramatized comparison between characters and figures of speech and the literalization of tropes in the characters' metamorphoses raise the question of a subject's construction. While problematizing characterization by mechanizing protagonists or by making them undergo various transformations (while they still claim to tell a true story) may be parodic of E.T.A. Hoffmann's inventions, in the sense of critically altering them, this strategy simultaneously emphasizes the narrative construction of history and the semiotic construction of the subject.

In addition to the self-reflexive questioning of the formation of literary characters, Carter's automata lead back to the problem of writing. To write means to trope, to make characters out of language, to give language a face and to portray the "inscrutable mechanics" of one's "interior" (Carter, *Fireworks* 75). What emerges strongly in Carter and E.T.A. Hoffmann is the notion of the artist as an alchemist, as a master of transmutations, someone who can imagine world and identity anew. This romantic notion is both portrayed as the artist's idealized self-image and criticized as self-delusion in Carter's novel and in many E.T.A. Hoffmann stories. But, furthermore, in Carter's metaphorization of literary characters and in her revision of fairy tales one finds a double allegiance to the creative *and* experimental qualities of literature; her novel employs irony to point out the mechanics of literary devices and the limitations inscribed in the linguistic construction of life-like characters. Along with telling his story, the narrator-writer Desiderio is uncannily disturbed by the mechanizing power of his own language, a power that can turn him into a "daguerreotype" or a "statue" and relocate him into a "coffin" (*IDM* 14, 221). As narrative models for Desiderio's story, fairy tales trap him into an uncanny form *and* transform him into something new.

The Hoffman(n) Effect

Equally important to understanding the function of E.T.A. Hoffmann's fairy tales in Carter's novel, besides the way they are used to question and complicate characterization, is the effect on reading created by the fusion of many of these tales into one.

Christensen cogently shows how it may be more profitable to read Carter's novel with and against Hoffmann's "The Nutcracker" story than, for instance, his tale "The Sand-Man." However, I would like to propose a different understanding of the E.T.A. Hoffmann "connection" in which intertextual reading would not just be a matter of indicating which Hoffmann tale is more central to the novel or which offers more points of reference for interpretation. What could replace Christensen's perception of a one-way "connection" is a more thorough and literal understanding of the "Hoffman(n) effect." In Carter's novel "the Hoffman effect" refers to the all-pervasive power of the campaign that Doctor Hoffman launches in order to dissolve people's sense of all reality (*IDM* 13, 28). But intertextually speaking, I would like to argue that a literally polygenetic connection is at work, with texts embedded within each other in a potentially endless and all-pervasive combination.

All in all, it is possible to find in the novel the multidirectionality and heterogeneity of intertextual allusions, a dense networking of associations which occurs in single textual units and which are often impossible to trace to any single source. Both kinds of polygenetic allusion occur in the novel:

allusions where the same textual segment accommodates references to two (or more) otherwise unrelated texts, as well as allusions which occur as a "subtext in a subtext"—that is, as embedded texts nestled within each other in a potentially endless series, which gives the impression of a literally polygenetic connection (Tammi 192, 205). This polygenetic fusion of intertexts also affects the possibilities of thematic reading.

One textual model for such combination is Jacques Offenbach's opera *Les contes d'Hoffmann* (1881), the three acts of which are based on three different E.T.A. Hoffmann tales ("The Sand-Man," "A New Year's Eve Adventure," and "Rath Krespel" or "Councillor Krespel"). Furthermore, over the course of its narrative, Offenbach's opera evokes other E.T.A. Hoffmann stories such as "Nutcracker" and "Little Zaches." In Offenbach's version of these tales, the character Hoffmann, a young poet, sings about his three lost loves (Olympia, Giulietta, Antonia) to his companions in a dark wine cellar in Nuremberg. All three women have died or broken down, and at the end Hoffmann rejects the last love of his life, the superficial and heartless Stella, as a phantom. In Carter's *IDM* one finds a similar fusion of various E.T.A. Hoffmann tales and, in addition, a fusion of Hoffmannian characters and plot patterns with other fairy tales as well as with other kinds of texts. Susan Suleiman has referred to the possibility of the plurality of E.T.A. Hoffmann tales "behind" Carter's novel:

> the Tales of E.T.A. Hoffmann provide one structural model for the over-
> all story—a powerful father with magical powers keeps his beautiful
> but potentially deadly daughter (who is not necessarily human—she
> can be a doll, all the more alluring and deadly) tantalizingly out of the
> reach of a desiring young man, a situation that eventually leads to the
> death of the daughter (as in the tale titled "Councillor Krespel"), or
> the young man (as in "The Sand-Man"). Carter's novel conforms to the
> first pattern, but adds a new twist: it is the young man himself who
> kills the daughter, as well as the father. (129–30)

Carter's novel doesn't just evoke one or two Hoffmann tales but many, and engaging in this multidirectional reading, which the text activates, challenges, to a certain extent, Christensen's thematic interpretation of the E.T.A. Hoffmann "connection."

Christensen claims that E.T.A. Hoffmann was not "an apolitical defender of a dreamworld but rather a politically aware writer with a strong sympathy for the Enlightenment." He also cites Jack Zipes for whom E.T.A. Hoffmann was "just as much against the misuse of the imagination as he was against its abuse" (64–65).[3] For Christensen, Carter's novel is essentially a critique of an unreflective romanticism that points out the dangers of celebrating fantasy, even though he also remarks that its ending echoes that of E.T.A. Hoffmann's story in its "depiction of an incomplete victory over regression" (67). Yet, if one is to read Hoffmann's tale "Little Zaches, Surnamed Zinnober" against Carter's novel, a story that Christensen mentions only in passing in relation to Zipes's analysis of it, the thematic possibilities of *IDM* may become much more ambiguous.

The predominant target of irony in "Little Zaches" is the utopian orderly society which creates delusional structures of its own and takes narrowmindedness, servility, vanity, egotism, and greed to be forms of true civilization. The society that welcomes the tyrant dwarf Zaches as its new leader is based on the principles of the Enlightenment. Prince Paphnutius and his valet Andres, who introduced "Enlightenment" into their nation, plan to: "cut down the forests, make the river passable for ships, raise potatoes, improve the village schools, plant locusts and poplars, have the young people sing their morning and evening hymns in duet, lay out highways, and give cowpox vaccinations" (Hoffmann, *Three Märchen* 13). To the new rulers "poetry . . . is harmful" (85). Such a war of the worlds has not gone unnoticed by Zipes, who argues that "what once had been a paradise for poets, elves, fairies, i.e., the imagination, under the rule of Prince Demetrius, has been transformed into a police state by his successor Prince Paphnutius, who decides to introduce the principles of the Enlightenment into his kingdom" (*Breaking the Magic Spell* 86). Paphnutius's successor is Prince Barsanuph, and Little Zaches becomes his minister with the magic help of one of the last fairies in the kingdom, Fay Rosabelvedere, who takes pity on him.

To read *IDM* with "Little Zaches" shows that E.T.A. Hoffmann's as well as Carter's irony is profoundly multifarious. The similarities between these two texts also indicate that Christensen's arguments against reading "The Sand-Man" as a key text to *IDM* do not necessarily mean that "The Nutcracker and the King of Mice" is the right key; actually, similar arguments could be employed to support the importance of "Little Zaches" as an intertext. It is quite true that Christian Elias Drosselmeier has more control than Coppelius, and that in "The Sand-Man" "there is no overt battle between the warring conscious and the unconscious; no land of surfeit is depicted, and the hero dies rather than survives with his desires" (Christensen 68–69). Furthermore, Christensen convincingly argues that Drosselmeier, more so than Coppelius, "combines the opposite figures of liberation and control in a way similar to Carter's Dr. Hoffman" (68–69). But, in the same breath, is there as great a scheme of deception in "The Nutcracker" as in "Little Zaches"? Is there as clear a division into different notions of good society and different societal "campaigns" as in the Zaches story? Is there such biting irony involving writing and poets in "The Nutcracker"? Or does "The Nutcracker" have magical images that come alive or apparitions of the loved one comparable to those that the young Balthasar has of Candida, the daughter of the famous professor of physics Mosch Terpin, in the Zaches story? The making of a cultivated, rulable world—Paphnutius's destruction of the poetic and "nocturnal chaos"—has its equivalent, in Carter's novel, in the Minister's counterrevolution and doctrine of rational logic. The Minister's means of counterattacking Hoffman are barricades, directions and determinations, signs, computers, nominalism, scholastic philosophy, atheism, sobriety, Reality Testing Laboratories and the building of a coherent societal structure.

Furthermore, like Carter's Doctor, Zaches deceives all the people around him with magic tricks, creating thus an illusory world that enables him to fulfill his thoroughly bourgeois dreams of good marriage and social position. And like Desiderio, only the protagonist Balthasar, the gifted poet who is untouched by the spell, is able to see through the tricks and magic. As with the seemingly polar opposites of the Doctor and the Minister, in "Little Zaches" the figure of the "mad scientist" is also divided into two. On the one hand, there's the professor, Mosch Terpin, who knows how to convert physical experiments into clever tricks and has thus "condensed the whole of nature into a neat little compendium so that he could conveniently manipulate it at will" (*Three Märchen* 21), but who basically is a vain wine lover. On the other hand, Doctor Prosper Alpanus is a magician whose skills, as Zipes puts it, are "directed to offset repression and develop creativity so that hypocrisy and treachery will be exposed" (*Breaking the Magic Spell* 88). Like Carter's peep show proprietor, Doctor Prosper Alpanus possesses copper plates of spirits, images that can come alive, and he also has a crystal mirror on which Balthasar is able, with Alpanus's help, to project the image of Candida. Furthermore, the name "Prosper" is again a possible reference within a reference evoking in its turn Shakespeare's *The Tempest* and Duke Prospero, who is mentioned elsewhere in Carter's novel in an ironic take on the Doctor (*IDM* 200).

But perhaps more importantly, the sense of distance between the old, writing Desiderio and the young, adventuring Desiderio echoes the ironic narrative voice in E.T.A Hoffmann's "Little Zaches." In the beginning of Carter's *IDM* where the autobiographical narrative frame is revealed to the reader, the power of writing to transform experience and readership is exemplified by the narrator's ambiguous notions of his own text as prostituting him, as turning him into a public statue, as "whoredom," and as a "daguerreotype" (14). Towards the end of the novel, comments on the narrative itself become more frequent as the old Desiderio keeps addressing the reader and drawing attention to his plot and its lack of traditional denouement: "If you feel a certain sense of anti-climax, how do you think that I felt?" (*IDM* 218). Throughout "Little Zaches," in turn, the narrator pokes fun at all the characters including the protagonist Balthasar. For the narrator, Balthasar is someone who is completely possessed by his own poetry and by the image of the beloved: "extravagant poets like

Balthasar—they want the young lady to get into a state of somnambulistic rapture over everything they utter . . . or even to go blind for a moment at the peak of the most feminine femininity" (*Three Märchen* 32). At the end of the tale, the narrator makes it explicit that he prefers an ironic reading of his text: "If you, beloved reader, have now and again really smiled inwardly at many a thing, then you were in *that* mood which the writer of these pages desired" (105–06). The end of "Little Zaches" is marked by disillusionment comparable to that found in "The Nutcracker" and in Carter's *IDM*: the tale ends with a great funeral celebration for Zinnober, which is also a celebration of his "deep understanding, the depth of soul, gentleness, the unflagging zeal for the commonweal" (103), although only a moment prior to the funeral he was revealed to be an impostor. Wrongdoing is officially forgotten, the social forces purposefully maintaining a fake but glorifying image of a public person, similar to the falsely heroic image of young Desiderio.

These and possibly many other parallels can be drawn between *IDM* and "Little Zaches." For example, at one point Desiderio even seems to experience a Zaches-like state: "I was a naked, stunted, deformed dwarf who one day might begin to forget what purpose such a thing as a name of my own served" (*IDM* 190). Zaches is a deformed dwarf who changes his name into Zinnober.[4] However, to show the "origin" of the many Hoffmannian or other fairy-tale themes, structures, metaphors, and characters employed in Carter's novel can only be heuristic at best. Intertexts within intertexts accumulate over the course of her narrative, and the combination and coexistence of various intertextual threads is ongoing. E.T.A. Hoffmann's tale "Councillor Krespel" or "Rath Krespel" might also be one of the stories played upon in *IDM*: Councillor Krespel is a man full of mad schemes and whims who wants to alter reality according to his needs. He is also thought to be tyrannizing his daughter Antonia. However, it is finally the young men's and the narrator's love for the girl that is deeply destructive: when they want her to sing, they endanger her life due to the malformation in her chest from which her voice derives its wonderful power. "The Golden (Flower) Pot" and many other E.T.A. Hoffmann tales repeat the same pattern: a woman incarnates a mystical concept of love for the protagonist who, in pursuit of her, discovers his own identity often represented by the ability to write poetry, but who then loses her in the end.

Furthermore, other fairy tales alluded to in Carter's *IDM* mesh with the E.T.A. Hoffmann tale pattern. For instance, the "fairy play" *The Magic Flute* also fuses with the "Hoffman(n) effect." Much as Desiderio is deceived as to the real character of the Doctor—he assumes that the Doctor is much more poetic, romantic, and bohemian than he is[5]—the hero Tamino in *The Magic Flute* first maintains a false notion of the magician Sarastro. Desiderio thinks that the Doctor is initiated into the mysteries of desire and imagination while he in fact leads a rather mundane life—mundane other than the fact that he entertains himself with a perverse interpretation of "The Sleeping Beauty" theme. Specifically, the Doctor keeps the embalmed body of his dead wife in his castle. In *The Magic Flute* Tamino is led to believe that Sarastro is evil and that he keeps Pamina, the daughter of the Queen of the Night, in his clutches. Eventually, however, Sarastro and his priests open Tamino's eyes to a new mystical ideal: he will be initiated into the mysteries of Osiris and Isis, and he then discovers how the Queen and her ladies have deceived him. There are other references to the Mozart play in *IDM*: the first disruptive coup of Doctor Hoffman takes place during a performance of *The Magic Flute* (*IDM* 16–17). The play is Desiderio's special favorite and, as he grows more and more uncomfortable with his love for Albertina and her ideal of love suicide, he ends up associating her with the Queen of the Night (*IDM* 194). Carter's novel, however, reverses this fairy play by refusing to produce a happy ending or any kind of initiation into the mysteries of wisdom for its protagonist.

Such references and allusions form interlocking circles. The more the reader is familiar with the materials that *IDM* is made of, the more he or she is bound to find connections between different intertextual fields or "effects" functioning together. What I wish to emphasize, then, is a model of reading as circularity and metamorphosis. My intertextual reading of this novel develops through various interlocking links that promote a two-way movement among the multiple, simultaneous levels of reference as well as between past and present. Carter's novel prompts a kind of time and process of reading that plays with the sense of "timelessness" in the romantic German fairy tale as well as with the circular time of repetition which governs the archaic and alternative societies that Desiderio visits. The thematic opposition between stability and change (or metamorphosis) is doubled by the transformative, parodical and often critical intertextuality in the novel, such that differences between the German romantic fairy tales and Carter's novel are as important as their many similarities. *IDM* goes against what Zipes sees as the usual outcome or end situation of a romantic fairy tale (*Breaking the Magic Spell* 91): in Carter's novel there is no new, at least no unambiguous realm arising from the needs of the protagonist which would level false distinctions and create a more egalitarian society.

How to Read The Sleeping Beauty?

The revision of the German fairy tale tradition in Carter's *IDM* comes perhaps even more in focus when we consider her rewriting of the tale of "The Sleeping Beauty." "The Sleeping Beauty" story offers the mysterious princess as fairy-tale model for Albertina's character as well as a model for Desiderio's quest and the motif of the maiden found in a magic castle (N711.2). Albertina's transformations include becoming a black swan, the Doctor's ambassador, a woman in a pornographic picture, the male servant Lafleur, a doll of wax, a soldier, and a hermaphrodite. Yet what makes her change into a "beautiful somnambulist" called Mary Anne, an especially important reference in relation to Carter's novel, is that it thematizes sleeping as seeing, or as artistic creation, and poses the question of voyeurism and gender vis-à-vis the narrator's and the reader's point of view.

As is well known, in the Grimms' version of "Briar-Rose or, The Sleeping Beauty" the princess, in her fifteenth year, pricks her finger on a spindle and falls into a deep sleep, taking the whole castle into a dream with her. Only after the predestined hundred years have passed is a king's son able to pierce through the hedge of thorns, which have acted like deadly claws to the other candidates before him, and awaken the girl with a kiss. In many gender studies of classic fairy tales, the character of Sleeping Beauty has been taken as an example of idealized female passivity. For instance, in her analysis of this *Märchen* as an intertext to Marguerite Duras's *The Rapture of Lol V. Stein,* Jennifer Waelti-Walters has argued that the sleeping princess is someone who is cut off from perception, experience and language, and "whose entire well-being, entire identity, depends on her relationship with a man whom she loves" (73). According to Waelti-Walters, "deprived of the ability to articulate the relation of themselves with others, [the sleeping princess and Lol V. Stein] thus remain divided: an undescribed (and therefore undefined) self and a body described from the outside by others" (73). In this reading, the Sleeping Beauty is a victim and a metaphor for an ultimate state of passivity; she depends on a man to rescue her, and her whole psycho-sexual identity is a mere reflection of his desires.

Some ironic scenes of *IDM* seem to play upon such a feminist reading. In Carter's subversive rendering of the tale, Desiderio meets the mayor's daughter Mary Anne, who lives in a large house "quite forsaken for the extensive garden which surrounded it" (*IDM* 51). He makes love to this "beautiful somnambulist" when she is sleeping, then goes to see pictures of sleeping beauties in peep show machines the following morning, and is finally charged with the murder of this fairy tale-like woman who in fact was another apparition of Albertina. Desiderio also pierces his thumb on the thorn of a rose offered to him by the same woman.[6] One can clearly detect an intertextual irony directed at the convention of the female muse and the ideal passive woman, an irony similar to E.T.A. Hoffmann's parody of "extravagant" poets like Balthasar who want their young ladies to fall into a state of "somnambulistic rapture." And one can also recall, as I mentioned above, the Doctor's morbid wish to keep his wife's embalmed body in his castle. The Doctor's love for a corpse is another instance of necrophilia that, when compared with Desiderio's sexual act with the sleeping woman, portrays the hero as someone not so different from his enemy.

However, Carter's thematization of sleeping and spinning as artistic creation as well as source of subversive imagery complicates such a gender-based reading. As I see it, Albertina, the source of Desiderio's narrative and the object of his quest, never falls into a state of rapture but always slips away from Desiderio in a metonymic continuum of different forms thus keeping the hero in a constant state of awe. Albertina is also the most efficient weapon in Doctor Hoffman's campaign to disrupt the reality principle by means of fantastic imagery; she is not just a metaphor for passivity but intimately related to the realm of dreams and imagination.

Karen E. Rowe's reading of the history of "The Sleeping Beauty" and of the motif of spinning a yarn complicates the gendered analysis even further. Rowe traces "the complex relationship among spinning, tale-telling, and courtship" in the fairy-tale tradition in order to explain "why women (les vieilles), as figures within fairy tales, as frame narrators of them, or as actual raconteurs, are often considered les sages femmes" (64). She also argues that the rural version of "The Sleeping Beauty," from the Gatine district in France, implies traditional expectations of women: "that they be expert spinsters, judged suitably marriageable by virtue of their skill" (64). Another skill expected of such women is that they are good tale-tellers. For that reason it is important to notice that one of the central figures in "Briar-Rose" is an old woman spinning her flax in the tower of the castle; it is on her spindle that the princess pricks herself, and the old woman is most likely a shape taken by the powerful fairy who was angered that she was not invited to celebrate the princess's birth. The old woman's role as the spinner (of tales) and the controller of the princess's destiny relates her to famous female frame narrators such as Scheherazade and Philomela. The analysis of gender in this tale, then, should not just concentrate on the princess but should also include this seemingly powerful female character.

In its use of "Briar-Rose, or The Sleeping Beauty," IDM seems to be hinting that the old spinster is just as important as the princess and the prince. Besides punishing the princess, the old woman of the tower introduces her into a new world and thus transmits to her the secret truths of culture, truths concerning sexuality and death. Spinning flax is a metaphor for narrating and for transmitting knowledge of sex, love and death. Since Desiderio is the wounded one, Carter's version of the tale also asks whether it is really the prince who is sleeping. The narrator of IDM is male, but what is noteworthy in this novel is a kind of (de)gendering of the narrative act and frame through the unsettling identity of the male narrator as a "knitter" (and a sleeper). In the introduction to his story, the old Desiderio takes on the traditional female role of knitting and telling fairy tales. "I must gather together all that confusion of experience and arrange it in order, just as it happened, beginning at the beginning," as Desiderio describes his writerly task, "I must unravel my life as if it were so much knitting and pick out from that tangle the single, original thread of my self, the self who was a young man who happened to become a hero and then grew old" (*IDM* 11). Writing here as the unraveling of so much knitting is a form of the writerly self's becoming. The desire to narrate—that is, to make life meaningful in and through transforming language—is analogous to the profound transformation of the self. The forging of desire and memory into a new form enables writing and historical understanding. But at the same time, the act of narration may be misleading and painful. It may turn one into "posterity's prostitute" (*IDM* 14)—and one might see this metaphor as defining the princess's helpless state as well. The danger in transforming one's life into a narrative is to restrict one's experience and memory or to create a false identity and, thus, to use old Desiderio's metaphors, the story of one's life may enclose one in a kind of coffin (or even, to follow the Doctor's example, it may lead to turning oneself into a kind of embalmed holy relic).

However, it is difficult to understand the question of artistic creation and the act of narration as dramatized in Carter's novel through the rendition of "The Sleeping Beauty" without paying heed to the polygenetic intertextual play in relation to which the tale is situated. Most obviously, the relationship between Carter's novel and the romantic fairy tale must be read through surrealist and modernist aesthetics as well as through the predecessors of surrealism like Alfred Jarry, Lautréamont, the Marquis de Sade, and Raymond Roussel. Carter's text appropriates the romantic fairy repertoire of E.T.A. Hoffmann, the Grimm brothers, and *The Magic Flute;* fuses it with Jarryesque devices (punning, pronounced forms of intertextuality, machine-like characters, the depiction of desire-machines), as well as Roussel's and Marcel Duchamp's fantastic machines; and situates it in contact with surrealist/modernist concerns with the unconscious and the female muse (Albertina). Concomitantly, however, Carter's narrative distances itself significantly from its modernist and romantic precursors. And the surrealist notion of automatic writing or the vision of the invisible, in which one submits oneself to changes, is also critically duplicated in the text by the Doctor's emphasis of vision, the peep show machines, and the rewriting of "The Sleeping Beauty."

Carter's novel engages the idea that sleeping or, more generally, the unconscious is both passivity (and violation) and active creation. From the surrealist point of view, it is significant that the peep show proprietor, who works for the Doctor and who is another practitioner of (pata)physics, is blind. For the surrealists, of course, blindness was another metaphor for vision and artistic creation. André Breton, among others, embraced the absolute value of vision among the sensory modes, vision understood not as the seeing of exterior things mimetically but as an inner seeing that would offer a greater access to the libidinal and the unconscious. As Rosalind E. Krauss puts it, to Breton, automatism may be writing, but unlike the rest of the written signs of Western cultures, automatic writing should not be representation; it is rather a kind of presence, the direct presence of the artist's inner self (96). The goal of automatic presentation that taps the unconscious is to make the "human machine" write, to release the associative powers of creation, and to allow it to produce images of hybridity, polymorphosis, formlessness, and metamorphosis. Such images are products of unconscious or "surrealist" activity in which reason's role must be limited to taking note of, and appreciating, the phenomenon. Automatic writing is a form of sleeping and, explains Breton, it is especially conducive to producing the most beautiful images and to liberating rarely experienced desires (63–64).[7]

Like a surrealist, Desiderio the writer sees the image of desire, his muse Albertina, in fantastic apparitions and dreams. Yet, when this vision takes place at the end of the narrative, he seems to be rather controlled by his desires than to be someone who could manipulate them at will in order to write a personal history. In contrast to "The Sleeping Beauty" plot, it is not the prince here who journeys to awaken the princess but the "unbidden" Albertina who has the power to interrupt the old Desiderio's frame of narration and to take him back to the world of dreams, memories and imagination. When seen through Carter's narrator's predicament, the surrealist "inner seeing" (as well as T.S. Eliot's unconscious "concentration" outlined in "Tradition and Individual Talent" or Marcel's methods of reminiscence in Proust's *A la recherche*) seems to be not only a form of representation but also one that is tainted by illicit and uncontrollable forms of desire. Surrealism, like the pattern of the quest romance deployed in the German fairy tale and modernist aesthetics, is seen through a polygenetic textual operation, and must also be read through movements of revision and parody.

By playing with relationships within texts, with references within references, Carter's *IDM* prompts a sense of textual continuum that extends through the surrealists to their precursors like Jarry, Roussel, Sigmund Freud, Lautréamont, de Sade, E.T.A. Hoffmann and literary fairy tales, romanticism, Greek mythology, symbolism, primitivism, and Stéphane Mallarmé (I am thinking of Mallarmé's aleatory operations in the poem "Un coup de dés") in a seemingly endless chain that provides the reader with a history and a critique of modernist avant-garde. This critique runs parallel to what one learns about the Doctor's program: the effort to liberate libidinal forces is thoroughly fused with power and the abuse of power (as in rape, pedophilia, necrophilia, incest). Besides, as for surrealism, the focus of the critique is the male language of muse worship: the mystification of *femme (femme-enfant, femme fatale)*, and the image of the passive and/or mutilated woman as the ultimate object of desire. The violated female bodies and body parts in the first series of peep show machines (*IDM* 44–46) recall, unsettlingly, Hans Bellmer's mutated female puppets, Andre

Kertesz's photographs of female bodies in mirrors in his *Deformations* (1933), and Raoul Ubac's series of photomontages entitled *The Battle of the Amazons* (1939).[8] The surrealists' convulsive female object of desire is parodied in Carter's novel in the shabby archive of the peep show.

Another figure both evoked and critiqued through "The Sleeping Beauty" episode, the Desnos epigraph and Dr. Hoffman's character as well as through his alter ego the peep-show proprietor, is Marcel Duchamp. Duchamp's fantastic machines, ready-made intertextuality, eroticism and mutated female characters as well as his experimentation with (rhetorical) hermaphroditism—that is, with treating gender as a figure of speech—and his critique of binary oppositions, all come close to the Doctor's philosophy and aesthetics in Carter's novel. The most obvious link between Carter's novel and Duchamp may be the imagery of the peep-show machines. The first time Desiderio visits the peep show he sees a picture of the legs of a woman, "raised and open as if ready to admit a lover, form[ing] a curvilinear triumphal arch" (*IDM* 44). This image approximates the self-ironic dramatization of voyeurism and the male gaze in *Étant donnés: 1. la chute d'eau. 2. le gaz d'éclairage* (1946–66) and its lifelike relief of a female torso. Susan Suleiman has actually proposed that Carter's peep-show as a whole may be an allusion to Duchamp's *Étant donnés*, which literally makes every viewer into a voyeur (137). Like a peep- show machine, *Étant donnés* is based on the act of looking through holes (in this case through keyholes in a door) at a scene: a nude woman's body with spread legs, a woman who seems to act mechanically lifelike in showing so much (*Et tant donné*), her head and thus her eyes hidden by the brick wall. In an ironic move, in *IDM*, one finds behind a real door a life-size nude who is a dummy, holding a real lamp. The lamp is indeed significant as it may stand for seeing and thus emphasize Albertina's role as an object of seeing as well as the surrealist preoccupation with the gaze and gazing. Albertina is a cliché image, an epitome of a romantic or a surrealist female muse who inspires the male artist to tap the unconscious forces and to create art.

In *IDM,* Duchamp's fantastic "machine" for looking is a source of imagination and wonder, and yet the kind of looking it requires is rendered ambiguous and even suspicious. With regard to this theme of looking and the overall thick texture of male avant-garde works embedded in Carter's novel, the ironic treatment of Desiderio and Dr. Hoffman locates these figures in the history of modernism while it dismantles the male gaze behind the image of the muse and the mutilated female body. The surrealist muse worship, in turn, relates back to the ideal loves of E.T.A. Hoffmann's main male characters and the idealized women in the German romantic fairy tale: Candida, Olympia, Giulietta, Antonia, Serpentina, Pamina, and others.

Another way to describe this simultaneous appropriation and revision of the allegorical quest narrative and its ideal female characters at work in

Carter's novel involves what Brian McHale calls the postmodernist or Manichean allegory, an allegory that is a parody of allegory. The Manichean allegory reflects on the conventions of an allegorical narrative thus literalizing modernist-style mythic archetypes; the fictional world of the Manichean allegorical narrative, claims McHale, is a tropological world, a world within a trope (141). The ontological structure of a parodic allegory is dual: on one level (or frame) the trope, on the other the literal. In Carter's fictional world, these two levels are constantly intertwined—the text evokes a mythical background but simultaneously flaunts its metaphoricity. The characters are portrayed as figures of speech that may replace each other. In relation to Alexander Pope's (*The Rape of the Lock*) and Desnos's ("Le fard des Argonautes") mock-epics or E.T.A. Hoffmann's self-irony, however, Carter's novel has a quite different tone and perspective, especially with respect to the construction of gender positions in the text. If in *The Rape of the Lock*, which is one of the books that Desiderio reads (*IDM* 29), Pope parodies the idealized woman of the epic quest narrative, he also parodies "female" desires as such by revealing coquetry, vanity, pretension and immoderate pride as the reigning passions, or "little unguarded follies," of the female sex. In contrast, Carter's irony addresses the interdependence of the male narrator and the female muse, the notion of the idealized woman both as construction of the male "heroic quest" perspective and as the force behind the narrative's unfolding.

Sally Robinson's reading of the novel offers a helpful appendix to McHale's views when she proposes that Carter's critique of desire as domination works not only by literalizing the oppositions of a quest narrative but also by literalizing— or by de-metaphorizing—the structures of male fantasy that underlie traditional, and not so traditional, quest narratives (107). Robinson argues that *IDM* refuses to guarantee a voyeuristic or narcissistic position for its readers—male and female—because its metafictional strategies (like the treatment of characters as figures of speech) continuously disrupt the "pleasure" such positions traditionally afford (106).[9] The pleasure of the text is thus reformulated through its foregrounding of the enunciative apparatus behind the novel's inscriptions of desire and through its showing of desire and domination as complicitous. Desiderio as well as the reader are deprived of their climax. For Robinson, *IDM* is primarily a contorted oedipal narrative which foregrounds the question of gender by placing man in the position of a questing, speaking subject, and woman in the position of object who is subject to male regulation.

Robinson's analysis goes awry, however, in that it overlooks the fact that Albertina is not the only one put into circulation according to the logic of male desire: Desiderio himself is subjected to sexual exploitation, both literally and figuratively. Robinson never mentions that Desiderio is raped (117). Desiderio is also nearly stabbed to death by a young girl (91–92). Furthermore, like

Albertina, the main protagonist is captured and held hostage by the alternative societies of the pirates, the amazons and the centaurs. Robinson also claims that Desiderio's desire constructs women such as the gun artist Mamie Buckskin, or the Amazons, as "phallic in order to alleviate his anxieties over his own masculinity, evoked by the absence of his father" (113). It would seem rather that the lesbian Mamie Buckskin—who takes a liking to Desiderio because she admires "passivity in a man" (*IDM* 109) and thus performs the role of the active prince—is not simply a construction of Desiderio's male desires, but another figure through whom the narrative casts the male hero in an ironic light. All in all, Robinson's argument misses the point that Desiderio is not just the "one who desires" but also the "one who is desired" and, therefore, himself subjected to domination. Moreover, on the level of narrative construction, the young Desiderio, the "hero" of the quest, is dependent on the old Desiderio's critical narrative perspective and irony as well as on the limits of his memory.

Nevertheless, despite its shortcomings, Robinson's reading of *IDM* sheds light on the gender perspective of the traditional first-person romantic fairy tale and of the quest narrative as these are examined by Carter's novel as well as on the role of the erotic intertext embedded in some of the surrealist interpretations of the female body mentioned above. Through Desiderio's adventures and in their ironic treatment, the text seems to exhibit the "maleness" of its protagonist. The text also asks its readers to partake in an ironic treatment of this gendered perspective and of the figurative constructions created through it. As Robinson proposes, the novel invites the reader to occupy a position not sanctioned by Desiderio's narrative itself (105).

Thus, Desiderio's erotic adventure can never be entirely separated from questions of power, violence, and death. During his journeys and visits to various alternative societies and social groups, Desiderio's behavior is revealed to be triggered by illicit desires that are often contaminated by his need to have power over others. Ricarda Schmidt has noticed that the first time Desiderio acts upon his desires in his waking life, he re-enacts the fairy tale of "The Sleeping Beauty." This re-enactment is not innocent but, instead, dismantles desire as sordid necrophilia (Schmidt 57). Desiderio makes love to the sleeping "beautiful somnambulist" and, on the following day, finds her dead and himself charged with murder. Here, besides casting the protagonist in an ironic light, the story of "The Sleeping Beauty" is connected with voyeurism and sadism. This becomes even more obvious in a series of pictures in the Doctor's peep-show machines where the peeping Desiderio sees a sleeping young girl's "most significant experience in lifelike colours," which turns out to be a killing embrace (*IDM* 58–60). It is told in the title of one image that this picture girl could be awakened by a kiss—but when a lover awakens her he loses all his flesh and becomes a skeleton. Another such fusion of desire and power occurs soon after when

Desiderio, now visiting the river people Indians, engages in a pedophilic affair with a little girl who is planning to kill him for a cannibalistic ritual.

One may conclude then that in Carter's *IDM* desire takes both productive and destructive forms, and that it interrupts the scene of writing, questioning the power of narration and the role of the reader of a romantic fairy tale and quest narrative. The female muse, who escapes the hero and finally also the narrator, is at once the narrator's object of desire, the reason for his narrating, and the force that interrupts his act of narration. Yet, at the same time, the hero, young Desiderio, is shown to be the object of desire for the other characters and also, at the metadiegetic level, for the narrator, the old Desiderio, who wants to find the "original thread" of himself. By interrupting and metaphorizing the act of narration through uncanny notions like coffin-making or turning oneself into a statue and by hindering the plot development and climax through ironic commentary, the novel also unsettles the role of reading. *IDM* portrays the reader of the quest narrative as someone not so distanced from the predicament of old Desiderio. The reader's position is projected as oscillating between the poles of voyeurism and its critique, as moving between passive and active forms of "sleeping," between the states of being violated and of condoning violence.

I have explored here three intertwined literary devices that affect the reading of fairy tales in Carter's novel. First of all, the treatment of characters as figures of speech raises the questions of the construction of the subject and of the role of writing as troping. This self-reflexive aspect of the text resists the generic expectations of clearly identifiable characters and of an "omniscient" narrator whose desires apparently never interfere in the narrated events. Second, the narrator's unreliability is emphasized in the text through other means as well: the old Desiderio constantly redefines the nature of his task and lets himself be intercepted by the object of his desire or reason for his narrative. Through the uncertainty and ambivalence of its narrator, the text not only foregrounds the gendered narrative perspective of fairy tales, but also explores the many latent possibilities within this genre. An example of this is the old spinner figure, who is both empowered by her story and subjected to it, thus thematizing the power and dangers of narration. And last, the multiplication of textual allusions within single units, while recalling a literary tradition, creates unexpected thematic possibilities. The alternative readings made plausible by the polygenetic intertextuality in the novel accompany the structural reversal or transformation of certain essential story elements (e.g., the "prince" pricks his thumb on a thorn; the one who kisses the "princess" may lose his flesh). The unexpected possibilities include, as I argued in relation to the "Hoffman(n) effect," an emphasis on the potential in the romantic fairy-tale pattern for a critique of both unreflective romanticism and Enlightenment utopianism; a critique of the female muse tradition; the question of sleeping and spinning as metaphors for the creative narrative act; the problematic status of the female muse and of the "enemy," Dr. Hoffman, as driving forces behind the hero's quest; and a questioning of the notion of reading as an act of "timeless" repetition and circularity.

Notes

1. It is Drosselmeier, argues Christensen, who takes us on dangerous flights of fantasy (65). In Carter's *IDM* there is a character called Dr. Drosselmeier, a scientist and an assistant to the Minister, who sets up a model of the unreality atom but who then goes mad and blows himself up (*IDM* 23, 28). Soon after, Dr. Drosselmeier appears again in the novel through an indirect reference in a metamorphic figure: in the original E.T.A. Hoffmann tale one of Drosselmeier's figurations is the big gilded owl which perches on top of the tall clock in the toy room; the owl figure reappears in Carter's text (*IDM* 26, 59). Christensen proposes that Dr. Drosselmeier and Dr. Hoffman are intimately linked in *IDM*: "one scientist figure dies early, leaving another, his enemy, Dr. Hoffman, to be pursued by the hero throughout the rest of the narrative" (65).

2. The treatment of characters as figures of speech or as automata is frequent in all of Carter's novels. In *The Magic Toyshop* the puppeteer treats his family as (less than) puppets. In *Nights at the Circus* the character Fevvers's slogan "Is she fact or is she fiction?" is an advertising ploy she uses to attract audiences and to sustain the enigma of her difference—but the American reporter Walser takes it literally. In *The Passion of New Eve*, Eve realizes that the character called Mother is a mere figure of speech (184). The character Jewel in *Heroes and Villains* is constructed as "a sign of the idea of a hero" (22). A similar association of automata, puppets and figures of speech is included in Carter's short story "The Loves of Lady Purple," where, as in *IDM,* the affinity between subjects and artificial constructions is portrayed as something unsettling and uncanny. The narrator inquires about the marionette that has come alive: "Had the marionette all the time parodied the living or was she, now living, to parody her own performance as a marionette?" (*Fireworks* 39).

3. See Zipes, *Breaking the Magic Spell* 35–37. Christensen refers to E.T.A. Hoffmann's Enlightenment-minded call for imaginative restraint in dealing with the world. Through his automatic characters, Christensen argues, Hoffmann warns us that people are being turned into automata and that machines are being credited with inordinate value (64–65, 69). Subsequently, Christensen sees that Hoffmann's tale "The Nutcracker and the Mouse King", rather than celebrating a fantasy land (like the Tchaikovsky/Petipa adaptation of the story), points out its dangers (68). E.T.A. Hoffmann's tale ends with a reference to Marie's and young Mr. Drosselmeier's wedding, where there "danced two-and-twenty thousand of the most beautiful dolls and other figures, all glittering in pearls and diamonds; and Marie is to this day the queen of a realm where all kinds of sparkling Christmas Woods, and transparent Marzipan Castles . . . are to be seen—by those who have the eyes to see them" (*Best Tales* 182). The question is: are we to celebrate with Marie or has she simply gone mad?

4. Another way to see an intimate connection between Carter's *IDM* and "Little Zaches" is to emphasize how these stories generate certain historical allegories and comparisons, in that they both depict the powers of the police state. Zipes finds two

main levels of meaning in E.T.A. Hoffmann's fairy tale that illustrate the point. First of all, for Zipes, on the level of the fantastic, "Little Zaches" is "the conventional romantic story of the aspiring young poet who falls in love with the seemingly unattainable beauty from the upper class, a 'princess,' and there is a magician who helps him not only to win the princess but to become a full-fledged poet" (*Breaking the Magic Spell* 89). On a different level, as Zipes sees it, this Hoffmann tale is a story about police repression in Prussia. Carter's *IDM*, in turn, is situated in a totalitarian state in South America.

5. Desiderio realizes how everything in the castle is safe, ordered and secure (*IDM* 197); how the Doctor has a chaste, masculine room where he reads mainstream magazines like *Playboy, The New Yorker, Time* and *Newsweek* (*IDM* 199); how lonely Dr. Hoffman is (*IDM* 199); how nothing in his castle is fantastic (*IDM* 200); how Albertina, like the Doctor, lacks a sense of humor (*IDM* 203); how not magic, but some incomprehensible logic rules over the castle (*IDM* 204); how Hoffman is a totalitarian and a hypocrite (*IDM* 207); how Hoffman probably just wanted power under the disguise of his program for libidinal liberation (*IDM* 209); and, finally, how Hoffman examined the world by the light of intellect alone (*IDM* 212).

6. Another instance of *IDM*'s ironic treatment of its protagonist's relationship vis-à-vis his dream lover occurs when Desiderio is at the home of the doll-like Mary Ann. Desiderio's description of the night at her house ends self-reflexively: "The night sighed beneath the languorous weight of its own romanticism" (*IDM* 55). One may infer from this self-ironic comment, as Christensen's reading suggests (69), that Carter's novel constitutes a critique of unreflective romanticism and of surrealism, which glamorizes hallucinatory experiences, mental disorders, and images of meta- and polymorphosis while promoting the image of a female muse.

7. In trying to give surrealism an aura of scientific experimentation, Breton takes on Pierre Reverdy's definition of the image and develops it as a critique of the traditional metaphoric comparison in his first *Manifeste du surrealisme* (1924). For Breton, "the image is a pure creation of the mind," and "it cannot be born from a comparison but from a juxtaposition of two more or less distant realities." Furthermore, "the more the relationship between the two juxtaposed realities is distant and true, the stronger the image will be—the greater its emotional power and poetic reality" (38). This implies that the poet does not evoke these images; rather, they come to him—the images appear to the poet, as Breton explains through a reference to Baudelaire, "spontaneously, despotically" (62).

8. The debate on how much of this imagery is gender-based is ongoing. Rosalind E. Krauss reads, in her essay with Jane Livingston, the mutated bodies of Bataille, Bellmer, Brassaï, Ubac and Kertesz as purely genderless or protofeminist images. Krauss assumes that the surrealist photomontage made signification a political act, by revealing the constructedness of and the illusion of presence in photographic representation, by dismantling the experience of the real itself as a sign (104, 107, 109, 110). Yet Krauss may not fully realize that most of these bodies can be identified as female. Rudolf E. Kuenzli strongly rejects Krauss's reading of Ubac, Kertesz, Bellmer, and Georges Bataille's notion of *informe* as critical in their deconstruction of gender categories and the representation of the human body in traditional realistic photography. Kuenzli claims that Krauss does not see the violent, sadistic dismemberment of the female figure (23–25).

9. Robinson describes the disruption of identification with the male protagonist as a

tripartite structure: (1) while Desiderio is so clearly complicitous in his adventures, a reader who identifies with him will uncomfortably share in his complicity; (2) the text makes explicit the economies of male desire behind representations of women (their construction); and (3) the text makes explicit the "underside" of narrative and history through the use and abuse of pornographic narrative conventions (meaning the violence and de-humanizing tendencies of these fictions) (105).

Works Cited

Breton, André. *Manifeste du surrealisme. Poison soluble.* 1924. Paris: Eds. Kra, 1930.

Carter, Angela. *Fireworks: Nine Profane Pieces.* 1974. New York: Penguin, 1987.

————. *Heroes and Villains.* 1969. Harmondsworth: Penguin, 1981.

————. *The Infernal Desire Machines of Doctor Hoffman.* 1972. London: Penguin, 1982.

————. *The Passion of New Eve.* 1977. London: Virago, 1982.

Christensen, Peter. "The Hoffmann Connection: Demystification in Angela Carter's The Infernal Desire Machines of Dr. Hoffman." *The Review of Contemporary Fiction* 14.3 (Fall 1994): 63–70.

Grimm, Jacob and Wilhelm. "Briar-Rose or, The Sleeping Beauty." *The Brothers Grimm: Popular Folk Tales.* Trans. Brian Alderson. London: Victor Gollancz, 1978. 39–42.

Hoffmann, E.T.A. *The Best Tales of Hoffmann.* Trans. Major Alexander Ewing, J.T. Bealby, Alfred Packer, and Thomas Carlyle, 1967. New York: Dover, 1986.

————. *Three Märchen of E.T.A. Hoffmann.* Trans. Charles E. Passage. Columbia: U of South Carolina P, 1971.

Krauss, Rosalind E. "The Photographic Conditions of Surrealism." *The Originality of the Avant-Garde and Other Modernist Myths.* Cambridge: The MIT P, 1985. 87–118.

Krauss, Rosalind E., and Jane Livingston. "L'Amour fou: Photography and Surrealism." Exhibition catalogue. Washington: Corcoran Gallery of Art, 1988.

Kuenzli, Rudolf E. "Surrealism and Misogyny." *Dada/Surrealism* 18 (1990): 17–26.

McHale, Brian. *Postmodernist Fiction.* New York: Methuen, 1987.

Mozart, Wolfgang Amadeus, Carl Ludwig Giesecke, and Emanuel Schikaneder. *The Magic Flute.* Trans. Edward J. Dent. Cambridge: W. Heffer & Sons, 1913.

Offenbach, Jacques. *Les contes d'Hoffmann.* Trans. Ruth and Thomas Martin. New York: G. Schirmer, 1959.

Robinson, Sally. *Engendering the Subject: Gender and Self-Representation in Contemporary Women's Fiction.* Albany: State U of New York P, 1991.

Rowe, Karen E. "To Spin a Yarn: The Female Voice in Folklore and Fairy Tale." *Fairy Tales and Society: Illusion, Allusion, and Paradigm.* Ed. Ruth B. Bottigheimer. Philadelphia: U of Pennsylvania P, 1986. 53–74.

Schmidt, Ricarda. "The Journey of the Subject in Angela Carter's Fiction." *Textual Practice* 3.1 (Spring 1989): 56–75.

Suleiman, Susan Rubin. *Risking Who One Is: Encounters with Contemporary Art and Literature.* Cambridge: Cambridge UP, 1994.

Tammi, Pekka. "Seventeen Remarks on Poligenetichnost' in Nabokov's Prose." *Studia Slavica Finlandensia* 7 (1990): 189–232.

Thompson, Stith, ed. *Motif-Index of Folk-Literature.* 6 vols. FF Communications 117. Helsinki: Academia Scientiarum Fennica, 1936.

Waelti-Walters, Jennifer. *Fairy Tales and the Female Imagination.* Montreal: Eden, 1982.

Zipes. Jack. *Breaking the Magic Spell: Radical Theories of Folk and Fairy Tales.* New York: Routledge, 1979.

Betty Moss

Desire and the Female Grotesque
in Angela Carter's
"Peter and the Wolf"

Angela Carter's artistic evolution moves toward the realization of an alternative vision of creative desire as positive and productive rather than driven by Lack—as in the dominant traditions of Western thought since Plato; Carter develops a fictional idiom adequate to the expression of such desire. This distinctly Carterian idiom participates in the aesthetic of the grotesque and inflects the grotesque in a specifically feminine and feminist way, maximizing its potential as an instrument of social and personal transformation. Integrating the feminist discourse of Hélène Cixous, French writer and critic, with the theory of the grotesque advanced by Mikhail Bakhtin, renowned Russian literary and cultural critic, opens a useful way to explore Carter's fiction.[1] Carter's admiration for, appropriation of, and reinvention of wonder tales demonstrate her regard for realms of the fantastic, a category intrinsically connected with the grotesque. While any of her tales can be approached through the lens of the grotesque, her wolf stories offer one of the most elemental of grotesque figures: the part-human, part-animal; as Bakhtin points out, "[T]he combination of human and animal traits is . . . one of the most ancient grotesque forms" (*Rabelais* 316. Subsequent citations of Bakhtin refer to this text unless otherwise indicated.). Carter's wolf-narratives both deconstruct received assumptions of gender and desire, and offer alternative possibilities for understanding and constructing desire and sexuality.[2]

Marvels & Tales: Journal of Fairy-Tale Studies, Vol. 12, No. 1 (1998), pp. 175–91. Copyright © 1998 by Wayne State University Press, Detroit, MI 48201.

Traditional tales of wolves (and werewolves), such as "Little Red Riding Hood," cast the wolf as masculine threat and danger, a force to be fought on its own terms of violence and dominance. Carter's re-visionings both appropriate and work against this tradition; her "Peter and the Wolf" in the collection *Saints and Strangers* is one such tale. Given her use of the same title, Sergei Prokofiev's popular musical score *Peter and the Wolf,* written for children in 1936 as an instructional guide to musical instruments, undoubtedly served as at least partial source material for her re-visioning.[3] Prokofiev tells a story of masculine initiation: Peter, the youthful hero, proves his own masculine (predatory) power by capturing the predatory wolf. Prokofiev's well-known hero exhibits time-honored traits of a folktale's hero—courage and cunning—to rid his community of their enemy, the wolf; for his actions Peter is duly honored.[4] Carter's story appropriates the masculine initiation narrative, but her Peter does not function as a heroic guide for children's socialization. Indeed, Carter's Peter exists as hero insofar as he challenges his community's traditions; after much unease and uncertainty, he repudiates the options offered him by tradition and accepts initiation into unmapped territory. In his reaction to encounters with the grotesque wolf-human, a girl-child, he subverts prevailing masculine conceptions of desire and sexuality, and offers an initiation story for the adult reader, not the child. My essay presents a reading of Carter's "Peter and the Wolf" as a tale in which the female grotesque, as a representation of otherness or difference, profoundly confuses Peter, ultimately propelling him, and the story, into the potential of an other desire. Preceding that discussion is a foundational accounting of matters relevant to that reading: Carter's insistence on the need for re-visioning; her feminist position regarding desire and sexuality; an integration of Bakhtin's and Cixous's theories; Carter's critical regard for the tale as genre; and an important connection between the tale as genre and Bakhtin's grotesque.

Carter understands that transparent realism—that category of fiction which renders events "as if" the reader is looking through a window at the familiar world—is bound to ideological presumptions of what constitutes reality; that is, it reflects a familiar, consensual reality, thereby implicating itself in dominant political and social conventions. She elects to explore possibilities for discovering, even inventing, alternative realities, ones not bound to convention or assumption. She does not presume to display a familiar "real life" and thus avoids the possibilities of indifference or, perhaps worse, of misleading readers into believing they are reading a representation of actual lived experience.[5] Carter's retelling of "Peter and the Wolf" deconstructs and defamiliarizes original tales, most recognizably Prokofiev's, thus calling attention to both literature and reality as constructs or perceptions. In the tale itself, Carter textually reveals the operation of defamiliarization through the story's setting, the mountains of the Alps. The narrator notes that "with familiarity, the landscape ceases to provoke awe and wonder and the traveller sees the alps with the indifferent eye of those who always live there" (59); at the conclusion of the story, after Peter experiences the "vertigo of freedom," we are told that "for the first time, he saw the primitive, vast, magnificent, barren, unkind simplicity of the mountain" (67). In her retellings, Carter defamiliarizes well-known tales, bringing both deeper understanding and renewal of those earlier versions.[6]

As a feminist writer, Carter particularly seeks to expose the constructed character of cultural representations of gender. While Carter does not presume to convey a "reality" of sexuality and desire, she does offer new, sometimes tentative, sometimes startling, ways of understanding and conceptualizing how they work. In opening new possibilities, Carter's appropriation of the wonder tale provides a genre within which she can deconstruct and subvert cultural mythology, leaving the reader the opportunity to consider alternative realms of desire. Carter engages the reader as a participant who is continually challenged, within and beyond the text, to expand possibilities of knowing and understanding the world—and other worlds—through story.

Recognizing that "[l]iterature is an inseparable part of the totality of culture and cannot be studied outside the total cultural context" ("Notes" 140), Mikhail Bakhtin theorizes grotesque realism as a mode which "discloses the potentiality of an entirely different world, of another order, another way of life," for it is "always conceiving" (48, 210). His belief in the transformative power of literature not only compares with Carter's creative desire but also corresponds to Hélène Cixous's utopian vision of the potential for cultural transformation contained in feminine writing: "Her [the feminine writer's] libido will produce far more radical effects of political and social change than some might like to think" ("Laugh" 339). Cixous contends that a feminine text poses a certain challenge to the reader: "A feminine text goes on and on and at a certain moment the volume comes to an end but the writing continues and for the reader this means being thrust into the void" ("Castration" 488–89).[7] With the sense of ongoing movement, this void becomes one of potentialities; the reader must take the leap into this Cixousean void of potentialities, becoming a participant in the movement toward a potentially renewed futurity. In contrast to the obsession with the negative (death, loss, fear) that masculine writers evince, Cixous declares that feminine writers "have no womanly reason to pledge allegiance to the negative" for "they do not fetishize, they do not deny, they do not hate," and "Wherever history still unfolds as the history of death, she [the feminine writer] does not tread" ("Laugh" 341, 348, 348). Masculine desire—as Lack in Western tradition—implies a void of finality in contrast to Cixous's void of *potentiality* which parallels Bakhtin's theory of the grotesque as a site of another way of life always conceiving.[8] I contend that Carter's narrative of "Peter and the Wolf" depends upon an aesthetic of the grotesque inflected by a feminist desire for transformation, and that the theories of Bakhtin and Cixous provide an avenue for articulating that narrative's movement.

In the Afterword to her short fiction collection *Fireworks: Nine Profane Pieces,* Carter mentions two aspects of the *tale* as genre that link her creative aesthetic with the grotesque: first, tales are not implicated in deceptions of realism, and, second, they provoke an unease. To begin, she tells why short fiction, broadly considered, is an important genre to her: "The limited trajectory of the short narrative concentrates its meaning. Sign and sense can fuse to an extent impossible to achieve among the multiplying ambiguities of an extended narrative" (*Fireworks* 132). This relatively uncomplicated fusion of sign and sense in her short fiction allows a sharp, intense narrative focus on particular aspects of desire and sexuality. Then, adding further to an understanding of the operation of her short fictions as a genre, she identifies those in *Fireworks* as *tales*, not *short stories*, a distinction that extends to her other short fiction collections as well. She defines what, to her, is the important difference: "Formally, the tale differs from the short story in that it makes few pretenses at the imitation of life. The tale does not log everyday experience, as the short story does; it interprets everyday experience through a system of imagery derived from subterranean areas behind everyday experience, and therefore the tale cannot betray its readers into a false knowledge of everyday experience" (*Fireworks* 133). The tale, as she distinguishes it from the short story, is overtly interpretive, not descriptive of everyday life; it thereby offers an exploration of experience without presuming to convey either a projection or a reflection of lived experience. As Carter constructs tales that carry the reader into unfamiliar daily worlds of the marvelous and the fantastic, these worlds necessarily depend upon the tradition of the grotesque to plumb the "subterranean worlds of everyday experience." Carter's grotesque subterranean worlds are relevant to lived experience and to the production of desire because they open avenues to the discovery of other ways of living and thinking; they toss the reader into a Cixousean void of potential.

Also in the Afterword to *Fireworks* Carter reflects back to another teller of tales who influenced her strongly: Edgar Allan Poe, creator of "Gothic tales, cruel tales, tales of wonder, tales of terror," as she describes him (*Fireworks* 132). Noting his use of the tale as genre, she also maintains that the Gothic tradition of which he (and she) are part "retains a singular moral function— that of provoking unease" (*Fireworks* 133). In all her works, Carter, as "Peter and the Wolf" exemplifies, embraces the value of "provoking unease," an unease produced when expectations of how the world operates are called into question or even shattered. Such unease prompts one of two reactions: either rejection of the "subterranean" or grotesque areas being explored, or the opening of different ways of understanding the world. Since the Gothic literary genre is inextricably bound to the grotesque for its effects, the *unease* that Carter designates as an effect of Gothic literature can be validly understood as indicative of the *ambivalence* which, as Bakhtin observes, is provoked by the grotesque. Bakhtin views ambivalence as regenerative and as central to understanding how the grotesque functions to achieve a transformative vision in literature. As struggle is set in motion, ambivalence liberates an energy that upsets and topples stasis. While regeneration is not certain, it is made possible by struggle. Ambivalence, equated here with the *unease* that Carter recognizes, denotes conflicting and/or confusing emotions; central to understanding the grotesque as an aesthetic category is the ambivalence it both constructs in the text and provokes in the reader. In Carter's "Peter and the Wolf," the figure of Peter textually dramatizes this ambivalence, not the bravery of Prokofiev's Peter. Concurrently, the ambivalence aroused in the story's reader opens the way into the Cixousean void of potentiality, thereby setting in motion the transformative power of the grotesque.

Carter's "Peter and the Wolf" tells of an infant girl who was stolen and raised by wolves in the mountains of Eastern Europe. She had been living in a remote cabin with her parents when wolves attacked, killing the parents. The wolves did not mutilate the mother's corpse, but left only "a gnawed foot in a boot" as evidence of the father's probable defensive ferocity and his brutal death (59). When the story opens, eight years have passed since the girl's abduction. Her cousin Peter, only a year younger at seven, spies her one day while guarding his family's goats; he sees "the thing he had been taught most to fear advancing silently" (59). Carter's revisioning of wolf mythology underscores that fear is *taught*, and that fear, in its elemental magnitude, suppresses other ways of thinking. In "The Company of Wolves," a tale in *The Bloody Chamber* that revises "Little Red Riding Hood," the granddaughter dares to laugh at the wolf and at its representation as masculine predator, knowing that "she was nobody's meat"; she then sleeps "sweet and sound . . . between the paws of the tender wolf" (118). The granddaughter reconceives what she had been taught to fear and opens new ways of thinking about desire and sexuality. Similarly, Peter has been taught to fear the wolf; operating subtextually is that he has also been taught to fear the feminine, for it is the girl-child who is "advancing silently" with her wolf family. In this tale the grotesque and the female merge, creating a female grotesque that offers an other vision of sexuality and desire.

When Peter spies the wolves, Carter reminds us textually, as she did with the mountains, that familiarity risks the loss of discovery: "If they had not been the first wolves he had ever seen, the boy would not have inspected them so closely" (60). As a result of his close inspection, Peter discovers that "the third wolf was a prodigy, a marvel, a naked one, going on all fours, . . . hairless as regards the body although hair grew around its head" (60). When Peter later tells his grandmother that " 'There was a little girl with the wolves, granny,' " the narrator wonders, "Why was he so sure it had been a little girl?" for Peter would not have been able to see the genitalia since she was walking "on all fours." Carter, while understanding gender as constructed, retains an enigmatic, elemental bodily link to sexuality with Peter's recognition of the girl's sex; the narrator speculates only that maybe "her hair was so long, so long and lively" (60). Although she hints here at a trace of body-inscribed sexuality, Carter comprehends the constructed nature of gender as, paradoxically, both determinant and potential. Contrary to prevailing, universalized notions and attitudes, Carter insists that gender and sexuality are not fixed according to anatomy or essences. In her "Polemical Preface" to *The Sadeian Woman,* Carter begins by voicing rejection of Freud's assertion that "anatomy is destiny": "My anatomy is only part of an infinitely complex organisation, my self. The anatomical reductionalism . . . extracts all the evidence of me from myself and leaves behind only a single aspect of my life as a mammal. It enlarges this aspect, simplifies it and then presents it as the most significant aspect of my entire humanity" (*Sadeian Woman* 4).

The grandmother, hearing Peter's story, knows this girl-wolf to be her grandchild—Peter's cousin—and goes with Peter and his father to seize the wolf-child and bring her to the home. The ensuing ritualistic capture hyperbolizes the brutality of masculine containment of the feminine: "[S]omebody caught her with a sliding noose at the end of a rope; the noose over her head jerked tight. . . . The girl scratched and fought until the men tied her wrists and ankles together with twine and slung her from a pole. . . . Then she went limp . . . [and] pretended to be dead" (61). Even in all her ferocity, this girl-child does not, of course, stand a chance against several powerful men with their instruments of control. When a "big, grey, angry bitch appeared out of nowhere" and "Peter's father blasted it to bits with his shotgun" (61), Peter also witnesses the fate of a grown female wolf who challenges the men's power. Such scenes dramatize the logical extreme of masculine power allied with violence: utter repression or annihilation, the void of negation or Lack.

The particulars of the wolf-girl's body, pivotal to this tale, comprise a central component of the grotesque; as an analytical category the grotesque is represented by the body, and the metaphorical extensions of the grotesque body include the textual body and the social body. Bakhtin explains the importance of the grotesque body: "In grotesque realism . . . the bodily element is deeply positive. It is presented not in a private, egotistic [contained] form" but represents "the epitome of incompleteness" (*Rabelais* 19, 26); it is "a body in the act of becoming. It is never finished, never completed" (317). Extended to the textual body, Bakhtin's celebration and elaboration of the grotesque body parallels Cixous's determination that a feminine text—a textual body—goes on and on; she extends the metaphor to include the reader who is catapulted into a void by the textual body's continual movement. Bakhtin contrasts grotesque bodies with those he refers to as existing in the "new bodily canon" (320) of the post-Renaissance modern world. These modern bodies are smooth and finished, and are reflected in "verbal norms of official and literary language" (320). He elaborates:

> In the modern image of the individual body, sexual life, eating, drinking, and defecation have radically changed their meaning: they have been transferred to the private and psychological level where their connotation becomes narrow and specific, torn away from the direct relation to the life of society and to the cosmic whole. . . . [T]hey can no longer carry on their former philosophical functions. . . . All actions and events are interpreted on the level of a single, individual life. They are enclosed within the limits of the same body, limits that are the absolute beginning and end and can never meet. (321–22)

The modern, individuated bodies cannot merge with the metaphoric social or cosmic body as does the grotesque body.[9] Bakhtin asserts: "This bodily participation in the potentiality of another world, the bodily awareness of another world[,] has an immense importance for the grotesque" (48). Having developed the wolf's movements and habits, the girl-child of "Peter and the Wolf" has transgressed boundaries and fused with a disparate and alien realm, thus representing the potential inherent in the grotesque. When Peter "reads" her body, he will be tossed into a void; if he does not deny the implications of the grotesque body as "always becoming," as not static, a potential will be generated in the void.

In an article that became part of her full-length exploration of the female grotesque, Mary Russo imagines a study that would explore the grotesque body in opposition to the modern idealized (static) body: "This category [of the female bodily grotesque] might be used affirmatively to destabilize the idealizations of the female beauty or to realign the mechanisms of desire" ("Female" 221). In "Peter and the Wolf" the girl-child's grotesque body does indeed both destabilize notions of female beauty and realign the mechanisms of desire, as Peter's reactions and actions indicate. Fundamental to Russo's category is the contrast of the static, closed, contained body of masculine idealization with the dynamic, open, boundless body of the female grotesque as it writes itself in feminine texts. Cixous maintains that the woman writer involved in feminine writing "will return to the body which has been more than confiscated from her, which has been turned into the uncanny stranger on display," a display constructed by the male imagination ("Laugh" 337); in Carter's reinvented story of "Peter and the Wolf," as in most of her fiction, the female body is a crucial site of transformation. In her essay "Coming to

Writing," Cixous describes the initial stages for (her)self of a process that is a personal "prospect of transformation," the body that begins to write: "And in my body the breath of a giant, but no sentences at all. Who's pushing me? Who's invading? Who's changing me into a monster? Into a mouse wanting to swell to the size of a prophet? A joyful force" (10). Perhaps not coincidentally, Cixous's (feminine) written expression of her own transformative process relies on grotesque images: a giant, a monster, a mouse/prophet. Similar to Cixous's employing grotesque images to represent her feminine creative desire, Carter employs the female grotesque as a powerful catalyst for transformation. As "reader" of the female grotesque, Peter is catapulted into territory that indeed realigns the mechanisms of desire.

When Peter first views his cousin, she "was running . . . with her arse stuck up in the air" (60). A crucial quality of the grotesque body as Bakhtin describes it is its openness to, and connection with, the social and material world through its emphasis on the lower rather than the higher regions. Because the lower regions such as the "arse" are closer to the earth, they suggest the possibility of regeneration, whereas the upper region—the head—has traditionally represented the mind and its tendency toward abstraction and consequent universalized "truths" and essences. Further, the lower regions signify an important attribute of the grotesque body: degradation. The narrator exclaims, "[H]ow filthy she was! Caked with mud and dirt" and, bluntly, "She stank" (61). When Peter's father unties the wolf-child in the home, "[I]t was as if he had let a fiend loose" (62); not only does she ravage the room, but "[s]everal times, her bowels opened" (62). Filth and stench align and fuse the wolf-girl's body with the material world; she is even marked by the earth with "every inch of her chestnut hide . . . scored and scabbed with dozens of scars of sharp abrasions of rock and thorn" (61). In a surreal gesture, Carter further links this scene of degradation to the earth and its abundance when the wolf-child knocks over the meal barrel in her frenzy, and "the flour settled on everything like a magic powder that made everything strange" (62); the strangeness is both a defamiliarization and a blending of the profane (excrement) with earth's abundance (the magic powder of flour). The degradation of the family's simple home connects to the earth and potential regeneration, and displaces the sanitized and reified official world, thereby opening a space for transformation.

The climactic moment in the home occurs as the seven-year-old Peter, who is watching his cousin howl, views for the first time the female sex: "Her [vaginal] lips opened up as she howled so that she offered him, without her own intention or volition, a view of a set of Chinese boxes of whorled flesh that seemed to open one upon another into herself, drawing him into an inner, secret place in which destination perpetually receded before him, his first, devastating, vertiginous intimation of infinity" (63). With this powerful image, Peter encounters the female folds of flesh as signifier of infinity. For Freud, this moment of viewing female genitalia inscribes masculine fear of castration—the fear upon which masculine desire is constructed and from which springs a desire for control and containment; the Freudian female sex registers negation or Lack. Carter's retelling, however, turns this theory on its head, since Peter does not experience his first view of female genitalia as Lack but as Abundance. In a compelling essay, Jean Wyatt elucidates this moment: "[W]hen Carter's little boy, Peter, catches a glimpse of his girl cousin's body he sees what *is* there," for " 'Peter and the Wolf' attempts to revise this founding narrative [the Freudian narrative] of sexual difference by articulating the female genitalia as material presence," not Lack (550, 551). Peter, unlike Freud's little boy, "doesn't reduce female difference to a logic of the same (having/not having the penis)," and thus "He enters a world unmapped by linguistic and doctrinal meanings, a world wide open to his discovery" (551, 552).[10]

Carter deploys the transformative possibilities of a specifically feminine grotesque, and offers another possibility of desire. Peter's story dramatizes a movement from the void of emptiness or Lack—the masculine void which originates in fear and manifests itself in the desire to contain or even to annihilate—to Cixous's void of potentialities and abundance. The female body in this story—a "secret place" of boundless movement without destination—recalls Cixous's description of the feminine textual body, the story that goes on and on, tossing the reader into a void. In his ambivalent reaction, Peter conceivably parallels the reader of the feminine text: "Peter's heart gave a hop, a skip, so that he had a sensation of falling; he was not conscious of his own fear because he could not take his eyes off the sight of the crevice of her girl-child's sex. . . . It exercised an absolute fascination upon him" (63). Peter is both frightened and fascinated; he has entered the world of the grotesque with its consequent unease—or ambivalence—that offers a potential realignment of desire and of categories of gender. If he should succumb to fear of this infinity, he will perpetuate masculine desire as founded upon Lack; if he resists fear, he will open other possibilities.

Soon after Peter's view of the female sex, a wolf-pack breaks into the home and reclaims its human member. When the "wolves were at the door" before breaking through to reclaim the girl-child, bringing with them "Dissonance [and] Terror," Peter "would have given anything to turn time back, so that he might have run, shouting a warning, when he first caught sight of the wolves, and never seen her" (64). His ambivalence when he is confronted with the grotesque is apparent; he is besieged with both fascination and terror—as well as a futile, nostalgic desire to turn back time. Wolfgang Kayser, whose important study of the grotesque Bakhtin both appreciates and writes against, unconsciously and ironically demonstrates this ambivalence in his own admitted confusion as he explores the grotesque. Kayser perceives the site of the grotesque as an estranged, frightening, other world: "[T]he [perceived] order [of the world and of thought] is destroyed and an abyss opened where we thought to rest on firm ground" (59). He maintains that "The grotesque totally destroys the order [of recognizable reality] and deprives us of our foothold" and "We are unable to orient ourselves in the alienated world" (59, 185). The ontological uncertainty provoked by the grotesque disturbs Kayser's fascination with and appreciation of the grotesque.[11] Movement into an alien world necessitates a change in perception; transformation, which always involves a rupture with known reality, can be so frightening as to precipitate strong resistance in a desire to maintain order.

Kayser's discomfort with the power of the grotesque to disorient, combined with his fascination, demonstrates a reaction intrinsic to the grotesque: ambivalence. Even as he senses the grotesque as foreboding, he determines that "[i]n spite of all the helplessness and horror inspired by the dark forces [of the grotesque] . . . [its] truly artistic portrayal effects a secret liberation" (188). However, Kayser's fear eclipses the sense of liberation and manifests itself in a desire for order and control, for a hold on known reality and recognizable ontological categories. Kayser, fulfilling his own fear-induced desire to maintain control, emphatically sums up the grotesque in a final interpretive comment: "[W]e arrive at a final interpretation of the grotesque: AN ATTEMPT TO INVOKE AND SUBDUE THE DEMONIC ASPECTS OF THE WORLD" (188; capitalization in original). This final comment signals his fear of and successful retreat from the transformative power of the grotesque; Kayser resists falling into the "abyss" and regains his ontological footing through certitude and finality. Bakhtin, who views Kayser as mistakenly projecting his own fear onto the grotesque and as possessing a "somewhat distorted interpretation," disputes him by rejoining that "[t]he existing world suddenly becomes alien . . . precisely because there is the potentiality of a friendly world" and that "[t]he world is destroyed so that it may be regenerated and renewed" (46). For Bakhtin, Kayser's fear represents "the extreme expression of narrow-minded and stupid seriousness" (47). The estranged world as Bakhtin perceives it can be productively compared to the Cixousean void into which a reader is catapulted and into which Peter is tossed following his second and final encounter with the grotesque female figure of his cousin.

In his grappling to understand his experience with the grotesque, Peter initially moves toward succumbing to fear and its resultant desire for containment and certitude, as exemplified by Kayser's reaction. A few months after the wolf-child has escaped with the wolf pack, the grandmother dies from a festering wound sustained when she had been bitten by her granddaughter wolf-child.

Peter, "consumed by an imperious passion for atonement" as a result of his sense of responsibility for the grandmother's wound, asks the local priest to teach him to read so that he can pore over the Bible "looking for a clue to grace" (65). Peter seeks a traditional path to alleviate his troubling experience with the female grotesque—the path of transcendent religion, or, in this case specifically, a search for God's blessing on Man. For Carter, transcendence as traditionally understood is a dangerous illusion because it renders the physical, social world as relatively insignificant. Carter understands that meaningful transcendence can be effected, paradoxically, only via the material.[12] Not to contextualize desire or sexuality materially is to universalize them and thus to close them to transformative possibilities. Carter notes that "There is no way out of time. We must learn to live in this world . . . because it is the only world that we will ever know" (*Sadeian Woman* 110). And in an interview (1988), she speaks of her antipathy toward religion: "How do we know what is authentic behavior and what is inauthentic behavior? It's about the complex interrelation of reality and its representations. It has to do with a much older thing. I suppose it comes back to the idea of mythology and why I talk so much against religion. It's because it's presenting us with ideas about ourselves which don't come out of practice; they come out of theory" ("Interview" 16). Sexuality and desire are processes shaped by particularized social and bodily conditions; they are not determined essences. Peter initially elects to deny the flesh, the physical here and now, and enter a world of abstraction—the world of universal "truths" and core essences.

Carter's fictions work against this repressive universalizing, seeking to represent particularized voices of desire and sexuality. Peter's movement toward religion—metaphysical transcendence—denies his experience with the female grotesque. Striving to repudiate the flesh which irrevocably connects him to his wolf-cousin, he "fasted to the bone" and "lashed himself" (65). However, his path is marked by unease for, "as if to spite the four evangelists he nightly invoked to protect his bed, the nightmare regularly disordered his sleeps" (65); the unspecified nightmare signals his internal wrestling with his fears. Such dissonance and disorder characterize the grotesque in that they signify a disruption of stasis or containment. Peter, in striving to give himself up to religion, is seeking to contain, or explain, his encounter with the female grotesque, but he is later unable to do so.

At age fourteen, Peter sets off to study for the priesthood but remains ambivalent: "In spite of his eagerness to plunge into the white world of penance and devotion that awaited him, he was anxious and troubled for reasons he could not explain" (65). Peter has decided to enter the seminary to seek penance and to dissipate or control his fear of the world around him, particularly as provoked by the grotesque figure of his cousin. Bakhtin discusses fear's relation to orthodox seriousness: "[C]osmic terror . . . is the fear of that which is materially huge and cannot be overcome by force. It is used by all religious systems to oppress man and his consciousness" (12). Peter's plan to enter the seminary—a symbolic metaphysical space—promises to offer sanctuary from his fear, but its form of protection is suppression.

On his way to the seminary, Peter pauses to wash his face at a stream and once again sees his cousin, who, lapping the stream's water, projects "a different kind of consciousness," one that might have existed "before the Fall" (66); this female wolf-human suggests the possibility of an other story following the Fall—with accompanying new stories of desire and sexuality. When two cubs roll out of the bushes, Peter "began to tremble and shake. . . . He felt he had been made of snow and now might melt" (66); any ontological certainty he was previously trying to maintain begins to dissipate. His wolf-cousin again strikes a grotesque figure at the stream with her wolf-cubs: "Her forearms, her loins and her legs were thick with hair and the hair on her head hung round her face . . . She crouched on the other side of the river . . . lapping up water" (64). When "[t]he little cubs fastened their mouths on her dangling breasts" (65), Peter stumbles toward them, "intending to cross over to the other side to join her in her marvellous and private grace, impelled by the access of an almost visionary ecstasy" (66). Peter experiences an epiphany but not one founded upon abstraction; Peter does not find the grace he seeks in the Bible's transcendent God but rather in the half-animal fleshly figure of the female grotesque. Even though his wolf-cousin and her cubs flee at his sudden movement, Peter has experienced a material transcendence—a "visionary ecstasy"—as effected via the flesh, the body. Sensing his own indissoluble connection to this alien figure, he apprehends life's abundant potential.

The visionary ecstasy inspired by the compelling elemental grotesque of the half-human/half-animal defeats the cosmic terror from which Peter suffers, and propels him into possibilities; he wonders, "[W]hat would he do at the seminary, now? For now he knew there was nothing to be afraid of. He experienced the vertigo of freedom" (66). Years earlier, the sight of the female grotesque had filled him with a vertiginous intimation of infinity, a void that could possess either negation or potential. With his second sighting of the female grotesque, Peter experiences the void as freedom or potential; he gains the liberation that Kayser only sensed. Peter then "determinedly set his face towards the town and tramped onwards, into a different story" (67). Revised by Carter, the story of Peter and the Wolf goes on and on. Whereas Prokofiev's Peter marches triumphantly carrying the captured wolf, thus fulfilling the expectation of a happy ending, Carter's Peter abandons tradition and journeys into unmapped territory—"a different story" or, as Bakhtin designates the grotesque, "another way of life."[13] The ending to Carter's wonder tale is triumphant in Peter's rejection of tradition. His initiation into a different story coincides with the reader's dizzying movement into the Cixousean void of potentialities as written into this text. The reader can understand the story as a representation of process; the story does not conclude but continues on and on. Peter (likewise Carter) repudiates the story a masculine tradition had scripted. The female grotesque— the unfamiliar, the other—shatters his known world and propels him first into fascination, ambivalence, and fear; when fear is replaced by an understanding of profound connection with the female grotesque (the Other), Peter is liberated and moves into other possibilities of living. He, like the reader, is then enabled to reconstruct, or rewrite, his desire and his story; there is no conclusive ending, only the potential of process. Carter writes in her story "Wolf-Alice" that if the wolf-child could be transported back to Eden, "she might prove to be the wise child who leads them all" (121); the same can surely be said of Peter's cousin— the female grotesque.

The Cixousean void is not meant to invoke a metaphysical, transcendent space; indeed, such a space would be anathema to Carter. I like to think of the Cixousean void as analogous to the void of quantum physics, which, paradoxically, possesses the whole of potential reality—a space not of emptiness or Lack but of an energy that creates all potential manifestations of reality. In *The Tao of Physics,* Fritjof Capra, exploring a comparison between the mystical Buddhist void and the quantum field of subatomic physics, notes that both conceptualize "a Void which has an infinite creative potential" that shapes the essential nature of reality (212). The physical vacuum of quantum physics pulsates endlessly in a rhythm of destruction and creation. This dynamic quality of continual death and regeneration is reminiscent of the grotesque, which both destroys and regenerates. Sexuality and desire cannot be adequately represented by static or contained forms but require continual transformation and movement into diverse shapes and forms. Confronting the grotesque text, the reader does not find a closed world of finitude, negation, or certainty; s/he is tossed into a dynamic void of regenerative potential. Through her re-visionings of tales, Carter reveals that continual reinvention—or process—imparts new possibilities. For Carter as a writer, continual exploration and regeneration are an imperative responsibility; as the reader celebrates a transformative narrative, s/he is propelled into realizable worlds of an other sexuality and desire that offer the possibility of social transformation.

Notes

1. In her study of the female grotesque, Mary Russo indicates the feminist need for modifying Bakhtin's theories of the grotesque: "Bakhtin . . . fails to acknowledge or incorporate the social relations of gender in his semiotic model of the body politic, and thus his notion of the Female Grotesque remains in all directions repressed and undeveloped" (*Female* 63). Cixous provides abundant theory on the social

relations of gender, while Carter's fiction abounds with (feminist) configurations of a complex female grotesque that incorporates social relations of gender.

2. In his Introduction to the complete collection of Carter's short stories, Salman Rushdie mourns the loss of Carter to an early death and longs for the "full-scale wolf novel she never wrote" (xii).

3. In her 1986 review of Carter's story collection *Saints and Strangers,* Ann Snitow also assumes Prokofiev's *Peter and the Wolf* as Carter's primary folktale reference source for "Peter and the Wolf." However, the earliest sources of stories about shepherds, wolves, and boys are Aesop's fables, another probable source for Carter to have closely explored. Further, the enduring success and fame of Prokofiev's composition, for which he wrote both the text and musical score, is attributed to his high regard for the childhood imagination and to his lifelong love of fairy tale and fantasy. As one biographer puts it, "His interest in the fanciful manifested itself throughout his life. . . . He was very much attracted by myths, tales, *bylini,* and fantasies of all kinds. He conjured up in his music . . . images from such wonderful storytellers as Andersen and Gozzi, Perrault and Bazhov, as well as from ancient Slavic mythology and Russian, French, and Kazakh folk tales" (Nestyev 457). As I do with Carter, then, I also assume as highly likely Prokofiev's familiarity with Aesop's fables. Relevant fables—those that tell of wolves, shepherds, and boys— exist in almost any collection of Aesop. For example, Jack Zipes's collection includes "The Shepherd Boy and the Wolf" (72) and "The Wolf and the Shepherd" (201); the former tells the familiar fable of the shepherd boy who cried "Wolf," and the latter tells of a shepherd who foolishly comes to trust a wolf, only to have the wolf devour his flock. Joseph Jacobs's 1966 collection includes "The Wolf and the Kid," in which a boy spies a wolf from atop his family's cottage, not unlike Prokofiev's Peter who, peering from behind a protective gate, spies a wolf (40–41). Aesop's kid chastises the wolf, only to be scorned by the wolf who knows that the boy, from his distance, is not a danger. In Prokofiev's tale, however, the young Peter climbs a tree in order to lasso the wolf and save the smaller vulnerable animals. In "The Shepherd and the Wolf," an Aesop fable found in the Spencer Collection of the New York Public Library (92), a shepherd raises a wolf cub with his dogs, but must kill the wolf when he discovers it murdering his sheep; this fable's moral validates the notion of "unchangeable nature." Certainly, Carter subverts this notion with the wolf-child of her story, who, though human, reveals no "human nature." (None of these fables, though, gives a name to the boys or shepherds; Prokofiev assigns the name "Peter" to the character in his narrative, as does Carter.) With such wide-ranging source material, any speculation here as to specific source(es) for either Carter or Prokofiev is just that—speculation.

4. Prokofiev wrote the character of Peter as a Pioneer, a member "of a Soviet organization for children of grammar-school age—a sort of politicized Cub Scouts" (Robinson 321). The construction of Peter as hero is reflected in Prokofiev's original title for the composition: *How Peter Outwitted the Wolf.* Prokofiev was a Russian nationalist who, unlike other Soviet artists or intellectuals (such as Bakhtin), determined "to become more deeply involved in the Soviet musical establishment" (Robinson 285); indeed, *Peter and the Wolf* was written in 1936 for the Moscow Children's Musical Theater.

5. Carter writes in the Introduction to a collection of her essays, *Expletives Deleted,* of her mother's cautions regarding realistic fiction: "My mother preferred Boswell,

Pepys—she adored gossip, . . . but she mistrusted fiction because she believed fiction gave an unrealistic view of the world. Once she caught me reading a novel and chastised me: 'Never let me catch you doing that again, remember what happened to Emma Bovary'" (1). But Carter also tells us, "Don't think I don't like real novels, though . . . I *do* like novels! I do! In spite of my mother's warning. Although, if a comic charlady obtrudes upon the action of a real novel, I will fling the novel against the wall amidst a flood of obscenities because the presence of such a character as a comic charlady tells me more than I wish to know about the way her creator sees the world" (3).

6. For an exploration of the historical intertextuality of the postmodern fairy tale, see Cristina Bacchilega's recently published book *Postmodern Fairy Tales*. Observing that "by working from the fairy tales' multiple versions, [the postmodern revisionist is] seeking to expose . . . what the institutionalization of such tales for children has forgotten or left unexploited," she contends that such a project does more than "interpret anew or shake the genre's ground rules. It listens for the many 'voices' of fairy tales as well, as part of a historicizing and performance-oriented project" (50).

7. Cixous does not restrict *feminine* writing to women. In an interview, as well as in other writings, she repeatedly makes the point that "I do not equate *feminine* with woman and *masculine* with man" ("Exchange" 154). She explains:

> the preliminary question is that of a "feminine writing," itself a dangerous and stylish expression full of traps, which leads to all kinds of confusions. . . . The use of the word "feminine" . . . is one of the curses of our times. First of all, words like "masculine" and "feminine" . . . that are completely distorted by everyday usage,—words which refer, of course, to a classical vision of sexual opposition between men and women—are our burden. . . . I speak of a decipherable libidinal femininity which can be read in a writing produced by a male or female. (129)

8. Margaret Atwood writes of the masculine construction of and fear of the void—a void that she says woman doesn't understand. Pointing to the masculine desire to divide, to arrange categories, to be "objective," she concludes that

> This is why men are so sad, why they feel so cut off, why they think themselves as orphans cast adrift, footloose and stringless in the deep void. What void? she says. . . . The void of the Universe, he says, and she says Oh and looks out the window and tries to get a handle on it, but it's no use, there's too much going on, too many rustlings in the leaves, too many voices. . . . And he grinds his teeth because she doesn't understand, and wanders off, not just alone but Alone, lost in the dark, lost in the skull. (*Good Bones and Simple Murders* 76)

Atwood's female character's perception of "too much going on, . . . too many voices" corresponds to Cixous's void of potential.

9. Bakhtin's celebration of the grotesque body in opposition to a sanitized body has been discussed in relation to the fact of Bakhtin's writing during the time of Stalinist Russia; in part he was reacting against Stalinist tyranny over the masses. (Compare with Prokofiev's position in Russia, endnote 4.) For instance, in their comprehensive study of Bakhtin's work, *Mikhail Bakhtin: Creation of a Prosaics*, Gary Saul Morson and Caryl Emerson point out that "[i]f Socialist Realist art (and what today might

be called fascist art) emphasizes the clean, closed-off, and narcissistic body, the art of the grotesque stresses exchange, mediation, and the ability to surprise" (449). Bakhtin, as a persecuted intellectual during the Stalinist regime, would celebrate the grotesque as a strategy of subversion.

10. Wyatt's essay, which only touches upon "Peter and the Wolf," provides a cogent critique of castration images in two of Carter's novels, *The Magic Toyshop* and *The Passion of New Eve*. Pointing out that Carter understands Freud's narratives of sexual difference "as powerful ideological tools for inscribing and so insuring women's inferiority," Wyatt draws upon Lacan and Irigaray as she explores how Carter employs the "castrated" female body to envision new possibilities for both the masculine and the feminine (549–50).

11. For another explication of Bakhtin's "positive" grotesque in relation to the "negative" grotesque of the post-Romantic (Kayser's position), see Heather Johnson's essay "Textualizing the Double-Gendered Body: Forms of the Grotesque in [Carter's] *The Passion of New Eve."* Johnson uncovers elements of both the positive and negative grotesque forms in that novel, specifically as configured in the bodies of the two central hermaphrodite characters.

12. In a passage from *The Sadeian Woman,* Carter subtextually links the body with God via writing. For her, writing "turns the flesh into word" (13). The "word" in this transmutation reshapes the metaphysical metaphor of "In the beginning was the word, and the word was God," that is, the metaphor of the transcendent authority of language, the authority of language to reveal the world. For Carter, the word— language—is the body transformed. The word might indeed reveal God, but God is the flesh, the body, the earthly—not a metaphysical non-presence. The flesh, being of the world, knows the world, and will discursively reveal, and re-create, its knowingness. For Carter, narrative enactments—words as story—deploy bodily pleasure (or displeasure). Cixous also develops her theory of *écriture féminine* on this supposition. For Carter and Cixous, desire and sexuality are inextricably bound both to the flesh and to language in their material contexts.

13. Regarding Prokofiev's conclusion in which there is "the victorious procession of the brave Peter and his hunter friends leading the captured wolf away," Nestyev writes, "[W]hile all the principal characters pass before the listener, Peter's theme is transformed from a light, carefree tune into a pompous, sharply accented march" (281). In its conclusion, Prokofiev's tale glorifies, in both text and musical composition, the masculine story of dominance and control.

Works Cited

Atwood, Margaret. *Good Bones and Simple Murders.* New York: Doubleday, 1994.

Bacchilega, Cristina. *Postmodern Fairy Tales: Gender and Narrative Strategies.* Philadelphia: U of Pennsylvania P, 1997.

Bakhtin, Mikhail M. "From Notes Made in 1970–71." *Speech Genres and Other Late Essays.* Trans. Vern W. McGee. Ed. Caryl Emerson and Michael Holquist. Austin: U of Texas P, 1986. 132–55.

———. *Rabelais and His World.* Trans. Helene Iswolsky. Bloomington: Indiana UP, 1984.

Capra, Fritjof. *The Tao of Physics: An Exploration of the Parallels Between Modern Physics and Eastern Mysticism.* 3rd ed., exp. Boston: Shambhala, 1991.

Carter, Angela. Afterword. *Fireworks: Nine Profane Pieces.* By Carter. 1974. New York: Penguin, 1984. 132–33.

————. *The Bloody Chamber and Other Stories.* New York: Penguin, 1979.

————. *Expletives Deleted: Selected Writings.* London: Vintage, 1992.

————. "An Interview with Angela Carter." *The Review of Contemporary Fiction* 14.3 (1994): 11–17.

————. *The Sadeian Woman and the Ideology of Pornography.* New York: Pantheon, 1979.

————. *Saints and Strangers.* New York: Penguin, 1985.

Cixous, Hélène. "Castration or Decapitation?" *Contemporary Literary Criticism: Literary and Cultural Studies.* Ed. Robert Con Davis and Ronald Schleifer. New York: Longman, 1989. 479–91.

————. *"Coming to Writing" and Other Essays.* Ed. Deborah Jenson. Cambridge: Harvard UP, 1991.

————. "An Exchange with Hélène Cixous." 1982. *Hélène Cixous: Writing the Feminine.* Verena Andermatt Conley. Lincoln: U of Nebraska P, 1984. 129–61.

————. "The Laugh of the Medusa." *Signs* 1.4 (1975): 875–93. Rpt. in *Feminisms.* Ed. Robyn Warhol and Diane Price Herndl. New Brunswick: Rutgers UP, 1991. 334–49.

Jacobs, Joseph, ed. *The Fables of Aesop.* Ann Arbor: University Microfilms, 1966.

Johnson, Heather. "Textualizing the Double-Gendered Body: Forms of the Grotesque in *The Passion of New Eve.*" *The Review of Contemporary Fiction* 14.3 (1994): 43–48.

Kayser, Wolfgang. *The Grotesque in Art and Literature.* Trans. Ulrich Weisstein. Bloomington: Indiana UP, 1963.

Morson, Gary Saul, and Caryl Emerson. *Mikhail Bakhtin: The Creation of a Prosaics.* Stanford: Stanford UP, 1990.

Nestyev, Israel V. *Prokofiev.* Stanford: Stanford UP, 1960.

Prokofiev, Sergei. *Peter and the Wolf.* Virgin Classics Ultraviolet, 1994.

Robinson, Harlow. *Sergei Prokofiev.* New York: Viking, 1987.

Rushdie, Salman. Introduction. *Burning Your Boats: The Collected Short Stories.* By Angela Carter. New York: Henry Holt, 1995. ix–xiv.

Russo, Mary. *The Female Grotesque: Risk, Excess and Modernity.* New York: Routledge, 1994.

————. "Female Grotesques: Carnival and Theory." *Feminist Studies/Critical Studies.* Ed. Teresa de Lauretis. Bloomington: Indiana UP, 1986. 213–29.

Snitow, Ann. "The Post-Lapsarian Eve." *The Nation* 4 Oct. 1986: 315–17.

Spencer Collection of the New York Public Library. *The Medici Aesop.* Ed. Everett Fahy. Trans. Bernard McTigue. New York: Harry N. Abrams, 1989.

Wyatt, Jean. "The Violence of Gendering: Castration Images in Angela Carter's *The Magic Toyshop, The Passion of New Eve,* and 'Peter and the Wolf.'" *Women's Studies* 25 (1996): 549–70.

Zipes, Jack, ed. *Aesop's Fables.* New York: Signet, 1992.

Janet L. Langlois

Andrew Borden's Little Girl: Fairy-Tale Fragments in Angela Carter's "The Fall River Axe Murders" and "Lizzie's Tiger"

Introduction

Angela Carter's works are new to me.[1] Although I had seen the 1984 film, *The Company of Wolves,* I had not read her "Little Red Riding Hood" rewrite on which it was based until recently. Although I have used Robert Coover's and Anne Sexton's revisions of literary *Märchen* in my courses on "Folklore and Literature," I had never assigned students any of Carter's tales until recently. I wonder now at my own resistance. Letting go and reading her short story collections has catapulted me, somewhat late, into Angela Carter fandom. I am particularly intrigued with her apparent *move away* from literary fairy tales, represented in her classic 1979 *The Bloody Chamber,* toward other narrative forms in her later collections, notably her 1985 *Black Venus* (published in 1986 in the United States as *Saints and Strangers*) and her 1993 *American Ghosts & Old World Wonders.*[2] "These stories, written late in Angela's life, are about legends and myths and marvels, about Wild Western girls and pagan practices," notes Susannah Clapp in the introduction to this last story collection (ix). Carter sensed this "move away" herself when she told Anna Katsavos in a 1988 interview, "I've noticed a very definite shift in my works, a most definite shift" (15).[3]

In one sense, reasons for this shift are not difficult to see. Critics have remarked that, in her earlier work, Carter's goal as a writer lay in contextualizing the literary *Märchen* she drew upon, often to expose their underlying patriarchal

Marvels & Tales: Journal of Fairy-Tale Studies, Vol. 12, No. 1 (1998), pp. 192–212. Copyright © 1998 by Wayne State University Press, Detroit, MI 48201.

foundations. Mary Kaiser sums up what she calls Carter's "deuniversalizing of fairy tale plots" in *The Bloody Chamber*: "Situating her tales within carefully defined cultural moments, Carter employs a wide-ranging intertextuality to link each tale to the zeitgeist of its moment and to call attention to the literary fairy tale as a product, not of a collective unconscious but of specific cultural, political and economic positions" (35). Cristina Bacchilega extends Kaiser's apt perception by regarding Carter's intertextual rereadings/rewritings of fairy tales as implicit criticism of monologic readings that disregard multiple folk and literary versions and their various social contexts. For Bacchilega, Carter's complex postmodern rewriting is "fairy-tale archaeology" that recuperates (in a good sense) these absent generic/gendered voices (50–70).

Although Bacchilega sees Carter's work in *The Bloody Chamber* as focusing more on narrative genealogy than on historical accuracy per se (61), I am not surprised that Carter turned eventually to rewriting American and European historical accounts and legends as these are narrative forms already contextualized by definition. When Salman Rushdie writes in his introduction to the 1995 collected short stories, *Burning Your Boats,* that the later stories "eschew fantasy worlds; Carter's revisionist imagination has turned towards the real, her interest towards portraiture rather than narrative" (xiii), he notes Carter's trajectory out of *Märchen* and into legend. He reinscribes Jacob Grimm's often-quoted 1844 statement that "The fairy-tale flies, the legend walks, knocks at your door; the one can draw freely out of the fullness of poetry, the other has almost the authority of history" (qtd. in Dégh 72).

In another sense, however, reasons for Carter's ostensible shift from "the fullness of poetry" to "almost the authority of history" must be perplexing to critics who value the writer for just those qualities she apparently left behind in her later works.[4] In response to interviewer Anna Katsavos's question, "What sort of games do you most enjoy playing with the reader?" Carter answered in part that "I'm doing it less, actually, because I have less time. . . . I find myself thinking much more simply because I'm spending so much time with a small child" (Katsavos 15). Notwithstanding the very real parenting issues facing her, I sense that Carter's pragmatic response might be amplified in theoretical ways. My project here, then, is to explore some of her later, "simpler" stories that resonate with and around History.

Rushdie comments that some of the best stories in these later books are portraits, "portraits of Baudelaire's black mistress Jeanne Duval, of Edgar Allan Poe and of Lizzie Borden" (xiii). Perhaps because both Carter and I have been drawn to American women who "took an axe . . ." and carved their way into a certain historical consciousness (Langlois), I focus here on the portrait of Lizzie Borden, who may or may not have murdered her father and stepmother in Fall River, Massachusetts, in 1892. Although, for some years before her own death in 1992, Carter was considering writing a novel about Lizzie Borden, for whatever reason, whether for practical constraints on her time or for reasons of philosophical/critical position, the short stories, "The Fall River Axe Murders" and "Lizzie's Tiger," rather than that (unwritten) novel, are the texts before us.[5] Earlier versions of both stories appeared in 1981,[6] but "The Fall River Axe Murders" was technically the first to be published, for it appeared as the last story in *Black Venus* in 1985 (reprinted in the 1995 *Burning Your Boats*) and as the first story, somewhat altered, in *Saints and Strangers* in 1986 (*SS* hereafter). Published in *American Ghosts & Old World Wonders* in 1993, "Lizzie's Tiger" was also reprinted in 1995.

"The Fall River Axe Murders": The House on Second Street

Both versions of "The Fall River Axe Murders" present such a realistic picture of the day of the murders, 4 August 1892, that readers might accuse Carter of paraphrasing somewhat too closely the casebook studies that document the famous event.[7] Historical accuracy per se appears uppermost. Historical sources confirm, for instance, that it *was* a scorching day in the New England mill town. Carter's British version begins: "Hot, hot, hot . . . very early in the morning, before the factory whistle, but, even at this hour, everything shimmers and quivers under the attack of white, furious sun already high in the still air" (300). Her American version amplifies: "Hot, hot, hot. Even though it is early in the morning, well before the factory whistle issues its peremptory summons from the dark, satanic mills to which the city owes its present pre-eminence in the cotton trade, the white, furious sun already shimmers and quivers high in the still air" (*SS* 9).

Writer Rikki Ducornet, who has written one of the few critical pieces on this short story, highlights this particular image as informing the rest of the story to follow: "At the story's center, the sun's vortex gyres" (37). The summer heat wave marks the contrast between this story and the crystalline winter scenes sharply etching Carter's *Märchen* such as "The Bloody Chamber," "The Company of Wolves," "The Snow Child" and "The Werewolf" (Bacchilega 36–38, 59). It anchors the story in social realism, in the quotidian stink of bodies: of workers' bodies sweltering in the heat of New England mills, of mill owners' bodies (and those of their wives, daughters and servants) sweltering in Victorian cultural codes. Yet, in the passage quoted from the American version, Carter's allusion to Blake's prophetic vision of the Industrial Revolution hints at her "reformist imagination" at work, positioning Lizzie Borden, a mill owner's daughter, at the nexus of social, political and historical forces but in league with the devil.

Both versions of the story layer stifling historic detail upon detail.[8] Carter focuses on the Borden house, for example, "narrow as a coffin" (301; *SS* 10) and as airless on that too-hot morning when family members will wake sickened by food tainted by the heat: Lizzie, a thirty-two-year-old spinster still living in her miserly father's house (her older sister Emma, also a spinster, is gone visiting); her father, Andrew Jackson Borden, the entrepreneur and patriarch; her hated stepmother, Abby Durfee Gray Borden; John Vinnicum Morse, her deceased mother's brother on a visit; and Bridget Sullivan, their Irish housemaid and cook. (Dis)located on Second Street in the "flats" down among the middle-class Irish residents near the town's business center rather than up on the "Hill" where Fall River's Yankee elite lived and the Bordens' social standing would have allowed them to reside (Robertson 363–68), the house stands as mute testimony to the family's dysfunction. Carter notes accurately: "One peculiarity of this house is the number of doors the rooms contain and, a further peculiarity, how all these doors are always locked. A house full of locked doors that open only into other rooms with other locked doors, for, upstairs and downstairs, all the rooms lead in and out of one another like a maze in a bad dream. It is a house without passages" (304; *SS* 13). Details pile up and are caught in the early morning *before* the murders occur. The story is as still and oppressive as the day, the house and the characters themselves. The story is plotless because it stops *before* it can build to narrative. It is literally a "Mise-en-Scène for a Parricide," the first title under which "Fall River Axe Murders" was published in 1981. It exemplifies, in an ironic way, Jacob Grimm's comment that legendary material is more "fettered" than *Märchen* "but more home-like" (qtd. in Dégh 72).

The Borden house, "cramped, comfortless, small and mean" (302; *SS* 10), appears the very antithesis of the castle in "The Bloody Chamber": "The faery solitude of the place; with its turrets of misty blue, its spiked gate . . ." (117). Carter echoes this contrast when the narrator accurately notes that Lizzie had a chance to leave the narrow house in "the sweating months of June, July and August" when "few of their social class stay in Fall River" because she "was invited away, too, to a summer house by the sea to join a merry band of girls." But Lizzie, enmeshed, refuses the offer: " . . . but, *as if* on purpose to mortify her flesh, *as if* important business kept her in the exhausted town, *as if a wicked fairy spelled her in Second Street*, she did not go" (302; *SS* 10; my emphasis). Yet the incremental repetitions of "as if" pull the domestic space of Victorian house and the *Märchen* world closer together for Lizzie, the omniscient narrator and the reader alike in what must be a typical Carter tease.

Carter reiterates the triply-closed system of the Borden house, Lizzie's prospects, and the story frame when the narrator refers to a European tour Lizzie had taken two years earlier in 1890 with other "girls" who would not marry: "It was a sour trip, in some ways, sour; and it was a round trip, it ended at the sour place from where it had set out. Home, again: the narrow house, *the rooms all locked like those in Bluebeard's castle*. . . ." (314; *SS* 28; my emphasis). This allusion also opens up intertextual references to the *Märchen* world in the parallel space of simile; it aligns the Bordens and those unhappy families "never more than one step away from disaster" that Carter saw depicted "in the traditional tale, no matter whence its provenance." It specifically links the Bordens' case to those fairy tales that "offer evidence that even widely different types of family structures still create unforgivable crimes between human beings too close together" (Carter, *The Old Wives' Fairy Tale Book* xviii–xix). And it indicates that "The Fall River Axe Murders," as so many traditional tales before it, ends "at the sour place from where it had set out," a situation Ducornet recognizes in the short story's multiple levels of circularity and enclosure (37–39).

That these embedded fragments of the fairy tale Carter ostensibly left behind indicate her fusion of the fantastic and the everyday must come as no surprise to Carter aficionados who have long acknowledged her propensity towards magic realism (Kendrick). Yet how she plays out the idea that Jacob Grimm had already noted a century and a half ago that *Märchen* and legend could "by turns . . . play into one another" (qtd. in Dégh 72) is a process worth attending to more closely. Agreeing with Walter Kendrick's assessment that she "suspends time, lets murderer and victims sleep, while she ponders, digresses, speculates . . . broods over the legendary house at 92 Second Street, Fall River," I argue that "The Fall River Axe Murders," "a bizarre amalgam of tale and essay, delicacy and grossness," becomes a meditation on the liminal spaces between these genres (66).

Carter speculates on different ways one might "*Märchen*-ize" Lizzie Borden's story, in mirror imagings of Bacchilega's and Kaiser's readings of her historicizing literary *Märchen* in *The Bloody Chamber*. She does this through focusing on portraiture, as Rushdie noted. "The Fall River Axe Murders" contains many verbal portraits of Lizzie, some complementing, others contradicting each other. The pivotal first portrait presented, like that of the stifling Second-Street house discussed above, builds on historical detail; it concentrates on what Lizzie will wear that hot, fateful day; it depicts her through action strangely static because set in the future tense:

> On this morning, when, after breakfast and the performance of a few household duties, Lizzie Borden *will murder* her parents, she *will*, on rising, don a simple cotton frock—but, under that, went a long, starched cotton petticoat; another short, starched cotton petticoat; long drawers; woollen stockings; a chemise; and a whalebone corset that took her viscera in a stern hand and squeezed them very tightly. She also strapped a heavy linen napkin between her legs because she was menstruating. (300–01; my emphasis)[9]

From this point, however, Carter presents two divergent lines of possible representation. The one she considers first is the grass-roots, folk or popular depiction of the legendary Lizzie that segues from the description above: "In all these clothes, out of sorts and nauseous as she was, in this dementing heat, her belly in a vice, she will heat up a flat-iron on a stove and press handkerchiefs with the heated iron until it is time for her to go down to the cellar woodpile to collect the hatchet *with which our imagination*—'Lizzie Borden with an axe'— *always equips her,* just as we always visualize St Catherine rolling along her wheel, the emblem of her passion" (301; *SS* 10; my emphasis). The ubiquitous children's folk rhyme, the epigram which heads both versions of the short story and whose first line Carter quotes above, is simple and illustrative.[10] It positions Lizzie as murderer and, through the polishing effect of repeated transmission, it hones down the voluminous Borden case documentation to the "emotional core" of elemental family conflict—a daughter's "whacking" her parents to death.[11] Carter's apparent writerly digression, while cataloging family members in the house on 4 August, only highlights the emblematic qualities of this time-polished (re)visioning:

> Write him out of the script.
> Even though his presence in the doomed house is historically unim-peachable, the colouring of this domestic apocalypse must be crude and the design profoundly simplified for the maximum emblematic effect.
> Write John Vinnicum Morse out of the script. (302; *SS* 10)

Ducornet reads Carter's story, in fact, as an emblem book for Anger, summer heat transmuted into Passion; she writes that "Lizzie is emblematic and exemplary; she is reduced to sign—the ax she carries within her grinding madly," in a pun literalizing the folk metaphor worthy of Carter herself (37).

Here, Lizzie's story takes on the patina of *Märchen,* an emblematized form itself for many folktale scholars.[12] I think that Carter, who would have appreciated the current fate of "the doomed house"—opened as The Lizzie Borden Bed and Breakfast in August 1996, a piece of cultural tourism still scripting the legend ("Inn Cold Blood"; Witchel)—may have been thinking of a once-favorite quote from Jean-Luc Godard's *Alphaville:* "There are times when reality becomes too complex for Oral Communication. But Legend gives it a form by which it pervades the whole world" (qtd. in Katsavos 12). Godard echoes Jacob Grimm's observation that "As the fairy tale stands related to the legend, so does legend to history. . . ." (qtd. in Dégh 72).

Carter clearly supports these "legends of people," to borrow a phrase from anthropologist Bruce Kapferer, for she accepts the basic premise that Lizzie did it, as did the working classes of Fall River who "viewed the case as yet another example of the rich literally getting away with murder" (Robertson 362). She does not accept what Kapferer calls "myths of state," in this case the official verdict of acquittal of a good, Christian woman of high social standing in the June 1893 trial, a "myth" or verdict supported by jury, judges, journalists and others, including suffragettes of the day (who, however, with other elites, ostracized Lizzie once the trial was over) (Robertson 362). She eschews the underlying mythic narrative operating at the trial for both prosecution and defense with somewhat different inflections: the fate of Lizzie as a "damsel in distress," a heroine of romance who could not have committed such brutal crimes, or, at least, not easily (Jones 221–22; Robertson 391–416).[13] She also disregards other voices, contemporary and current, that develop alternative theories of who might have killed the Bordens if Lizzie did not.[14] In this respect, she reverses the process of recuperating multiple voices in literary *Märchen* but, in doing so, gives credence to a folk voice.

Then, Carter turns from the emblematic legend of "Lizzie Borden with an axe," "with which our imagination always equips her," to the second line of representation with which our imaginations have not dealt so easily: *why* she killed (Schofield 92–93). The narrator, in discussing why all the doors, inside and out, were locked in the Bordens' house, accurately reviews a burglary that predated the double murders by several years and that has been seen by many as a prelude to them. The burglar took Mrs. Borden's jewels, then urinated and defecated on the Bordens' bed. Andrew Borden, "a man raped," nonetheless, stopped the initial police inquiry and locked the doors, a clear sign to current scholars, but not to contemporary observers, that he thought it an inside job; most agree that he knew or suspected that it was Lizzie herself who was also a kleptomaniac and may have had "hysteric spells" close to her menstrual periods like her mother had before her (304–06; *SS* 16–17). At the time of the burglary, Mr. and Mrs. Borden were away from the house; Emma and Lizzie were at home. The narrator muses:

> The girls stayed at home in their rooms, napping on their beds or repairing ripped hems, or sewing loose buttons more securely, or writing letters, or contemplating acts of charity among the deserving poor, or staring vacantly into space.
> *I can't imagine what else they might do.*
> *What the girls do when they are on their own is unimaginable to me.*
> (304; *SS* 13; my emphasis)

Yet the rest of the "The Fall River Axe Murders" resonates with imagining just what Lizzie Borden did on her own to bring her to parricide. Carter broods over this "blank page" and constructs portraits of Lizzie that are not unsympathetic and which address feminist debates both about her own writings and about the Lizzie Borden case (Altevers, Bacchilega, Duncker, Jones, Kaiser, Robertson, Schofield). Feminist critics have read Carter's treatment of locked-up women in different ways. Her focus on the Bordens' locked house and on the restrictive clothing Lizzie will wear seems to confirm Patricia Duncker's broader critique of Carter's stories in *The Bloody Chamber* that she ultimately reinforces gender stereotypes, despite her innovative prose techniques, by choosing "to inhabit a tiny room of her own in the house of fiction. For women, that space has always been paralysingly, cripplingly small" (12). But for Mary Kaiser, Carter's representations are culturally and historically sound because they accurately present women's conditions in the time periods portrayed in her stories. And for Ann Schofield, "The Fall River Axe Murders" is one of a small body of twentieth-century fiction dealing with the Lizzie Borden story as a feminist quest, one that "portrays Lizzie Borden as an individual oppressed by historical circumstances and struggling to break free of social restraints," one that simultaneously breaks free of gender stereotypes itself (95–96).

Regardless of the positions taken, the critics above might agree that Carter plays with the dialectic between constraint and freedom for women in some complicated ways as the story draws to its close. Part of this play involves an intricate overlay of the *Märchen* world with that encased in 92 Second Street, Fall River, in a much more specific and focused way than earlier. The short story spirals back to its beginning with an extended description of Lizzie sleeping in her locked room, the room she loves, "a pleasant room of not ungenerous dimensions, seeing the house is so very small," on that hot morning *before* she rises and dresses in the first portrait discussed above. In its privacy, she is wearing "a rich girl's pretty nightdress, although she lives in a mean house, because she is a rich girl too": "The hem of her nightdress is rucked up above her knees because she is a restless sleeper. Her light, dry, reddish hair, crackling with static, slipping loose from the night-time plait, crisps and stutters over the square pillow at which she clutches as she sprawls on her stomach, having rested her cheek on the starched pillowcase for coolness' sake at some earlier hour" (309; *SS* 23).[15]

"Sleep," the narrator tells readers, "opens within her a disorderly house" (310; *SS* 24). Her "nightdress rucked up above her knees" and her hair "slipping loose from the night-time plait" suggest a lessening of restrictions/constrictions in the dream world of sleep. Yet "her room is harsh with the metallic smell of menstrual blood" (309; *SS* 24). Carter seems to superimpose the image of the vampiress's blood-flecked nightgown in "The Lady of the House of Love" from *The Bloody Chamber* over this bedroom scene, and so disrupts Lizzie's harmless sartorial attempts to offset her father's conflicted Victorian codes and shifts her towards butchery (195–209). Rushdie notes this double (con)fusion of menstrual and murder victims' blood, and of historical personage and dramatis personae of fairy tale when he writes, "Beneath the hyper-realism, however, there is an echo of *The Bloody Chamber;* for Lizzie's is a bloody deed, and she is, in addition, menstruating. Her own life-blood flows, while the angel of death waits on a nearby tree" (xiii–xiv).

Intertextual references to *The Bloody Chamber* move so dangerously close to the story's surface now that its still waters writhe with the bloody storm that is to come. Carter takes two extensions of the portrait of Lizzie sleeping, her actual photograph and her image in a looking glass, and breaks their surfaces with fairy-tale shards. In the first instance, the narrator asks readers to imagine finding a surviving daguerreotype of Lizzie Borden: "If you were sorting through a box of old photographs in a junk shop and came across the particular, sepia, faded face above the choked collars of the 1890s, you might murmur when you saw her: *'Oh, what big eyes you have!' as Red Riding Hood said to the wolf,* but then you might not even pause to pick her out and look at her more closely, for hers is not, in itself, a striking face" (315; *SS* 29; my emphasis).[16]

In the second instance, narrator and readers watch Lizzie watching herself in her bedroom mirror:

> There is a mirror on the dresser in which she sometimes looks at those times when time snaps in two and then she sees herself with blind, clairvoyant eyes, as though she were another person.
>
> "Lizzie is not herself, today."
>
> At those times, those irremediable times, *she could have raised her muzzle to some aching moon and howled.*
>
> At other times, she watches herself doing her hair and trying her clothes on. . . .
>
> She is a girl of Sargasso calm. (315; *SS* 30; my emphasis)

In both instances, Carter sets up a dual image—Lizzie as the wolf in fairy tale, Lizzie as an ordinary person—that opens up the "disordered house within her" despite locked room and choked collar. The overt reference to "Little Red Riding Hood" conditionally connects Lizzie's story, not to the literary fairy tales of Perrault and Grimm, but to Carter's three dark rewrites in *The Bloody Chamber*: "The Werewolf," "The Company of Wolves," and "Wolf-Alice," whose richness, complexity and subversion Bacchilega reveals in her analyses (50–70). Lizzie is in the company of wolves. She, perhaps, has most in common with the female characters in "The Werewolf" who seem to be "sheep" (grandmother and granddaughter in their respective, appropriate feminine roles in a harsh economy) but are hidden "wolves" (the grandmother a were-witch, the grand-daughter her possible killer who prospers in a most masculine way) (Bacchilega 59–62). Ducornet writes that Lizzie "is in fact a werewolf ruled by the moon" whose "anger has made her supernatural" and who literally "cuts loose" from her "coffin house" by hacking its occupants to death (39). Cara Robertson, in assessing cultural representations of Lizzie at her trial, notes that the economic imperative—to fall heir to her father's fortune kept from her while he was alive—is an obvious motive not, however, recognized by either defense or prosecution, who could not fully accept that "the angel in the house" might also be "the madwoman in the attic" (Gilbert and Gubar). Carter's reference to Jean Rhys's rewriting of *Jane Eyre* from a viewpoint sympathetic to the madwoman ("a girl of Sargasso calm") suggests just this association, however.[17]

It is this sympathy for the "wolf" in Lizzie, not its condoning but its understanding, that ties "The Fall River Axe Murders" to "The Company of Wolves." Bacchilega argues that the latter rewrite draws on the folk traditions that werewolves were melancholy creatures to be pitied as well as feared (62). "The Fall River Axe Murders" focuses near its conclusion on an incident presented as the immediate cause for Lizzie's flailing out against her parents: her father butchers and her stepmother eats in a pie the pet pigeons that were her only consolation. "At home all was blood and feathers." Although "she doesn't weep, this one, it isn't her nature, she is still waters, . . ." she picks up the axe her father used and remembers (316; *SS* 30–31). Feminist critics, Joan N. Radner and Suzanne Lanser, draw on a remarkably similar story, Susan Glaspell's 1917 "A Jury of Her Peers," in developing their analysis of women's folk coding as strategies within patriarchal discourse. In Glaspell's story, farmers' wives decode signs of a neighbor woman's disordered kitchen, including a dead canary in its cage with neck wrung, as evidence that she is the one who has killed her abusive husband. Their husbands, acting as sheriff and deputy, do not see these signs; the women remain silent, complicitous, empathetic in allowing the farmwife her probable freedom (1–3). So, perhaps, for Lizzie.

Lizzie, who is "the wild card" in the Borden house (314; *SS* 29), is also something like Carter's "wild child," Wolf-Alice. Both are menstruating and both confront their own reflections in the patriarchal mirror (Bacchilega 64–66). However, while the fairy-tale heroines'/wolves' initiations ultimately open them up to sensual and nurturing encounters in the cold winter of Carter's *Märchen* rewrites, no such maturation process touches Lizzie Borden, constrained in her father's house. "The Fall River Axe Murders" resolutely focuses on family dynamic and submerges sexual connection. Little Red sleeps between the paws of the tender wolf before her own transformation in "The Company of Wolves"; Wolf-Alice licks the vampiric Count into humanity; Lizzie Borden stares into the mirror where "time goes by and nothing happens" (315; *SS* 30). Sometimes she might howl, alone, at "the aching moon" yet her icy demeanor, noted by journalists at her trial, remains despite summer heat.[18]

Carter's hyper-realism and her dark ironic literary *Märchen* here converge on Victorian conventions of the feminine. Carter takes what Cara Robertson sees as complementary ideologies sometimes called forth and sometimes suppressed in Lizzie Borden's trial—the born criminal "who has remained animalized" (378), the female hysteric whose "duality" threatened Victorian divisions between virtuous and decadent women (386) and the periodic insanity due to menstruation making violent crime possible (387–91)—as valid explanations for Lizzie's actions. Carter, in fact, carries the prosecution's unsuccessful arguments further than the state was willing to go in assessing motivation. She suggests that Lizzie's gender-bending blood-lust might grant her freedom; her dual image might confound the mirror; her axe might break open a door on Second Street, but that "a free woman in an unfree society is a monster" (*The Sadeian Woman* 27).

When Robertson writes of the trial, "In a sense, the Miss Lizzie of the defense plays Jekyll to Lizzie Andrew Borden's Hyde as conceived by the prosecution" (411–15), the "*Märchen*-izing" of Lizzie Borden's story comes full circle.[19] Not only Carter's not-so-simple versions of "The Fall River Axe Murders" but also the Commonwealth of Massachusetts vs. Lizzie Borden partake of "fiction" in the broadest sense. Carter's story points to the *Märchen* world, on the one hand, but also toward the social and narrative constructions of the historical record in the Borden case, on the other (Robertson 356; Schofield 98–101). She gives readers a concrete example of Jacob Grimm's comment partially quoted earlier that "As the fairy-tale stands related to the legend, so does legend to history, *and (we may add) so does history to real life*" (qtd. in Dégh 72; my emphasis).

"Lizzie's Tiger": The Cottage on Ferry Street and the Circus Tents

Ann Schofield makes a telling comment about "The Fall River Axe Murders" when she writes that, when it concludes "with violence summoned, Lizzie's future is left to the reader" (95). Carter does focus relentlessly on the past, probing its crevices and permutations for answers, perhaps, to the enigma of Lizzie's character and motivations. Carter's second story, "Lizzie's Tiger," constructs a day long before the murders when Lizzie, then a four-year-old child, escapes her restrictive home, at the time a cottage on Ferry Street, to go to the circus.[20] It more clearly exemplifies Alison Lurie's comment that Carter "weaves intricate fantasies around historical characters" (11) as no historical documentation supports the liminal moment when Lizzie confronts a caged tiger after her own mother, Sarah J. Morse Borden, has died and before her father marries her stepmother, Abby Durfee Gray Borden. Although Schofield notes that "The Fall River Axe Murders" escapes the "Freudian family romance" which drives many twentieth-century reworkings of the Borden story (91–96), this second story picks up familial threads in the first which, if not distinctly oedipal, point to significant emotional experiences for its protagonists: Lizzie's mourning the loss of her mother (310; *SS* 23–24), her father's conflicted adulation of his youngest daughter despite his miserliness, and Lizzie's youthful recognition of her power to manipulate her father for small change (314; *SS* 19).

Social realism and literary *Märchen* interpenetrate in this second story, too, but in more subtle and pervasive ways. As the story begins, the description of the Borden cottage illustrates this muted intertexuality. Carter writes: "The hovel on Ferry stood, or, rather, leaned at a bibulous angle on a narrow street cut across at an oblique angle by another narrow street, all the old wooden homes *like an upset cookie jar of broken gingerbread houses lurching this way and that way,* and the shutters hanging off their hinges and windows stuffed with old newspapers, and the snagged picket fence . . ." (322; my emphasis). The Borden home is located both in the worst slum area of Fall River, down near the Taunton river where the shacks of newly-arrived Portuguese and French-Canadian mill workers stand close to the mills (Robertson 366), and in the dark forest of "Hansel and Gretel." Like the house on Second Street which Ducornet called "the gingerbread house," punning again on Victorian architecture and the Grimms' witch's enticing dwelling (38), it embodies all the anxieties about changing family relationships, blended-family tensions and hinted-at incestuous desires with which contemporary folk-tale scholars and writers have imbued the Grimms' tale.[21] The narrator, strangely positioned somewhere between omniscient and family storyteller, only comments about Lizzie and Emma, "Such was the anxious architecture of the two girls' early childhood" (322).

Like the siblings in the fairy tale, Lizzie escapes the edible/devouring house, but only for a brief moment. She and her sister Emma, thirteen at the time and too young for all the household duties, see a circus poster "showing the head of a tiger" tacked on their fence one midsummer day (322). The poster, more symbolic than realistic because its image is stylized and fragmented, creates another place that foreshadows the alternative world of the circus (Bouissac 176–90). It draws Lizzie, stubborn as her father, out of her bed after supper and out the back door on a fairy-tale quest. As she moves alone through the cityscape to the forbidden circus, the Victorian middle-class conventions her father imposes on her, despite their impecunious living situation, fade for her. The child becomes a small, female version of the nineteenth-century aesthete *flâneur,* walking through the city, watching, observing and interacting in ways and in places proscribed by her father's aspirations, the gender role assigned her, and the bourgeois repression of carnival (Stallybrass and White).

Carter honors the nineteenth-century conception of the city and its spaces as she tracks Lizzie's progress *down* through geographic space and social class, illuminating a semiotically-charged urban landscape. "A gaggle of ragged Irish children from Corkey Row" take her to the field on the edge of town where the circus tents have been set up, and one of the boys swings her up on his shoulders since she is too small to keep up with them, foreshadowing the contact she will have with man, boy and tiger later in the evening but not again (323). Once in the big top, "a red and white striped tent of scarcely imaginable proportions, into which you could have popped the entire house on Ferry, . . ." she finds herself among those immigrant millworkers—Lancashire, Portuguese and French-Canadian—her father both lives in the proximity of and disdains. Within its expansive canvas walls, class, ethnic, and gender oppositions melt in carnival. "All unnoticeably small as she was, she was taken up by the crowd and tossed about among insensitive shoes and petticoats, too close to the ground to see much else for long. . . ." In "the frenetic bustle of the midway," Lizzie experiences sensuous delights of smell, taste and touch which counteract and subvert her gaze (323–25). She comes under the spell of what Rushdie calls "Carter's other country": "the fairground, the world of the gimcrack showman, the hypnotist, the trickster, the puppeteer" (xi). Carter and Lizzie revel in Bakhtin's carnivalesque "lower bodily orders."

Following a piglet more sensuous than the snow white bird that guides Hansel and Gretel, Lizzie runs out of the big tent and beyond the circus grounds to "an abrupt margin of pitch black and silence" where the sensual landscape becomes further eroticized for her. Before she sees a couple coupling in the grass and a dwarf somersaulting across her path, she experiences the tiger trainer's lust firsthand as he "took firm hold of her right hand and brought it tenderly up between his squatting thighs." The narrator notes that although she does not mind this act of sexual abuse, Lizzie does mind when the trainer asks her for a kiss: "She *did* mind that and shook an obdurate head; she did not like her father's hard, dry, imperative kisses, and endured them only for the sake of power" (325–26). Juxtaposition of the tiger trainer's and Andrew Borden's kisses projects the Ferry Street cottage onto the dark spaces around the circus grounds with that breath of incest that intrigues and troubles Carter and other scholars in the Borden case (Robertson 406–09; Schofield 92–93).

A smaller tent behind the large striped tent draws Lizzie. She follows the tiger trainer to the back of this smaller tent whose pulsing "bright mauve, ammoniac reek" marks the tiger's range.[22] When the narrator comments that the trainer fumbles at this tent's flap as he had fumbled earlier at his trousers, readers must guess that the tiger "burning bright" within is Blakean experience writ large. Carter makes this phallic (and paternal) connection obvious and overblown, seemingly parodying Freudians' projective readings of folktales: "The tiger walked up and down, up and down; it walked up and down like Satan walking about the world and it burned. It burned so brightly, she was scorched. Its tail, thick as her father's forearm, twitched back and forth at the tip" (328). A French-Canadian boy, there to see the tiger with his large family, has picked Lizzie up in his arms so that she, too, can see the beast despite his mother's ironic warning that Lizzie, mudstained and tousled, might harbor lice herself. When Lizzie is drawn towards the beast and the beast is drawn to the child in a way that frightens the boy holding her and that catches the attention of the raucous crowd, Carter writes, "Time somersaulted. Space diminished to the field of attractive force between the child and the tiger. All that existed in the whole world now were Lizzie and the tiger" (328).

Lizzie's encounter with the tiger thrusts readers, too, even further into alterity; they are thrown into the *Märchen* world of "Beauty and the Beast," particularly into that of "The Tiger's Bride," which I find the most openly sensual of Carter's rewritings of the ancient animal husband's tale (154–69). Both stories share protagonists: a miserly father in one, a profligate father in the other; daughters caught in commodity brokerage; and the tigers, raw sexual energy paradoxically harnessed in a cage in one and in a civilized suit and mask in the other. Both stories share the same language, especially in the attraction between girl and beast. In "The Tiger's Bride," the girl ultimately chooses the Beast her father initially forced upon her. Naked, filled with fear redolent of "Hansel and Gretel," she comes to the Beast: "Nursery fears made flesh and sinew; earliest and most archaic of fears, fear of devourment. The beast and his carnivorous bed of bone and I, white, shaking, raw, approaching him as if offering, in myself, the key to a peaceable kingdom in which his appetite need not be my extinction" (168). The tiger crawls towards her; "the reverberations of his purring rocked the foundations of the house" and prove her "as if" offer valid. "And each stroke of his tongue ripped off skin after successive skin, all the skins of a life in the world, and left behind a nascent patina of shining hairs" (169).

Bacchilega's reading of "The Tiger's Bride" as subversion of a patriarchal order, itself subverted by Beauty's moment of hesitation, is particularly apt when applied to "Lizzie's Tiger" (95–102). If "The Tiger's Bride" "liberates women only partially within a genre which . . . is often used to constrain gender" (101–02), then how much less liberating is Lizzie's story (first published in *Cosmopolitan*)? The child, constrained by the Canadian boy, by the trace of incest prohibition (if parody can be in deadly earnest), by "all the skins of a life in the world," cannot transform completely into the Beast's feline mate although her love drew it, too, purring, on its belly towards her over gnawed bloody bones, "the serpentine length of its ceaselessly twitching tail" behind it (328–29). The narrator's "as if" musings are horribly ironic in this case, in the light of the axe murders to come: "It was . . . as if this little child of all the children in the world, might lead it towards a peaceable kingdom where it need not eat meat. But only 'as if'" (328).[23]

Crack! The spell broke.
The world bounded into the ring. (329)

The tiger trainer's whip as he jumps into the cage signals his confrontation with the tiger and his mastery over it, in what Paul Bouissac sees as the basic semiotic text of the circus act (90–107). Yet, as psychoanalytical readings of fairy tales prepare us (Carter seems to take them straight as the story draws to its finale), both characters can be seen within circus ritual, meant to confuse the human and the animal, as aspects of the same familial/familiar person writ large (Bouissac 108–22). "Then he placed one booted foot on the tiger's skull and cleared his throat for speech. He was a hero. He was a tiger himself, but even more so, because he was a man" (329). For a moment, tiger/man re-establishes the fearful rule of the patriarchal father. When the French-Canadian boy tries to kiss Lizzie on the forehead before he sets her down, her shouts break her cover and the crowd recognizes her because she is "the most famous daughter" in the whole town: " 'Well, if it ain't Andrew Borden's little girl! What are they Canucks doing with little Lizzie Borden?' " (331). Lizzie Borden is caught in a way the heroine of "The Tiger's Bride" is not; she is still "daddy's girl" (Bacchilega 73).

The story ends with the freedom of circus and carnival dissipating, with the child Lizzie doomed to return to the succession of Victorian gingerbread houses which will ultimately bestialize her. For she will take back to the Ferry Street Cottage and to the house on Second Street "the sudden access of enlightenment" she gained as the tiger trainer spoke of his control of his cats: "I have established a hierarchy of FEAR . . . because I know that all the time they want to kill me, that is their project, that is their intention . . ." (330–31). "Her pale-blue Calvinist eyes" will take on the qualities of the "flat, mineral eyes of the tiger" (328). As she hugs the family cat, Miss Ginger Cuddles, as she climbs "kitten-like" (322) into her father's lap to ask for money, she will remember that " 'The tiger is the cat's revenge' " (330). Like the nineteenth-century women labelled as hysterics by Freud and his predecessors, she will internalize the frenzy of carnival until, repressed, it will return 4 August 1892 in an individual, bloody act of resentment (Stallybrass and White).[24]

In "Lizzie's Tiger," Carter takes up what Bouissac has called "the link between children and the circus" in the Western tradition (122) and makes further links to the *Märchen* world of "Hansel and Gretel" and "Beauty and the Beast," possibly two of the most-discussed fairy tales in the western canon of children's literature. The intricate linkage holds possible sexual abuse and father-daughter incest just below the surface of Lizzie's story, however. And Carter seems to ask readers to consider the implications of such family dysfunction and sexual tension whether in childhood fantasy or experience, a question haunting readings of her works, literary *Märchen*, psychoanalytic and social work literature still.

Conclusion: Maplecroft on the Hill

Although Carter's stories about Lizzie Borden are quite different from each other, my analysis has focused on what seem to be Carter's similar narrative strategies in both; she spins out intertextual *Märchen* threads in both stories to lead protagonist and readers momentarily and paradoxically out of closed cultural, historical and literary frames into the more open spaces of "once upon a time" or "as if," and then she shuts the door. We, as readers, are caught in a dialectic "archi'text'ure" that encloses in "The Fall River Axe Murders" and that runs at oblique angles in "Lizzie's Tiger."[25]

I can only imagine a third story about Lizzie Borden that Carter might have written had she lived. It would have been about Lizzie's life after her acquittal. She and her sister Emma bought a thirteen-room mansion that stood on "the Hill" on French Street in the upper-class section of Fall River with part of the quarter of a million dollars inherited from their father's estate. Lizzie, who changed her name to Lizbeth, named the house "Maplecroft" and lived there until her death in 1927, despite the probably appropriate social ostracism she endured. What Joyce Williams calls "the only extant expression of what Lizzie wanted," the house has many windows that looked out "in marked contrast" to the hovel on Ferry Street and to the narrow house on Second Street. At Maplecroft, Lizzie actually had two bedrooms—one for winter and one for summer—and the front (winter) bedroom extended the width of the house with eight windows (Emma took a small interior bedroom that might have been slated as a maid's room) (Williams 233–39).

I imagine that Carter would pull readers once again into contemplating this new short story about Lizzie and "The Lady of the House of Love" as intricate palimpsests. In the latter story, "the beautiful queen of the vampires sits all alone in her dark, high house" with "her own suite of drawing room and bedroom" (195) as Lizzie might have in her spacious rooms. Yet the Countess opens up "the long-sealed windows of the horrid bedroom" and "light and air streamed in" as signs of her self-annihilating love for the innocent British soldier (207). Lizzie's open windows, allowing sun-lit reflections on the chandeliers and crystal within, seem to give evidence of her conflicted feelings about her parental homes (Williams 233) and of her own self-construction (Jones 232–33).

No such story will be written, yet Maplecroft itself stands as an emblem of Carter's postscript to *The Sadeian Woman:* "History tells us that every oppressed class gained true liberation from its masters through its own efforts. It is necessary that women learn that lesson. . . ." (151). That Lizzie Borden had to learn that lesson through the probable murder of her father and stepmother suggests that she has become "one of the dark ladies [with] unappeasable appetites to whom Angela Carter is so partial" (Rushdie xi).

Notes

1. I thank writer Anne Finger and our student Mary Kathryn Keith who indirectly introduced me to "The Fall River Axe Murders" and colleagues Andrea di Tommaso, Ross Pudaloff and Anca Vlasopolos for their allusive help. I also thank Cristina

Bacchilega, Kathleen Manley and Danielle M. Roemer for their introducing me to "Lizzie's Tiger" and for their bibliographical information, critical comments and support.

2. All collections (except *Saints and Strangers*) have been republished together in 1995 as Carter's *Burning Your Boats: The Collected Short Stories*. All page references will be to this edition unless otherwise noted.

3. In all fairness, I may be taking Carter's statement somewhat out of context. The shift to which she refers may be read as a move from the more "speculative fiction" of her earlier novels to that of "a kind of down-to-earthness" in the short stories in *The Bloody Chamber*. It may also be read as a move from a certain complex verbal game-playing in the *Märchen* to the more "simple" narrative structures of her later collections (Katsavos 14–15). The first reading contradicts the argument being presented here; the second complements it.

4. Judging by the far greater number of critical pieces on *The Bloody Chamber* and by Rushdie's statement that this collection is Carter's masterwork (xi), I conjecture that such critics' responses may correspond to the general devaluing of legendary forms in comparison to *Märchen* in much folk narrative scholarship.

5. Clapp writes, "The stories are quite different; both are characteristic. Taken together, they show what a fine, fierce book we might have had" (xi). Rushdie echoes her sentiments: "One hankers for more; for the Lizzie Borden novel that we cannot have" (xi).

6. An earlier version of "The Fall River Axe Murders" appeared as "Mise-en-Scène for a Parricide" in the *London Review of Books* in September 1981; a version of "Lizzie's Tiger" was first published in *Cosmopolitan* in September 1981, and broadcast on Radio Three in Britain (Carter, *Burning Your Boats* 461).

7. Although a number of case studies were published in 1992, the centennial year of the Borden murders (Kent, Rappaport, Ryckebush), studies by Pearson; Spiering; Sullivan; and Williams et al. would have been available to Carter earlier.

8. Hereafter, the first page number will refer to the version published in Carter's *Burning Your Boats,* the second to the version published in Carter's *Saints and Strangers* (SS). Significant differences in quotations will be noted in the text or in endnotes.

9. The version in *Saints and Strangers* is similar but more didactic. It reads in part, "On this burning morning when, after breakfast and the performance of a few household duties, Lizzie Borden will murder her parents, she will, on rising, don a simple cotton frock that, if worn by itself, might be right for the weather . . ." (9).

10. The full text reads:

> Lizzie Borden with an axe
> Gave her father forty whacks
> When she saw what she had done
> She gave her mother forty one. (300; SS 7)

I learned it with a slightly different first line: "Lizzie Borden took an axe." Although most evidence suggests that Abby Borden was killed first with nineteen blows to the head and then Andrew Borden with ten, the rhyme reverses the sequence and exaggerates the number. At present, I have not located further information on the provenance of the rhyme.

11. Allusions to the rhyme abound in scholarly and popular book and article titles. Ann Schofield's "Lizzie Borden Took an Axe: History, Feminism and American Culture" and David Gates's "A New Whack at the Borden Case" are examples.

12. The concept of *Märchen* as emblem is represented by Lüthi, but other European scholars of folk narrative have recognized possible shifts in local legends to a more polished fairy-tale form, what Swedish folklorist Carl von Sydow characterized as a migratory legend. Lüthi notes that the violence, destruction and mutilation of legend is transmuted and stylized in fairy tale, and so it is a relief for listeners and readers to turn from the former to the latter; fairy tale empties legend of reality and fills it in altered stylized form (83–94). Cara Robertson uses the term in a slightly different way when she writes, "For Fall River and most of America, the murders became emblematic of the perils of foreign immigration, social disorder, or feminine transgression" (352).

13. Interestingly enough, Ann Schofield characterizes a number of twentieth-century fictions about the guilty Lizzie Borden falling into the same romance stereotype (91–93).

14. Bristol Community College in Fall River hosted a centenary conference 3–5 August 1992 in which participants discussed theories concerning the case, including those which variously put Bridget Sullivan, John Vinnicum Morse, Emma Borden, a Portuguese immigrant and others in the murderer's seat. See Ryckebush. Karen S.H. Roggenkamp asks questions that Carter does not: "I'm also interested in how Borden's modern reputation came to be formulated. It would seem to me that most people, if they know of Borden, think she did in fact kill her father and stepmother. . . . My own work has concentrated on the journalistic casting of the Borden trial, and if we can trust those at all, the VAST majority of people CLEARLY believed in Lizzie's innocence—the journalists most certainly did. . . . So how did a heroine of 1893 become a dark folk figure in a rhyme?" As noted in the text, Robertson documents coverage in Fall River's Irish popular newspaper, *The Daily Globe,* for its anti-Borden sentiment.

15. In the British, but not the American version, the narrator ironically interpolates "Look at the sleeping beauty!" before this passage (309).

16. Such photographs exist as part of the collection of the Fall River Historical Society. While writing this, I am looking at a reproduction of a portrait photo circa 1890 (Robertson 354).

17. I am, of course, referring to Jean Rhys's *Wide Sargasso Sea* (London: Deutch, 1966). Carter's portrait of Lizzie Borden comes close to that of Jeanne Duval in her *Black Venus* in which she highlights the Afro-Caribbean woman's enclosure in Baudelaire's apartment in Paris with the windows painted over (231–44).

18. See my analysis of "Lizzie's Tiger" for a discussion of possible incestuous relations between Andrew Borden and his daughters.

19. William R. Espy writes that "A Jekyll and Hyde is a person who is alternately completely good and completely evil. In Robert Louis Stevenson's *The Strange Case of Dr. Jekyll and Mr. Hyde* (1886), the gentle and proper Dr. Jekyll discovers a potion by means of which he can change himself into the monstrous Mr. Hyde and back again. He is ultimately trapped in the Hyde personality" (140).

20. This is one point where Carter's historical accuracy fails. Lizzie, born in 1860, would have been four years old in 1864 in the middle of the Civil War. Carter positions the time period some ten years earlier: "In another ten years' time, the

War between the States would provide rich picking for the coffinmakers, but, back then, back in the Fifties, well—" (321). The Bordens did live on Ferry St., however, until they moved to Second Street in 1871 when Lizzie was eleven years old.

21. Bruno Bettelheim reads "Hansel and Gretel" as a warning against a child's regression to the oral stage of development and a fixation on the mother as he/she works towards maturity (159–66) while social historian Robert Darnton sees it, with other tales, accurately reflecting starvation issues and multiple marriages in early modern Europe (9–72). Anne Sexton in *Transformations* (101) and Robert Coover in *Pricksongs & Descants* (see 75) each develop probable incest themes projected into the arena of food and eating metaphors in their rewrites. To my knowledge, Carter has not rewritten this tale in any of her literary *Märchen* collections.

22. The position of the tiger's tent, accurate for the layout of typical traveling circuses, also marks a deepening of illicit pleasure as it has something in common with the "back rooms" of bars, bookstores, video stores, etc.

23. With one of Edward Hick's paintings of "The Peaceable Kingdom" before me, I cannot believe that Carter was not playing on the double entendre of the verb "to lie down with" in Ezekiel: "The wolf also shall dwell with the lamb, and the leopard shall lie down with the kid; and the calf and the young lion and the fatling together; and a little child shall lead them" (11.6). Lizzie leading, rather than the Christ Child, is Satanic reversal indeed.

24. It may be significant that one of the contested etymologies for "carnival" is "farewell to the flesh."

25. I lift the term "archi'text'ure," most appropriate for the fusion of cultural space theory and textual production, from the title of a conference on feminist texts to be held at Emory University in the spring of 1998.

Works Cited

Altevers, Nanette. "Gender Matters in *The Sadeian Woman.*" *The Review of Contemporary Fiction* 14.3 (Fall 1994): 18–23.

Bacchilega, Cristina. *Postmodern Fairy Tales: Gender and Narrative Strategies*. Philadelphia: U of Pennsylvania P, 1997.

Bettelheim, Bruno. *The Uses of Enchantment: The Meaning and Importance of Fairy Tales*. New York: Vintage, 1977.

Bouissac, Paul. *Circus and Culture: A Semiotic Approach*. Advances in Semiotics. Bloomington and London: Indiana UP, 1976.

Carter, Angela. *American Ghosts & Old World Wonders*. London: Chatto & Windus, 1993.

———. *Burning Your Boats: The Collected Short Stories*. New York: Henry Holt, 1995.

———. Introduction. *The Old Wives' Fairy Tale Book*. Ed. Angela Carter. The Pantheon Fairy Tale and Folklore Library. New York: Pantheon, 1990. ix–xxii.

———. "Mise-en-Scène for a Parricide—a Story by Angela Carter." *London Review of Books* 3.16 (3–16 Sept. 1981): 21–24.

———. *The Sadeian Woman and the Ideology of Pornography*. New York: Pantheon, 1979.

———. *Saints and Strangers*. 1986. New York: Penguin, 1987.

Clapp, Susannah. Introduction. Carter, *American Ghosts & Old World Wonders* ix–xi.

Coover, Robert. *Pricksongs & Descants*. New York: Penguin Plume, 1969.

Darnton, Robert. *The Great Cat Massacre and Other Episodes in French Cultural History*. New York: Basic, 1984.

Dégh, Linda. "Folk Narrative." *Folklore and Folklife: An Introduction.* Ed. Richard M. Dorson. Chicago and London: U of Chicago P, 1972. 53–83.

Ducornet, Rikki. "A Scatological and Cannibal Clock: Angela Carter's 'The Fall River Axe Murders.' " *The Review of Contemporary Fiction* 14.3 (Fall 1994): 37–42.

Duncker, Patricia. "Re-Imagining the Fairy Tale: Angela Carter's Bloody Chambers." *Literature and History* 10.1 (1984): 3–14.

Espy, William R. *Thou Improper, Thou Uncommon Noun: An Etymology of Words That Once Were Names.* New York: Clarkson N. Potter, 1978.

Gates, David. "A New Whack at the Borden Case." *Newsweek* 4 June 1984: 12.

Gilbert, Sandra M., and Susan Gubar. *The Madwoman in the Attic: The Woman Writer and the Nineteenth-Century Literary Imagination.* New Haven: Yale UP, 1979.

"Inn Cold Blood." *People Weekly* 46 (5 Aug. 1996): 65.

Jones, Ann. *Women Who Kill.* New York: Holt, Rinehart and Winston, 1980.

Kaiser, Mary. "Fairy Tale as Sexual Allegory: Intertextuality in Angela Carter's *The Bloody Chamber.*" *The Review of Contemporary Fiction* 14.3 (Fall 1994): 30–36.

Kapferer, Bruce. *Legends of People, Myths of State: Violence, Intolerance, and Political Culture in Sri Lanka and Australia.* Washington, D.C.: Smithsonian Institution, 1988.

Katsavos, Anna. "An Interview with Angela Carter." *The Review of Contemporary Fiction* 14.3 (Fall 1994): 11–17.

Kendrick, Walter. "The Real Magic of Angela Carter." *Contemporary British Women Writers: Narrative Strategies.* Ed. Robert E. Hosmer, Jr. New York: St. Martin's, 1993. 66–84.

Kent, David, ed. *The Lizzie Borden Sourcebook.* Boston: Brandon, 1992.

Langlois, Janet L. "Belle Gunness, the Lady Bluebeard: Symbolic Inversion in Verbal Art and American Culture." *Signs: Journal of Women in Culture and Society* 8.4 (Summer 1983): 617–34.

Lurie, Alison. "Winter's Tales." Rev. of *Burning Your Boats: The Collected Short Stories,* by Angela Carter. *New York Times Book Review* 19 May 1996, natl. ed., sec. 7: 11.

Lüthi, Max. *Once Upon a Time: On the Nature of Fairy Tales.* Bloomington and London: Indiana UP, 1976.

Pearson, Edmund, ed. *Trial of Lizzie Borden.* Garden City, N.Y.: Doubleday, 1937.

Radner, Joan N., and Suzanne S. Lanser. "Strategies of Coding in Women's Cultures." *Feminist Messages: Coding in Women's Folk Culture.* Ed. Joan Newlon Radner. Publications of the American Folklore Society. New Series. Urbana and Chicago: U of Illinois P, 1993. 1–29.

Rappaport, Doreen. *The Lizzie Borden Trial.* New York: HarperCollins, 1992.

Robertson, Cara W. "Representing 'Miss Lizzie': Cultural Convictions in the Trial of Lizzie Borden." *Yale Journal of Law & the Humanities* 8.2 (Summer 1996): 351–416.

Roggenkamp, Karen S.H. "Re: Lizzie Borden." E-mail to the author. 11 Aug. 1997.

Rushdie, Salman. Introduction. Carter, *Burning Your Boats* ix–xiv.

Ryckebush, Jules R., ed. *Proceedings: Lizzie Borden Conference.* Portland, Maine: King Philip, 1993.

Schofield, Ann. "Lizzie Borden Took an Axe: History, Feminism and American Culture." *American Studies* 34.1 (Spring 1993): 91–103.

Sexton, Anne. *Transformations.* Boston: Houghton, 1971.

Spiering, Frank. *Lizzie.* New York: Random, 1984.

Stallybrass, Peter, and Allon White. "Bourgeois Hysteria and the Carnivalesque." *The Cultural Studies Reader.* Ed. Simon During. London and New York: Routledge, 1993. 284–92.

Sullivan, Robert. *Goodbye Lizzie Borden*. Brattleboro, VT: S. Greene P, 1974.

Williams, Joyce G., J. Eric Smithburn, and M. Jeanne Peterson, eds. *Lizzie Borden: A Case Book of Family and Crime in the 1890s*. Bloomington, IN: T.I.S., 1980.

Witchel, Alex. "Sleeping, Fitfully, Where Lizzie Once Did." *New York Times* 18 Sept. 1996, natl. ed.: B1+.

CRISTINA BACCHILEGA

In the Eye of the Fairy Tale:
Corinna Sargood and David Wheatley
Talk about Working with Angela Carter

When I found myself really wanting to go to Mont Saint-Michel because of Angela Carter's "The Bloody Chamber," I knew that her words had touched me in an unusual way. And when at dusk on the ramparts of this *merveille,* I listened for the cry of seagulls, I was not disappointed by the ghostly appearance and shifting feeling of the place: "Sea; sand; a sky that melts into the sea—a landscape of misty pastels with a look about it of being continuously on the point of melting. . . . his castle that lay on the very bosom of the sea with seabirds mewing about its attics, the casements opening on to the green and purple, evanescent departures of the ocean, cut off by the tide from land for half a day. . . . That lovely, sad, sea-siren of a place!" (*Burning Your Boats* 116–17). Carter's topography has little to do with realism: Mont Saint-Michel houses an abbey. But her images of that island, as of London or of Northern Italy, are vivid in a powerfully personal way which does feed on distinctive, actual details. Just as dreams and fairy tales do. Corinna Sargood's illustration of "The Bloody Chamber," published for the first time in the present volume, picks up on that multiple resonance of Carter's images: the seabirds in it are Arctic skuas, specifically because of their "dashing, hawk-like flight."

"I always think first in images, then grope for the words," Carter said (Paterson 43). Italo Calvino too claimed that each of his first three novels developed from a single image. Not accidentally, both writers had a passion for fairy tales. They embraced storytelling as a proliferation of borrowed images

Marvels & Tales: Journal of Fairy-Tale Studies, Vol. 12, No. 1 (1998), pp. 213–28. Copyright © 1998 by Wayne State University Press, Detroit, MI 48201.

and words, Calvino with an eye to systematizing it, Carter with the urge to further its unruliness. But it also worked the other way around: she exposed the rules of re-production, and he played with its possibilities. If, as Carter wrote, stories—especially fairy stories—are "part of the invisible luggage people take with them when they leave home" (*Virago Book* xiv), images are the visible, but even less sharable, luggage we carry.

To begin exploring the significance of the fairy tale as a specifically visual component of Carter's writing, I talked with two people who worked with her intensively on image-centered adaptations of her fairy-tale-based work. Corinna Sargood, a London-born artist and longtime friend of Carter's, illustrated *The Virago Book of Fairy Tales* (1990) and *The Second Virago Book of Fairy Tales* (1992). Working from Carter's 1967 novel, award-winning David Wheatley directed the film *The Magic Toyshop* in 1986 for Granada television and then made it into a feature film which was also distributed on video. In both interviews, I focused on the process of collaboration between the writer and the illustrator or director; Sargood's and Wheatley's understanding of and involvement with fairy tales, independent of Carter; and these visual artists' fascination with Carter's work as well as their knowledge of Carter's "luggage" of images. A third person, Kate Webb, kindly agreed to contribute to this collage of inter-views. To shift from illustration to film, I will later quote from Webb's unpublished paper "Rewriting the Script: Angela Carter and the Cinema" because she helps to identify Carter's film-related "luggage" and to place Carter's fascination with film in a larger context of image and word re-production.[1]

Surrounded by Mexican and Italian folk art, I sit with Corinna Sargood in her kitchen-dining area in Frome, Somerset; I have placed the tape recorder and the two Virago books (reprinted in the United States, the first as *The Old Wives' Fairy Tale Book* and the second as *Strange Things Sometimes Still Happen*) on the beautiful inlaid-wood table her partner Richard Wallace has made; when I look up, a giraffe and other painted animals are peeking down at us from an untypically-English clear blue sky—one of the many trompe l'oeil in this wonderful house. It is 7 May 1997, Angela Carter's fifty-seventh birthday.

Bacchilega: How did you and Angela Carter work on the two *Virago Books of Fairy Tales*?

Sargood: [She speaks softly, in a lovely staccato, a spark in her eyes.] We just more or less knew what we liked, because we'd been to exhibitions together, and we'd known each other a long time, thirty years, so there wasn't a lot of discussion to be done. We were both very much influenced by those wonderful books of Dulac's, which were a treat to look at, and still are a treat to look at.[2] I had to work out some sort of visual vocabulary to go with the stories in Carter's collections—what I was going to illustrate and how. It was understood that this visual vocabulary wasn't for children because these stories aren't for children, although they are obviously read by children. In fact, some people bought the books and complained, particularly to me, that they were quite unsuitable for children, which of course they are. For the first book, Angela was away for three months at the time that I was working on it, and when she came back, she was really pleased. I suppose she was quite confident by the time she left. I mean, whimsy was out.

Bacchilega: Were there any stories that you discussed in particular for either of the books?

Sargood: Yes, only what she found particularly salacious or funny. She would ring me up and say, "Hey, read this one!" These stories, the funny ones that amused her, were a challenge to illustrate because you can write in more details with words than if you actually start to illustrate. People start to get hot under the collar. . . . Say, the Eskimo story, I can't remember what it's called—

Bacchilega: "Blubber Boy" [*Virago Book* 31–32]?

Sargood: Yes. I thought that was quite tastefully done, quite decent. And this, "The Pupil" [see *Virago Book* 60], is the explicit one, about which there was a serious committee meeting at Virago to decide whether they could use it.

Bacchilega: In contrast, when you illustrated "Sermerssuaq," you certainly chose not to go into any details that might upset people here [*Virago Book* 1]. Why this particular illustration?

Sargood: [She reads the short text and examines her illustration.] Well, because unless you're going to start by drawing a clitoris, and that's very difficult. . . . So I just drew a picture of the fox that would cover it. I think nowadays I might do something quite different, having quickly reread the tale.

Bacchilega: But the fox works well because of all the wily and smart characters that follow.

Sargood: Yes, maybe I like foxes. Oh, dear, dear. It's marvelous, this tale.

Bacchilega: Did the two of you talk about these fairy tales while she was selecting them? Or did you send each other stories?

Sargood: She'd send me stories. And she used to send me a lot of pictures. I still have hundreds and hundreds of pictures she sent me. Oh, when I first started to do the illustrations, she sent me masses of pictures, and I went to her house and looked through books, and she had a new photocopier which she learned to operate. So a lot of pictures were photocopied for reference, and I also have a lot of books which I use for reference all the time. . . .

Bacchilega: What kind of illustrations or pictures did she send you?

Sargood: Oh, a huge variety, from abstract African patterns to Japanese tattoos, wood carvings, anything that intrigued her or amused her. She would make a copy, and I was very pleased to receive these pictures.

Bacchilega: The first book opens with the image of a tattooed woman's body: why?

Sargood: Well, I mean, it is a Virago book of fairy tales, and it seemed appropriate to have a woman's body. Like Angela, I am really interested in tattoos. I just liked the idea of this illustrated body, which in a way is a bit of a pun on what an illustration is, or what the book for me was meant to be. As for the *Second Virago Book,* she wrote to me while I was in Mexico regarding these illustrations, "Could you do the body of a man, or a tree of life?" So I combined the two as a tattoo, with the tree of life being like a tattoo. But I was inspired by some sixteenth-century murals from the little town in which we were staying in Mexico. Those highly skilled craftsmen willfully misinterpreted Christian symbolism. You see the Grim Reaper in the tattoo? Although considered to be tasteless in our western society, this would be a perfectly acceptable way in another culture to indicate that we knew Angela was going to die soon—she certainly understood. And she asked for the tailpiece, another illustration some people found offensive [*Second Virago* 231]; she asked for a Mexican Day of the Dead as a tailpiece; and that I did with a skeleton, with an Easter bonnet and a frilly skirt, who is throwing a book into the air.

Bacchilega: And grinning.

Sargood: With a smile, yes. You always go out with a smile on your face, which I felt was—no, she didn't go out with a great smile on her face, alas. Actually, I had the end of the book in mind! That was the last picture I did before she died.

Bacchilega: Did she see the illustrations for the second book?

Sargood: I sent them all to her. She saw them a week before she died. Her husband said she was very pleased with them.

Bacchilega: What about the full-page illustrations that introduced each section?

Sargood: Each was meant to tell the whole story of a particular tale I enjoyed in the chapter, in a sort of little frame. And I also liked doing these illuminated letters at the beginning of each story.

Bacchilega: So there is a narrative structure to the full-page illustrations?

Sargood: Yes. . . . I love Angela's chapter headings, the categories. Before this interview began, we were talking about the feminist, new fairy tales, but I don't think you can have a fairy tale without it being seen from the woman's point of view. Women are the main storytellers for children and for everybody, but this doesn't mean to say that these women are victims.

Bacchilega: Can you say more about that?

Sargood: Well, I read a book in Mexico by a young American anthropologist who had stayed in a village to work on his thesis; he came alone, which would have been quite difficult, I think; he did a survey and lived there and did very well, and began to question women about various aspects of their lives, and he came to the conclusion that they were not only sexually very, very repressed, but they also got ill because they were so dissatisfied with their lives. This is very well-received research. It goes down very well, and I think it does because of people's ideas of what women in these countries are. Being a married woman, I could talk to the married women there, and they do have very hard lives. I met women with eighteen children, and they said it's very hard. But they are certainly not victims, whatever their lives are or however unsatisfactory their husbands may or may not have been. They are very vigorous and amusing, and strong women. They are . . .

Bacchilega: Resourceful.

Sargood: Absolutely, yes. So I mean, it's no good taking my experience and saying that's how it is, but generally I do think women are very resourceful.

Bacchilega: And that's what comes out of these fairy stories, very much so.

Sargood: Yes, all over the world, women have to be resourceful.

Bacchilega: You lived in Mexico and before that in Peru. Did those experiences affect your illustrations of Carter's books of fairy tales?

Sargood: I think the whole feeling of a place does influence you, and I had just come back from Peru when I did the first book. For three months, I had been in the Amazon rain forest, on the banks of the river, drawing; and that's a strange place, very sensual, very green, very flat. In Mexico instead you get a much more open, lighter feeling. Apart from that, in Mexico there is the enormous weight of input, of the extraordinary things you see and experience. When Angela was ill, we corresponded enormously. She just said, "Do Mexico for me. I won't get there." [She looks through *The Second Virago Book of Fairy Tales* and points to 72– 73.] I like "The Witchball," which is from the United States. In Mexico, images of God have what looks like a jelly [donut] on his hat. I was very pleased to be able to draw a picture of God in the sky, with the sun and the moon and the stars, in connection with a fart. And as I

"The Sleeping Prince" by Corinna Sargood. Copyright © Corinna Sargood. Reproduced with permission.

said, I am also influenced by Mexican ideas of death, the double take of both enjoying and grieving.

Bacchilega: What about your use of mirrors? There are a number of mirrors in the illustrations to both volumes.

Sargood: I suppose it's a useful device, but I like mirrors, and I like it that, in these illustrations for instance, what you see reflected is different—the reflection is not of what or who is looking into it. I mean, I like the change.

Bacchilega: Right. We see it in your illustration of "The Mirror," another story in *The Second Virago Book* [118]. Actually, I was also thinking of how important mirrors and seeing yourself are in Carter's work, especially in *The Bloody Chamber,* and then they are also important in fairy tales, of course. The magic mirror.

Sargood: Yes. I suppose it's a symbol of how what you see is only a perception. A mirror in an illustration like that one is useful because you can condense more than one perspective.

Bacchilega: You can have more than one reading.

Sargood: Yes. [She is flipping through the pages and stops to look at "The Sleeping Prince," 123–25. See illustration on facing page.] Here's another one.

Bacchilega: That's a beautiful use of reflection.

Sargood: That's actually a washstand from a kitchen in Puglia. . . . If we disagreed on anything, Angela and I, I think it was that she was less bloodthirsty than me. "Mr. Fox" [*Virago Book* 8–10] is an incredibly bloodthirsty story, so I did a linocut which she thought was really a little too much. I think I did a big, full-page illustration which she didn't like—it was the only one she didn't like. But, you know, when you have to illustrate something which ends up by saying that the heroine's "brothers and friends drew their swords and cut Mr. Fox into a thousand pieces" [*Virago Book* 10], how are you going to get round violence and blood? I did another illustration, and I do like it.

Bacchilega: You told me earlier that you have done some reading on fairy tales. Was it in preparation for these illustrations?

Sargood: No, I've always been interested in fairy tales, and fairy-tale books specifically. The Dulac books, which I love, have always been very special; it was a special time when, with clean hands, I could take them out of my grandmother's shelves. And, during the war, my father used to read the *Grimms' Fairy Tales* out loud. It was wonderful. And funnily enough, I think the only stories that really upset me when I was a child were Hans Christian Andersen's. I had the mistaken idea that they were fairy tales. They're not. They are morbid tales. I mean, to think that he was writing for children. He should have been stopped. But I did go on to read. I read Bruno Bettelheim who sees the fairy tale from children's point of view, and that's because he worked with children living under appalling conditions. The difference between Hans Christian Andersen, his tragic tales, and fairy tales is that in fairy tales having been taken on this path of disaster, things turn out all right. You're taken through all sorts of feelings, and the tales demonstrate that you can actually get past tragedy and grief. I like this idea.

Bacchilega: When you listened to fairy tales or read them yourself, images must have formed in your mind. Is there a connection between fairy tales and your imagination?

Sargood: Well, I have a visual imagination so I have very vivid pictures of these stories. "The Juniper Tree" is one I remember most clearly from being only three or four, because the war was still on. The picture was so vivid that when I came to illustrate it, I could just turn up my own photograph in my mind and go from there; . . . it was the same story [*Virago Book* 183–91]. And I think that story has affected me a lot.

Bacchilega: It's a story about transformation—

Sargood: Yes, wonderful. And also about the tenderness between the brother and sister, which is something that is often lost these days, I think.

Bacchilega: Carter talked about fairy tales as "dreams dreamt in public" [*Virago Book* xx], and she also focused on the significance of images in fairy tales. Could you say more about this?

Sargood: I think the images of our imaginations are the most powerful thing. I'm not so sure that the imagination should be somehow scooped up and locked away from everything else. I mean, it's everywhere. If you go to a shop, it's imagination: who has put things in the window and how. But, in the West, it seems that the imagination has been removed from the whole and put into a place, because it is very dangerous for people trying to run a capitalist economy and society.

Bacchilega: When you read *The Bloody Chamber,* for instance, what was your reaction?

Sargood: I loved it. For me, she is a very visual writer, but that may be my interpretation. And as you said, she can be read on a lot of levels. She's also a very amusing writer. I'm terribly fond of *Wise Children* because I think it's really, really funny as well as being a serious book, and maybe people—I don't know if people feel comfortable with the serious, intellectual level and the very playful one riding the same horse. And in *The Magic Toyshop,* a wonderful book, I enjoyed the symbolism. I enjoyed it a lot. She wrote in a very fluid way; in a film the director points you to what she or he wants you to see, whereas the book sort of rolls on and you accumulate images in your mind.

Bacchilega: You did the paintings and the poster for the film adaptation of that novel. It's certainly a book where the paintings and the visual images play an overt and significant role.

Sargood: Yes. Oh, they are visual jokes, just that.

Bacchilega: And in her introduction to *The Virago Book of Fairy Tales,* Carter made a connection between the fairy tale and jokes: overused fairy tales have become jokes; they circulate among adults as jokes, you know. And soap operas, too.

Sargood: Yes. I slightly disagree with her about soap operas, but they are having to discuss all sorts of serious issues—like laboring the point that all violent men don't come from out of a coal-mining family and they can come from rich, educated families. Soap operas are quite didactic, but maybe that's what fairy tales are too. But in the soaps, there's never a happy ending because they go on ad nauseam. . . .

Bacchilega: What about Carter's own interest in painting and images? You mentioned you went to art exhibits together and—

Sargood: We used to go to exhibitions and have lunch or coffee together. She liked a lot of things I liked, not necessarily all of them. She liked the bizarre, which I do as well, and I think I like odd paintings more than she did.

Bacchilega: Is there something else that you want to say about her?

Sargood: Well, I think our friendship was sort of a domestic friendship. I am an illustrator, not a writer. Just talking with her about problems was a good opportunity. She was very supportive. And I hope I was a bit supportive to her. I mean, you know, nobody's life runs totally smoothly, or if it does, those must be dreadful people. And she had an amazing sense of humor. She said there was no good joke without it being malicious, and I remember trying to think of good jokes that weren't malicious, and it's really quite difficult. There aren't funny, kind jokes. We used to go to the films, lots and lots of films, especially Svankmajer's.[3] He's a wonderful cartoon filmmaker. We used to go on Sunday afternoon to the National Film Theatre, and it must have been cheaper to go on Sunday afternoon, because there are an awful lot of bag ladies in the cinema, [laughter] so we used to say we were practicing for when we were bag ladies.

Cinema, I think: Carter loved it, and it's all transformations, wonder, illusion, rooted in fairy-tale magic. Laura Mulvey writes: "Transformations and meta-morphoses recur so frequently in Angela Carter's writing that her books seem to be pervaded by this magic cinematic attribute even when the cinema itself is not present on the page" (230). Kate Webb puts her finger on what else motivated Carter's passion for film: "Carter who wrote in praise of 'recycling' and 'mutability' was inevitably drawn to the cinema, the bastard art based on re-writing, re-drawing, re-imagining the work of others. It appealed to her, too, as a collective art, not reliant upon some Master Author" (2–3). Webb's informative and evocative recollection in her "Rewriting the Script: Angela Carter and the Cinema" makes the scene for this recycling come to life:

> By the Seventies, [Carter's] own outings to the cinema, often with the novelist Paul Bailey, were to the smorgasbord of independent houses in London which catered for every kind of taste. Carter enjoyed sampling the delights of all these tatty, rundown palaces of light. She was a regular at the Little Bit Ritzy Cinema in Brixton in the early Eighties when I was working there as a projectionist, and I remember her announcing with relish to other horrified customers that there were fleas jumping off the seats at the Electric Cinema in Notting Hill Gate, . . . There was also The Everyman in Hampstead for the nobs; or The Scala, home of the queens in King's Cross, or just a short trip away, five stops on the Northern line from where she lived in Clapham, there was the National Film Theatre beside the Thames. All of these were running varied repertory programmes, projectors turning incessantly, for all-nighters as well as for evening shows and matinees.
>
> In the space of a year an avid watcher like Carter could get an education in the history of cinema: see the early greats—D.W. Griffiths and Eisenstein; the Hollywood vamps of the Twenties; the German expressionists of the Thirties; Hollywood film noir of the Forties; Italian neo-realists of the Fifties. Or, if you preferred them, there were weird 3D Sci-Fi movies from America, with their cold war plots and atomic threats, films which seemed quite literally to break down the border between the world on the screen and real life, vomiting projectiles out onto the audience. There was the gritty, Northern realism of English cinema in the swinging Sixties; and then, bringing you smack bang up to date, there was De Niro walking the *Mean Streets* of the Seventies. At the Ritzy where films frequently broke down during change over from reel to reel, a member of the audience might get up and tell jokes or play rock'n'roll music on the clapped-out piano at the side of the stage. (Webb 1–2)

It is with this kind of (in)visible luggage that Carter comes to the making of "her" first film, *The Magic Toyshop*.[4]

It is 4 June 1997, and I have just watched the film on video at David Wheatley's house. We are sitting in his spacious living room, full of morning light. We drink coffee. He is animated as he answers questions, trying hard to recall details of a long-past project.

Bacchilega: How did you get to know Angela Carter, David, and why did you start working together on *The Magic Toyshop*?

Wheatley: I only got to know her through working. I made a film about the Brothers Grimm, a drama about the meanings of enchantment, not along Bruno Bettelheim's lines, but an attempt to get at the root at what fascinated people about fairy tales. You see, I started off at the Royal College of Art making a film about Magritte, the painter; and the reason I'm telling you this is that I think that by fluke I came into a kind of magical—I don't like that phrase much—magical realism. I came to it through people who were inspired by extraordinary images. So I was curious. As part of this magical tradition, you place an object to surprise people, make them aware of the world around them, and Angela definitely does come from that kind of tradition, and also the women's movement and lots of different things, you know. Extraordinary mind, as I already said to you on the phone. Well, you interview people— I've made documentaries about some: Borges, the Argentinean poet and writer; Ray Bradbury. . . . I think they've got a door in their mind. They're able to step into their subconscious and access something there to create these odd associations. Angela, I think, had a mind like that.

Bacchilega: On the phone, you said something about her mind being. . . .

Wheatley: She was like a jigsaw because you could never completely fathom where she stood on anything. And that's what was wonderful about the woman—that you'd think because you had heard one or two of her views about the women's movement, that she would think one thing, and then she would throw you and talk about an issue in a completely different way. You should have seen her house, because I don't know why it didn't collapse. It had things like fairground horses in the living room—see [pointing], she brought me that little Spanish dog. She loved those kinds of things, and *Toyshop* is full of those kind of magical elements. With that amount of books, the amount of wood pulp, her house should have come crashing down to the basement. And it was an eclectic collection of topics, including underwear through the ages or perceptions of women in connection with popular images of women. Her mind was like a library, and she had a wicked sense of humour—I called her a wild witch, and she liked that. [Pause.] See, you got a sense of my tradition, my interests. The way the whole project started. . . .

I had worked with Steve Morrison at Granada television: a film about George Orwell, *The Road to 1984,* and it had been a good experience. We were looking around for another project to do, and I had read Michael Ende's *Momo.* That's quite an enchanting book as well, because Michael Ende's father was a surrealist, and I think he was influenced by his own father. Anyway, the rights had been taken by someone in Germany, so I was looking for a book with the similar tone, and a friend suggested Angela Carter's novels. I read *The Magic Toy Shop.* . . . It was a difficult film to try and make. I think a number of people had tried to make it previously. It wasn't a feature film. It became a feature film. We blew it up to a thirty-two-millimeter film from sixteen-millimeters. It was only supposed to be a television movie, and we just didn't have the money for the movie. We had a television budget. The special effects budget was nine thousand pounds, which wouldn't buy a cup of tea in Hollywood, you know, so we had to use some pretty amateur techniques, really, to try and make it work. Anyway, it was commissioned, and I said to Angela, "How do you want to go about this?" She said, "Just tell me what you want." She had kind of a surprising way about her. I said, "Well, I'll go through the book and just select what I think some of the major scenes would be." "That's great," she said. When I went to see her about it, she said, "I'm bored with this book. Should we start again?" And I said, "Angela, we've been commissioned to start a script based on your book, your work, so I think we'd better try and stick to it a little bit." So we began a routine. We went through the novel—she worked incredibly fast. She would sit at the typewriter and just write. . . . She introduced me to Corinna through *The Magic Toy Shop,* because Corinna did the paintings, and she did the poster. I can show you the poster. A very good imagination, building on folk art traditions. I did like her. [Pause.] I joked with Angela once: "Is this book really a book about the Protestant Englishman in Ireland, and uncle Philip is the oppressor of the Irish?" And she laughed and said, "Possibly." So that might have been one reading. Anyway, one of the problems I had was the end of the book. I said, "It looked to me like you just got bored with all the characters and sent them out of the house. What happened to them all?" She said, "Oh, they were safe, they got married, and Margaret went to another place." And I said, "But Angela. . . . Reading the novel, you probably gather all that, but the thing about making a film is we have to make these things specific."

Bacchilega: Could you talk about the issues involved in adapting a novel into a film?

Wheatley: Adaptations from a novel are always a problem—it's like people say, "The pictures look better on radio." I mean, specific images in film challenge people's opinions because they say "That's not how I saw the book, that wasn't my interpretation." There's not one film, anyway. You come out of the cinema, and you listen to people talk—everyone has watched a different film because we're all living in three spaces simultaneously. It's now, this second; but at the same time, you're colored by your experiences and what brought you to this moment; and also you're thinking, what's going to happen next? So when you're watching a film, all that is going on inside you, and each image in that film is having a different effect on you because you brought your own set of experiences. Or you cough and you look down and you miss things. So it's always a strange experience to sit in a cinema and view a film with other people. [Pause.] I think Angela was happy with the film. I mean, I did explain to her that some of the effects were . . . as good as I could make them with the money and resources I had. I was quite pleased with it in the end. But it gets a bit tricky. I thought the film *The Company of Wolves* was flat. There was extraordinary imagery and I think he [Neil Jordan] is a fantastic filmmaker, but because it was a short story. . . . I think there is a danger in Angela's work that when you dramatize it, you stretch the drama. It's like a row of pearls. You stretch it so thin, if you're not careful, it is just beads, and it no longer—you lose the narrative drive, with incidents colliding into one another. And I think there's a slight danger even with the novel actually, but it is easier to compress a two-hundred-page novel than to work from a short story.

Bacchilega: What did you do about the ending of *The Magic Toyshop*? The novel ends with: " 'Nothing is left but us' [says Finn to Melanie]. At night, in the garden, they faced each other in a wild surmise" [*Magic Toyshop* 200]. They're almost like Adam and Eve.

Wheatley: How, why, where are they safe? And what about the other characters? We [in the film] kept true to her image; for instance, you see Margaret going away with the child [Victoria], Margaret looking like some kind of spirit, with the hair almost looking like wings. The actress [Patricia Kerrigan] stood on this little platform on wheels; we attached a fan to it and pulled it back with a rope—a special effect!

Bacchilega: It's a beautiful image, and from it we know that she has the power to make her own space.

Wheatley: Yes, magic, that's right. She's a witch. She's a creature from another world that has been released when they removed the choker. And I thought we needed to see the demise of uncle Philip. So we see him spun around in the shop, and all the children take revenge on him. We want to see evil vanquished, and that is to do broadly speaking with the fairy-tale tradition. I think with changing the end, we almost went back to the folk/fairy tale where the evil character was vanquished by his own creations who all come alive and take their revenge on him, which again I suppose is a magical occurrence.

Bacchilega: What about magical objects in the film? You mentioned earlier that she was interested in them.

Wheatley: Well, I think they are true to the folk/fairy-tale tradition. These stories were stories about ordinary people. Look at some of those magical objects: which people invented the porridge producers? No rich people would ask for that! You put an object in the middle of the story and make it magical because you want to make it more memorable and more surprising. . . . In the film, when you see the magical choker—which was a symbol of oppression—being thrown away, it vanishes into the sky; it's a bit like when you see the house go tumbling in *The Wizard of Oz*. Basically, you put a camera on the roof of the studio, and you watch the object drop away from you. But you get a sense of how it goes into the sky; the supernatural starts to take over as well. So the image enhances the notion that these people are supernatural, and that the symbol of evil has been dealt with supernaturally.

Bacchilega: And then there was the dog leaping. . . .

Wheatley: Oh, that's right. The dog leaps through the painting. You see, the dog again is almost a symbol of uncle Philip, and, I suppose Angela would say, isn't it nice that his best friend betrays him, because the man wasn't worth being loyal to. And there's the magic fiddle. And the staging can be magical too—when Melanie looks down on the theater set, and suddenly the room almost vanished, or there were parts of the room only, and they are at a huge beach by the sea. I think it's not just magical objects, which you do get, but the magical objects are there to underline what's going on in terms of each character's development, in terms of their relationships and what oppresses them and their emotions, yeah. I hope I've answered that question.

Bacchilega: Did you talk about the story of "Bluebeard" when you were working on the film with Carter?

Wheatley: Yes. Uncle Philip in a sense is Bluebeard, but she said uncle Philip, in another interpretation, could be the Irish Protestant. But it could be the legend of Bluebeard, and basically the house is a chamber of horrors, you know. It's like 10 Rillington Place.[5] And everyone in that house is oppressed. I think the difference is that Bluebeard murdered, while Uncle Philip kept everyone alive. I think she's borrowing from all kinds of traditions of male oppression.

Bacchilega: That's also clear from one of the early scenes, when Melanie is looking at herself in the mirror and posing as different ideas of femininity.

Wheatley: Yes, ideas of femininity. Well, for one split second, there is a little bit of pubic hair revealed on Melanie. When the film was shown in Japan [at the tenth Pia Film Festival in 1987], they scratched out the pubic area with a pin. . . . It was the most problematic thing I've ever seen, because suddenly it looked like there were maggots dancing all around this girl's pubic area. To me, it was a much more pornographic image than the image that was portrayed originally in the film.

Bacchilega: How else did you prepare yourself for directing *The Magic Toyshop*?

Wheatley: I asked Angela, "What were you doing when you wrote the book?" And she said, "Actually, I was actually writing about film, a feature film review." And I said, "Could you make a list of films that you were reviewing during that time?" And there were some very strange films: *Valerie and Her Week of Wonders;* Walerian Borowczyk's *Goto, Island of Love.* . . . *Valerie and Her Week of Wonders* is one I quite liked. . . . We just sat down and watched all these films together, and I'd never heard of some of them. I will look and see if I can't find. . . . It was like a reading list. I was trying to get to where her mind was at when she wrote the novel.

When David Wheatley found the list, it included Roman Polanski's *Repulsion* (1965), George Franju's *Judex* (1963), Jiří Menzel's *Closely Watched Trains* (1966), Michael Powell's *Peeping Tom* (1960), . . . and Michael Powell's and Emeric Pressburger's *The Red Shoes* (1948) and *Tales of Hoffmann* (1951).

Notes

1. I am grateful to Corinna Sargood, Kate Webb, and David Wheatley for their generous collaboration. I also wish to thank Kathleen J. Cassity for transcribing the interview tapes.
2. Sargood is referring to Edmund Dulac (1882–1953), who illustrated a number of deluxe *Christmas Gift Books*, including fairy-tale books like *Stories from the Arabian Nights* (London, 1907) and *The Sleeping Beauty and Other Fairy Tales* (London, 1910).
3. The Czech director Jan Svankmajer is known for his surrealistic films, some of which mix animation and live-action scenes.
4. Providing a careful introduction to the themes of the film, Laura Mulvey foregrounds both wonder and social struggle. First made for television, *The Magic Toyshop's* first public showing was at the London Film Festival in November 1986; the film was dubbed an "adult fairy tale," and it was praised by most reviewers

for its richness and dreamlike quality. Wheatley said then, "[The novel *The Magic Toyshop*] follows the plot of a classic fairy tale. Most fairy tales come in when the central character's parents are dead or dying, when they've suffered some fall . . ." ("Dream Machine" 12). In another article, Carter commented: "[T]here are times when I think that the barmier [sic] aspirations of romantic fiction and romantic movies are very important. Having some sort of dumb aspirational illusions may well be the trigger that makes you do what you wouldn't do otherwise. Not the women's magazine romance of the Fifties and Sixties type where the message was essentially 'settle for what you can get.' But the wilder shores of romance that promise that Cinderella will go to the ball, Snow White will defeat her wicked stepmother" (Paterson 14).

5. The site of the John Christie murders in London during the late Forties. In 1970, Richard Fleischer directed the film *10 Rillington Place,* based on this famous murder case; the cast included Richard Attenborough and John Hurt.

Works Cited

Calvino, Italo. *I nostri antenati.* Torino: Einaudi, 1960.

Carter, Angela. *Burning Your Boats: Collected Short Stories.* New York: Holt, 1996.

————. *The Magic Toyshop.* London: Heinemann, 1967.

————, ed. *The Second Virago Book of Fairy Tales.* Illus. Corinna Sargood. London: Virago, 1992.

————, ed. *The Virago Book of Fairy Tales.* Illus. Corinna Sargood. London: Virago, 1990.

"Dream Machine." *City Life* 9–23 Oct. 1987: 12–13.

The Magic Toyshop. Scr. Angela Carter. Dir. David Wheatley. Perf. Tom Bell, Caroline Milnoe, Kilian McKenna, and Patricia Kerrigan. Prod. Steve Morrison. Granada, 1986.

Mulvey, Laura. "Cinema Magic and the Old Monsters: Angela Carter's Cinema." *Flesh and the Mirror: Essays on the Art of Angela Carter.* Ed. Lorna Sage. London: Virago, 1994. 230–42.

Paterson, Moira. "Flights of Fancy in Balham." *Observer* 9 Nov. 1986: 42–45.

Webb, Kate. "Rewriting the Script: Angela Carter and the Cinema." Unpublished.

"The Werefox" by Corinna Sargood. Copyright © Corinna Sargood. Reproduced with permission.

ROBERT COOVER

Entering Ghost Town

Angela Carter and I first encountered one another in the landscape of the tale, somewhere between Pricksongs & Descants and Fireworks, published a year or so apart, discovering therein an immediate affection for one another's imaginations. We corresponded for two years before we actually met and became lifelong (alas, not so long) friends, and in that time confirmed that we shared much as writers and differed little, if at all, and thus what either of us might write might seem a message or a tribute to the other.

Here it's the tale as shared vocabulary. In the "Afterword" to Fireworks, Angela confessed to a fascination with "cruel tales, tales of wonder, tales of terror, fabulous narratives that deal directly with the imagery of the unconscious," for the tale "cannot betray its readers into a false knowledge of everyday experience [as realism does]. It retains a singular moral function—that of provoking unease." In a letter to me she wrote: "I'm interested, then, in a fiction that takes full cognizance of its status as non-being—that is, a fiction that remains aware that it is of its own nature, which is a different nature than human, tactile immediacy. I really do believe that a fiction absolutely self-conscious of itself as a different form of human experience than reality (that is, not a logbook of events) can help to transform reality itself." That is to say, in the end, after all the fireworks, Angela Carter was, as am I, an intransigent realist, angry with most so-called realist works for their perpetuation and reinforcement of the old fairytales, including the dogmas of form.

The folktale (or "children's story") was well suited for Angela's favorite themes (and mine) of ending willful innocence—the victim as culprit in preserving the oppressive system—and the power of patterns of history over people (having to live in the dreams of others). "Wake up, wake up!" more than one of her characters has insisted. *"I had played a game in which every move was governed by a destiny as oppressive and omnipotent as himself,"* says the narrator of the title story of The Bloody Chamber, *one caught up but heroically escaping another's fiction, "I only did what he knew I would." But no longer, she's outa there.*

Thus, so many of our heroines and heroes have found themselves, as does mine here, entrapped in the dreams of others and suffering the sudden blunt challenge faced by little Red Riding Hood in Angela's "Werewolf" story: "Go and visit Grandmother." Okay, kid. It's your turn now.

Not that Angela Carter was a didactic writer with a "program" or a "message," her appetite for irony and paradox made sure of that. She told stories, and had a good time doing so, so her narratives do not surrender easily to neat allegorical or interpretive schemes, even though her very clear worldview necessarily informed all her tales. First and foremost came the plunge into story. To wake, as she might have said, one must first remember the dreams.

○　○　○　○　○

[Editors' Note: In the Summer-Fall 1975 issue of Iowa Review *(6.3–4: 125–62), Coover edited and introduced "The Angela Carter Show" which featured three stories and two poems of hers "threaded together . . . by running commentary as though in a public reading, and most of that commentary was extracted, with her [Carter's] permission," from the two writers' correspondence (e-mail to Bacchilega, 3 October 1997). The passage quoted above "from a letter" is part of that metafictional, reflective dialogue ("Notes on the Gothic Mode" 133). Coover, then fiction editor of* Iowa Review, *chose this form, much "like a good solid hour-long public reading with questions-and-answer time thrown in," because he found it "particularly suitable" for Carter, "an English writer, who works in a variety of forms, . . . who is articulate about what she is doing and why, and whose talent and performance far exceed her reputation, at least in the United States. She's been with us, after all, for ten years now, has seven books of fiction in print, a radio play in production at the BBC, poems and essays hither and yon, regular columns in magazines—where have we been?" (125). And that was in 1975! What follows here are the beginning sections of Robert Coover's* Ghost Town, *a recently published novel.]*

Bleak horizon under a glazed sky, flat desert, clumps of sage, scrub, distant butte, lone rider. This is a land of sand, dry rocks, and dead things. Buzzard country. And he is migrating through it. Because: it is where he is now, and out here there's nothing to stop for, no turning back either, no back to turn to. His lean face is shaded from the sun directly overhead by a round felt hat with a wide brim, dun-colored like the land around, old and crumpled. A neckerchief, probably once red, knotted around his throat, collects what sweat, in his parched saddle-sore state, he sweats. A soft tattered vest, gray shirt, trailworn cowhide chaps over dark jeans tucked into dust-caked boots with pointed toes, all of it busted up and threadbare and rained on, dried out by sun and wind and grimed with dust, that's the picture he makes, forlorn horseman on the desert plain, obstinately plodding along. He wears a wooden-butted six-shooter just under his ribs, a bowie knife with a staghorn handle in his belt, and a rifle dangles, barrel aimed at his partnering shadow on the desert floor, from the saddlehorn. He is leathery and sunburnt and old as the hills. Yet just a kid. Won't ever be anything else.

It wasn't always like this. There were mountains before, a rugged and dangerous terrain, with crags and chasms, raging rivers in deep gorges, and dense forests, unsociably inhabited. He's known rattlesnake bites, grizzly attacks, blizzards and thunderstorms, frostbite, windburn, gnats and mosquitos, wolves, too, arrow wounds—a black-haired scalp, hair braided with shells and beads, is strung from his gunbelt, though if asked he couldn't say where it came from, just something that happened, must have. Back then, he was maybe chasing someone or something. Or was being chased, some vague threat at his back, that's mostly what he remembers now from that time, an overwhelming feeling of danger, or else of despair, that filled the air whenever the sky darkened or the trail petered out. He had to bury someone on one occasion, as he recalls, someone like a brother, only the dead man in the hole he'd dug wasn't really dead, but kept moving blindly, kicking the dirt away, in fact he was himself the one who kept twisting and turning, the one blindly kicking, he was down in the burial pit with dirt peppering his face, but then he wasn't again, and the one who was was crawling out suddenly to flail at the air, flesh sliding off the bone like lard off a hot pan, so he left that place, to go chase someone, or to be chased, or finally just to move on to somewhere else, not to see things like that.

Then one day, climbing up out of a steep canyon cut by a wild frothy river way down below, struggling all the while against some kind of unseen force pressing down on him, almost palpable, as if a big flopping bird were expiring on his chest, having to dismount finally and haul his shying wild-eyed horse up through the last fierce pass, he found himself out upon this vast empty plain, where nothing seems to have happened yet and yet everything seems already over, done before begun. A space there and not there, like a monumental void, dreadful and ordinary all at once. As if the ground the horse treads, for all its extension, might be paper thin and stretched over nothing. He doesn't expect to come to the end of the world out here, but he doesn't expect not to.

What he's aiming at is a town over on the far horizon, first thing he saw when he rose up out of the canyon and the canyon shut itself away behind him. The town's still out there, sitting on the edge like a gateway to the hidden part of the sky. Sometimes it disappears behind a slight rise, then reappears when that rise is reached, often as not even further away to the naked eye, his naked eye, than when last seen, like a receding mirage, which it likely is. Sometimes there's no horizon at all, burned away by the sun's glare or night's sudden erasure, so no town either, and his goal is more like the memory of a goal, but he keeps moving on and sooner or later it shows itself again, wavering in the distance as if made of a limp sheet that the wind was ruffling. He doesn't know what it's rightly called, nor feels he need to know it. It's just the place he's going to.

Maybe he dozes off between times, but out here it seems always to be either dark and starcast or else the sun is directly overhead, beating down on him as though fingering him for some forgotten crime, just one condition or its contrary like the two pictures on a magic lantern slide, flickering back and forth, as he opens and closes and opens his eyes. Nothing much could sneak up on him out here in all this emptiness as long as he's mounted above it, so in the saddle is where he does most of his sleeping, his eating too, which is largely confined to the strips of old buffalo jerky, black as tar and half as tasty, that came with the horse. He could use a watering hole, a bit of forage for the beast between his legs, the best prospects for which would seem to be that town on the horizon, unsubstantial though it appears. Out here, nothing but stumpy cactus and tumbleweeds and a few old dry bones, provender unfit for the dead.

Who haunt him, or seem to, whispering at his back like a dry wind with eyes. That feeling of eyes in the air gets so potent at times that he has to stretch round in his saddle to cast his gaze on what's behind him, and one day, bent round like that, he discovers another town on the opposite horizon, a kind of mirror image of the one he's headed toward, as if he were coming from the same place he was going. A vapor of the atmosphere, he supposes, but next time he looks it's back there still and clearer than it was before, as if it might be gaining on him. Which is the case, for as the days, if they are days, go on, the town behind him closes upon him even as the one in front recedes, until at last it glides up under his horse's hoofs from behind and proceeds to pass him by even as he ambles forward. He tries to turn his horse around to face this advent, but the creature's course is set and it is clearly past considering further instruction. It's a plain town that comes past, empty and silent, made of the desert itself with a few ramshackle false-fronted frame structures lined up to conjure a street out of the desolation. Nothing moves in it. In an open window, a lace curtain droops limply, ropes dangle lifelessly from the gallows and hitching posts, the sign over the saloon door hangs heavy in the noontime sun as the blade of an ax. A water trough catches his eye as it drags lazily by, and he spurs the horse forward, but he cannot seem to overtake it. The whole dusty street heaves lazily past like that, leaving him soon at the edge of town and then outside it. He halloos once at the outskirts, but without conviction, and gets no reply, having expected none. He is alone again on the desert. The town slowly slips away ahead of him and grows ever more distant and finally vanishes over the horizon and night falls.

o   o   o

There's a dull flickering light on the desert floor as if a decaying star has slipped from its rightful place and he follows it to a warmthless campfire where a group of men huddle under serapes and horse blankets, smoking and drinking and chewing, bandits by the look of them.

Look whut the cat drug in, one of them says and spits into the low flame.

Reckon it's human?

Might be. Might not. Turd on a stick more like.

He's just stood in his stirrups to ease himself down out of the saddle, but he changes his mind and rests back down. A tin pot squats at the edge of the smoldering fire, leaning into it as though in mockery of the squatting men and emitting a burnt coffee stink that mingles unfavorably with the viscid reek of burning dung.

It dont make a damn t'me, says another without looking up from under the wide floppy hat brim that covers his lowered face, lest I kin neither eat it nor fuck it.

Dont look much good fer one'r tother. Lest mebbe it's one a them transvested pussies.

Yu reckon? Little shitass dont look very beardy at that.

C'mere, kid. Bend over'n show us yer credentials.

Ifn they aint been down outa that saddle in a spell, I misdoubt I wishta witness em.

The men hoot drily and spit some more. Whut's yer game, kid? the one under the floppy hat asks into the fire, his voice gravelly and hollow like one erupting from a fissure in the earth deep below him. Whuddayu doin out here?

Nuthin. Jest passin through.

That also seems to amuse them all for some reason. Lordy lordy! Jest passin through!

Ifn that dont beat all!

A one-eyed mestizo in a rag blanket lifts a buttock and farts fulminously. Sorry, boys. That one wuz jest passin through.

Just as well to keep moving on, he figures, and to that purpose he gives his mustang a dig in the flanks, but the horse drops its head in solemn abjuration, inclined, it seems, to go no further.

So whar yu passin through to, kid? asks a wizened graybeard in filthy striped pants, red undershirt, and a rumpled derby. Next to him, the man in the floppy hat is deftly rolling shredded tobacco into a thin yellow leaf between knotty fingers.

That town over thar. His rifle is off the saddlehorn now and resting on his thighs.

Yu dont say.

Wastin yer time, boy. Nuthin over thar.

Then nuthin'll hafta do.

Yu'll never git thar, kid.

Aint nuthin but a ghost town.

I'll git thar.

Hunh!

Ifn they's any gittin to be done, son, says the graybeard in red skivvies and derby, I'd advise yu hump yer green ass back home agin. Pronto.

Caint do that.

No? Floppy hat licks the tobacco leaf, presses it down. Why not, kid? Whar yu from?

Nowhars.

Nobody's from nowhars. Who's yer people?

Aint got none.

Everbody's got people.

I aint.

That's downright worrisome. The man tucks the thin yellow tube away under the overhanging hat brim at the same time that a tall ugly gent in a flatcrowned cap, much punctured, and with stiff tangled hair spidering down to his hairy shirt, stuffs a fresh chaw into his jaws and asks him what's his mustang's name.

That's it.

Whut's it?

Mustang.

Shit, that aint nuthin of a name. He spits a gob against the tin pot to fry it there.

Dont need no other.

Dont fuck with me, son. Hoss must have a proper name.

Ifn he does, he never tole it to me.

That boy's a real smartass, aint he?

Either him or the hoss is.

Tell me, kid, says floppy hat, holding an unstruck match out in front of his fresh-made cigarillo. And I dont want no shit. Dont keer fuck-all about the damn hoss. But whut's yer name?

Caint rightly say. Whut's yers?

We call him Daddy Dunne, says a grizzled hunchback with greasy handlebars sloping to his clavicle like a line drawing of the hump behind him. On accounta he dont do no more. And they all laugh bitterly again, all except the man under discussion, who is lighting up.

So why dont yu git down off that mizzerbul critter'n come set with us a spell, says the one-eyed mestizo, unsmiling.

He watches them without expression, knowing what must come next, even while not knowing where that knowing has come from.

Yu know, that young feller dont seem over friendly.

Looks like he's plumb stuck on that dang animule.

Looks like he's hitched to it.

Lissen, boy. I ast yu a question, floppy hat says, straightening up ever so slightly, so the glowing tip of his cigarillo can be seen in the voided dark beneath the broad brim, both hands braced like talons on his knees.

The rider shifts his seat for balance, his finger edging up the rifle stock toward the trigger, and in the fallen hush the saddle creaks audibly like a door suddenly opening under him. And I done answered it, ole man, he says.

Nobody moves. There is a long direful stillness during which a wolf howls somewhere and stars fall in a scatter, streaking across the domed dark like flicked butts. Then that dies out, too, and everything stops. It goes on so long, this star-stunned silence, it starts to feel like it won't ever not go on. As if time had quit on them and turned them all to stone. The rider, the horse under him gone rigid and cold, feels his own heart winding down. Only his hands have any action left in them. He uses them, struggling against the torpor that fetters him, to raise his rifle barrel and shoot the man in the floppy hat. The impact explodes into the man's chest and his hat flies off and his mouth lets go the cigarillo and he pitches backwards onto the desert floor. With that, things ease up somewhat, his mustang snorting and shifting under him, the skies awhirl once more, the others watching him warily but returned to an animate state, more or less. Chewing. Spitting.

Yu shouldna done that, kid, grumbles the ugly man with the spidery hair.

He rests the rifle back on his thighs again. Warnt my fault. He shoulda drawed.

Shit, sumbitch warnt even armed.

He's blind, kid. Stark starin.

Wuz.

The man he's shot lies arms asprawl on the desert floor, staring up at the night sky with eyes, he sees, as white as moons.

Yu shot an ole unarmed blind man, son. Whuddayu got t'say fer yerself?

He walks his horse over to the dead man, bends down from the saddle, and picks up the fallen cigarillo. Not a bandit, as he'd supposed, after all. Wearing a sheriff's badge, the star pierced by his rifle shot and black with blood. Probably he should shoot them all. Maybe they expect him to. Instead, he tucks the half-spent cigarillo between his cracked lips, sucks on it to recover the glow, and, without a backward glance, quits their wearisome company and slowly rides away.

Marina Warner

Ballerina:
The Belled Girl Sends a Tape
to an Impresario

Angela Carter

The Bloody Chamber *wasn't the first book by Angela Carter that I read, but it was the one that turned the key for me as a writer. It opened onto a hidden room, the kind that exists in dreams, that had always somehow been there, but that I'd never entered because I'd been afraid. It is this room of her title that all her fictions inhabit: the centre of the labyrinth of desire, the eye of the stormy journey towards self-knowledge, the ruelle by the side of the bed where the deepest intimacies are exchanged, the cheval glass—called in French un psyché—of our inner selves. I say, our, but the way Angela Carter retells familiar fairy tales in* The Bloody Chamber *casts them as female stories, takes their heroines as the eyes and tongue and ears of the tales, and lifts the barriers that had come down to ringfence them for the polite bourgeois nursery, that setting for the "toilet training of the id" (one of Angela's many brilliant, dry reproofs of pedagogy).*

I first met Angela Carter in the Sixties, in the offices of Vogue, *a magazine she continued to write for rather surprisingly through to the Nineties, when she contributed a characteristically sharp-eyed piece about the new "skirtless" fashion in leggings. Angela Carter was already known in the Sixties, and this early success did not help her later, when she appeared to be from an earlier generation to writers who merely started later—like Rushdie (only six years her junior). She was already a prize-winning writer from the darker side of swinging London, who penetrated mysteries with a unique command of passion and its perversities, who was making in one fiction* after another, a new, fierce, interior map of women's curiosity and sexuality. The early novels—The Magic Toyshop, Love, Heroes and Villains—drew me as well as thousands of others into an expertise about the twists and knots of the psyche that was stunning, alarming, and thrilling. She had red hair then, and had just come back from Japan, where she'd fled with the proceeds of the Somerset Maugham prize, to escape her first marriage, she used to say. Her first collection of short stories, Fireworks, recounts some of her experiences there. Japan was tremendously important in the development of her writing, for it gave her, she said, a viewpoint outside England from which to look back at its familiar contours; she turned herself into a stranger in her own country, its traditions and its culture, and was able to explore it as an anthropologist might, and set out its oddnesses, its preconceptions, now to mock its hypocrisies, now to freshen its poetry. With these stranger's eyes, she was able to look again at stories everyone knows, that everyone is brought up on, and open them like quivering oysters. In many ways, The Bloody Chamber stands as the metafictional counterpart of the commentaries on lipstick, D.H. Lawrence, music hall, Kurosawa, that she wrote for New Society and were collected as Nothing Sacred.

I had always loved fairy tales—which I'd principally read in the Andrew Lang Fairy Books editions, where Angela Carter also first found them in any quantity—but I felt ashamed of liking them, of fantasizing in the enchanted forest of dogrose and secret princesses arrayed in dresses the colour of time. The shame took two forms, really: at the time, it didn't seem grownup enough to continue thrilling to "The Maid Without Hands"—when I was also reading Vanity Fair (Thackeray's), Gone with the Wind, Rebecca, Silas Marner. Babyish, and girly, too. Fairy tales were deemed lacking that signature of genius, that uniqueness of the true work of art—they were interchangeable, scanty, predictable, repetitive—and somehow, in spite of all their aristocratic preoccupations (or perhaps because of them) they were a literature of the poor and ignorant. Angela Carter, in her later introduction to the Virago Book of Fairy Tales, points to just this aspect that attracted her to the genre: it has been made by those people "whose labour made our world," she writes. But later, when I still loved fairy tales, with their fatal structure, their recurring enchanted motifs, I did not explore my feelings or write in response to them, but resisted and repressed them because in those days, the late Sixties, when I was first writing as an adult, "Cinderella," "Snow White," Perrault, the Grimms, et al. were coming under bitter attack from women who felt the fairy-tale heroine was a simple tool of male hegemonies who wanted a Stepford wife, or a blonde bimbo, or a Bobbsey twin, as in Anne Sexton's mordant variation on Cinderella. Princess Diana has since fulfilled the most doomladen of these strictures.

But Angela specialised in provocation; she had a way of tilting her head, lifting the corner of her lips on one side and lowering her eyes as she delivered softly, in her near stammer, some delicious, poisoned barb at the pieties or thoughtless prejudices of her interlocutor. For this reason, she had an uneasy relationship to mainstream feminism in its Seventies shape: far too curious about perversity, masochism, collusion in women, far too enthralled by make-up and fashions and spectacle and performance for those days. "Glamour" was a word she particularly liked, for example, and an appropriate liking for someone so in love with language, for "glamour" derives from "grammar," which used to confer status on its users.

The Sadeian Woman was a calculated affront to orthodox reformers and campaigners for female emancipation. I was frightened by it, and wasn't altogether sure I understood it. But The Bloody Chamber was another matter, for here were nursery standards rewritten in the light of her sadeian woman, and they flung open that door in my head, on to the possibilities of women's reimagining the material that lies all about, readily to hand. There was no need to tunnel into the depths and darkness of the past to recover a different story for women: you could improvise it from what you already knew and liked. "This is how I make potato soup," she wrote about the telling of old tales differently, in that same introduction.

She didn't like my first novel, but she liked my last, which she read just before she died, and because she knew she was dying, it was overwhelming for me that she did so, that she rang me to tell me so. She had sent me a postcard a year or so before, from a Hindu scroll in the British Museum, the kind of narrative prop that the storytellers in the bazaar unroll as they spin out the episodes, pointing to the figures and the settings as they go. It showed a great white sea monster, who became, in Indigo, the cannibal fish Manjiku who terrorizes the islanders. I had begun writing short stories, too, that attempted to give voice to the heroines of well-known stories: Ariadne, Susannah from the Old Testament, Martha from the New. "The Belled Girl" forms part of this sequence; its immediate inspiration was a bronze sculpture called "Ballerina" by the Spanish contemporary artist Juan Munoz which shows a girl with staring eyes and bells for hands, but it echoes the theme of the maid-without-hands, a story much older than the Grimms' version. La Manékine, a medieval French poetic romance by Philippe de Beaumanoir already tells it: the heroine Joie slices off her hand to avoid marriage with her father. I wanted to express a contemporary twist on this sexual fear and place it in the context of today's emphasis on appearances and image: the culture that has produced beauty pageants for six-year-olds, and murdered child beauty queens like JonBenet Ramsey, though I had already written the story before her death.

Angela Carter's effect on me, and on so many writers, goes beyond the way she unlocked the magic, light and dark, of everyday life, the way she showed up the unnecessary orientalism of fictions that go far and wide in search of new experience. The enchantments of the most familiar will meet all needs (Wise Children triumphantly conveys her baroque and extravagant celebration of the mundane). It even goes beyond the way she voiced female desire. She is a consummate writer of the English language: syntactically innovatory, verbally fertile, with a thousand registers and tones and cadences, comic and heady and poignant; it is simply the most dazzling prose. I used to look up words all the time when reading her; but I also had to look *up things she would mention, needing an illustrated encyclopaedia to understand the references to items and cuts of dress, to technical tools, to flora and fauna. I discovered what "purple loosestrife" is from one of her books: it has always seemed apt that she should have known this wanton and lovely name for a wild flower, a native to England, which self-seeds and flourishes near flowing streams.*

[Editors' Note: The following story first appeared in a slightly different form in Silence, Please, *edited by Louise Neri, New York and Zurich, 1996.]*

To Lynton Orlowski, Esq.,
The New Stage Company
London WC1

From Prof. Sir Scott Mandell
Royal Cary Hospital
Clepton Shallett
Gloucestershire

December 29

Dear Mr. Orlowski,

Ms. Phoebe Jones is a patient who has been in my care for several years now. She saw you interviewed on BBC2's Late Show the other night about your recent production (as did I) and your message about the therapeutic power of performance and participation in the theatre struck a chord with her, for reasons which will become clear when you listen to the enclosed tape, as I very much hope you will do. I also hope that you will not find this approach an unwarranted intrusion, for may I say that I too was very impressed—and indeed, moved—by the way you reached out to those who are so often kept out of the light, as if society (and we are none of us free from blame) were ashamed of admitting them as members as one of us, as *mon semblable, mon frère,* you know what I mean. (I need hardly tell you that the disorder from which this patient suffers—formerly known as dysmorphophobia, but since redefined, more properly, as body dysmorphic disorder—does no harm to anyone except the patient herself.) Through your work you are making splendid moves to turn this tide of prejudice and change attitudes and I and my colleagues here and, indeed, in psychiatric hospitals all over the world are deeply sensible of your pioneering enterprise.

I wish you much continued success with 'The Gentle Giant' and hope that you will be able to listen to Phoebe's account of her life. I think you will find it fascinating. As they say, *Nihil humanum* . . . you are doing wonderful work.

Yours sincerely,

Scott Mandell, Kt., Prof. MD

Dear Mr Orlowski, I hope you will listen to me on this tape I am sending it to you, Dr Mandell says he knows how to get it to you, he nodded when I said you would understand me because I understood everything you said, every single thing you said speaks straight to me; you and me are brother and sister, flesh and blood, or perhaps born at the same hour on the same day, you in Kansas City (I think you said you were born in Kansas City) and me in Bristol. Star twins, that's what we are. From what you said, I know we have identical souls and that you could take me away from here like you took those boys you were talking about away from the place they were sectioned, no, perhaps not sectioned, but kept. I am kept here, too, and I could do things for you like they did. I can speak, you are hearing my voice on this tape, I hope it sounds nice—I'm talking to you now, I have a nice voice, everyone tells me so, it has a tinkling sound, like spring water, like fairyland! But I'm running ahead of myself, I must take things one at a time and try and not things get jumbled up. . . . More haste, less speed, that's what the nurses like to say. You said that one of the boys you took away from the place where he was kept couldn't even talk at all when you started. You made noises and suddenly you screwed your face up, your mouth and eyes all twisted to show us how difficult it was for him to make words. Your face looked so different when you were showing us his handicap (handicapped—that's the word for it, that's something else I'm going to come to, in a moment). At one moment you were calm and beautiful, your face smiling and smooth like the angel with the candle in the chapel here where I go sometimes to ask that someone like you comes and lets me out of here. You drew with your finger in the air a cube and you said it was made of glass and sparkled and that your theatre was like that, an imaginary place where everything was clear and pure and safe and beautiful and then you showed us a photograph of him, of the Gentle Giant in your play. Casey, his name is, you said, and you could hear what he was saying through all those funny noises, that heehawing and spluttering—Amy who often sits beside me in the day room does that too, sometimes, when we're meant to be having quiet time. But you could understand what was lovely and wise and deep underneath and in the heart of him, trapped inside that horrible mumbling and stuttering Casey was doing. And he was only twelve years old then, eight years ago, you said, when you first took him in. The audience loved it when you told how you had asked the judge if you could adopt him and the judge had said, No, he'd have to go to a home but you said it would cost the state so much more money to do that than to let him go home with you instead. It was easy to see you loved him. Well, I know you could understand me even more because I . . . you see, I can talk to you. And I can perform—you wouldn't even need to teach me to dance and play I can do lots of numbers, I've had lessons. I can twirl and ring the whole of The Beatles's first album: She Loves You, Yeah Yeah, Love, Love Me Do, Money, That's What I Want, and I Wanna Hold Her Hand—that's funny, really. But my audience like it. I'm used to tumultuous applause. I'd spin round and round and take my curtain call dizzy from the public's love. Casey you said was a star, you made him the star of your show, there was a photograph of him, sultry eyes, big slick quiff of hair and snaketight jeans on a throne with a long drape flowing down the stage from beneath his feet and the light falling on him like a halo. Well, I would do anything for you if you did all that for me. Because I loved you when I first saw you last night on the telly. And you haven't tried the same with a girl, not yet, have you? Well, I am the one, Lynton, Mr Orlowski. I'll be much better than Casey who couldn't speak, not properly at least. You can hear how well I talk, I swear this is all just coming out, without anyone helping me, no doctors around, I'm on my own, just you and me and the machine. I can also scat a bit when I sing too, I am fearless when I am in front of my public. I will be perfect I will perform I won't flag I'll dance and sing: here, Listen! Just a verse so you know what I can do.

She loves you, yeah yeah
Hear the bells?

This is for why: I'll tell you the story, it's simple really but lots of people don't believe me when I tell it. That's why I'm sending you this, because you will. Like you could see through Casey's noises, you'll see me. And then you'll know I'm made for you to take away with you. That it wouldn't be like two people together, but just one person. Two bodies, yes, but joined in one soul.

I was living in Bristol, I think I mentioned that, in a small house with a garden front and back, no weeds in the tiled path to the front porch, my mother always hung the washing low so that neighbours wouldn't get a peek at our underwear, so she said. The school bus stopped just down the road, and I had time to run out when I heard the driver turn the corner, changing gear and throbbing. I'd plaits then, which Mum used to do for me, with ribbons tied over elastic bands, otherwise they'd fall off because my hair is really silky. And when she did her nails, she'd let me do mine, too, dab it on for me I liked the smell when I waved my fingertips about to dry them, like Mum did. Frosted Rose was her best colour, I think, but Cinnamon Gold was good, too. Sometimes I'd do different nails different colours, you know, to try them out.

On Thursdays, I wouldn't come back with the others on the bus, but go to my ballet lessons. Miss Morris, she used to tap our feet with a little wand to make us stick them out at the widest angle and hollow our backs and pull in our bottoms. Tuck that tail in! she'd bellow. I had very expressive hands, she would say to the class, and point at them with her wand, and sometimes lift my arm a little with it to adjust the pose in the mirror. Sometimes she put one of my hands—they were small and quite pudgy then—in her palm and then she'd stroke it smooth, like it was covered in velvet with the pile running one way, and then she'd bend the fingers down and lift my arm and check in the mirror and tell the whole class to look at my *port de bras* and stop being such hephalumps and take a cue from Phoebe Jones. You can see I was her favourite.

Miss Morris has small feet and the elastic of her ballet slippers made her instep into two plump mounds like the halves of a peach—she wore thick pinky brown tights too. She was a character dancer when she was young; she once danced a mad nun who tore her clothes off at the Royal Opera House. Her brother—you probably know him—is the actor who plays Kevin in Streetwise at 5:15 on Thursdays with a repeat on Monday I always miss because it's my time in the hot baths here. Miss Morris smelt of fags and talcum powder all mixed up. One day she came home to see Mum and Dad and told them I had a future and should go to a proper dance academy. So that's how I came to go to London when I was still titchy.

My hands were my 'passport to success.' More than my legs, Miss Morris knew. She advised me to build on my strengths. "They're your capital, darling," she'd say. This was when things got weird. You see whatever people were saying about them I couldn't believe. Friends in class would hold theirs up next to mine and the nice ones would groan and cry "It's not fair!," and the not so nice ones would look squintily and tighten their lips and I could feel their hate slam down on my hands like a hammer. I won't repeat what was said—you'd think I was boasting. My boyfriend then was Lucas Tring, one of the Tring family, you know them, too, that meant something to me, music hall, circus, dance, show biz, for generations, and he wouldn't let me do anything, kept looking up insurance brochures to see what was the best deal he could buy to 'cover any loss.' He stopped me even washing up my tights in the basin saying he'd do all that for me so that my hands wouldn't spoil. He and I were renting together off the Earls Court Road and that's when things began to go *really* weird. No, I suppose they had been for a while, as I said, except that I hadn't noticed. He was an artist, he kept on saying, and I was his muse. He was planning a show, he wanted to be someone like you, Mr Orlowski—I hope you're still there—he was designing the lights and the choreography, it was a puppet version of The

Little Mermaid, with my hands in whiteface dancing the parts in a black box like a Punch and Judy booth. But I kept not doing the movements right. I kept falling over myself. I was all fingers and thumbs! And he was shouting at me. Then he'd grab my hands and massage them with oils and breathe on them . . . and he wouldn't let me use them even to . . . you know when we were in bed. He'd wrap them in silken bags with ribbons at the wrists.

I knew my hands were deteriorating every day, minute by minute, that if Miss Morris saw them now she'd notice they were getting wrinkled like an autumn leaf and the pores showing like someone has pricked out a paper pattern in the skin. The joints thickening and the tips flattening and the colour changing under the makeup, so that liver spots were just round the corner. I was beginning to find it hard to show them at all. I began pretending I had cramps so that I could get out of appearing, not have to perform any more. I stopped functioning, really. Then one morning I woke up and I couldn't move. I could not lift a finger, literally.

While I was lying in bed, though it felt as if I was lying kind of above the bed, suspended like the girl who gets sawn in half at the circus, a doctor came to see me and he gave me the idea for the cure. He said I should have a transplant, it would be simple. Plenty of people would be glad of a pair of hands like mine, they'd be very useful to someone, even if they didn't do me any good any longer. He had a big black hat with a wide brim and silver buckles on old-fashioned shoes and black stockings and he spoke in a soft voice—he was an American, like you! I helped him draw a circle round me with white chalk in my space above the bed and then I closed my eyes. There was no blood. He put my hands in a shoe box, wrapped in the neckerchief he had been wearing, and they did look beautiful, the knuckles dimpled just so, the backs smooth as ivory and each finger gracefully angled in relation to its neighbour. I was proud to be giving them away to someone who would know how to use them.

My bells play very prettily. You know bells are very unusual instruments, lively, with lots of character. My left bell rings in C and the other in F sharp which makes a lovely, solid chord, rings of sounds that go out and out for miles around me, humming high and low and just a little bit dissonant, which gives an edge to my tinkling, I can tell you! I can play almost any song-and-dance routine you care to name, and I'd be pleased to—especially for you. So I'm still a wonder of the world—a singing, ringing girl. Lucas always said I was his muse. But I'd rather be yours, Mr Orlowski. Oh do write back, dear Mr Orlowski, and take me on. I'll be a star, promise.

CONTRIBUTORS

Editors

CRISTINA BACCHILEGA, a professor in the English Department at the University of Hawai'i at Mānoa, is interested in contemporary fiction, folklore and literature, the fairy tale, and feminist theory and literature. She has published on Margaret Atwood, Angela Carter, Italo Calvino, Robert Coover, Maxine Hong Kingston, Dacia Maraini, women writers and the fairy tale, and fairy tales in Hawai'i. Her work in progress includes a study of the representation of place in twentieth-century narratives that adapt native Hawaiian, and more inclusively Hawai'i's, traditional stories. She is also the review editor of *Marvels & Tales: Journal of Fairy-Tale Studies* and continues her research on contemporary literature and fairy tales, especially in connection with women's sexuality and narrative.

DANIELLE M. ROEMER is an associate professor in the Literature and Language Department at Northern Kentucky University, where she teaches folklore and literature courses. She has published in sociolinguistics, on the use of semiotics and Bakhtinian perspectives in the study of graphic folklore, and on folklore and literature connections in the fiction of Julio Cortázar and J. D. Salinger. She is also interested in the use of folklore in the Vietnam War stories of Tim O'Brien and continues to investigate the role of substantive ornament in Angela Carter's literary fairy tales.

Authors and Illustrator

JACQUES BARCHILON founded *Marvels & Tales* in 1987 and edited it until the end of 1996. A professor emeritus at the University of Colorado, he is the author, in both French and English, of many articles along with a few editions of and volumes of criticism on the fairy tale and seventeenth-century French literature. His contributions include a volume on the history of the French fairy tale, *Le Conte merveilleux français* (1976), a biography of Charles

Perrault (1981), as well as an edition of Perrault's *Pensèes chrétiennes* (1987, in collaboration with Catherine Velay-Vallantin). His two-volume critical edition of Madame d'Aulnoy's complete tales (in collaboration with Philippe Hourcade) was published in 1997–98.

STEPHEN BENSON is a lecturer in the English Department at Brunel University (UK). He has published on contemporary literature, narrative theory, and the folktale. His current interests include literature and music in the twentieth century.

ELISE BRUHL is a judicial clerk for the District Court of the Eastern District of Pennsylvania. She has taught both at Harvard University and at the University of Michigan, where she received her master's degree in English and a juris doctor from the University of Michigan Law School.

ROBERT COOVER is the author of such works as *Pricksongs & Descants, The Public Burning, A Night at the Movies, Pinocchio in Venice,* and most recently *Ghost Town.* His novel *John's Wife* is dedicated to Angela Carter and to Ovid.

ANNY CRUNELLE-VANRIGH is a professor of English at the University of Paris, Nanterre, and a research fellow at the Centre d'Etudes et de Recherche sur la Renaissance Anglaise, University of Montpellier, France. She has published essays on Renaissance drama in *Cahiers Elisabétains, Etudes anglaises, The Shakespeare Yearbook,* and *Renaissance Forum.*

MICHAEL GAMER is an assistant professor of English at the University of Pennsylvania, currently finishing a book manuscript titled "Gothic Receptions and Romantic Productions: Making Poetry in the Age of Radcliffe."

JANET LANGLOIS is an associate professor of English at Wayne State University in Detroit with an interest in folk narrative theory—especially contemporary legend studies, folklore and literature connections, ethnographic issues, women's studies, and cultural studies. Her publications include *Belle Gunness, the Lady Bluebeard,* "Mother's Double Talk," in *Feminist Messages: Coding in Women's Folk Culture,* and articles in *Contemporary Legend, Journal of American Folklore,* and *Signs: Journal of Women in Culture and Society.* Her current projects include a study of horror films as ethnographic critique and work on narratives of racial passing and on personal experience narratives of angelic encounters.

KATHLEEN E. B. MANLEY recently became professor emeritus of English at the University of Northern Colorado, where she taught both folklore and literature courses; most of her work explores the relationship between the two disciplines. Some of her recent publications are: "Native American Writing," in *Encyclopedia of Folklore and Literature* (1998), "Atwood's Reconstruction of Folktales: The Handmaid's Tale and 'Bluebeard's Egg,'" in *Approaches to Teaching Atwood's* The Handmaid's Tale *and Other Works* (1996), "Decreasing the Distance: Contemporary Native American Texts, Hypertext, and the Concept of Audience," in *Southern Folklore* (1994), "Women of Los Alamos during World War II: Some of Their Views," in *New Mexico Historical Review* (1990), and "Leslie Marmon Silko's Use of Color in Ceremony," in *Southern Folklore* (1989).

KAI MIKKONEN is a professor of comparative literature at the University of Helsinki. His *The Writer's Metamorphosis: Tropes of Literary Reflection and Revision* (1997) focuses on the temporal aspects of narrative and intertextuality in the work of Michel Butor, Angela Carter, Maxine Hong Kingston, and Philip Roth. He has published articles in various American and international scholarly periodicals (*Style, Literature and Psychology, Diderot Studies, Critique*) and is currently writing a study on the question of literature and technology in the fin-de-siècle French novel.

BETTY MOSS is visiting assistant professor in the English Department at the University of South Florida. She teaches contemporary literature and cultural studies and serves as director of University of Southern Florida's Suncoast Writers' Conference. The author of several articles on contemporary literature, as well as a book-length manuscript on Angela Carter, Moss is currently working on a book that explores the visionary impulse in several contemporary writers.

CHERYL RENFROE received her Master of Arts in English from the University of Hawai'i at Mānoa. She is interested in feminist approaches to literature and theology, folklore, modern/postmodern women writers, and fiction writing.

LORNA SAGE is a writer and critic and a professor of English literature at the University of East Anglia in Norwich (UK). She first wrote on Angela Carter twenty years ago and has often done so since, most recently in *Angela Carter* (1994). She edited *Flesh and the Mirror: Essays on the Art of Angela Carter* for Virago Press the same year. She has most recently edited *The Cambridge Guide to Women's Writing in English* (1999). Her *Bad Blood: A Memoir* will be published in 2000.

CORINNA SARGOOD is a London-born artist who has lived in Bristol, southern Italy, Peru, Mexico, and Somerset. She illustrated Angela Carter's *The Virago Book of Fairy Tales* and *The Second Virago Book of Fairy Tales*. She is working on a special illustrated edition of Carter's "The Bloody Chamber."

MARINA WARNER's most recent books include *No Go the Bogeyman: Scaring, Lulling and Making Mock* (1998) and *Six Myths of Our Time* (1995). Her *From the Beast to the Blonde: On Fairy Tales and Their Tellers* (1994) has been translated into Japanese and Portuguese. She has edited *Wonder Tales: Six Stories of Enchantment* (1994 UK; 1996 US), and her collection of short stories *Mermaids in the Basement* has also appeared in French (*Sirènes en sous sol*). She is now working on a novel, "The Leto Bundle."

JACK ZIPES is a professor of German at the University of Minnesota and has previously held professorships at New York University, the University of Munich, the University of Wisconsin, and the University of Florida. In addition to his scholarly work, he is an active storyteller in public schools and has worked with children's theaters in France, Germany, Canada, and the United States. His major publications include *The Great Refusal: Studies of the Romantic Hero in German and American Literature* (1970), *Political Plays for Children* (1976), *Breaking the Magic Spell: Radical Theories of Folk and Fairy Tales* (1979), *Fairy Tales and the Art of Subversion* (1983), *The Trials and Tribulations of Little Red Riding Hood* (1983), *Don't Bet on the Prince: Contemporary Feminist Fairy Tales in North America and England* (1986), *The Brothers Grimm: From Enchanted Forests to the Modern World* (1988), *Fairy Tale as Myth. Myth as Fairy Tale* (1994), *Creative Storytelling: Building Community, Changing Lives* (1995), *Happily Ever After: Fairy Tales, Children, and the Culture Industry* (1997), and *When Dreams Came True: Classical Fairy Tales and Their Tradition* (1999). He has translated *The Complete Fairy Tales of the Brothers Grimm* (1987) and *The Fairy Tales of Hermann Hesse* (1995), and he has edited *Spells of Enchantment: The Wondrous Fairy Tales of Western Culture* (1991) and *The Outspoken Princess and the Gentle Knight* (1994). He coedits *The Lion and the Unicorn,* a journal dealing with children's literature, and has written numerous articles for journals in the United States, the United Kingdom, Germany, Canada, and France. He is the general editor of *The Oxford Companion to Fairy Tales,* which was published in January 2000.

Index